# THE DHAKRIS AWAKENING

Elizabeth Geeslin

The Dhakris: Awakening is published under Enigma books, sectionalized division under Di Angelo Publications INC.

DI ANGELO PUBLICATIONS
A Houston-based Publishing Firm

ENIGMA BOOKS

an imprint of Di Angelo Publications The Dhakris: Awakening. Copyright 2016. Elizabeth Geeslin in digital and print distribution in the United States of America.

Di Angelo Publications
4265 San Felipe #1100
Houston, Texas, 77027
www. diangelopublications. com

**Library of congress cataloging-in-publications data**
The Dhakris: Awakening. Downloadable via Kindle, iBooks and NOOK.

Library of Congress Registration
Paperback
ISBN-10: 1-942549-27-x
ISBN-13: 978-1-942549-27-7
Layout: Amit Dey
Cover: Di Angelo Publications
Edition 10 9 8 7 6 5 4 3 2

1. Fiction——Young Adult——Mystery
2. Fiction——Fantasy——United States of America with int. Distribution.

# DEDICATION

To my readers, thank you for being who you are, and for reading and giving life to this book with your imagination.

To my children. Without you, I could've been lost, unfocused and I could've settled for a life of mediocrity. You have been my driving force to ensure mediocrity is never an option.

To my truest supporters and believers, you will know exactly who you are if you read this. If we didn't talk for months, it didn't matter because our friendship is stronger than a calendar. You are the ones who loved to dream with me and talk about life and its meaning. You are the ones who never, ever doubted me. You are the ones who truly love me. You never, ever brushed off my vision as irrelevant or insignificant. You were never pretentious or condescending in any way, ever. Not once did you ever judge me or any of my decisions. You never wavered. You held my hand when I went through the worst of times. You didn't disappear because my life inconvenienced you or I didn't follow an imaginary narrative you had devised in your own mind about how life should be. You loved me for who I am.

# TABLE OF CONTENTS

**Part I—The Catalyst** . . . . . . . . . . . . . . . . . . . . . . . . . . **1**

Chapter 1. . . . . . . . . . . . . . . . . . . . . . . . . . . . . . . . . . . . 3

Chapter 2. . . . . . . . . . . . . . . . . . . . . . . . . . . . . . . . . . . 15

Chapter 3. . . . . . . . . . . . . . . . . . . . . . . . . . . . . . . . . . . 28

Chapter 4. . . . . . . . . . . . . . . . . . . . . . . . . . . . . . . . . . . 38

Chapter 5. . . . . . . . . . . . . . . . . . . . . . . . . . . . . . . . . . . 50

Chapter 6. . . . . . . . . . . . . . . . . . . . . . . . . . . . . . . . . . . 58

Chapter 7. . . . . . . . . . . . . . . . . . . . . . . . . . . . . . . . . . . 66

Chapter 8. . . . . . . . . . . . . . . . . . . . . . . . . . . . . . . . . . . 84

**Part II—Knowing** . . . . . . . . . . . . . . . . . . . . . . . . . . **113**

Chapter 9. . . . . . . . . . . . . . . . . . . . . . . . . . . . . . . . . . 115

Chapter 10. . . . . . . . . . . . . . . . . . . . . . . . . . . . . . . . . 129

Chapter 11. . . . . . . . . . . . . . . . . . . . . . . . . . . . . . . . . 143

Chapter 12. . . . . . . . . . . . . . . . . . . . . . . . . . . . . . . . . 161

Chapter 13. . . . . . . . . . . . . . . . . . . . . . . . . . . . . . . . . 166

Chapter 14. . . . . . . . . . . . . . . . . . . . . . . . . . . . . . . . . 189

Chapter 15. . . . . . . . . . . . . . . . . . . . . . . . . . . . . . . . . 197

**Part III—The Deal.** . . . . . . . . . . . . . . . . . . . . . . . . . . **205**

Chapter 16. . . . . . . . . . . . . . . . . . . . . . . . . . . . . . . . . 207

Chapter 17. . . . . . . . . . . . . . . . . . . . . . . . . . . . . . 214

Chapter 18. . . . . . . . . . . . . . . . . . . . . . . . . . . . . . 223

Chapter 19. . . . . . . . . . . . . . . . . . . . . . . . . . . . . . 247

Chapter 20. . . . . . . . . . . . . . . . . . . . . . . . . . . . . . 253

Chapter 21. . . . . . . . . . . . . . . . . . . . . . . . . . . . . . 257

Chapter 22. . . . . . . . . . . . . . . . . . . . . . . . . . . . . . 263

**Part IV — Timelines. . . . . . . . . . . . . . . . . . . . . . . . . . 273**

Chapter 23. . . . . . . . . . . . . . . . . . . . . . . . . . . . . . 275

Chapter 24. . . . . . . . . . . . . . . . . . . . . . . . . . . . . . 282

Chapter 25. . . . . . . . . . . . . . . . . . . . . . . . . . . . . . 293

Chapter 26. . . . . . . . . . . . . . . . . . . . . . . . . . . . . . 313

**Part V — Awakened. . . . . . . . . . . . . . . . . . . . . . . . . . 325**

Chapter 27. . . . . . . . . . . . . . . . . . . . . . . . . . . . . . 327

Chapter 28. . . . . . . . . . . . . . . . . . . . . . . . . . . . . . 335

Chapter 29. . . . . . . . . . . . . . . . . . . . . . . . . . . . . . 346

Our soul is cast into a body, where it finds number, time, and dimension. Thereupon it reasons, and calls this nature necessity, and can believe nothing else.

— Blaise Pascal

# PART I

# THE CATALYST

# CHAPTER 1

They say the only way out of my condition is suicide, but I'll just come back as the same damned thing. I am what I am, and I have come to terms with that. This is the story of my awakening; my becoming the Dhakris.

I didn't always know what I was, or what my abilities entailed, but when I first began having the cyphs, as they call them, I knew for sure that I was either on the verge of insanity or about to die.

I shook off the feeling of a brain zap as I stood up quickly to walk to the door of the guidance counselor's office. I had dubbed the sensation I felt a brain zap because it felt as if my head had morphed into a lightsaber from Star Wars. During these brain zaps I could see what colors music played for a brief moment. My despondence due to the phenomena had been happening more often ever since Emily, my older sister, had disappeared.

I greeted the guidance counselor with a smile as she passed the plastic bag containing my cap and gown to me over her desk. She gave me a smirk, wrinkling her face up enough to reveal her cigarette stained teeth. My last day of school in Eddinsville was turning out to be much like the rest; a blur through which I had to suffer, trying not to focus on the strange sensations I felt dwelling within me.

I often thought of Emily, but lately, it was all I could do just to keep her out of my mind. She had been too young, much too young to simply vanish without a trace. There had been no indication whatsoever of where she had gone. Everyone around me had handled it differently.

My father hid inside himself. My mother chose to just live in denial. Friends decided to compensate for my loss by patronizing me and essentially overloading me with attention. And I, well, I changed completely.

Here one day and gone the next. It had never added up to me. In the first few months after she disappeared I would dream of her and not think much of it. I knew her too well to believe she had run away. I closed my eyes and lifted my face toward the sun, letting the red light filter through my closed eyelids. I half expected to see her face emerge from the red glow, but it didn't.

After Emily's disappearance, there was the community outpouring. You never truly realize how involved people will get in your life until something tragic happens. There was more cobbler and casseroles sent to our house from concerned friends and neighbors than the three of us could ever eat. Unfortunately, our appetites weren't exactly themselves.

"We'll find her," our friends would say, or "Don't ask why—the why is what will make it hurt the most."

Yes, that why; that unbearable and ineffable why was the scariest part of all. It was meant to be that way. Everything that had happened was exactly what was supposed to have happened.

The memories of police officers and search volunteers coming in and out of our home danced through my mind, parading the heaviness of loss through my heart. There were times when we had hope, but it just led to more sadness. Once, they found a girl's body in a bayou in Houston who almost matched her description. My parents and I even went to check to see if it was her. They didn't want to let me in, but I remember insisting and pushing my way through. What I saw was a grotesque image I'd never be able to unsee. The poor young woman was bloated with discolored grey skin that was peeling away, with large gaping holes in all sorts of places, and her face was so swollen that her tongue was protruding outward as were her bulging eyes. That's how I knew it wasn't Emily. This girl had deep brown eyes, glossed over with the stare of death and permanently fixed with a look of horror. They yanked me out of the room before I could look any longer.

When the investigators left us for the final time, they parted with a nod and some mumbling about how that was the age that a lot of young people decide to just disappear, start a new life somewhere else, and that maybe we should check with the big cities in the region to see if she had shown up somewhere. They never mentioned dead or alive, and that was what made the entire situation more impossible to deal with than it already was. There was no closure.

I mulled the implications of their words over and over in my mind. Their words coupled, with my own personal feelings and experiences over time, kept leading me to the same conclusion; no one ever just disappears, do they? That one thought lingered behind my waking consciousness, haunting me day and night. Something has to happen to someone. It wasn't in Emily's character to just vanish into thin air.

My mother decided to leave my sister's room just the same as she had left it. Even the rumpled sheets remained the

same. I thought it was my mother's effort to fight off the inevitability that she wasn't coming home. Something in my mother's eyes told a different story, but I wasn't sure what to make of it at first. I avoided the subject and avoided the room.

My father, always closed off to begin with, maintained his fortitude and solidarity. Without showing emotion, I suppose he dealt with it the only way he knew how, away from the rest of us. It had to have killed part of him inside, not knowing where his teenage daughter had gone or why she would have decided to leave, who she would have met up with. He kept working and taking care of all of us, his only means of purpose in a world that had taken away something so precious to him.

In the grand scheme of things, it didn't matter much anyway—she was another missing seventeen-year-old. We were close enough to Houston and only hours from Austin or Dallas; she could have gone anywhere. The thing about East Texas, at least where we lived, is its mixture of everything: weather, cultures, people and beliefs. There are so many different elements merging all at once that it's impossible to know what could make a person vanish. The investigators knew that much.

The thing that no one knew, what I could never tell anyone, was what I had witnessed the day before she disappeared. I had reluctantly ridden with her that day to Beaumont—particularly to the side of the city that we generally did not enter.

It was almost an hour drive, and it was definitely off the marked path. The area was worn down, with cheap apartments and abandoned shopping carts scattered around the shady looking corners of the streets. And the heat, I remember the heat that day, burning in through the windows of the car. Hot and sweltering, making me feel even dirtier than the neighborhood looked.

She parked the car outside of a shop in a desolate strip mall and turned off the engine. I noticed that some stores weren't even in business. The whole area looked dead. I shifted uncomfortably in the passenger seat.

With a very serious expression, she turned to face me, shocking me with her cold, grey eyes, always clear and glass-like. She took me by the shoulders and whispered, "You cannot, under any circumstances, tell anyone about where we are right now. It doesn't matter what happens. I need you with me though. I didn't want to go in alone."

I looked at the beads hanging from her rear-view mirror. They were still swinging from the abrupt way she'd stopped the car. She looked at them too, noticing my distraction.

"Jessica, I mean it. I need you to promise me you're with me on this."

I looked back at her with wide eyes. "Okay, Emily. I won't tell anyone we're here."

I was so shocked at her level of seriousness. Nobody I knew took anything that seriously, not at our age. I understood she wanted to sneak into town—I didn't understand why she was absolutely beside herself about it. If she didn't want anyone to know, why bother bringing a witness?

"None of your stupid little friends need to know either," she mumbled as we climbed out of the car and slammed the doors.

I wasn't planning on telling them. I didn't want anyone to know where I was. When my friends and I drove to Beaumont or Houston, it was to a mall where we could snag the latest and greatest name brands. This was no shopping mall, nowhere even close. This was a sad lookingshop, something botanica, yerberia, something that had to do with plants from my recollection of Spanish class.

I reluctantly followed her inside, clutching my purse to my chest and clinging to it for dear life. I remember the smell upon entering the store. It hit my nostrils with a stinging punch. It wasn't necessarily bad, just a mixture of exotic aromas combined into one invisible cloud.

A woman who looked to be in her thirties sat behind the counter on a stool. I remember the first thing I noticed about her were her long red fingernails. You could tell they were real and not the acrylic material that everyone religiously wore in our home town, a mark of a woman who pampered herself. Her eye makeup was thick with layers of black eyeliner. She reminded me of the ancient Egyptians, trying to ward off evil spirits. The thought made me smile to myself as we walked up to her.

"Don't laugh," Emily shushed me.

"I'm not," I said with a giggle, finding the laughter harder to stifle once I had started.

"Hello," she greeted us emotionlessly in a thick Spanish accent as we approached the counter.

"I came to see Doña Carlota," Emily said matter-of-factly. It was obvious she'd been there before.

"Ah, jes, come through here. Follow me. But just ju. This is your seester? Let her stay in the front," they both looked back at me. I looked at them and shrugged in agreement with my exclusion from entering the back of the store. They turned and exited through a doorway covered with a thick veil of beads.

Left to myself, I roamed the strange store, sniffing bags with herbs and exploring each aisle. There were all types of plants, large and small. There was a wall lined with an abundance of different colored candles. Some candles were encased in glass containers that had pictures of Jesus, some had different saints. The candles were different colors and scents. Everything was printed in Spanish. There was a display of incense that I walked by. I picked up the patchouli and sniffed it cautiously, it smelled warm, inviting. Even now, I think about that moment anytime I smell patchouli. It reminds me of a simpler time before my life got so complicated.

The woman with the red nails had returned to the front and had taken her seat back at the counter. Oddly, I hadn't heard the beads when she returned through the door. I glanced at her just as she looked over at me and waved with her long nails. She seemed nice enough, but as I wandered down the aisles of the strange shop I felt the woman's eyes digging into the back of my skull. I didn't have to turn around and look at her to know she was watching me.

I twirled my long, golden hair around one finger as I perused the aisles of bottles and salts. Some bottles were labeled Florida water. I found that amusing. Why would water from Florida be any different than water from Alabama, or Texas? Strange. There were a variety of oils such as rosemary, sage, and lavender stored in simple phials and, again, labeled in Spanish.

On the aisle closest to the front window the sparkle of crystals caught my eye. There were all different kinds of quartz assembled in rows along the shelves. I walked over to get a closer look at them when I heard the beads from the back entrance rattle with movement.

"Let's go now," Emily commanded rather than said, motioning towards the front door and moving at a quick pace.

We opened the doors and plopped back into the oven of a car. I watched as she tossed a cheap velvety black pouch in the back seat.

"What did you do back there?" I asked as she reversed from the parking space and began retracing the route back to our home in the woods. "Who did you come to see?"

"If I told you what was going on, I don't think you'd believe me," Emily said condescendingly. Ever since we were in high school together she had talked to me like that, as if somehow my presence would ruin her reputation. If anything, I probably would have helped it.

"Why don't you just tell me so I can decide for myself whether or not I believe you?" I replied, widening my eyes to express the obvious to her.

"Well, I have a hard time trusting you," she replied in the same sneering tone as she looked ahead at the road.

"Why wouldn't you trust me? What have I ever done to you to make you not trust me? And what is it that you don't want me to tell anyone? You trusted me enough to bring me with you…."

"Look, Jess," she interrupted, "things didn't work out for me the way I'd planned…and now graduation is coming up, and I've got to do something before it's all over with. I know it sounds strange, but sometimes you have to take matters into your ownhands. I've been looking into some stuff—doing some research on my own—of how to get what you really want in life."

I looked at her for a moment, admiring the shine in her long dark waves. Her skin glowed from the humid weather. Her eyes were sad though, lost in her thoughts. They were focused on the road, but I saw a longing in their depths.

"What is it that you want for your life?" I asked, hoping to illicit a useful answer from her from her dreamy babbling.

"I want Jeremy Mullins to love me back, the way I love him, and I'll do whatever's necessary to get him to feel the same," she snapped, taking her right hand off the wheel and waving it in the air in a flustered manner.

I threw my hands in the air in exasperation, making her lean away from my reach. "A guy? Seriously, Emily? What the hell!" I couldn't believe she was being so weird about someone she probably wouldn't even see again after graduation. Small town or not, it was easy for people to get out and never come back. I glanced back at the black velvet bag and wondered just exactly what she was planning as part of her necessary endeavor. "Who did you go to see and what is in the bag?"

"I knew you wouldn't understand," she mumbled. Then more agitatedly, "You've never been like me. This is what I meant about trust. It's just a feeling I have. You don't understand what it's like!" The condescending tone was back. She pressed her pretty lips together, thinning them into a straight line while grasping the steering wheel with white knuckles.

"What what's like?" I asked, trying to understand her.

"To want someone like I want him! I have dreams of him, they're so realistic. I wake up and I hurt from the pain of not actually getting to be with him. We were together, you know, like briefly," she explained as she turned at a traffic light near the road that would take us home. I knew we had at least a few miles left for me to talk to her. When she said together, it could have meant a variety of things. I wondered if they'd kissed, hooked up, had a deep conversation about their hopes and dreams—but that was doubtful knowing Jeremy.

She sighed heavily. "But he just didn't love me back the same way I loved him."

I shrugged my shoulders. "Well, I've had dreams about guys before, I know what it's like to be secretly in love with someone," I lied. I had no idea, really. My friends and I always went on meaningless group dates— well they were meaningless to me.

"No, no," she shook her head emphatically, "It's more than that. If I don't at least try to be with him somehow, I know I'll regret it for the rest of my life. I had my chance with him that night at the party, and I didn't take it. Now I'll never know unless I try."

"Try what?"

"To make him want me too, the same way I want him. There's got to be a connection anyway or I wouldn't be having dreams like I do. It's like he's sending them to me, but maybe he doesn't even know it. It's all for a purpose. It all means something, I just don't know what, "she rambled.

I could tell that it was consuming her like a fire from within. I could see that in her face. She burned from inside herself. I may not have known much about love, but I knew a thing or two about the intensity of a crush. I had one or two of them at that point in high school, but she was right, this was completely different.

"Emily, you're seventeen. Not eighty-seven. There are going to be other guys, other parties, other people," I tried explaining. I couldn't believe she was that obsessed with a guy. I knew how she could be from growing up with her. It had been bad enough seeing her worship the teen heartthrob posters that littered her walls when she was thirteen. Now her obsessions were real, with real people. What made it even worse to me was that she was pretty and could get a normal guy in a normal way without being crazy about it. She just couldn't see that.

"So what's in the bag?" I asked, hoping I could discourageher.

"Things that I need for tonight."

"What are you going to do, exactly?" I asked. I was beginning to feel very uneasy about what her plans might entail.

She drew in a deep breath and explained, looking straight ahead as she drove. "Right before midnight, I'm gonna leave the house, but I have to go out of the window so mom and dad don't hear me. I'm going into the woods."

"Emily, are you out of your mind?" I was exasperated. "Those woods are freaky. It could be dangerous. You're stupid. I heard there are panthers and we just don't see them. Mason Jeffries' dad said he saw one while he was hunting last season…and the hogs.

They kill dogs, you know?" I stopped myself from continuing to berate her. I could see that nothing I said would get through to her.

"That's the perfect time and place. There's energy out there—good energy that I need to harness. I need to be in that setting for everything to go as planned," she said with determined tone.

I couldn't believe what I was hearing but didn't want to insult her so badly that she'd cut me off completely. "Who told you about the energy? The person you went to see at that shop? Who did you talk to, Emily?"

Emily stared straight ahead but I could tell she was considering the questions and how much information she was willing to give me. "I went to see a curandera. She helped me learn a spell. That's what's in the bag. A potion for a spell." Emily had whispered the last sentence.

"A what?" I managed to squeak. I could see Emily grinding her teeth in frustration at my reaction.

"She's a sort of witch doctor," she said with a roll of her eyes. A wall of silence shot up between us, separating us in the small space of the car. I sat in the passenger seat so astonished that I was speechless. Who was this person next to me? How could this same person be the sister I had grown up with? I finally found my voice again. "Can I go with you?" I offered quietly, all the while knowing I had no desire to sneak out with her. At the very least maybe I could talk her out of it. I couldn't leave her alone.

"No," she replied coldly. "I need to be alone when I do this."

That was three years ago, and that was the last real conversation I had with my sister before she disappeared.

I snapped out of my memory to realize I had walked to my car and was sitting in it, feeling the same pounding heat radiate through me like the last day I was with Emily. The plastic bag filled with my wrinkly graduation gown and cap was lying in the passenger seat. This had been the norm since Emily vanished. I would find myself thinking of her, recalling our last conversation, and the next moment I would awake, as from a dream and find I had continued my life on the outside but inside I was with Emily. Nothing had been the same and nothing would ever be since her disappearance. People treat you differently when they know you've suffered a loss, and they treat you with contempt when you start to make things change around you. I realized that every time I had ever heard that everything happens for a reason, it was true.

# CHAPTER 2

"I know this is going to be hard for you, graduating today."

I looked at Sarah, one of my closest friends, as she tried her best to be caring. She just didn't have the knack that most people do for tactfulness. She had come over so that we could get dressed for graduation together. That was how things always were. We always did everything together. It made it really difficult for me to completely be myself when I was always surrounded by her or other friends of ours.

"Yeah, it's sort of sad. Seeing me graduate will remind my parents about Emily and I just really don't want to deal with all of that emotion today," I said in a low tone as I fumbled with my makeup. I said it deliberately, because I knew it was exactly what she wanted to hear.

Sarah leaned over in the mirror of the vanity in my bedroom and continued curling her shiny, dark hair with a large barrel curling iron to create lustrous waves. "I still can't believe they still haven't found anything after all this time."

*Really*? I thought. *This again, today*? "Yeah I know. All I knew was that she wanted to go out into the woods that night. Alone," I said softly. I wasn't about to disclose Emily's affinity for voodoo magic that she had brought with her that night—especially not to someone like Sarah. She may have been one of my best friends, but her outlook on most things was through a pretty narrow tunnel.

"I'm sorry I brought it up. I don't want to upset you. I was just thinkin' about it. I know it's not something you want to talk about," Sarah said, setting the curling iron down with apologetic gentleness.

"No, it's cool. It doesn't bother me. I mean, it's hard but I can talk about it and be fine. I'm a normal person," I replied, rubbing my cheeks with bronzer and checking the symmetry of my work.

"Why do you think she wanted to go out in the woods alone that night?" Sarah asked, taking my reply as an invitation for more questions.

I let out a big sigh. It was always like this with her, a judgmental investigation. "I don't know. She wasn't afraid of things like the woods, I guess," I stood up and went to turn on my TV. I needed something to distract us from the grim subject.

"Do you think she was meeting someone out there?" Sarah asked. She had that gleam in her eye of salaciousness. She also had a knack for asking questions to which she already knew the answers. We had discussed Emily's disappearance before. None of this was new information. I fumbled with the remote and pressed the power button. The TV emitted a loud pop. Startled, I jumped back from it, dropping the remote on the floor in my surprise. The TV crackled on but with a snowy screen. The TV was set on Channel 6 and I could barely see the afternoon news team through the snow. I grabbed the remote from the floor and began searching for a channel that would help get Sarah's mind off of questions.

"The detectives asked us about it. They asked me if I knew anything. I told them she was going out into the woods and wanted to go alone. They thought she was going to meet someone out there, like a guy. But she wasn't seeing anyone at the time."

"Ugh what's wrong with your TV? Can't you get a new one?" complained Sarah. "Maybe she just didn't tell you, or anyone. Maybe it was a secret. She could have been taken by someone that no one else knew about," Sarah said as she began to dab shimmery highlighter onto her cheekbones.

"They checked her email on her phone, her phone calls, and her online activity. There was never any evidence she was talking to anyone other than her usual friends," I told her, fiddling with the channels. I knew my voice sounded distracted. I backed away from the TV and noticed the screen clearing up to reveal a normal picture.

"It's just such a mystery," Sarah said, oblivious to my electronic difficulties. "I liked your sister; she was always so cool compared to other people. She was like, a natural beauty."

Such lies. Sarah and all my friends thought my sister was weird. I knew they thought I was too, but wouldn't say it. They liked me because I looked like them, did things they did, and I had a car. I took a step closer to the TV, watching the screen turn to snow. Sarah didn't notice a thing. "Yeah, not like me. I couldn't live without the convenient beauty tools of today."

It wasn't true. I really didn't look anything like my sister, but I didn't need the full beauty regiment either. I liked to skip makeup when it was socially acceptable. UnlikeEmily's dark, shiny mane that she kept trimmed with virtually no split ends, I grew my blonde hair out down to my waist. It had many shades of blonde in it that became wavy the longer it grew. I was always accused of dying it or wearing extensions, however no one usually believed me when I refuted their claims. Sarah and the rest of my friends liked to refer to me as their resident hippie. I tolerated the title without complaint. It gave me free range to be weird when I needed to be.

Sarah looked down at her phone. "Ugh, it's Michael again. He's blowing up my phone today. I already told him we'd meet him at the stadium at six. You're so lucky you don't have a high school boyfriend.

I turned away from the TV and looked at the clock. It was 5:40. "Lucky? There just wasn't anyone for me I guess," I replied, my mind on why my electronics were screwing up. The few dates I'd been on with everyone had usually not led to anything I considered romantic. They were all the same. They all went hunting and fishing, which wouldn't have been so bad except for the fact that they couldn't maintain a conversation much beyond the content of such activities. Sometimes they could carry on about other things like wrestling on TV or the latest sports clip from ESPN, but other than that, their topics of interest were slim to none. I just couldn't talk to them. On special occasions they wore starched jeans and boots. If they weren't into the country vibe they thought anything from Hollister at the mall was dressing up. They thought chewing tobacco was all the rage and disregarded how disgusting it was. I always imagined I'd meet a guy in college and that would be where I fell in love, not in high school.

"Well, Michael is being so possessive. I think it's because we're graduating and obviously going to different colleges. I wouldn't go to Louisiana with him, and he's still pissed about it."

I sort of laughed. "But doesn't he understand that it probably won't even work out when you guys start your first semester of college?"

"Ugh! Jess! That's really messed up of you to say," Sarah whined. "We have a history together."

*Yes, a very in depth and meaningful history*, I laughed inside my head. It didn't occur to me that I had hit such a sore spot with her. I was confused by her reaction. She complained about him, yet couldn't deal with me saying that they weren't meant for each other. I wondered why she actually thought we were friends sometimes.

"I'm sorry, Sarah. I didn't mean it like that. It may work just fine. I only want the best for you."

She shrugged and returned to the mirror as she suggested nonchalantly that we hurry and leave.

Once we arrived at the stadium, we had the pleasure of being inspected by Mr. Miller, our principal. He walked around scrutinizing all of us as we stood around and slid into our graduation gowns.

As I stood with my classmates, listening to the shallow talk of other peoples' outfits and how tacky they looked, my mind began to drift to thoughts of my sister. I closed my eyes again, as I liked to do when I thought of Emily and searched for her face in filtered light through my eyelids. She didn't get to experience any of this, and it would have been something she would have loved.

Love. That's what stopped her. What happened to her three years before had obviously taken place because she thought she was in love. I never told my parents about our trip to the creepy yerberia, or her uncanny crush on Jeremy Mullins. I kept that part of the promise because I thought she would have been embarrassed when we found her, for them to know about her obsession with a guy and a visit to a shop where we had no business going. Telling them she went into the woods that night was the most I could do to help without hurting her dignity.

I knew what I should have done, but I didn't do it. I didn't tell them that she had probably bitten off more than she could chew by visiting a Mexican witch doctor. Now, I felt as though too much time had passed to dig up an old grave, so to speak. Jeremy Mullins had graduated with my sister's class. He'd left for the Navy shortly after and only returned for short visits. As far as I or anyone else knew, he didn't know how my sister felt about him and definitely didn't know that he might have been part of the cause in her disappearance. I often wondered what he would think if he knew she disappeared trying to make him love her. I wondered what had happened between them for her to obsess over him so deeply. Had they really had something? Had he told her he would call her back and never did? There was no way to know now.

I checked my phone out of habit. There was nothing new to see because everything being posted or shared was happening all around me. I only knew the people that were there with me. Then I felt it again—that buzz in my head. It set of an alarm within my mind. I had an epiphany of sorts. It had been so long since anyone had checked… but what had my sister been doing on the Internet before she disappeared? They said they checked her phone and her laptop history, but did they really? She had to have been doing some research that would have been red flags. There had to be something that would help me understand exactly what she was doing that night.

In that moment, I wanted nothing more than to return home and look for something, some kind of clue. Someone had missed something, or worse, not checked at all. I felt an urge to go into her room. I never went in there; no one did. I knew my mother would freak, but it had to be done. Mom was so obsessed with leaving her room exactly as it had been that she hadn't really combed through all of her belongings and had given very little to the investigators. Everything was exactly the way Emily had left it.

I was ranked fourth in my class so my appointed roll in the graduation ceremony was to deliver the benediction. It was a public school, but in South East Texas it was expected that a Christian blessing was to be given at every event and no one would say anything about it. Everyone belonged to either the Baptist, Methodist, Church of Christ faiths or some other denomination along those lines, and would undoubtedly be offended if there wasn't a proper Christian prayer, even though it bordered on infringement of separation of church and state. After hearing my voice echo across the football stadium, I walked back to my seat and returned to my impending thoughts. Throughout graduation, even as I walked across the makeshift stage and awkwardly shook hands with a member of the school board, all I could think about was getting back to my house. The urgency clawed at me.

A sea of flying red graduation caps soared into the air, signifying our transition to the next chapter in life. Mine dropped directly down beside me. Families scattered frenziedly around the field, taking pictures of everything and everyone. I smiled with friends and family, forcing the expression on my face to be one of excitement-something I was good at anyway with the company I kept. People walked up to greet me. Friends cried. I didn't cry. I had a mission now and I needed to get it accomplished quickly and capably.

"Are you going to the all-nighter?"

The words snapped me out of my daze. One of my other friends, Melanie, looked at me expectedly. I had forgotten all about it.

"Yeah, I'll be there. I need to run home first."

"Do you want me to pick you up?" Melanie asked eagerly, bouncing on her toes in a

dance of enthusiasm.

"No, thanks," I said distractedly. "I'll take my car. I'll be there soon."

"Well, don't forget the bottle," Melanie reminded me with wide eyes, nodding her head up and down for added emphasis of its importance.

"I won't."

She was referring to a bottle of whisky that her brother had bought for her and she had hidden in my room. I was supposed to bring it so we could drink during the all-nighter. She couldn't hide it at her place because her mother was an obsessive cleaner and a staunch Baptist and was sure to find it anywhere that Melanie attempted to stash it. During Melanie's pleading testimony stating all of the reasons I should hide it for her, she mentioned that if her mom found it, she'd probably force her into church camps all summer, thus ending any summer fun she had planned for herself. I assured her that boys at church camp couldn't be all that bad, but she grabbed my arms and begged with watery eyes, whimpering at the thought of being forced into encampment.

My parents had taken my visiting family out to eat at a restaurant for traveling to watch me graduate. Since I had given the benediction at the graduation, they had all come to listen. They were also there for moral support, since I was my parents' only child to graduate. Aunt Kathy was the only one who couldn't make it, and I was disappointed because she was really the only family member I wanted to see. They knew I couldn't go eat with them because I was expected to get to the all-nighter and help set up, and be there the whole time. The time between that exact moment after graduation and before the all-nighter was my only opportunity to run home and get into Emily's room unnoticed.

I pulled up into the driveway with a screeching break and threw the gear into park. I opened the front door as quickly as I could and ran upstairs, straight to Emily's room. I opened her bedroom door with a force, the door hitting the wall with a slam, unsettling papers that were still attached to her wall and I flipped on the light.

I stood in the door and scanned the room, slightly stunned to actually be in it. It was the first time I had really looked at it in a long time. The musty smell of unwashed linen filled the air as I took in a deep breath. Her baby blue sheets were ruffled in an unmade bed. There were pictures on the wall of her with friends. At her vanity, her hairbrush and makeup bag sat untouched. There was her bookshelf, full of books from her early childhood on up. I ran over to the shelf and started pulling books. She was somewhat of a packrat. I shook them out, flipped through pages and tried to find books on things related to her black bag of magic. She had kept that part of her life concealed, evidently. I wasn't finding anything. I shoved the books back and looked around.

I crawled over to her bed and pulled up the bed skirt. There were shoes scattered around and a couple of purses. I took them and dug through them. They were full of change and receipts, old lip glosses…absolutely nothing that could help me. I sat up and tilted my head back, huffing in the dusty hair.

Her laptop sat on the foot of her bed. Unplugged.

I walked over to it and plugged it up. I wasn't sure if it would even work, it had been so long since it had been used. I listened as the fan and hard drive began to buzz and I felt its warmth as it began to start up. I needed to get it out of her room so I could inspect it properly. I was sure that my mother would notice if it was gone. She didn't go into her room often, but I had seen her in there before at odd times, times when she must have needed to be around Emily's things. She'd notice if it was missing

I ran down to my room and grabbed mine. It was the same color and size, difficult to detect when swapped. Taking one last look to make sure everything looked in place, I turned off her light and closed the door, taking Emily's laptop back to my room and placing it where I usually keptmine. Every move I made was precise and careful. I plugged it into my wall charger and continued the start up. It prompted me for her password and I hit a brick wall of complications.

Her password could have been anything she liked at that time. Considering the interest of girls in their late teens, I was at a loss. I knew what she had liked, and especially towards the end. But a password? Impossible. Normal things people used like birthdays were out. Her favorite book was impossible to tell as her collection was quite eclectic. Music, maybe. People's names were a possibility, and anything that had to do with Jeremy Mullins would be useful. Then I thought of James.

James graduated with me and would perhaps be at the all-nighter. He had made himself into a complete computer expert by the end of our senior year by his own learning. If there was ever a chance I could get into her laptop, it was with his help. The trick would be getting him to even listen to me.

I loaded it in my car and drove over to the all-nighter. It was being held at a local church venue that people could rent out for different events. There were basketball courts, a room to lay sleeping bags, rooms to play video games, and every sort of mundane activity to keep us from having drunken bonfire parties in the woods all night.

I pulled into the parking lot and Melanie immediately came out of the door of the building with a plastic cup in hand and approached me as I was getting out of the car with the laptop.

"You got it? Let's go sit in your car for a minute."

"Got what?" I asked, having forgotten completely about her request.

"Shit! Well, there goes the night. You forgot it!" She threw her empty hand up in the air and went back inside to disseminate the news that no one would be able to get tipsy because of me.

I breezed past her with Emily's laptop, looking for James.

"Hey," I asked Sarah when I saw her. "Do you know if James Milton is here?"

"James?" She furrowed her carefully sculpted eyebrows upward in confusion. "Why would I know if James Milton is here?" She said his name with such distain, squinting her eyes shut with each syllable as if it hurt to even speak it.

"Just, have you seen him?" I rolled my eyes at her. Now was not the time to question my allegiance to someone over my friends. "I have a computer problem," I said, holding the laptop up for proof.

"Really? You have to get your laptop fixed tonight?" Sarah asked, following me as I walked past her in search of his whereabouts.

"Well, when else am I gonna see him again?" I asked, irritated.

"True. We are all now graduates. This is our last night together." The cheesiness in her words pained my ears.

"Okay well I'm going to find him then I'll catch up with y'all later," I said, trying to get her to find something else to worry about besides what I was doing.

I found him in the corner of the video game room, with his own computer set up and running.

"James?"

"Yeah," he glanced up at me with a bit of irritation at the distraction.

"I really could use your help with something if you have a minute. You see, I'm locked out of this laptop," I said, holding it with the hope that he would feel my dedication to the issue.

"Oh, really? Well that's funny how you only come around to talk to me when you need your computer fixed," he replied sarcastically.

I looked at him, confused. His sandy brown hair covered his focused blue eyes as he sat before me making me feel like a complete idiot for bothering him.

"James, I—I never asked for you to fix my computer before," I assured him, trying to pinpoint the origin of his negative disposition.

"Well, no, maybe not you, but your friends. Your kind," he replied, looking back at his screen. "Besides, I'm in charge of the gaming for tonight."

"Okay," I said, trying to think of how to introduce my conundrum. "Well, I'm not them. I may look like them, talk to them, hang out with them. But I'm not them. I could really use your help." I didn't want to give him too many details.

I knelt down beside him so that no one else could hear what I had to say. Everyone in the gaming room had headsets on anyway, so I didn't have too much to worry about.

"It's Emily's laptop," I whispered, looking eagerly at his face for a reaction. I pleaded with my eyes.

He looked away from the screen, then over to me with his eyes, not moving his head.

"Your sister, Emily?"

"Yes."

"I'm sorry, but the same one who went missing?" he asked quietly.

"Yes, the only sister I have, had, have," I stuttered. I didn't know how to talk about her, even after three years. I didn't have the sort of closure I needed to use a specific tense about her.

"Is this legal?"

"I don't know. But I need you to try."

At this point James was looking directly at me, thinking while considering the implications of what I was saying.

"Well, I have some things I can do. Can you leave it with me?"

"Yes, but can you keep it quiet?" At the very least his offer was promising. "And take really good care of it. It's my only hope."

"Of course, but I don't guarantee I can get in."

"It's fine, whatever you can do I appreciate it," I said, wishing for some sort of gratitude karma.

I spent the rest of the night with my friends, laughing, making it seem like I was completely in the moment. I let myself become immersed in the world that had seemingly forgotten my sister. I danced and sang karaoke with Sarah and Melanie. When it was my turn to choose the track to sing to, I touched the screen and the TV went blank. I jumped back a little and felt a buzz in my head. Everyone seemed to sigh a unified disappointment as I shrugged and laughed. A teacher ran up to try and fix it and was able to get the thing working again.

I hugged everyone and laughed as my mind churned with possibilities. I had my happy graduation, my college scholarship, dreams of a big future, but ultimately, none ofthese would matter. You're never who you think you are in life when you're eighteen.

# CHAPTER 3

"I got in."

That was the text I received from James a few days after graduation night. My stomach sank. I knew that it meant I had to go deeper into Emily's world—the world from which she never came back.

"When can I meet you?" I texted back, eagerly awaiting his answer.

"My house now, if you can."

"Sure. Kingsland Street, right?" I asked.

"That's it, white house on the left," he responded.

It had been quite some time since I'd been to his house, but I knew where it was. Everyone knew where everyone lived in our little town. I knew that he had done something tremendous, and I needed to get over there. I had a feeling deep down that I couldn't explain. As I pulled up to his home, I felt my stomach flutter. Now was the time I had really dreaded for three years, to know any sort of truth of my sister's true existence.

I knocked on the door and James' mother let me in.

"Hey Jessica," she greeted me.

"Hey Mrs. Milton. Thanks for letting me come over!" I gushed, slightly embarrassed that I was there at that moment, so awkwardly awaiting his help.

"Sure, we're glad to have you," she said, leading me down a narrow hallway lined with family photos to James' room.

I entered James' room with a gentle knock and saw him seated at his computer portal. There were two large, flat monitors and all sorts of equipment, most of which was unidentifiable to me. I suddenly felt small and impotent in my mission. It looked like he subcontracted for NASA out of his bedroom.

"Hey," I greeted, taking a seat on the foot of his twin size bed near the station he had set up. It was so dark I felt like I had entered a different dimension, lost in time. The windows were covered by layers of blankets and probably an original layer of curtains somewhere beneath it all.

"Hey," he said with slight distraction, clicking computer windows closed and evidently closing out of whatever it was he had been working on before I arrived.

"So," I started, with drawn out hesitation, "were you successful?"

"Success is always relative," he replied, spinning around in his office desk chair to face me, his sandy brown waves of hair falling partially over his eyes. "But I think you'll be pleased with the results."

"Really?" I asked rhetorically, feeling a rush of adrenaline flood through my body. My heart twisted with the thought of what I might find.

"Yep. Look, don't go spreading it around that I can do this sort of thing, and most definitely not for free. This sort of thing is illegal and can be pretty expensive when done for legit purposes. So, don't run and tell your friends that I can hack their boyfriends' email accounts or whatever," he said. "I don't really want to deal with anyone else's problems or create any for myself."

"James, this isn't the sort of thing I want to advertise anyway. No one knows I brought it to you," I said with my head down. I felt bad.

"Do you even know what to look for when you get in?" he asked, attempting to not sound condescending. He knew I probably wouldn't know where to start.

"The internet history, that's where I thought I'd start," I confessed with a big sigh, feeling my confidence drain again in the presence of such a whiz.

"Okay, well, do you want me to show you?" he asked, this time with more compassion.

"Sure. That'd be great!"

At least he was kinder than the people I had been running with for the last few years.

He pulled out the laptop and popped it open, placing it on his bed so that the two of us could look at it. We got down on our knees at the bedside and crowded the screen as it warmed up.

"I'm going to show you the steps to take, then it's all yours," he explained as we waited on the startup process to complete. "It's pretty slow," he added, "this software is super out of date."

"Can I ask you something?" I questioned, looking over at him.

"Sure," he said as he scrolled through the data and highlighted sometext.

"Why'd you do this for me?"

"Well, I guess I felt like it was my own little way of helping, you know, if it does help in anyway."

"I hope it will, I really think it will. Mom never touched any of her stuff. The cops? They said they looked but, nothing," I murmured.

"I knew they never found your sister. I thought about it a lot, still do actually. I'm sorry that it happened. You never really asked me for anything else before. You never really even talked to me much. It sort of shocked me that you'd come to me with it. I had always wanted to help if I got the chance to."

"James, I'm sorry. I didn't mean for it to seem like I never talked to you," now I felt really terrible, like he thought I was just using him for free help.

"No, no that's not the point," he laughed. "I just mean, I wanted to do you the favor."

"Well, thank you. Really."

He smiled, satisfied with my answer. "Okay, let's see what we can find."

I watched as he clicked and scrolled through the search history, our faces aglow from the bright screen. Seconds felt like minutes as I watched him pull up information.

"Your sister was into some strange, um—things." James mumbled as he looked through the list of webpages that she frequented the most. I looked at him without saying a word. The silence was tense.

"I'm sorry, I don't mean to be offensive," he apologized. "But look, right here," he pointed at the screen. "She was a member of several groups on Wicca, witchcraft and Santeria. It—it's all right here," he stuttered a little.

"No, it's okay. That's what I need to know," I assured him. I knew what I had seen the last day I was with her, but this was a discovery of epic proportions.

"Do you think this had something to do with her disappearance?" He asked.

"I don't know for sure, but that's what I need to find out. I don't understand why the detectives didn't think it was at all out of place that all of her computer history mainly dealt with witchcraft," I said confused, putting my head in my hands for a second of decompression.

"I guess they just wrote it off as kids being weird, like the whole 'boys will be boys thing'," he answered and shrugged.

"If they even looked at all…," I muttered.

"Here, I'm writing down the instructions for finding all of the history, web pages and everything. I have some passwords I was able to detect with my retroactive key logger, if you need to log in as her," he explained as he went over to his desk again to retrieve the information.

"I designed the key logger myself. It detects algorithms of all the most used key strokes in the hard drive's history, then matches the key strokes with words, phrases and number matches. This list I'm printing has the top twenty hits. Try those first and see if any of them work for her accounts. If you don't have any luck, shoot me a text, we'll try the next twenty."

"Thanks. I really can't thank you enough," I said to him, my ears abuzz from all of the tech talk.

"Like I said, I wanted to help. You're welcome. Let me know if you run into any problems," he reassured, walking me out of his door back into the photo-speckled hallway.

I said my goodbyes to his mother and left through the front door. It was a warm night, and I could feel the humidity immediately stick to my skin. It felt like stepping into a sauna with clothes on.

I got in my car, setting the laptop carefully on my passenger seat. I looked down at it and after thinking for a moment, I decided to strap it in with the passenger seatbelt in case I had to slam on my breaks for any reason. I needed it to be as protected as possible. I turned on the radio, hoping to find a song into which I could lose myself for a short while. Commercials. I changed it to another station, then another as I drove down the street. I settled with an old Celine Dion song that I could belt to as I drove, my steering wheel was an excellent audience for my vehicular solo performances. As I emoted into the bolting lyrics, gripping the steering wheel with my private concert, static rushed through the speakers and flooded out the melody to the song. It jolted me with fear. I hated that sound, the sound of static. I had the music up so loud it was even worse than if it had happened at a normal decibel. I stopped at a traffic light and changed the station, something about the static wasn't normal. Each station I tuned into began with clarity and suddenly snapped into static—a hissing, crackling static. I heard behind it a voice, barely audible.

"CB radios," I calmed myself. The cross-road truckers' radios could sometimes interfere with anything related to the radio. But this was different. I started scanning through the stations, desperate to make it stop. Nothing was functioning.

I hit the power button. It wouldn't stop. It should have turned off. The crackling static and the strange voice, almost robotic in its timbre, kept seeping from my car's speakers. I heard honking behind me. The light had turned green.

I screamed and stepped on the gas, completely horrified at the noise. The robotic sounding voice became clearer and I heard the words clearly come out in the terribly mechanical tone

"Jessica…is there…is the one…"

It all stopped with a loud pop. All of the noise stopped. The radio was completely silent, power off. I trembled as I drove. The last thing I wanted to do was stop the car. I had to keep going. When I arrived home, I walked through the door with the laptop hidden in my tote bag, questioning my own sanity each step of the way.

My mother was on the sofa watching TV and said something about us having to go out to dinner with our relatives the next day. I mumbled an acknowledgment to her and rushed up to my room, passing Emily's closed door along the way.

I opened the laptop on my desk and began scrolling through the list of frequently visited websites that had been left open. Much of the pages consisted of old threads in forums and discussion boards on topics such as spells and experiences in using magic. I felt overwhelmed. There was just so much through which I needed to sort and at that point, I truly couldn't fathom how I would find anything helpful. I only knew I had to try.

The subject of witchcraft, and the practice for that matter, was one with which I had little to no familiarity. I was terrified of the implications and being labeled by my peers. No one talked about that sort of stuff at school and the only kid who ever claimed to be a Wiccan was bullied to the point of switching schools. Furthermore, my parents would likely consider sending me to a convent to repent my evil ways if they ever thought that I had an interest in such things, and we weren't even Catholic. But regardless of any of my reservations, I knew I had to overcome them if I was going to find anything else about how my sister thought and what she did to get herself into a situation where she had literally vanished from humanity.

My first time reading about witchcraft felt surreal. It was just like reading about any other study of a religion. There were rules that some followed that others didn't. Some experts said that whatever spell you cast on others would come back on you three fold, others said nine fold. I wasn't disturbed by it all until I started reading about how those who believe in it were the ones that were affected by it. It was one thing if someone didn't believe in any of it and someone put a hex on them, but it was completely different if the person being hexed believed in it. Some people had died because they heard they'd been cursed and believed it to the point that they essentially caused their own death. Believers and practitioners shared stories and experiences. They claimed to be able to manipulate reality and emotions. People warned against messing with someone's free will—evidently love spells were the worst about doing that.

For every webpage that my sister frequented for spells, incantations and readings, I had to open a different tab to look up terms and research what everyone was talking about. It was, in a nutshell, quite the undertaking. I made notes as I read, writing down points that I needed to look up later to further understand, such as Wiccans and the difference between witchcraft and devil worship.

It was an overwhelming brain squeeze of information that took an insurmountable amount of energy for me to continue. I had my phone, my tablet, and the laptop all overloaded with tabs and videos and articles while I scribbled into a notebook.

I found a website where my sister had actually contributed information. It was a spell trading website with networking for local groups to come together. They had given her information about love spells. Some told her which ones worked better thanothers, and they offered to help her out. I needed to talk to these people. I needed to know who knew her. I wondered if they were still around after three years.

"Emlove" was my sister's username. I checked my list from James for passwords. I typed in the first one, Emiloveone. Incorrect. The next on the list was oneloveem16. That wasn't it either. I tried the next one and the next one. I got to the seventh one and typed it in. EmilytheDiety. I closed my eyes as the browser processed. I was in. James' algorithms really worked.

I looked at her previous posts to see who she was communicating with the most. It was hard to tell. There was NellyJelly from New England. They had corresponded back and forth on a message board thread, but that person had been inactive for a while. I kept scrolling. There was a post about a meeting of locals in a city park, Caraway Park, in Beaumont, a town within an hour drive from us. She would have had to lie to mom and dad about where she was going if she had gone to these meetings by herself, which would have taken her away from home for more than two hours. We had gone to Caraway Park as a family when I was little. Willow trees and ancient live oak trees decorated with Spanish moss shaded the park. Little Pine Bayou ran through the middle of the park and the city rented paddle boats, canoes and kayaks from a concession stand that also sold sodas and ice cream. I remember Emily and me climbing on live oak limbs that were so old and heavy they touched the ground. We would gather Spanish Moss and put the grey strands on our heads and pretend to be fairies.

My phone rang as I was looking for information. Only zeros appeared on the caller ID. I answered quickly, anyway.

"Hello?" I mumbled, tired from my work.

Nothing. No voice, no breathing. Then I heard the crackling. Static—the exact same static I had heard before on the radio.

"Hello!" I shouted into the phone, irritated this time.

There was more static and crackling. Then faintly, barely audible, in a very robotic voice I heard "road is dangerous".

I let the phone fall to the floor. I didn't know who had contacted me, or what. But I felt that someone knew exactly what I was doing. I needed a rational explanation for it. If I could explain it, I could get a better grip on reality. I dropped down on my knees to the floor to pick up my phone.

I sat it back up on its holder by the laptop at my desk and set it to play music. I wanted as little to do with electronics as possible at that point. I opened a new tab on the screen. I needed to know now more than ever where these people were meeting. Wherever it was, if I could find them, I could find out something about Emily.

In a new tab, I opened the current threads of the same website to see where they were currently meeting. Hardly anyone from the years before was still using the forum, but there were a few I recognized as users from the older thread that my sister had used. I couldn't be active on the threads unless I was a member.

"Well, here I go," I said to myself. I really didn't have another option other than become a member.

Carmichael, our last name. It didn't reveal whether or not I was male or female. I decided to go with it. I didn't add a photo, but I did put my age. After I completed the sign in process, I clicked back into the active meeting discussion board thread. Now I could interact with them, not just read.

"Tomorrow, Caraway?" Wrote a user named Danamite. She had been in the older posts.

"There might be rain, but let's go ahead and say 3:00 PM for everybody," wrote a different user, Yaborgh. I didn't know where I could find them in the park.

"Where are we meeting in the park?" I typed with apprehension.

Within a few seconds, I had a response.

"Where we always meet. On the North side," wrote Yaborgh.

I guessed that they weren't going to be any more specific than that. I'd have to just find them by myself. Satisfied with a meeting date, I kept reading as much as I could to make sure I was as well versed as possible when I met everyone the next day. I schooled myself on everything from the Wiccan belief system to astral projection, which was my personal favorite. Before my eyes closed with the heaviness of reading screens for hours, I decided that if I could make myself do anything amazingly unreal, it would be astral projection.

# CHAPTER 4

I stood in front of my mirror and mindlessly brushed my hair, examining the long, stringy tips. It was 1:30 PM the next day, and I had some driving to do if I was planning on getting to the meeting in time. I didn't know what to wear, how to look, how to dress, how to smell. What if I wore too much perfume? What should I say to these people? Questions flooded my mind as harshly as the static that kept haunting me every time I was around something with a broadcast signal.

I told my parents I'd be back later, in time to eat with them. They probably assumed I was going shopping with Sarah or Melanie; that was the norm. I breezed out of the front door and into my car, cranking it with a push of the button and enjoying the feeling of thawing from air conditioning into a warm car in the early summer. I typed the park address into my navigator and listened to it direct me where to turn—silently praying there would be no interference. So far, my phone and laptop had been alright, but I worried they'd be the next victim to my electronic interference.

I wasn't halfway out of town when I got a call from Sarah, so I turned on my Bluetooth to talk to her.

"Hey," I made sure I sounded cheerful; using my best forced caring voice. If I didn't, she'd ask what was wrong and then from there it would be a massive cover up to deter her.

"Hey! Where are you?" frantic irritation erupted from her voice.

"I'm driving," I replied calmly. There was no way I would tell her where I was going.

"Where are you going right now? There's a pool party at Melanie's boyfriend's house."

"Where?" I asked, her voice crackled through the speaker.

"Melanie's boyfriend's house. You gotta come—it's happening today," she explained desperately.

"Really? It's already the afternoon," I said. A pool party sounded horrible to me. People drinking and canoodling, I wasn't into it. I was so focused on Emily I didn't want to bother with anything else.

"Yeah, yeah, his parents are leaving around three to go out of town for the weekend, it's going to be an afternoon then into the night party. Tell your mom you're staying with me, leave your car at my place, then we'll all ride over with Melanie. If they drive by they'll just think mine's parked in the garage." She explained, spurting excitement through her words.

"Oh, okay. Yeah, I think I'll be late, but I'll try to make it," I lied.

"You're not going to lay out with us then?" I could hear how annoyed she was with me.

"Lay out? No, I'm headed to Beaumont. I won't be back in time," I lied.

"Why?" her nosiness oozed.

"I have to run an errand for my parents. It's a long story."

"Well, hurry up and get back. You don't wanna miss this, it's supposed to get crazy. I've gotta have you there. I don't know if I can stand Michael all by myself tonight, you know?"

"He's your boyfriend, Sarah," I laughed. "If you can't stand him, why don't you break up with him?"

"I guess you're right, but it's just harder than that. I guess I'd freak if I saw him with somebody else, you know? He was my first...never mind. You know what I mean—well maybe you don't. Until I find someone else, I'd be crazy jealous if I saw him with another girl," she explained.

"So, you're not quitting one job until you've been hired for the next, then?" I joked, not letting myself become insulted by the fact that she had moved fast with Michael and felt that she was the more experienced one out of the two of us with regard to life and love.

"Exactly. Besides, the whole college thing coming up, you know? Orientation is coming up soon, who knows who I'll meet there. You're coming with, right?"

"Yeah, I was planning on it. It's next week, right?"

"No, the week after."

"Okay, well, let me call you on my way back. These roads scare me," I said, trying to get off of the phone with her.

"Call me when you're home. Let me know which swimsuit you end up wearing. I'll text you what everyone else has on later. Bring an extra one for me, in case I need to change into something else."

"Okay. You got it," I was relieved to end the conversation. Swimsuits. Pink bikinis, green ones, polka dotted ones...we had to make sure we all wore different ones. No one could be seen in the same one. Oh, no. That would be disastrous. A bikini was like a trademark at a pool party. If you had the same one on as someone else, you'd lost your individuality.

I drove into the city of Beaumont, past the merging of the freeways and signs that directed drivers to Louisiana. As I turned off into the park area, I looked at my car's navigator for the north side; I saw that I could circle around the outer area of the park until I got to the north side. There was a parking lot where I saw a few cars scattered in spots. I decided to go ahead and park there in case I couldn't find anything else, so that I didn't have to circle around again. It was 3:01.

I got out of my car and walked across the slick grass. The spring weather had not brought nearly enough rain, but here, on the day I needed to sit in the park, it was wet. I realized I hadn't brought anything on which to sit during our meeting. I groaned at the thought of dusty jeans or standing awkwardly the entire time.

I made my way through the park anyway, looking for any group of people that I could find. There was a group of five people in an area with thicker foliage. They sat beneath the trees near the low live oak branches and had a spread of snacks, sort of like a picnic. I walked up to them slowly, hoping I'd found the right place.

They looked up at me, strangely but not surprised. Each individual had a different look, and all of them were completely opposite from me.

"Hi," I introduced myself. "I'm Carmichael, from the discussion board? Jessica Carmichael."

"Carmichael?" asked the first girl, sitting down smoking a cigarette. She had short black hair with blue tips on the front ends. Her skin was very pale, and she had on heavy eye makeup. Her clothes were all black, and she wore a pair of black converse with the bottoms painted green. "I thought you were gonna be a dude."

"Yeah," said the girl sitting next to her. She was less severely made up with black eyeliner, and she had a bit more color to her face. She had on dark blue skinny jeans and black converse shoes with a large flannel shirt. Everything about her screamed 90's to me. Her light brown hair was long and stringy, not too different than mine, like she hadn't trimmed it in a few years. It was beautiful though, she pulled the look off well.

"We were expecting a guy I guess," she smiled, speaking softly.

"Well, I didn't want to reveal too much before I met y'all," I said, thinking that it was a lie. I was all over social media with my friends. I was no secret to anyone who wanted to find me.

"Cautious much?" asked the first girl. "I'm Dana. This is Chandra," she introduced, gesturing to the 90's girl through her billowing cigarette smoke.

"Nice to meet you both," I replied, walking up awkwardly to shake their hands. I walked to the other group members too and shook their hands.

"Chris," the guy next to Chandra offered as he shook my hand.

"Vanek," announced the guy next to Chris. His eyes startled me as they were strangely clear blue. He looked more like a Viking than I thought a person could ever look, very blonde and with sharp features—almost scary. It wasn't that I was scared of Scandinavians—this guy just had something about him that was different. His eyes glowed with a piercing blue that shook me.

"Josie," mentioned the girl beside Vanek.

Chris and Vanek wore jeans and t-shirts, both looked like they shopped frequently at thrift shops. Everything looked vintage. Chris had wavy dark brown hair cut into a sort of shag. He had tattoos that I could see going down his forearm onto his wrist. I couldn't tell what they were. Vanek looked more reserved, quiet. I could tell that he didn't dye his hair that color, his eyebrows and lashes matched his light hair. Josie also had the thrift store look, wearing a large Pink Floyd T- shirt with jeans. *Sarah would have a heyday*, I thought to myself. These were definitely not the crowd with whom I would have normally associated myself. I didn't care how different I seemed to them, I wanted to see what they were all about. Some of them knew Emily, and that was all that mattered to me at that moment. I could hear footsteps in the grass behind me, and I saw their faces turn and look to see who was coming.

"Dominic!" Chandra jumped up from her pallet to greet him, throwing her arms around him. I turned around and felt my stomach drop to my feet, or maybe into a bottomless pit that never quite ended. The inevitable rush of adrenaline that followed filled my face with heat.

As far as I am concerned, the only real magic that had ever happened around these people was happening there, right in front of them. But they didn't see it, because that was when I first saw him, and that was where he first touched me, and where I first found reality.

The heat of the day had set in. The moisture from the Gulf of Mexico made the air sticky and humid. I could feel my shirt sticking to my back as I watched them all greet him kindly as he joined the circle in the shade. I began to kneel down, accepting that my jeans would just become dirty. None of it mattered though;everything in my mind was swirling in a whirlpool of emotions as I tried to pull myself together.

"No, wait," Chandra chirped, looking right at me with a smile. "I brought an extra-large towel just in case. Just come over here and share this one," she said with self-assurance.

"Thanks," I accepted, moving over to sit beside her. The sound of the cicadas in the trees hummed loudly as I watched Vanek take a deck of cards out and begin to shuffle. I wondered if we were all going to play a game of spades or if he was going to do magic tricks. Maybe he was going to read them like tarot cards.

"So," Chandra began, "I'd like to start today. I think I did something wrong. I worked a spell the other night to see a spirit in the mirror. It really broke me, I had to ground myself right afterward. I was wondering if any of you had a similar experience. I was so exhausted," she explained.

It was like an AA meeting for witchcraft, except no one was trying to get away from the practice of it or try to discourage it. They wanted to be better at it.

"You should probably try grounding yourself before you try anything like that," suggested Dana. "I take a salt bath with Florida water, then practice breathing and connecting myself to the ground before I begin. You're going to get better results that way regardless of what you're doing. And get some obsidian or tourmaline to hold when you're working like that, you need protection from anything negative.

*Florida water, so that's what it's for*, I thought to myself. One mystery solved. But that guy, Dominic, had just thrust a new mystery right into my head. I had never wanted to stare at someone so badly before in my life.

Vanek kept gently shuffling his cards and looking down. I looked down and then tried to sneak a look at Dominic. He was unlike anyone I'd ever seen, and I just couldn't help myself. He was looking at me. I noticed his eyes were piercingly clear green—like mine. They looked exactly like mine. They were enhanced by his dark lashes and eyebrows. His hair, dark brown and longer, over his ears in a bit of a shag, helped them stand out even more. He looked away when he noticed my glance. I'd never seen eyes like that before, except in the mirror. But eyes framed by a face like his made it impossible to resist looking at him. I gave in and just looked for a moment. He had a perfect jaw line, chiseled but not hard. It made no sense not to just look for a moment.

"What was it that you wanted from the spirit you were conjuring?" Dana asked Chandra.

"Hmmm," she hummed, thinking out loud. "I really just wanted to see what would happen. I've read about it and I wanted to have a cool experience with it, just to see if I could do it."

"Don't you realize what you could have done?" Vanek snapped, not once looking up from his shuffling. He didn't have to use his eyes; his tone was piercing enough.

Startled by his gruff tone, all she could muster was a meek, "What?"

"You could have let something into your house that you can't get out by yourself. You say you want to know what it's like, but what if it's something you can't handle? Then what are you going to do? Ask us all to come over and help exorcise a demon from the house and risk all of our lives?" he sneered, stopping his shuffle and glaring over at her.

"But I didn't conjure a demon," she assured with a hurt look on her face at his scolding tone.

"Well, if you don't know what you're doing then you don't know what you're getting either," he continued. "I sometimes wish I didn't still bother with you people."

The group fell silent. The humming of the cicadas began to roar in my ears. I was stunned by how straightforwardly rude he was to her out of seemingly nowhere.

"So, Jessica," Dana interrupted with her raspy smoker's voice. She seemed too young to have such a rough look, but who was I to judge? I looked at her and awaited her question.

"Where are you from?"

"From the north side, out in the woods," I answered.

"So, not a city girl," she commented. "Dominic used to live up that way, right?"

He nodded his head in agreement.

"I moved to the city a couple of years ago when I started college," he explained. "But I live back home now."

"You in school?" Dana asked.

"Just graduated," I replied.

"Huh. Well, what brings you to our meeting today?" She was tapping out another cigarette and lighting it.

"I just wanted to learn more. I'm new at all of this," I answered, not really able to articulate anything anymore. None of what they were saying felt relevant.

"Yeah, we were all new at one time or another," Dana said, taking a long drag and letting the smoke slowly filter out of her nostrils. "Are you trying to be Wiccan?"

"No."

"So. you're just a practitioner then, no alliance per se."

"I guess not, no. Are you all Wiccans?" I asked the group ignorantly.

"No," Vanek answered. "Only Chris, Dana and Josie are. I'm not, neither is Dominic or Chandra. But we all share a common interest, so this is our group. Some of us are old, some of us newer," he glanced at Chandra, "but we're pretty much the only group around these parts that deals with this topic."

"Wait, wait," interrupted Chris. "I'm more of a chaote, I'd say."

"Whatever," Vanek snipped.

"Oh, okay," I nodded my head. I felt so unprepared.

I'd never felt so stupid in any social situation before in my life. I had always fit in everywhere. This was difficult.

"So what experiences have you had?" Dana continued her impromptu interrogation.

"Um, none as of yet. I'm really just trying to learn what I can," I replied hesitantly, looking around the group. Chris checked his phone. Josie picked her black fingernail polish off and smiled as I responded.

"Well you've come to the right place then," Dana welcomed. I felt relieved that her inquisition had stopped. It was difficult to gauge the group. Everyone seemed like they were there but not there. I didn't know who to trust. Chandra seemed flighty, ditzy and persuadable. She seemed to like Dominic. I saw her touch his back while we were talking. Vanek appeared to harbor some sort of disdain for everyone there but came out of some sort of obligation—for what I couldn't determine. I wasn't sure about Chris, he was hard to read. He seemed more interested in his phone than where he was at the moment. He was almost too well dressed to be there. Josie was quiet, withdrawn. I figured this was probably as social as she got. Dana was like a ring leader, at least in the sense that she seemed like an older, more established member. Dominic was just as hard to read as everyone else. He listened to what everyone had to say and didn't really participate. But the magnetic attraction from me to him was undeniable. I was more taken aback at how I reacted to him than to anything the group had discussed. They could have been talking about flying dragons that were headed our way to carry us away from the Rapture, and I still would have been more intrigued by him.

When it was my turn to talk about something, I had to think fast. I had been lost in thought. "Astral Projection," I said. "I want to learn how to do it."

Chris looked up from his phone. "It takes a lot of practice. But you can totally do it. We've all done it," he said, glancing around through his hipster glasses for reassurance.

"When you go to sleep tonight, say a little prayer. Ask for protection and guidance as you leave your body. It happens between the awake and sleep state. Sort of like a dream," Dana explained.

"Also very important—when you feel the buzzing on your body, like a painless electrocution, don't stop. People get scared, and they don't follow through. When you feel it and hear it, go with it. Let go of yourself," Chris explained.

"What can I do once I'm doing it?" I asked.

"Depends on where you want to go," Dominic piped up.

"What do you mean?" I looked at him, taking in a breath.

"In the astral state, you can go anywhere, see anything, anyone. You can learn information that way as well. You can start small, in your own house. Once you get comfortable, you can move on from there, to another familiar place—or person," he explained.

"Okay. I guess I'll try it tonight then," I decided out loud, satisfied with the information I had gained. I looked at my phone, it was almost four. I had a couple of text messages from Sarah and Melanie. I started to scroll through them, anticipating their incessant questions and demands.

"Jess, where are you? Pool party is starting! Melissa and Brooke both have on little pink bikinis. SO WEAR YOUR BLACK ONE." Oh, the urgency.

Melanie's text was next. "Jessica…when you get here, Rob's friend Ryan wants to meet you. He's a sophomore at State, plays on some team, baseball maybe, IDK. You WANT to get here soon."

As I stopped reading, the group began to disseminate. Everyone was starting to stand up and stretch.

"Okay same time next week," I heard Chris telling Dana.

"Yeah, I'm gonna bring some cool shit—hopefully some EVP's for us to listen to," Dana said as she walked away.

Josie climbed onto a bicycle and began to ride off, waving at the group. Chandra started walking with Dominic over to the parking lot near where I had parked. Vanek went further into the park, down a trail. I watched him walk away until I couldn't see him anymore.

I began walking to my car, thinking about what I had just heard from these new people, and then my mind was rushing with thoughts about Melanie's boyfriend's party. There would be lots of booze and debauchery, that much was for sure. I didn't know if I felt up to it, but I felt the obligatory pressure to attend and show face. I thought about what Dominic had explained regarding astral projection. More than anything, I just wanted to go home and practice it, not stay up partying with a mix of college people and risk getting caught drunk by my parents or the police.

I walked up to my car, unlocking it as I approached. As I reached for the door handle, I felt a hand touch my shoulder. A surge of energy penetrated my whole being.

I gasped, spinning around. I thought I felt someone behind me, but I had been looking at the phone. It was Dominic. I thought Chandra had walked him over to his truck. I didn't expect to see him. I was sure that whatever I had felt was something that would just pass, but I was completely wrong.

Now the embarrassment having stared at him rushed into my face, overcoming everything else.

"Um, hey," I greeted, looking around nervously. I was afraid if I stared into his eyes again I wouldn't be able to stop, ever.

He smiled, almost laughing. "Hey. Sorry to sneak up on you like that," he said, rocking back on his heels, hands in his pockets.

"What's up?" I asked, not sure if I needed to look busy, pretty or just stop everything altogether. I didn't know how to act, I realized. He made me feel out of sorts—in a good way. I went with the latter. I slowed myself down, sucked in a breath, and let my eyes meet his.

"I know who you are," he confessed. "You're Emily Carmichael's little sister."

# CHAPTER 5

Hearing his words ring in my head I was reduced to a roaring silence. I couldn't think of any clever or intelligent retort. I could only look at him with a shocked expression of bewilderment. I thought I was ready to know things, but maybe I wasn't.

"I—I have to go," I turned away from him and fiddled with the door handle to open it as quickly as possible and drive away, but I didn't want to go. He had just given me exactly the thing I had come for. His penetrating eyes looked disappointed, and I was immediately ashamed with myself for saying that I needed to leave when it wasn't what I wanted. Something like a magnet in my gut made me feel like I needed to be right up against him.

"Wait, don't leave," he pleaded, furrowing his brows with concern. "I didn't mean to make you worry."

"It's just...I didn't want anyone to know who I was."

"No one knows who you are—except me. Don't worry."

"But how?" I asked, wishing we could just talk about something else, something more normal.

"Well that's why I came," he said, "I came to find you."

"Find me? It seems like you always come, they all know you."

"You mean you don't know yet?" he asked. Now his eyebrows had changed into an upward slant of genuine surprise.

"Dominic, I have to go," I said, choking out the words in more of a whisper.

"Wait," he asked as I opened my door and got in. I hesitantly rolled down the window. "I wanted to tell you why I started coming in the first place—how I knew."

"I…I can't right now," I said, and I put my car into reverse, leaving him standing there.

He watched me drive away, and as I drove away looking in my rearview mirror I was completely terrified that he knew exactly who I was. But I didn't understand what I didn't know already.

My phone rang and the sound of it startled me to attention.

"Hello?" I answered with a panicked tone.

I heard laughter and crackling through the speakers. The static sent chills down my spine.

"Not again," I whimpered.

"Jessica!" Sarah shouted with laughter through the phone. I had heard only pool party

noise—no terrifying voices.

"Hey!" I shouted back at her, trying to get her attention through the laughter.

"When are you gonna get here?" she asked with nagging irritation.

"I'm on my way back now. I'm driving!" I yelled through bursts of static and interference.

"Melanie says to bring that bottle that you forgot the other day," she said, chatting with the people around her while yelling into her phone at me. I could tell by her voice she was already slightly inebriated.

"Tell her I will. I'll be there in like an hour," I responded, turning off the Bluetooth. My obligations to my friends were beginning to irritate me. The only positive attraction to the situation was that I at least wouldn't have to be alone with my thoughts.

I arrived at my house and ran upstairs, racing past my parents without saying much more than a hello.

As I was changing into my bikini and pool clothes in my room, my mother knocked on the door.

"Where are you going, hun?" Her tone was mainly of disinterest, as if she was only asking me because that's what she was supposed to do.

"To Sarah's. We're all going to hang out and spend the night," I replied, covering my swimsuit straps so that my mother wouldn't suspect that I was lying to her.

"Oh, well your gonna miss dinner with everyone. How was your day?" she asked.

"It was…fine. I'll be back in the morning. I can't sleep late over there," I explained. The doctor must have upped her dosage—the one she'd been given ever since Emily disappeared. Her voice was empty, and I was surprised she didn't care that I wasn't going to eat with everyone. I reached under my bed for the bottle of whisky that Melanie anticipated so badly and slipped it into my tote bag. I opened the door and my mother was waiting, staring me down like she knew something. The party. I thought. She must know something.

"Take care of yourself, Jess. You're getting older now, things change," she counseled. I couldn't figure out her motives. I hugged her, told her to tell everyone at dinner I said hello, and walked away silently, questioning whether it was meds or something else.

The bass of my music rattled through my speakers as I drove to Melanie's boyfriend's house. His parents had a place out in an exclusive subdivision with large houses and expensive cars.

I pulled up to a large, two-story brick house with a three-car garage to the side. If it hadn't been for all of the cars parked in the driveway I would've been lost—all of those houses seemed to look the same. Big, brick and boring.

I walked around the side of the house to where I could hear the music and opened the gate slowly.

"Jessica!" I was greeted with immense squeals from my friends.

"Come on! Get in the hot tub with us! Where the hell have you been?" Melanie bombarded me as she took my tote bag and searched for the bottle.

She pulled it out and yanked my shorts on one side, encouraging me to strip down. I slipped out of my clothes and received some enthusiastic yelling from some guys in the swimming pool. Sprinting for the track team had my physique in pretty good shape.

"We're in the hot tub, over here," Melanie pointed, wearing a lime green bikini and showing off her prom tan. Her slender frame was like that of a model, with her bleached, blonde wavy hair bouncing around as she walked. She obviously hadn't been swimming at all yet; she still had on a full face of makeup.

"Ryan, this is Jessica. Jessica, Ryan," she said, motioning towards us with a grand Vanna White gesture as she said our names.

"Ahh, the pretty one with the crazy cool eyes," he said, holding his drink up to toast my entrance into the hot tub.

"I've been shown some pretty hot pictures of you."

"Well, filters really exaggerate our best features," I said with a menacing smile at Melanie, getting into the hot water slowly and wanting to yank Melanie's hair for whatever she had shown to this stranger. Melanie poured the whisky into red plastic cups and distributed them to everyone as we sat in the steaming water. The tips of my hair dipped into the water, and I looked down at them and watch them sway peacefully back and forth, not really wanting to look at Ryan in the face. I hated set ups. They made me so uncomfortable. She'd tried to set me up back in the fall, and I had to just ghost the guy after a while.

The guys she knew always wanted easy girls who drank beer and liked to sit in deer stands. I wasn't an easy girl, and I had better ways of spending the waking hours of winter weekends. Melanie was right about Ryan though—he was extremely well built and attractive. He was as tan as I was and obviously worked out frequently. He had dark blue eyes and sandy colored hair that he styled in the perfect way for his bone structure. Overall, Ryan was an Abercrombie model incarnate, as if he'd just stepped right off the side of a shopping bag.

"So, Melanie tells me you're single?" Ryan said, scooting over to sit beside me in the tub.

"Yeah, actually I am," I replied. Normally the hot water would have been soothing, but I felt more like I was in a boiling pot awaiting imminent death. Nothing he said really registered with me, I kept seeing Dominic's face popping up in my head.

"That's cool. I know a lot of girls fresh out of high school have their like, serious boyfriends that they don't want to hurt and shit," he laughed.

"Well, I lied, I do have one," I said coyly, letting the mental image of Dominic sink into my thoughts comfortably. I wanted to know what it felt like to say something like that out loud.

"That's cool, that's cool," he replied nodding, taking a sip from his drink.

"So you party much?" he asked me, undeterred by my boyfriend comment.

"Like, party party? Or party?" I said, trying to glean from him what exactly he was asking and not sound stupid all at the same time.

"Like this, you know?" he asked, holding up his drink and guzzling from it.

"Oh. Yeah, we drink sometimes. I don't really wanna get fat though, I know that happens to a lot of girls that drink all the time," I said, trying to be funny but still not really comfortable. I looked over at Melanie, she was completely tangled up with her boyfriend. The other two girls in the hot tub got up and left. It was admittedly a disgusting sight to see Melanie in that position, but I had grown accustomed to it since we were about sixteen. She and Sarah both took relationships to a whole other level really quickly when they thought they were in love. It was just the four of us now. I was even more uncomfortable, it looked like a set up for seduction.

"Yeah, you're not fat at all," he agreed with a handsome smile and grabbed me, pinching me playfully on my side and then sliding his arm around my waist. I could see where this was going. Disgust began to well up within me. My comment had not been an invitation for touchy-feely. I hated feeling used for the way I looked. I pushed myself up out of the water and murmured a quick "excuse me" without really looking anyone in the eye. "I have a boyfriend."

Melanie turned from her activities and mustered a drunken, "Where are you going? What? Since when?"

"I'll be back," I lied. What I thought I wanted, I now didn't understand. I thought I had wanted to be at all of the best parties and in the middle of everything. I thought I wanted everything I had. I thought my friends were really my friends. Now I just wanted to go home. My parents thought I was at Sarah's house. I'd just tell them I had a stomach ache and go back home.

I found my tote bag in the middle of a group of people at poolside table laughing and drinking. I wiggled through them as politely as possible and grabbed my bag. It was soaked with water.

"Ugh!" I grunted out loud. People looked at me funny. I was supposed to be the pretty girl having fun, not the Debbie Downer upset about a wet bag.

I grabbed my things and got in my car in my swimsuit. I looked down at my phone. I had an instant message sent to one of the apps on my phone.

"Hey…" it read.

I felt my stomach drop a little. The thought of who it might be rushed through me like fire. I knew who I wanted it to be.

I looked at the user icon. It was a picture of an Ace of Spades from a deck of cards.

"Hey, who is this?" I wrote back.

"It's Vanek. From the meeting today."

"Yeah, I remember. What's up?" I replied, thinking it was odd of him to message me. He had been so cold and rude.

"There's something about you that you weren't telling us today," he wrote.

My gut dropped as I started the car. Again, I felt I was being lambasted, as though I was keeping a secret. Had he talked to Dominic?After the incident at the pool party I was flustered and completely incapable of playing mind games with people. I decided to just put it out there.

"That I'm Emily Carmichael's sister?" I punched the message into my phone.

"Why were you at our meeting? Do you think someone there might know something about what happened to her?"

"I don't know. I just want to find out for myself, really."

"You're awful young to be delving into the unknown like that, don't you think?" he replied. I could feel his negative energy through the message.

"No, not really. Not much younger than you are."

"You really don't understand what you're getting yourself into, do you? And you don't know so much about me either…or anyone else who was out there today. You really don't know who to trust, do you?"

"No, I guess not Vanek," I replied, irritated with him.

"If I were you I would just stay away. Lest you want to end up like your sister," he responded quickly. Images of possibilities of her death flooded my mind and I shook from the thought of what had happened to her.

I threw my phone down in the passenger seat. Why was this guy being so weird? And hateful? And who still used "lest"? Did he know that Emily was dead and we didn't? I was flabbergasted as the possibilities flew through my mind. Putting my car into gear I headed home.

I got out of my car and threw on the t-shirt and shorts from my tote bag before I went in the house. They were still damp and uncomfortable from my bag getting wet earlier.

"What brings you back so early?" my mother said calmly, sipping a glass of cabernet sauvignon on the couch, seemingly not too surprised to see me.

"I had a headache. Stomach ache. Just tired." I said, passing by the living room where she sat.

She gave me a look through the side of her eyes as she took a sip. "I'm guessing you don't need anything?"

"No," I mumbled back at her as I headed for the stairs on a mission to get to my room. "Just need to shower and go to sleep!"

"You missed a great dinner with the family!" I heard her shout as I topped the staircase. I just needed to wash the ickyness of the day off of me.

I did just that. The steam from the shower felt great as it washed away the discomfort of the night. From the pool party, to being touched by a strange guy, to the bizarre texts from Vanek, I felt like I needed to wash it all away.

I fell into my bed, exhausted more than usual. Everything was weighing on me. Seeking total isolation, I shut my phone off and let myself melt into a deep sleep.

# CHAPTER 6

I woke up feeling like I was walking through molasses. I couldn't move very well at all. It was a struggle to open my eyes, like they had been glued shut. I forced them open and saw the tall pine trees towering around me. I was in the woods. It looked like it was dusk or dawn, very dimly lit. I saw a light in the distance ahead of me. Something compelled me to follow it. I tried to move, but I couldn't quite get the motion going forward. I looked around me, behind me. I could see there was a trail that led to this point. I whipped around to see the light again. It was getting farther away. I started trying to move towards it again. My movement started to change from slow, like running in water to quicker, faster. Then I was in full pursuit of it. I got close enough to it to reach out for it. As I did, a face appeared in the light. It was the most horrific face I had ever seen. All of the features were distorted and it looked like something straight from the depths of hell. The eyes were slits, but vertical ones, and the nose was the same. The mouth stretched unnaturally from ear to ear and gaped open, the jaw dropping in an unnatural position, showing rows of strange, pointy teeth. It was like whatever it was had on a mask of torn skin. Total darkness surrounded it. It was like it had emerged from a dark corner of a room and zoomed directly at me, faster than anything natural could move, and faster than I could escape it. It got so close to me, I could feel cold breath on my face. I stopped and screamed, shuffling backward clumsily, trying to back away from it.

Then I actually woke up. I had been sweating profusely in my bed. I looked at the clock; it was 10:27 A. M. I had slept all night and through to the next day without ever waking up.

The intrigue and fear of the dream kept me thinking about it all through the day. It seemed to me to be more than just a coincidence that I dreamed about the woods. It was as if the light in the woods came to me in my dream and beckoned me to follow it.

I lounged in my room reading The Mists of Avalon, thinking about Morgain le Fay and how her life had so many disturbing turns in it. The escapism of a good book was not quite enough for me though, which was upsetting because it was the first book I had made time to read outside of books for school and I had really looked forward to it. My mind wandered back to the dream and its meaning over and over again. The woods scared me. I hadn't been out in them once since the search for Emily ended, and I didn't want to go back now.

By the time night fell, I was still in bed ignoring my phone. I didn't want to see the messages from my friends, wondering where I was or why I had left the party. I didn't feel up to an interrogation about what was wrong with me, either. More than all of that, I didn't want to see anything weird from Vanek.

The day seemed to pass without any real meaning to it. My family stopped by to say goodbye before leaving town. I felt sleepy very soon after they left, and I headed to bed at an unusually early time.

My eyes fluttered open and I looked at the clock. Again, it read 10:27. I was wide awake after having done essentially nothing all day long. I looked out my window to the woods. It had to happen now, I thought. I slipped on my running shoes and threw on a light zip up hoodie, making sure to walk quietly down the stairs to the back door. I took a flashlight with me from the counter. I walked towards the trail that led down into the thick brush at the border where the trees met our property. The smell of pines in the air was aromatically appealing. Dry pine needles crunched beneath my feet as I cautiously started down the trail. I picked up my brisk walk and turned it into a jog. Mosquitoes nipped at the bare skin on my hands and face as I made my way down the trail. I wasn't sure exactly what I was looking for, but I wanted to see if there were any lights like I had seen in my dream. A flashback of the face made me stop for a moment, but I reminded myself it had just been a dream and I trekked on.

The humidity made my face feel damper than it really was. I wiped underneath my eyes with the sleeves of my hoodie to try and see better in the dark. I had reached the point of the trail where it split and went two ways. The woods had been a playground for me and Emily when we were little. I remembered that the left trail went to a creek bed and the right wentfarther into the woods. Hunters often had camps nearby that they would stay in during deer season, but that time of year was months away. Any sound I heard now could be any number of possibilities. There could be deer, rabbits, wild hogs, even those elusive panthers I had warned Emily of in the woods. I began to feel stupid for wandering out so far in the woods when I could be attacked by a wild animal.

Just as I had convinced myself to turn around and go back home, I saw a flicker of blue light down the trail to the right. My stomach dropped to my feet. I wanted to run away, but I couldn't let myself leave when I knew this was what I had ventured to see. I had already run away from Dominic when he was just about to tell me something important. I couldn't do something like that again. I went on several yards down the trail, to where there was a slight clearing in the trees. The blue light flickered like the flame of a candle, faint but visible. I thought maybe I was hallucinating or seeing the "gas" everyone claimed made lights appear in the woods in Texas. I crept up the trail a little bit more until I saw the small flame jump away farther into the trees.

*Could have been a firefly,* I thought to myself. There were fireflies this time of year. Maybe I wasn't seeing blue at all. It didn't make sense. But then again, it didn't make sense that I was out in the woods late at night. I stood in the clearing for a moment, perplexed at my odd behavior. My flashlight grew dim to the point that it no longer functioned. I had no room for fear. This defined what I would make of myself—run away or discover something.

I hadn't quite decided whether to return home or not when something made me drop my dead flashlight. There, before my eyes, was the blue flame. It was blocking my way back down the trail and slowly growing bigger. It swelled outward and I could feel heat radiating from it. It wasn't cold, like in my dream. Frozen by fear, I couldn't move away from it. I felt that its pulsing growth was about to overtake me and there was little I could do to escape its power. I trembled as it began to envelope my head, pulling me into its force.

"Look away!" I heard a voice yell and felt myself be tackled to the ground. I hit the pine needles with a scraping thud, too hypnotized by what had just happened to react to the fall.

"Are you okay?"

I looked up to see Dominic, breathing heavily and sweating profusely.

Bewildered, I sat on the pine needle floor of the woods and looked up at him. I couldn't believe he was there.

"How did you know I was here?" I finally managed to say through heaving breaths.

"Are you okay?" he repeated.

"I think so," I stammered, staring at him, scared that he had found me. A thousand thoughts rushed through my mind. Had he followed me? Was he a stalker? How did he know I'd be out here?

But deep down within me I knew none of those things were true.

"I didn't mean to scare you. I had a feeling you'd be coming out here soon," he replied. His breathing had steadied back into normalcy.

"A feeling?" I couldn't hide my fear in my tone.

"Look, it's not safe out here. These woods are cursed."

I had so many questions for him, but the cluster of things running through my mind was hindering my ability to articulate my thoughts to him properly.

"Why are you—how did you know to find me here?" I asked, still sitting. He knew where I would be earlier that day and now this.

He reached his hand out to me to pull me up. I looked at him with slight distrust, but completely enthralled with his eyes.

He smiled, motioning for me to take his hand. "Let me help you up."

I took his hand, reluctant for help. When my hand touched his, it was the same sensation as static electricity without the painful pop. I couldn't explain it, but it felt perfect in some way.

He pulled me up with surprising strength. I started dusting my pants off, and he took my hand to lead me back out of the small clearing down the trail back to my house.

"I'll explain everything," he started, "but I want to get you home first. You and I, of all people, should not be out there in those cursed woods right now."

This sort of thing wasn't supposed to happen. It was something I had seen in corny movies or read in books. No good looking stranger was ever supposed to rescue me.

We reached the clearing near my house, and he gently ushered me with his hand on the small of my back until we reached the back porch of my parents' house. He sat down with me on the steps to the back porch.

"Thank you," I said, wanting to say much more with those two words.

"You're welcome. I'm sorry if I scared you—again," he said.

"You stopped that light. What was it?" I asked. I felt like a fool.

"I told you, these woods are cursed. There are things out there not explainable. I grew up around here too, on the other side of the woods."

"Yeah, I grew up out here, too. But I never heard of any curse. I remember you said you grew up across on the other side, at the park today. That still doesn't explain how you knew I would be out there, out here. . . ."

"You probably wouldn't have heard the woods are cursed. Not from this side. If I tell you, you might think it's a little strange," he said, smiling.

"No stranger than everything else that's been happening," I shrugged.

"I dreamt about the woods last night. I've known these trails since I was a kid. I knew the spot where you were, the clearing. I saw you in my dream, looking for your sister. But I also saw danger. It was too realistic to ignore. It was like a message was being sent to me. I wasn't going to actually come all the way out here, but I was compelled. I had to. That's what I wanted to tell you at the park. I'd seen you, in dreams."

Somewhat shocked that I'd been in his dreams, I stopped for a second and thought about what to say next.

"I had a dream too," I confessed, looking off into the woods. "That's why I came out here. But you weren't in it. No one was. Just me—and...."

"And what?" he asked. I could hear the intrigue in his voice and I wasn't sure what to
make of it.

"And that blue light. But it turned into something. It was a terrifying, horrible face. I'll never forget it no matter how much I'll try. It had slits for eyes and a gaping mouth. The whole thing was—distorted. The soulless eyes spread vertically across the face, and it looked like it was coming after me. I felt like it wanted to hurt me. I have a feeling that whatever that thing was took my sister."

"Well, that's another reason I wanted to talk to you, but I couldn't when I first saw you," Dominic explained.

"Yeah that meeting was—not the right place to talk," I shrugged. "It seemed like everyone there was a mismatch."

"That's why I wanted to talk to you alone. Your sister didn't disappear. She was taken. It's happened here before, around here and it will continue to happen if it isn't stopped."

"Where was she taken?" I asked, incredulously.

"Somewhere we can't travel to the usual way," he replied.

"What does that even mean? And who else was taken? Is she alive?" I asked, desperation cracking my voice.

"I'll come back to you soon, and we can talk more about it. Get some rest, make sure you don't go back out there alone."

I nodded that I agreed, furrowing my brows at him, trying to gauge everything with logic and reason.

He reached into his pocket. "Here's my number. Call me if you need me," he responded, handing me a piece of rumpled up paper. He walked away into the darkness of our road, avoiding the side of our land that met the woods.

I sat there for a moment, completely taken aback at what all had just befallen me. Not only had Dominic saved me, but now he was going to help me. I had so many unanswered questions that it made my head hurt—or maybe it was from the tackle in the woods. Either way, I needed to sleep. I pulled myself up holding onto the porch railing and snuck inside as quietly as possible.

I replayed what had happened over and over in my head, combing through every detail I could recall. I didn't know what to think; all I knew was that I was thankful. There was something in the woods. That was for certain. What it was exactly still remained a mystery.

# CHAPTER 7

The heat of the summer had begun to creep in with the heavy humidity that lines the gulf coast each year in June. Summer clouds developed and sprinkled an afternoon shower as I sat in my room with the TV sounds posing as a background noise for my ever-developing thoughts. I kept my distance from it in order for it to work. Each time my phone would buzz with a message, my stomach would turn with wild fury at the thought of who it might be. It had been a week since the pool party, and I had been ignoring my friends ever since. I thought of ways to search the woods and find what could be lurking in the midst of the forest.

I looked at Dominic's number and typed it into my phone a few times, but I couldn't figure out what to say or do.

I sat at my sister's laptop and searched for answers on the internet, finding only generic clues to what lay dormant. I had to keep it plugged in, the battery would drain almost immediately. The same was happening with my phone but at least I could use it for a little while before I had to plug it up. I found stories and books of Bigfoot sightings and haunted houses, but nothing about witchcraft or any other type of spirit that reminded me of what I encountered in the woods before Dominic had stopped it. It wasn't Bigfoot. It was something otherworldly.

Thunder gently rolled outside my window as I continued my research. Irritated, I looked down at my phone as it buzzed with another message.

"Can you come to another meeting tonight?" It was Dana.

Her unexpected invitation made my heart flutter with anxiety. I had only met her the one time, and I wasn't entirely sure of trusting the group after Vanek's slew of strange messages to me. "How did you get my number?" I asked.

"You gave it to me, remember?" Dana said in her gruff tone.

"No, I don't."

"Wait, no, I got it from Vanek, yeah, that's how I got it," she said.

Hearing his name made me reconsider meeting up with the group again. I didn't bother asking anything else. I took a deep breath.

"When and where?" I asked, hoping it wouldn't be anywhere where Vanek might be.

"Chris' apartment. Around 9, that's when he gets off work. It's not far from your side of town I don't think...not as far as the park was anyway," Dana replied.

I was terrified, but I accepted the invitation. Dana and Chris seemed harmless, just a little strange. I wanted to see what else they had going on besides Chandra's rambling at our last meeting.

My mind raced with all of the different possibilities the night held. I wondered what they had planned and hoped they didn't have any sort of initiation requirement. Maybe they wanted to go ghost hunting or something, hopefully nothing sinister. After all, some of them were Wiccan and they professed to be harmless.

I told my parents that I was going to Sarah's house and left at 8:30. They gave their usual goodbye reminders to call or text and let them know where I would be.

Pulling up to the address, I saw that the apartment was part of an older home that had been broken into smaller apartments. As I entered the front door area, I realized that it probably housed only seven other apartments. There were four doors on the bottom and stairs that led up to four other doors. I walked up the creaking stairs to the second floor and knocked lightly at 4B. The smell in the air was of antique wood and old carpet. The aromas created an air of spookiness in the old building, but I liked it. It made me feel like I was somewhere with a history.

I heard the locks coming undone and the sound of the hinges squeak as Dana opened the door.

"Hey! You made it!" she exclaimed, as she held the door open and ushered me through it.

I was surprised by the warm welcome because it was so different than the first time. I guess they just needed to trust. The apartment was small—efficiency size. There was a futon couch and some paper lamps, a small television, and the kitchen was no bigger than the average apartment bathroom. But Chris had everything neatly stacked and hanging. Everything had a place in the lamp-lit room. The windows were open and in the distance the refineries were visibly twinkling. It was a very cozy little apartment.

"I love this apartment!" I confessed to Chris as he came out of his tiny kitchen to greet me. There were a few boxes of pizza stacked on the miniature sized counter area.

"Thanks. Yeah, I like it because it fits me. I don't need much space. Help yourself to some pizza." He motioned toward the boxes.

Out of the tiny bedroom area emerged Chandra and Josie, and I sensed the smell of some sort of herb burning. Dana noticed me sniffing the air.

"It's not weed, if that's what you were thinking," she assured, with a wry smile. "They're smudging the apartment with sage for a cleansing."

"No, I didn't think it was that!" I laughed nervously. I didn't like Dana thinking I was judgmental.

"We use sage as a cleansing tool, all practitioners use it to cleanse the space of negative energy. We've got the placecovered now," Dana explained, plopping down on the futon with a slice of pepperoni pizza.

"So, where's everybody else from the other day?" I asked, meaning actually to ask, where's crazy Vanek and the sexy guy Dominic that secretly saved me?

"Oh, yeah, Vanek doesn't always come around. He works and stuff. Dom's got some other obligations tonight. Not sure what. Anyway, we needed enough people for a séance. And you make the right number."

"I didn't know there was a right number," I said.

"There's not, actually, but you gave us good vibes the other day and we invited you," Dana replied wryly in her rough voice.

"Oh, okay. Well, thanks?" I wondered what Dominic's other obligations were, and I hoped Dana didn't see my face flush when she mentioned his name.

"Did everybody eat?" Chris asked, and the other girls grabbed what pieces were left over as we conversed about our day and what we had been doing since we last met. My mind wasn't there though, I was meta-cognizantly thinking of howthese people, the same age as my other friends and I, were not out drinking and partying. Instead, they were eating pizza and "cleansing" an apartment of negativity.

"Jessica?" Dana asked. My mind whipped back to the conversation.

"I'm sorry, what's that?" I asked, embarrassed for having been lost in thought.

"Have you ever done a séance before?" she asked.

"Oh, no. This is my first time," I confessed, nodding my head awkwardly. I had the strangest sensation that none of them really knew what they were doing, either.

"You haven't been drinking, taking pills, smoking pot— anything like that today, have you?" Chris asked.

"No, why?" I asked, surprised at the question and a little insulted.

"We've all got to be clear minded, as pure as possible for this to work. Alcohol and drugs like Vicodin, Xanax, marijuana, they cloud the mind too much for concentration," he explained.

"Oh, I see. Well no, I'm all clear," I smiled with awkward reassurance.

"Okay, guys, this place is supposedly haunted by a suicide. The people downstairs are complaining of hearing someone walk around and making noise while Chris is at work. They even called the cops about the noise when Chris wasn't here. Whatever it is, it's either up here in Chris's apartment or hanging around the whole joint," Dana began. "So, we're gonna try and use our skills to meet it, and get whatever it is to stop bothering the tenants here. Josie, do you have the recorder?"

"Yep," she quietly said and smiled. She stood up and set up a tripod with a video recorder and pulled a digital voice recorder from the pocket of her sweater.

"That's for the EVPs," Chris said to me as we all gathered in his tiny living room space to sit in a circle.

"EVPs?" I asked, clenching my teeth with a gentle grunt as I bent down to sit. My knee was bruised from the night before.

"Electric voice phenomenon. You can catch voices that we can't hear with our human ears on the recording. It's stupid awesome. I've got some amazing recordings you need to listen to sometime from a few sessions."

"Wow. That's amazing." My curiosity was piqued by how scientific they were making the whole event.

"Yeah, the spirit world is very closely aligned with ours, but they vibrate, resonate if you will, on a different level than what we are on right now. It gets into physics, really. If you're interested I can explain it all to you sometime."

"Yeah, sure," I said.

"Anyway, their voices vibrate at that different level in which they exist, so our eardrums can't pick up that vibration, but the recorder can. And we can magnify it on my equipment later, to hear what all was happening that we weren't' able to hear."

Dana lit candles and turned the lamps off. All of our faces were glowing around a candle in the middle of our circle that we had formed. She had candles lit in the kitchen and on the side table beside the futon for extra lighting. The five of us huddled together.

"Everyone here, clear your heads of thoughts of the outside world. Concentrate only on the flame that I have lit with the intention of calling the spirit world to us tonight. Think ofnothing else but the flame and the intention with which it burns, to bring to us the spirits that are around us right now."

I concentrated, feeling odd at first. Clearing one's thoughts is something quite difficult to actually do when compared to the idea doing of it. So many thoughts were clogging up my mind that I felt I was going to be a failure at concentrating. I didn't want to let the group down. I needed to figure out a way to get all of the thoughts out of my head. My sister, my parents, my friends, my newfound problem with Vanek....

I began to imagine each one of my thoughts as boats, and envisioned them sailing away from me, until all I was left with was still water that was empty. I stared into the flame as I concentrated on my still and empty body of water.

The flame in front of us started to dance wildly. There was no air current blowing through the apartment and I became excited at seeing a change in the atmosphere. I began to feel cold.

"If you're here, and I think you are, tell us your name. We want to hear your name," Dana said, speaking slowly and methodically.

"We want you to do something to us to show us that you are here. Come into our world and show us that you are here with us."

Nothing happened. I tried to keep myself focused and concentrated on our candle flame, which had settled down from its wild dance. Then I realized something. I had a calmness, a knowledge of some sort. I just knew. I stared at the candle and willed it to move. The flame jumped like it had been sprinkled with gasoline. I had a sudden onset of thoughts that changed everything. There was no spirit haunting the place. I knew that, as well.

"Oh, my God!" Dana exclaimed, "I've never seen that happen. If you are here, and you're haunting this place, please know that you can move on to the next phase. You can leave. You are not bound to this place any longer. Go to the light, I command you."

It was difficult for me not to laugh, because I knew what I had done. I wasn't trying to be cruel, but it was amazing how easily I was able to manipulate the flame.

Dana leaned over and blew out the candle, trying to stay true to her séance seriousness. I had a feeling come over me. I stared at it hard, seeing just a tiny ember burning out. I told it to flare up again. It grew back into the flame just as if it had been lit by someone. Dana stared, befuddled.

"I blew that out. You all saw me blow that out, right?" She looked around at each one of us. We nodded in unison. She blew it out again.

We sat silent for a moment in darkness. My eyes focused in the dark and for just a brief moment I thought about doing it one more time, but I didn't. They weren't nearly as experienced as they thought they were. Neither was I, but this was coming to me so naturally.

"What the hell?" Dana blurted out, irritated. Again, I didn't laugh, but I wanted to, and badly. I realized that they didn't know anything.

The light of the lamp was flicked on and everyone squinted. Chris got up with the recorder and took it to his laptop to connect it. Josie moved up to the futon to sit and Chandra went to the bathroom. I got up and sat next to Josie. I could overhear Chris asking Dana what she thought happened, in all of her expertise.

"So, how old are you?" I asked Josie.

She looked at me with her wide brown eyes. "Twenty," she said almost whispering.

"Oh, okay. Well, I'm eighteen. This is all pretty new to me. How about you?"

"Josie's not really new to all of it," Chandra interrupted, sitting down beside her. I was getting a bit burnt out already on Chandra. I didn't understand why she had to be so invasive.

Josie looked at her as if to say, "speak for me".

"Josie's been wanting to contact her family on the other side. Her family was involved with a tragedy a few years back; she doesn't really talk about it. So, she's here with us most of the time, waiting for them to come through," Chandra explained, putting one arm around Josie's shoulder as if to show just how supportive she was.

I wondered why they didn't seem to ever let her talk for herself. I started to realize that groups of people, regardless of their interests, were really all the same. My friends tried to speak for me and tell me what I wanted, and here they did the same thing to Josie.

"Oh, I'm sorry to hear about the tragedy," I apologized, wondering what could have happened. It was at that moment of wondering that I felt my head buzz like a light saber and I had a flash of a car accident. It startled me, and I sucked in a quick breath. I felt horrible for her.

In a split second, I saw it in my mind, just how it had happened. They weren't killed right away. No one knew where they were, on a road somewhere in the woods. Her father fell asleep. They veered to the left and he overcorrected, sending them down into an embankment. They hit a tree and broke so many bones they couldn't move. With punctured lungs, they drowned in their own blood. I could feel it in my throat, there was a pain in my chest. I glanced up to see Chris and Dana sitting on the foot of his small bed with the laptop trying to get the recorder to connect to his software for review.

"So, Chandra," I asked, trying to be friendly and shake off what had just happened. "Are you in college?"

"I've taken some classes at the community college, but I'm undeclared. I really just don't know what I want to do yet. "Her voice seemed to flutter as she spoke. I wondered if she'd managed to pass the classes she took.

"Oh okay. I'm supposed to start at State in the fall."

"Cool! So, you're moving then, away?" she asked, seemingly excited to know that I wouldn't be around.

"Probably. Just home on the weekends, you know?"

"Yeah," she said. "Do you have a boyfriend?"

I had been drifting from our conversation and reflecting on what I had just done. I realized I was still pretty stunned by what I had done and I snapped back into the conversation, trying to catch up to it. "Um, no," I responded, sensing where she was taking things.

"Oh," she said, attempting to hide thoughts of jealousy behind her curious eyes. I could sense that she didn't like any competition for Dominic's attention.

"My friends tried to hook me up with some guy the other night. After I met up with you," I said, trying my best to be friendly.

"Yeah?" Chandra's blue eyes lit up, suddenly much more interested in my story. Now I had her. Now I wanted to push it.

"Yeah, but I just really wasn't into it. It was weird. We were all at this pool party, we were in a hot tub…I felt like my friend was just trying to hook me up with him so she wouldn't be the only one with someone that night."

"But he liked you?" Chandra asked. She seemed to be hanging on to my every word, like she had never been to any sort of party with that sort of scene. Maybe she hadn't, I thought.

Maybe my story was a whole new world to her.

"I think he acted that way, but you know how college guys can be. I wasn't falling for it."

"Was he hot?" she asked with a squinty smile.

"I suppose so, you like the athletic, pretty boy type," I replied jokingly.

"I'm sure you'll meet a lot of those when you start school," Chandra said, smiling gently and nodding her head as if to tell me you'll meet other guys, lots of other people.

"Yeah I guess, but I'm going to be there on an academic scholarship, so I'm going to have to study more than party," I replied, thinking about how weird it was going to be in that new environment. "What about you?" I asked.

"What do you mean?"

"Well, are you seeing anybody?" I asked.

She looked down at her hands bashfully, then back up to me. "No. I mean, not yet anyway. I think there's something with this guy. Well, you met him. Dominic," she said with a goofy girlish grin at the sound of his name.

"Really?" I said, wanting to laugh. "Does he know exactly how you feel?"

"No. I haven't said anything to him, but I think there may be something there."

"What if he's just really nice?" I asked, surprised at my own ability to make her second guess herself. I felt like I was being cruel to her, but I couldn't make myself stop. Everything I'd ever learned from Sarah and Melanie was coming out of me like word vomit. I was protective, jealous almost. I realized he was the only one in the world I wanted to tell about my little candle trick. I didn't feel that she knew him at all, not like I felt I did.

"Who, Dominic?" interrupted Dana with her rough voice, stomping through the room with her heavy walk to get a drink from the kitchen. I was happy for the interlude. "Dominic is nice to everybody. That's just how he is. Don't read so much into that, Chandra," she chided bluntly as if she were scolding a silly child.

Chandra shut her mouth and sat silently. I really didn't know what to say either after Dana had so eloquently explained that Dominic wasn't really interested in her, but it made something within me light up with excitement.

We all chatted about what had happened, and I could tell the vibe was that they hadn't ever seen anything that weird before. We said our goodbyes and planned to meet again sometime. I left in my car, headed back home with more questions than answers about everything, and a nagging feeling in the pit of my stomach that I couldn't seem to ignore. I had decided when I got halfway home that I would tell my parents I was headed back from Sarah's, as it was about the equivalent travel time. I picked up the phone to call when I saw a call coming in from an unknown number. I answered with uneasy intrigue.

"Jessica, it's Chris. I got your number from Dana."

"Oh, hey," I answered, curious as to why he was calling.

"I don't mean to scare you, but I think you ought to come back over."

"What?" I asked, confusedly.

"There's something on this recording that I think you, and only you, should hear."

I turned around and called my parents to let them know I'd be late. I knocked on the door, already familiar with the smell of the old wood and furniture that permeated the air of the building. Chris opened it almost immediately.

"I'm sorry to have you come back so late," he mentioned hurriedly, almost frantically, ushering me in and closing and locking the door.

"It's okay, I wasn't more than halfway home when you called."

"I noticed it the first time I reviewed it, but I played it louder after everyone else left. I didn't want the others to get involved."

"Really?" I asked, my curiosity piqued.

"Yeah. Dana thinks she knows everything about everything. She's cool though, I love her to death, but I didn't want her to jump to conclusions. She'd have us all on her own ghost hunting show if she could. Josie is traumatized and won't talk, which defeats most of the purpose of her even being with us, and Chandra is just a dingbat."

Although I found his assessment of the group to be somewhat backstabbing, I couldn't help but laugh. "Dingbat?" I asked.

"Yeah. You heard the way she talks about Dominic and he isn't even into her. She was like that about me at first until I finally told her I was gay," he smiled.

"You're gay?" I had no idea. He dressed nicer than most guys I knew but I really didn't ever get the sense he was gay. Dressing nicely didn't really reflect his personal choices as far as I figured.

"You didn't know?" he asked with a smile.

"No. I don't really have gaydar, or whatever it is they call it. God, I hope that wasn't offensive."

He laughed. "No, it's not. It can be hard enough in these smaller towns with small minds. But Chandra doesn't have any sort of radar for anything anyone actually thinks. So, no worries."

As he set up his laptop with his good speakers I wondered about why he even hung out with the group at all.

"So why do you come to the meetings?" I asked.

"Well, I've known Dana a long time and there used to be more of us that would come. But things happen, you know? People can't come anymore, change their minds about things, get freaked out, find Jesus. Whatever. It is what it is. I still go because I have more in common with the people in the group than I do with any other people. We had one girl...she used to come but she... she disappeared."

"Disappeared"?

"Yeah, um...it was pretty tragic, actually, nobody knows what happened exactly. She was doing constant work on love spells. She heard that there was a ghost or something in the woods, and the last we heard, she was going out there to conjure it."

"So you knew her," I asked.

"My first meeting was her last, so not really. But it had me shook a little. It had us all shook. It was a reality check for what can really happen."

As he finished setting everything back up, I asked, "What do you think happened?"

"To be honest, I don't know. I just know that she was really determined. So, why'd you start coming?"

"Curiosity, mainly," I replied.

"You don't look like a witch. Or a person who's into it. You look more like my sister's Barbies. My sister had horrible taste on what to put on those dolls."

"Yeah, I get the Barbie thing a lot. It is what it is," I threw his words back at him.

"Okay, no more Barbie from me. Listen to this. When I heard it the first time I really didn't believe what it was that I heard."

I listened, through the electric buzzing of the speakers.

Jessica. It's Jessica. She must be stopped. They cannot come together…must be stopped…cannot come together…must be stopped…cannot come together…

The all too familiar chills returned to my spine. The voice was unlike that of any human voice I could have imagined.

"Jessica, it's saying your name. Whatever it is, it's not human. Look at what's registering over here on this chart," he said hurriedly and pointed to a display on his screen where the vocal resonance appeared as it played.

"Normal human voices are somewhere up here," he motioned to the middle of the chart. "This is somewhere up around here." he pointed to a lower range. "Only dogs can come close to hearing at that frequency."

"Okay. What does this mean?" not really sure that I wanted to hear the answer. I wondered how come I could know that the place wasn't haunted, but I couldn't sense whatever this voice was.

"There have been reports of this happening before. Entities that are not human spirits often register at this frequency range when they're recorded in EVP sessions. It's not unheard of, but usually there's something sinister behind it," he explained.

"No, I mean what does that message mean? I've had some weird things happen to me lately, but this is by far the strangest," I confessed, immediately regretting the decision to divulge any information about why I was there in the first place.

"Weird like what?" he asked in a flat tone.

"Like, something beckoning me to explore the woods out by my house," I said, covering the truth but giving enough information to at least feel like I was venting to someone.

"What's in the woods by your house? Where do you live again?" he asked, tapping his fingers almost impatiently and looking at me for an answer through his thick lenses.

I avoided looking him in the eye. "I live up north, about an hour away."

"Is that why you joined our group?" he asked.

"Mainly, yes."

"Have you gone out there?"

"No, no not yet. I wanted to find out more about what I was dealing with before I just put myself out there like that," I lied. He didn't need to know that Dominic had been in on it with me somehow.

"Look, Jessica, I don't think it's all that good of an idea for you to go out there alone. Not if this message is saying anything about you being stopped. If anything, we should go out as a group. Like the old member, she went alone...."

"Did anyone else know her?"

"Yeah, Dana an Vanek. But that was it. Dominic...I'm not sure."

I cleared my throat gently, nervous by the ambiguous talk about my sister. I wanted to tell him that Emily was the missing girl to whom he was referring, and that she was the reason I was there. But I felt that it would be better just left alone. If anything, I was going back out there with Dominic, no one else. Nevertheless, I felt that I had to assuage his desire to travel to the woods as a group. Deep in my bones I could feel that it wouldn't be safe for them. They didn't know what they were doing.

"Well, whenever y'all are ready, we could go out there as a group. That way no one would be alone. Sort of like a ghost hunt, you know, see what's out there," I suggested, but I didn't want that at all.

"Sounds good. I'm emailing you a copy of this sound file, so you can listen to it whenever."

"Oh, thanks. I'm sure I'll play it on replay to lull me to sleep," I joked.

He smiled somewhat half concerned. "Jessica, send me a text when you get home. This whole thing has totally given me the creeps," he said with an overly concerned expression on his face.

"You got it. Thanks Chris, I'm glad I have a friend to talk to about it," I smiled at him. But I knew there were things I just couldn't tell him and would never be able to tell him. In fact, I really didn't ever want to see him again, or anyone else in the group that had been there that night. They didn't know what was going on and anything Chris knew, I wanted him to forget.

As I got back in my car and headed back home, I reached the halfway point again where I called my parents to let them know I was leaving Sarah's place—again. Driving down the rural road to my parents' house I found that my eyes played tricks on me with the light and the reflection on the tall pine trees. Everything looked like it was something else. I turned my bright lights on so that I could better navigate the distance ahead of me and watch out for deer. Deer were the cause of many one-car accidents along the isolated stretches of country roads thatlead away from the city. I forced my eyes to focus on the winding road, letting the pine trees blur past me. As I pulled into our long driveway up to our house, I felt a chill run down my spine at the sight of the woods in the distance. I didn't even want to get out of my car and walk to the front porch, but I had to.

Pushing through the door quickly, I saw my mother asleep on the sofa in front of the TV. I assumed my father was already in bed. I went past them as quickly as possible, avoiding talking about what I had been doing.

Right at the moment I entered my room, my phone vibrated with a text message. I didn't know the number, but the message read, "How was the séance?"

I immediately called the number.

"Hello," I heard his voice on the other end of the line.

It was Dominic. I knew right away. "I got your number from Dana," I could hear him smiling through the phone.

"Everyone keeps getting my number from Dana," I sighed, not that I minded this particular call one bit. I let myself fall onto the bed. "How'd you know about the séance?"

"You think Chandra didn't invite me to that sham of a séance? And you hadn't called me yet, so I had to get your number somehow," he laughed.

"So you just didn't want to go," I said, ignoring the comment about not calling first. I hadn't had the nerve to do it yet.

"I've been to one of them before…Dana dominated everything and nothing happened. Well, until I wanted it to happen."

I sat up with excitement and propped myself onto my side. "Wait, what do you mean?" Had he done the same thing I had done?

He started to explain his experience. "There was a feeling, I don't know exactly how to explain it, and I put my mind to it, and I made the lights come back on in the room," he laughed as he finished his story.

I was laughing too, to the point where tears were coming out of my eyes because I was trying to stay quiet.

He stopped, letting his voice become serious and I felt like if he could see me, he'd be staring me in the eyes. "You did it too, didn't you?"

I paused for just a second. "Yes, but no. I made the candle light up again," and my giddy laughter returned and we both let it all out now that we knew the group had no clue what was going on.

I looked down at my elbows. Both of them were scabbed over from the light scraping they took on the ground in the woods. It snapped me out of my laughter for a second.

"What is this?" I asked him. I wanted to know how he'd respond. He had to feel what I was feeling.

"I don't know, not exactly anyway," he answered. "I don't want to say the wrong thing, "

"Me neither," I said, looking up at my ceiling and wishing I could see him.

"I just need you to know that for whatever reason, I knew to come to that exact place that night, and that you were in great danger," he paused, and I could hear his gentle breath through the phone. I could manipulate a candle flame, but I couldn't guess what would happen next.

"And now," he said, "I'm going to tell you goodnight because I don't want to keep talking and ruin any of this." I wanted to talk to him all night, but no words could come out of my mouth.

"I don't think telling you thank you is an adequate response," I said, laughing a little.

"It was the only thing I knew to do," he said. "I'll be seeing you," he said with a tone of gentleness.

I heard the phone go silent and I couldn't help but wonder why I couldn't get enough of him.

# CHAPTER 8

It was early morning. I had heard something and gone out of the house. Dominic walked up to me outside. I hadn't expected him to come over. I hadn't called him. I had his number but had been afraid to call. He had an expression of seriousness while at the same time looking focused. I walked down the steps of my front porch towards him. It was darker outside than what I had expected it to be, like a storm was brewing in the sky above us. The electricity in the air could be felt like static. Fresh wind blew my hair back as the clouds rolled overhead.

"I came by to give this to you," he confessed, his green eyes vibrantly intense as he reached out to embrace me. My nervousness melted away. I reached up to him and pulled my arms around his neck and felt him kiss me. The warmth of his lips against mine made my entire soul tingle. I breathed in his scent. I ran my fingers through his hair and made sure he felt that I didn't want it to stop. No words were spoken. I felt young and old at the same time. It was everything. I slightly moved away from him to look at his face.

I saw only my ceiling. The yearning to return to everything I had just felt made me realize the powerfulness of waking dreams. It had been a total of three days, twelve hours and twenty-two minutes since I had last heard from Dominic. All the while, he hadn't escaped a single thought of mine. I wondered how he managed to be so mysterious yet kind, so caring yet so hard to be around. Chandra obviously never heard a cruel word from him, he never pushed her away from him. He seemed caring like that. I replayed the incident in the woods over and over in my mind, then I did the same thing to our brief phone conversation. I kept wondering if I should have said this or that…or if I had seemed grateful enough for his help. I was totally blown away by the whole experience, and troubled that I had to keep it all cooped up within me. He was the only person with whom I could talk about the incident.

Just as I had fallen completely lost in thought, I heard a knock at my bedroom door as it simultaneously swung open.

"Sarah, hey!" I said, sitting up in bed a little straighter at the sight of her all decked out in shopping attire.

"What in the hell have you been doing? Do you not have a phone anymore? I haven't heard from you in like a week!" she barked at me. It had actually been more than a week. This was the week, I remembered, of early orientation week.

"Shhh! Don't be so loud, mom might hear you!" I said through clenched teeth and wide eyes.

"What? Why?" Sarah asked with a confused expression. "What are you hiding from them? Are you pregnant?" she whispered, leaning in closer my face pretending to be caring.

"What? No. No, I'm not pregnant. I've just been busy," I said, avoiding all eye contact and trying to discourage further investigation on Sarah's part.

"Well then who have you been with? Have you been hooking up with that Ryan guy? Because I heard he totally has a girlfriend back at school and that she gets really jealous and does horrible social media pranks on girls she thinks are after Ryan. I'd watch out if I were you. Like she will Photoshop you

onto some nudes and send them everywhere," she rattled off, making herself comfortable on the foot of my bed, popping her gum. She smacked it back into her mouth. The sound made me wince.

I shook my head with my brows furrowed, simultaneously wondering why Melanie had even bothered to introduce me to him if they all knew he had a girlfriend. "No. I don't know that guy. Melanie made me meet him that night at her party but that was it."

"Oh, okay. We all thought you went off with him somewhere," she sighed in relief. "But then we saw him later and not you, so we thought that maybe it was a hit and run sort of thing—like you wanted more but he was done."

The thought of that whole situation in the hot tub made me cringe. "I wasn't feeling very well these past few days, I—I think I have a stomach virus, I've just been sleeping a lot, you know, pain killers," I said, trying to stifle the irritation I had for her thinking I would actually sleep with a guy I had just met at a pool party. I thought she knew me better than that. I couldn't believe my friends would even put me in that situation.

"Oooh, do you have any left?" Sarah perked up excitedly.

"What?"

"The *pain*killers."

"No. I just had a few that my mom had left over from a kidney infection a few months ago," I whispered, realizing I had become a manipulator of lies.

"Oh—bummer. I want a Vicodin with some bevies later tonight for movie night."

I looked at her curiously as I tried to figure out what she even really wanted from me as a friend.

She noticed my lost look. "You're not coming over for movies?"

"I forgot," I mumbled.

She took in a deep breath and slapped her knees. "Well, babe, it's really not cool of you to ignore your friends all the time and not even return our texts. Melanie and I have both been talking about it and we really think that you're being a little bit of a bitch." She stood up and strutted across my room to the mirror.

"A bitch?" I asked. "Define bitch, please? Could you do that? Because I don't know when I've ever been a bitch to you. I've always been there for you. God, even when I shouldn't have. Even when I didn't want to be, because you were being so selfish and stupid."

"Wow, like, just effing wow. I can't believe you would even go there. After everything, and like, you don't answer your phone like you're too good for technology. You've been all like, quiet and not drinking or partying."

"Um…that's sort of the antithesis of bitch…if you even know what that means?" I retorted. I couldn't think of anything snarkier to say to her. Nothing would make a difference if she had already made up her mind. "Besides, I don't want to drink all the time Sarah, I never did that much anyway.

You're going to end up becoming everything you detest. You're going to end up as a fat, miserable alcoholic all at your own doing."

She rolled her eyes and scoffed. "Oh—well, whatever. Like you're any better than me. I have seen you do some stupid shit plenty of times." She stopped and laughed, shaking her head. "I just remember that one time at Logan's and you were like, vomiting all night. Who took care of you? I did. Besides, I'll never *not* look good, Jessica. It's not who I am. I know you don't mean that, but again, it's whatever. Look, I just came by to see why you were being so weird and to tell you that we're all going shopping tomorrow at the Galleria. Oh, and you missed our beauty night. We all got colored highlights," she picked through her perfectly curled hair to show me a streak of purple and red. "Everyone's got their graduation money and we're planning on going to Louis Vuitton and getting new bags. You should really get it together and come, too."

"Okay, what time?" I sighed, giving in a little and realizing absolutely nothing I had said really made a dent.

She wasn't nearly as upset as I would have thought.

"We're leaving around noon—we want to eat lunch at the Cheesecake Factory first."

"Okay, I'll let you know if I can make it," I said hurriedly.

"Let me know?" she whipped around from the mirror she'd gravitated back to and glared at me. She was fierce again. "You mean you don't even know if you're coming? What's to think about, Jess?"

"I don't know," I said with a little more irritancy in my voice. "I may be busy." I felt my jaw clench and my neck muscles strain.

"Busy? Doing what? You haven't even had time to come lay out with me, or go tan at the salon when it was raining. You've been a shit friend. And when's the last time we went to get pedicures? You obviously forgot about movie night. And besides, you *need* the Louis bag. What's going to happen in the fall when it's pledge time? We said we were going to rush Tri-Delt. Did you change your mind about that, too? We need new Louis bags and we need to be tan and we need to stick together so that college isn't some total, socially awkward disaster. It's Tri-Delts or nothing. They're the best there and they won't take us in if we don't fit their description. We're lucky our mothers were part of them. You want the best, don't you? Or do you want to be a total nobody in college? Or a fat, party whore in a different sorority that doesn't even count?"

I almost felt like I was staring at a complete and total stranger in my room, even though I'd known Sarah since first grade.

"No. That's what you want. Those are your plans. I don't care about rushing." I replied, not unlocking my eyes from hers.

Everything she was talking about just seemed so meaningless to me at that point. I didn't know what to say to her besides telling her that she sounded like the most utterly ridiculous person that I had ever heard speak and that I was surprised that she was even intelligent enough to have been accepted into a college. Sure, at some point in my friendship with her I had wanted most of the same things that she was ranting about in my room. But all of that was fading away—and fast.

I stood up and moved to my door, opening it for her to make her exit. I'd never been so brazen before, it felt strange to be rude. But I couldn't let her stand in my room any longer and dictate a life of pure shallow materialism to me, and I didn't have anything left to say to her.

I looked at her with a stern expression. She stared back as if she was in shock that I was motioning for her to leave. She breezed past me with quick steps and looked back as she stepped out of my door. "You're flushing our friendship down the drain, and for what? We used to tell each other everything. I just don't understand what could be more important than us and all of the plans we made. If it's some loser dude I hope he's worth it. You'll end up pregnant and married at twenty. You can think whatever about me, just because I know how to have a good time and you don't, but you're going to regret being like this. This is all on you, Jessica," she spat as she turned and left. I heard her footsteps go quickly down the stairs and felt relief at each one as she got further away from me.

I felt nauseated at the strangeness taking over me and completely invigorated as she left my room. I heard her car door slam and her engine crank as she left my house. I wasn't deliberately trying to be mean to her, but I felt the distance between us was growing larger each day. I just didn't care about the same things anymore. All I cared about was finding out what happened to Emily, and I knew I was going to have to follow much of her same footsteps to find the answer. It was going to besomething that Sarah couldn't understand. It would scare her. It would scare Melanie, too. They wouldn't like the other people, the other people I had met, mainly because they weren't in our same social circle. I also knew that they really wouldn't like me, who I was becoming. They would definitely not understand my attraction to Dominic. They couldn't see past those things. Frankly, if she couldn't see people for who they really were, then I didn't feel like any of my time would be well spent around her.

I threw myself down onto my bed and buried my head into my pillow in frustration. There just didn't seem to be a solution to any of my problems without choosing my current life over a new one. I checked my phone to see what she had been lambasting me about and there was a newly delivered text from her.

"EEW I saw that dude in that old truck pulling up to your house. Gross. That's why you're ditching us? He looks poor. Maybe you can live in one of those hippie villages together."

I started to text back and tell her they were called communes, then realized the pointlessness of replying.

"What?" I yelled out loud, jumping up to look out of my window.

I saw the truck pull up and park. A door shut hard.

From my room I could hear the echoing voices of my mother and someone talking downstairs. My mother seemed cordial. I quickly slipped on sweat pants and a light jacket over my pajamas, ran a brush though my hair, then tiptoed out into the hall. I crept down the stairs slowly and cautiously to spy on the conversation, still reeling from my visitation from Sarah.

I heard a familiar male voice speaking kindly to my mother. I came down the stairs a little further to see if I believed my eyes.

"Oh, there she is," my mother said as she turned to face me. "Honey, this nice young man has come to pay you a visit."

Dominic looked right at me, making my face flush and my body feel tingly. I tried to hide my obvious rush of embarrassment at seeing him at my front door conversing with my mother. My dream had been so real and so full of passion.

"Oh, hey Dominic," I tried to straighten out my sloppy attire. Evidently Sarah had passed him on her way back down my road. His truck was old, but well kept. At least it wasn't jacked up three feet higher than it should be with mud all over it.

"I told you I'd see you soon," he replied with a movie star grin.

My mother looked at me with a strange smile. I wasn't sure how to take it. "He said he was taking you to the library."

"Oh, really?" I looked at them both and tried to decide if it was weird or good that they seemed so in sync.

"Thanks, Mrs. Carmichael, I promise to have her back by dinner."

"I'm sorry, Dominic, I didn't get your full name," my mother queried politely.

"Dominic Taggart...I went to school in Langsbury, instead of Eddinsville."

"Ah, okay. Must be why we never saw you around town. Well, you've proven chivalry isn't dead after all. Oh, and call me Celia," she laughed, ushering us towards the door. "I'm just glad she's getting out of the house. This girl, she's usually gone all the time! But ever since graduation, she's stayed cooped up like a hermit. Where'd you two meet?"

I thought fast. "At Sarah's. He was friends with some of her friends."

"Oh, that's nice. I didn't think you young people still knew what libraries were," she attempted joking. I assumed at that point she'd already taken her meds for the day, not that she cared when I used to go running around with Sarah or Melanie, but she seemed delighted in some way.

"Okay, wait," I said, looking at both of them with some confusion. "I'll go change."

"Ha," my mother exclaimed. "You two have the same color eyes."

He was sort of old school, I thought. It was endearing. I followed him out of the house into the thick summer air. I liked his truck. He opened the door for me, and I glanced at him with a smile as I climbed in. As the door squeaked shut, my stomach fluttered as I remembered my dream. I felt like he knew somehow.

"I must admit I'm pretty surprised you came by today," I looked directly at him this time, letting go of the fear of meeting his eyes.

"Well, I told you I'd come back to talk to you, remember?"

He cranked the truck and the engine roared loudly, then settled.

"Yeah," I said, pulling my hair back into a ponytail as the wind from the windows being rolled down blew it around, "but it was still a surprise—especially after the morning I've had."

"What's up?" He asked, briefly glancing at me as he drove.

"I don't know. My friend, or at least she was my friend. She's upset I haven't been hanging out with her as much—at all, actually. The summertime used to be our time. We'd do everything together. Now, we don't. That's basically what my mom was talking about back there."

"Was that Sarah, the girl I saw leaving?"

"Yeah, actually. I've never fought with her before. I feel really crappy."

"Ahh, well, people change, I learned that the hard way. Your life changes, then your circles change. But that's when you pay attention to where people gravitate. Basic people will gravitate to other basic people, the great ones gravitate to the great ones. You'll see who someone's going to be by watching who they gravitate to," he replied, and I knew that it was true.

"Yeah, they sure do," I nodded. I looked out the window and watched the trees rush by us. "What's the difference between basic and great to you?"

"From what I've seen, and this is just my opinion, the basic people are the ones who need to constantly feel validation that they're someone, or something important. It could be some boring corporate job that pays their bills and sends them on some commercialized vacation every year to an all-inclusive resort, two cars, two kids and a mortgage, or constant posting on their pages to get people to see how great their life is, or it could be them thinking that because you chose to go a different route, you're somehow beneath them. But that's not how it is, not at all. The basics, they'll create a whole world built around pretentiousness. They never take risks. The great ones, they're the ones that don't ever settle. They don't just sit there and say 'this is it, this is who I am meant to be and life is what it is and we'll settle down and wait for retirement when we have arthritis to go and travel the world'. Great people do great things then and there, they don't wait or don't worry about society judging their decisions…crap like who they're seen with or what their friends decide to do."

"I never, ever heard it put that way," I said, blown away by his analysis. "I agree with everything, basically because that's exactly what I'm experiencing. She's pissed because I don't want to spend all my money on a purse and join a sorority with her."

He let out a laugh that he couldn't stifle. "You mean you don't wanna become part of a cool secret society that makes you chant a phrase in Greek, take all your clothes off and run around the beach at midnight with candles, then pretend that after you graduate, it will help you get some sort of awesome job?"

"Nah. I think I'm good. I don't really need to pay to make friends."

"Not to change the subject, but I actually came up here to the library yesterday and looked some things up for you. I wanted to save us some time and bring you here to show you what I'd found," he explained, wind blowing his dark hair around wildly as we drove down the country road. I had to talk loudly to be heard over the roaring wind whipping through the windows. I asked him why he was so interested in helping me.

"I have a pretty deep connection to the woods. I told you about me growing up near there."

"Yeah, I remember you mentioning it," I replied. "Why do you go to the meetings with Dana and everyone?"

"Well, I have sort of a history with the strange and otherworldly. It's what broke some of my circles growing up. It's what makes me different."

"What kind of history?"

"My family. My grandmother and my great grandmother were both *curanderas*. Do you know what that is?"

"No," I replied, but I felt like I'd heard it somewhere.

"Okay, well it's a Spanish word for witchdoctor, healer, sort of like a shaman. They're special, the real ones are, at least."

"Oh, so you're Mexican?" I asked.

"I'm half Mexican. My mother is Mexican and married my father who is white—well, of Irish decent. I prefer to say it that way."

I nodded with interest to encourage him to tell me more.

"Yeah, so I grew up across the woods from where you live now. I went to school in Langsbury, down the road. My dad would drive me because he said it was a better school. I had friends, played sports, hunted…did all the normal things that we do around here.

"I'm surprised I never saw you, that's not far, we played your school in football every year," I laughed.

"Yeah, I graduated a year before you, but I guess it is weird. But I never knew a lot of people from other towns. I was different. My mother would always tell me when I was younger that I had the sight, what my grandmother and great-grandmotherhad. But I overheard my family one night talking about me, and what they said sort of freaked me out."

"What'd they say?"

"Well, I was like seven years old, and I heard them discussing what my grandmother and great-grandmother did, you know, like spells and helping people. They were talking about how it was foretold that one of us would be born into the family, someone who had a gift beyond theirs."

"And that would be you?"

"That's what they say. When I was really little, younger than I can even remember, they said I could see dead relatives of ours. They said that I had conversations with them and knew that they were all right. I don't remember how I knew these things, it's just something I could always do. That was just the beginning of it though. The older I get, the more things I realize I can see that others can't. I realized one day that spirits and strange things just seem to be attracted to me. My grandmother still lives in Mexico, she wants me to come down there and study with her, but I really don't think I want to. At least, I don't want to leave now."

"Why not?" I asked. "Wouldn't that be the perfect getaway? Mexico, grandmother, and some freedom?"

"I thought so, too, at first. I took a semester off from college, moved back home. Then things started happening, and something, something deep inside me, is telling me not to leave yet."

He had me dangling for more. "What is it that's telling you?"

"It's all been coming about since recently. I started meeting up with the group a while back, my junior year, because I liked to hear what they were working on and how in touch they felt they were with the spirit world. I kept most of my experiences to myself. But when Emily disappeared, I felt really strongly that I knew she wasn't dead."

"What do you mean?" I asked exasperatedly.

"That's why we're going to the library. I want to show you some things that I've found—verified really— that have happened before. These are things that I've known about, or been told or contacted about over the last few years. I went to the library to search the records and verify the truth to justify that I wasn't just hearing voices or going crazy. I know this all probably sounds nuts to you right now, but something brought all of this together. I don't believe it was just a coincidence that I met you."

My heart was pounding in my chest. I was processing all of what I was hearing from him, but I wasn't sure that I was truly hearing what he was explaining. It was as if I was out of my body, watching myself obtain all of the new information that Dominic was giving me. If there was even the slightest possibility that my sister was out there somewhere, it seemed that Dominic may have any inkling as to where her exact location could be.

* * * *

We walked through the doors and the librarian nodded her head in a silent greeting. He took me by the hand, making my heart flutter a little, and led me to an area where it was quiet and there was a laptop sitting on a table with two chairs.

He pulled out one of the chairs for me to take a seat and I quietly accepted his gesture. He began to talk rapidly, almost manically, about the things he had read when he had come to the library before.

"I couldn't figure out what it was about the woods here. I looked at everything I could find that would explain what, first of all, has kept people off of that land as long as the area has been inhabited, and, second, why you and I can't seem to get away from it."

"Well, what is it?" I asked. I needed to know as much as he could tell me. Never mind I felt myself swimming in the pools of green water that created his eyes, I needed to know everything he knew.

"Why was your sister in the woods?"

I looked down away from him. There was no way I could really avoid the question. "I don't entirely know the truth. All I know is that she wanted to use the "energy" out there. To work some sort of magic she was trying to do."

He sighed one of those quick sighs, where it almost sounded like an ironic laugh underneath his breath. "Energy alright," he mumbled.

"What's that supposed to mean? What kind of energy is out there then?"

"I'm not completely sure. Growing up, my dad would always tell me that if I wanted to go hunting or fishing, to make sure I never went alone. He would go with me, or some of my old buddies. My mom to this day won't go out into the woods at all. She says she can feel its presence out there, but she never explains what "it" is. And my grandmother, well, she's absolutely horrified by the vibes she gets."

"Is it Native American?" I asked, knowing how many places were said to be cursed due to the tumultuous history of settlers invading the space of the Natives.

"I thought so at first. At least that's what made sense to me. But there aren't any Native American tribes that lived in this exact location. Up to the north of us there were the Caddo, and to the south there were the Karankawa, who were a bit more nomadic, but they lived off of the gulf lands. Here? Nothing, except for the Alabama-Coushatta reservation, but that isn't their original land. But, I think I figured out the reason for it."

More questions than answers pilfered my thoughts. "Then what's your theory?"

"It's more than a theory. There's a reason they never stayed within these woods. The woods here are already inhabited. The Native American tribes had to have known it, too. They never settled in the woods because whatever is out there is not only more ancient than them, but beyond our abilities to fully understand. Caddos moved up north like I mentioned, they all steered clear of this area. Apaches and the like were all further to the west. No tribe seemed to want to stay here. It's not human spirits, and it isn't anything that's angel or demon related either. It goes way back, to a history that's lost to us. Another thing that I found while digging in archives was a news article from way back, maybe a century past, about a girl that went missing out in those same woods. Her name was Carline Tarney. Her family had sent her to collect some sort of root or flowers or something. There wasn't much information on it, but she was never heard of or found either. I think that's more than a coincidence."

"Where did you get all of this information?"

"Some of it's as easy as just doing basic research on tribes and areas where artifacts have been found. The news is all archived. The librarian helped me with missing people. There are books on folklore I've read, too. But when my grandma comes up and visits, she always says that those beings in the woods were to be left alone, and not to be provoked in any way."

"What kind of beings?" I asked, thinking of everything from gnomes to Bigfoot.

"That's what I want to figure out. She would never go into detail about it, because she said that if you talked about them, they'd show up to start bothering you. She said they're all over the world in different areas and go by different names. She said they can be whatever they need to be at any given time, which makes them all the more dangerous because a person wouldn't know if one was dangerous or not. I think whatever it is that she was talking about has been taking girls. Your sister was especially vulnerable if she went anywhere out there to work magic. It would be bad enough unprovoked, but whatever it was she did out there, it could have opened a portal."

"Portal?"

"Yeah, like a doorway to their world. The world of the others."

"What are you thinking, then?"

He looked directly into my eyes, making my heart beat a little faster. "I'm thinking that nothing just happens; there's always a reason."

I shook my head in shame at myself. "I could have been taken the other night in the woods, too."

"Maybe, but maybe there's a reason you weren't. I think your sister is out there, but she's not on our timeline. She's trapped."

"Time dilations?" I asked, not really sure where I obtained that particular verbiage.

"Time dilation is a good way to put it," he said while simultaneously plopping a pile of books down in front of me. "Look, I've read all of these books. Most of them contain stories that are either identical or very similar to stories that I heard growing up with my family. My dad grew up with Irish stories, since his grandparents were immigrants from Ireland. There were stories about fairies and little people who would come out and then disappear again, but if one of them took you, you would be taken to their world, where time passed much slower than it does here, in our realm. So if you were ever to return, it could seem like you were gone for three days but really two or three hundred years could have passed. Either way, it makes for some really strange missing person cases."

"They believe in fairies?" I asked, amused.

"Fairies, gnomes, all sorts of creatures. There's a story about the land of Tir Na Nog, the best way to describe it would to be a parallel dimension where they can come and go into and out of our world as they please. But if you get taken, you might not come back."

"Tir Na Nog, huh."

"What? You think this is all crazy, don't you?" he asked straightforward.

"No—no not really. It's different, but it feels natural to talk about it. I want to find out what happened to Emily more than anything, and I know this is tied to it."

"There's more than just the portals and the Caddos and the energy. I was reading for hours and hours. Essentially every culture that exists—including Native Americans, Nordic culture, Islamic Culture, you name it— believe in an invisible world. They have always believed in it. It's a part of what they think exists around us at all times. I would think it was absolutely crazy if it wasn't such a widespread held belief. Some of these cultures didn't even have connections with each other for thousands of years. How can anyone explain that they essentially have the exact same beliefs? Some are on different continents. To me, it's like the Occam's Razor theory. The easiest way to explain it is that it actually exists, instead of trying to theorize why it doesn't."

I leaned over to look at all of the books he pulled.

"To add to this, and if you truly don't think I'm crazy, I can see them sometimes."

"Really?" my eyes widened. "What do they look like?"

"The ones I have seen are short, dwarf-like, similar to what you would imagine little creatures to look. But not all societies have the same concept of what they look like. It's like there are different races or something. Some are described as tall and beautiful, some are the same as us, some can change at any moment…it's not a concrete type of being."

"I've been seeing some things, too." I admitted.

"What sort of things?"

"Like at that séance, when I found out Josie lost her family, I had this flash, suddenly I knew exactly what happened to them, something you don't wanna see."

He looked down and nodded, almost like he felt sorry for me.

I hesitated, before I spoke. I knew it was now or never. I needed to tell him what I knew before I lost my nerve.

"I never told anyone this before, but the day before Emily went missing, she took me to some sort of witchcraft shop in the city. It was on a really scraggly side of town."

With widened eyes of interest, Dominic pursued the details.

"It was called Yerberia something Santa muerte I don't remember the exact words. Anyway, my sister went to see a woman named Doña Carlota. I never saw her, but she worked in the back of the shop. She gave my sister a bag, a strange little black velvet bag, and I never saw what was in it. I know that my sister thought she was in love with someone and that whatever was in that bag and whatever Doña Carlota had told her to do was going to help her get the guy to love her. She disappeared that same night, after she took the bag out into the woods."

Looking into his eyes I hesitated, but then said, "I wasn't being truthful with you when I said I had never heard of a...that word you said. I just couldn't remember what the word was. That's who Emily went to see. Dona Carlota is a..."

"*Curandera*," he finished.

I felt tears welling up in my eyes as I told the real story for the first time in years. I had never felt so vulnerable to emotion before.

I let it all out, quiet tears of remorse rolling down my face as I finished the details. "I told her not to go, I even asked if I could go with her so I could try and stop her. The worst part is I never told any of this to anyone, because she told me not to; she didn't want to be shamed and embarrassed for what she was really doing. I thought we'd find her and I didn't want her to think I'd betrayed her by telling people her darkest secrets. All I ever told anyone was that I knew she was going to the woods, but I didn't say why. I should have. I feel like if I had just stopped her, said whatever it was that I had to say to make her stay, she wouldn't be gone now. I was too freaked out to stop her. I didn't know what to do. I just let her go and covered for her. I hate myself for it."

By this time, my recollections had completely capsized my ability to stay afloat emotionally and I hunched over my knees and let my tears fall to the floor. Dominic leaned over me and I felt his arm come all the way around my shoulders as he whispered, "Shhh... it wasn't your fault. It wasn't your fault," over and over again gently to me, patiently waiting for my outpouring to subside.

The librarian, who had overheard my emotional tempest, brought over a box of tissue and walked away, looking down at me with a strange expression. Dominic handed me one as I blew out my snot with bellowing echoes in the quiet library.

I looked up at him, feeling the puffiness of my eyes making it difficult to blink.

"Jessica, it wasn't your fault. She was doing what she thought she had to do. You didn't make her go out there, and you probably couldn't have stopped her. Her intent was set." I noticed his arm still around me, pulling me to him. I let my head rest on his chest, releasing the stress I felt so heavily weighing upon me.

"Thank you," I said quietly.

"We don't have to talk about it anymore today, if you don't want to."

"I don't mind," I replied, looking back up at him. "It's just that I've never talked about it before, so I have been keeping all of this inside me for three years. When I opened the floodgates, it I couldn't close them."

"I understand. You know, I've never told anyone else but you about my grandma and great grandma, or seeing invisible people."

"Really? Why not?"

"Oh, you know how small towns are. I didn't want anyone to think I was weirder than I probably already was. I kept it to myself."

"I think it's pretty cool. What exactly do they do, the *curandras, cudandras*...."

"*Curanderas*," he amended with a smile. "Their purpose is to help people with sickness, pain, emotional problems- everything really. They have a gift of healing and know how to use natural methods to fix ailments. But some can go even further. Some read tarot cards, give advice from the spirit world, and break curses that people have had put on them. Then some cause curses. Some, like the one your sister probably went to if it had anything to do with Santa Muerte, do pretty much nothing but harm."

"Curses are real then?"

"I always say believe whatever you want to believe. I leave it up to a person's own choice and knowledge to decide. Who am I to tell someone what belief is valid? But enough things have happened to me and to others I've known that have led me to believe they're real."

"Then it's sort of like being a white witch?"

"Yeah, I guess you could say that. A true *curandera* or *curandero* won't ask for money. At least not in the sense of setting a fee for their work. They'll take donationsthough. Those who do more harm than good will charge a fee for everything, and they don't always really know what they're doing. My mom calls them *brujeras* or *brujeros*, which is just calling them a witch."

"So, what you were saying about you and your family is that would make you next in line to be a *curandera*?"

"*Curandero*, since I'm a guy—the "o" is the masculine term. But yeah, that's what my mom and grandma always said."

My mind churned with the adventurous ideas that began swirling as he finished talking. He was like a wizard from Harry Potter but he didn't even realize it.

"That's pretty amazing," I smiled.

"You think so?" he asked, raising one eyebrow sarcastically.

"Yeah, I do actually."

To say that I was grateful for the help that Dominic was giving was a gross understatement. Up until that point in my young life, I had merely been mindlessly floating along in a void of day to day experiences, none of which had meaning or significance. To talk to someone—really talk to someone—was the most fulfilling experience I had ever had. To be able to let go of the worry of judgment of others and just openly speak was invigorating. I felt truly alive.

"What if we go back and try to find that Doña Carlota woman?" I asked, hoping he would be willing to take the plunge into the unknown with me.

"I was thinking the same thing. Let me see what I can find."

While reading through some of the books on folklore and magic that Dominic had pulled for us to go through, my mind wandered to the possibilities of the existence of a world beyond our own. I couldn't shake the notion as I tried to read the book in front of me. I shook my head and asked, "Dominic, what was it that you said about portals? You said she could have opened a portal?"

"It's what I've heard happens. There are evidently ways to create openings into the other 'world' that exists around us."

"Like, what do you mean exactly? Spell it out for me."

"The first time I ever heard about it, I was really little and my grandma had come up from Mexico for a visit. She told us about an uncle of mine, my grandpa's brother, who had 'opened' a door he couldn't close. He went missing. No one in the family or from the surrounding area ever saw or heard from him again."

"So, what? He went into another world?"

"That's the theory," he brushed his shaggy dark hair out of his face, almost in exhaustion. "I mean sure, he could've just disappeared in the dessert or whatever anyone can come up with to explain how he went missing. But they knew what he had been doing. They knew that he had been playing with fire. He had been dabbling in the occult to try and become wealthier, from what she said. He was having hard times, and that was what he resorted to for a solution. There are a lot of different ways people try and do that. My grandma said that he chose to make a deal with an entity, not really a spirit, and for whatever reason the deal fell through. Whatever it was that he was dealing with took him in exchange."

I had sparks exploding inside my head. "Is that what you think could have happened to Emily?"

"It's definitely a possibility, especially if she was trying to get someone to love her. She could have made a deal with whatever it is that exists in those woods."

"That's exactly what I'm thinking. It's the only thing that makes sense," I said hurriedly. "Do you think we could find that woman she went to, Doña Carlota?"

"Do you remember what side of town she was on?" he asked.

"Not exactly. I sort of remember what it looked like, but I don't remember the exits or the streets that we took."

Dominic paused and thought for a moment, then turned to me.

"I think I know where this place is. I may be able to find her. I promise you if I do, we're going. But you have to promise me that you'll let me come with you. I wouldn't want you going anywhere like that alone."

"Deal. I wouldn't want to go alone anyway. Not after the incident in the woods."

I turned back to the book I was thumbing through. "I wish I could find out more about radio interference with this sort of thing."

He looked up at me with curiosity, "What do you mean radio interference?"

"Ever since I began this venture of trying to find out what happened to Emily, even before, really, I've had some strange occurrences when the radio is on in my car. And with my phone—which is tied to the airwaves too."

"Voices?"

"Yeah. They've said my name, stopped music, created static. …"

Dominic couldn't help but intercede, and I let him.

"There's this thing, in Italian it's called videopsicofonetica. I found it one day when I had some similar things occur around my TV. People have images appear in them, of people on the 'other side', people who have passed."

"Do you think that's something we could try?" I asked.

"There's something I don't trust about it. I think the images are either generated by our sheer will, or something else trying to pretend to be a loved one. Not everything out there on the other side is friendly. And by the way, I have some trouble with most electronics, too. I carry tourmaline around to help control it," he pulled out a black stone from is pocket and showed me. I admired it, but remembered something I needed to say.

"There's another thing," I paused—thinking of Vanek. I wanted desperately to tell him what he had said to me.

"What is it?"

"Vanek."

"What about that guy?" He tensed up at the sound of hisname.

I inhaled a large breath of stale book air. "I got a weird message from him a few days ago. He was almost... threatening," I said, not sure how Dominic would take the news. I didn't know how well he knew Vanek.

"What did he say?"

"Here, read them." I handed him the phone to let him see the vague warning to stay away from my search.

I watched Dominic's expression carefully, wanting to see exactly how he would react, even on the smallest level. If there was something that Dominic was thinking that he really didn't want to tell me, I wanted to search for signs of it in his eyes. Even the smallest twitch could give off a hint that something was awry. I hadn't ever felt the sort of sensitivity that I felt at that moment. It was as if my senses were becoming stronger, like I was suddenly much more in tune with my environment. His brows furrowed, he took in his breath more deeply and slowly.

"Something is off here—I can feel it," he murmured as he looked over the words.

"I know something's off, it's been off," I replied.

"This isn't good. This is a warning. I don't understand why he is involved, or how he knew who you were and what you wanted. I'm going to find out though. This isn't right."

"What if I see him?"

"Don't go to any more meetings."

"Why does he even go to those?"

"I was never really sure. He's always just sort of watched everyone, and warded people off from doing anything too deep. When Emily disappeared, a few people in the group wanted to have a séance to find her. He stopped them, wouldn't let it happen. I always thought that was a good thing, but maybe it was for a different purpose."

"What sort of purpose? Like an evil one?"

"Whatever it is, he's definitely more involved with this that he has been letting on. He's covering something up."

"What else do you know about him?"

"Nothing, really. He's always shuffling those cards, I always thought it was just a weird quirk. Maybe he's just quirky, but I can feel something that tells me it's much more than that."

I cracked my knuckles from nervousness. "Dominic, you're sort of scaring me."

"He's never seemed threatening. Just blunt with everyone," he sat back, thinking out loud. "It's like no one ever taught him basic social skills. We don't even know where he lives. He just sort of shows up and then leaves, he never has anyone with him or talks to anyone outside of the meetings."

Dominic looked at the messages again then handed my phone back to me. "I don't understand why he would care at all if you were interested in finding out what happened to your sister. Did you tell anyone else about this?"

"No, just you. I thought about telling Chris the other night. I listened to an EVP recording with him. Oh, that's another thing that had my name in it."

"Do you have it? I'd like to listen to it."

"It's at my house, I mean the file is on my laptop, which is at my house. We can listen to it when you take me home."

"What did Chris say?"

"He let me have a copy, and he was trying to decipher all of what was said on it. He thought it was strange that the voice would be calling me out in an EVP session where we were trying to contact a human spirit, but honestly, after what has happened to me with the radio, I really didn't think it was all that strange."

"Well it's something, alright. But I think we should keep it quiet. I wouldn't say anything else to Chris and Dana either."

"I won't say anything. It hasn't felt right. It's a gut instinct. I just feel like the fewer people who know, the better."

"Then we're on the right path."

We stood up from our table and collected our books. I noticed I came up to the top of his chest. He must have been around 6"2'. I felt like leaning against it again for comfort, but we had our work cut out for us. My damsel in distress time was up for the day.

We left the library, and he drove me back to my house. He walked me to the front door and made sure I was inside, as the luring glow of the sun through the evening woods filled the background behind us.

"Did you wanna come in and listen to the recording?" I asked. I felt like he would just follow me in, but he didn't.

"Yeah, I do."

He walked behind me through the door and up the stairs to my bedroom. I felt the excitement within me that he was with me and following me to my room, my private place.

"Here, listen carefully," I played the recording on the laptop.

I watched Dominic's expression as he listened to the strange interference of words.

Jessica. It's Jessica. She must be stopped. They cannot come together...must be stopped...cannot come together...must be stopped...cannot come together...

It stopped, and he looked up at me, clearly upset. His brows were furrowed fiercely. He took a deep breath in and stood up.

I stood up with him, looking up at him and searching his face for an answer

"This isn't good, Jessica. Whatever was speaking on this recording knew you were there at Chris' apartment. It followed you," he said, putting his hands on my shoulders. I took in a deep breath.

"Please don't go anywhere alone. I'm worried about how powerful this thing can get, especially if it's been interfering with your radio. What if it makes your car malfunction while you're driving?"

"I hadn't thought of that. Now I'm freaked out. I don't want to be alone," I reached up and touched his hand resting on my shoulder and squeezed it.

"You're not alone. Not in any way."

"I wish you could stay," I shut my eyes tight, surprised at myself for blurting that out. Who was I? I never wanted anyone to stay. Now I couldn't imagine the rest of the day without him.

"I hate having to leave you. Just, be careful in everything you do. I'll be back tomorrow. I'm gonna make sure you're alright."

I picked up my phone to text him as I watched his taillights fade away. "Thank you for today," I wrote. It wasn't all I wanted to write, but it was all I could manage to send.

I couldn't pretend anymore. Whatever it was about Dominic, I was falling for him. It was definitely something I had never experienced before until that moment.

Seeing him drive away made me miss him in a way I'd never missed anything or anyone before—completely different than missing Emily.

# PART II

# KNOWING

# CHAPTER 9

Emily looked down at me. I could see her in a blurry haze. My vision was corroded from having just woken up. I blink my eyes to clear the fogginess to see her more clearly. Looking into her sparkly eyes, I could see the life within them. I felt her hair brush my cheek as she leaned over me to whisper into my ear.

"Everything you thought you knew is wrong. Get ready for it."

I tried to look at her more closely, to see the details of her face as I awakened to realize she was real. I was just so groggy, it made even the slightest movement difficult for me. I reached up to touch her face as she pulled away from me. As soon as I touched it, she was yanked backward from me rapidly. I sat up, now able to move freely.

"Emily!" I screamed, "Where did you go!" I could see her with a horrid expression on her face, one of pure agony. She was being sucked away from me into a black mass of darkness coming from my window across the room.

I chased after her until she vanished, along with the black mass. I was alone now. I looked down. Below my feet I saw the ground and the light from the rising sun hitting the moist dew that coated the blades of grass and weeds. My feet weren't wet though, I was above all of it. I began to run through the tall grass, not feeling a thing. I then looked to the trees that lined the outskirts of the woods. That was where she went. That was where she was taken.

With a rapid snap I was back in my body. I awoke with a jolt, as if I had fallen back into my bed. My heart beat fiercely. I sat up and looked around my room cautiously. My dream had been more than just a dream. I knew that for sure. I reached for a pen and paper beside my bed and scratched down what I had heard Emily say to me. "Everything you thought you knew is wrong. Get ready for it."

I felt a keen sense of understanding; an understanding that I never had before. I knew more, I was more aware. I could hear the morning birds singing outside of my window, but I knew intuitively that they were calling the nature spirits to assist them with their day just as those people who say their morning prayers ask for a blessed day. It wasn't language, it was deeper than that. Something within me was changing. I listened and could hear my father preparing to leave for work. It wasn't that I had gained extra hearing—I was more in tune with the world. I looked at my clock—it was 7:21 in the morning. On a typical summer day, I was usually never awake so early, but I felt that it was for a good reason. I dressed myself and walked outside as the light from the rising sun began to warm the air around me. It was fresh and made me feel clean by just breathing.

I took a walk along the road that lead away from the woods. All around me I felt like I was part of where I was and what I was experiencing. It was a unique oneness that I had never known before. I approached the shallow creek that ran through the culvert underneath the road up to our home. Touching the water, I could feel the vibrations of its existence intertwining with mine. I looked up to the trees and inhaled their fragrance, stronger than I had ever noticed before. Its intensity intoxicated me. Everything around me seemed truly alive.

Walking back home, I contemplated the vision of Emily in my dream. She had come to see me. But then she was taken away. Closing my eyes, I could see her pure face, and I wondered if I'd ever really see it again. Could she be brought back from that place where she existed? Was she alive in another world? It seemed true; it seemed real, but for what, exactly, should I be readying myself?

I dialed the numbers and listened to the brief ringing before hearing Dominic's voice say hello.

"Sorry to bother you so early," I apologized before saying anything else.

"It's no bother, I was already awake. I'm sort of an early riser and a night owl all in one."

"I had a really strange dream last night. I wanted to tell you about it," I found myself almost shouting as the signal of my phone started crackling as I completed my sentence.

Through the static I heard Dominic say that he would come to talk to me. I didn't hear what time he would be there, so I was surprised when I saw him drive up only half an hour later.

I met him out on the front porch. "Hey," I said. "You got here quicker than I expected."

"I can come back later if you need me to. I just couldn't hear you and thought it might be urgent."

"Yeah I'm not sure what's going on out here with our phone signal. I've never had a problem before."

Dominic looked up and around at the towering pines. They swayed ominously in a gust of wind. "I know what it is," he said. "Come on and get in, we'll go get breakfast."

It was an unexpected invitation that I happily accepted. He drove us into town to Essie's Café. It was almost as old as the town but was the only place left with a fully functioning soda fountain from the 50's. It had the best root beer floats around. I was so happy to go there again. I hadn't been since I was a little girl, with Emily and our parents. Now, my parents never wanted to go, and my friends were too snobby to be seen there.

He chose a booth near the back, and we ordered greasy breakfasts with fresh juice and he ordered black coffee to go with his meal.

"I had a dream. Except it was more of an out of body experience," I started. He just listened intently, not judging or interrupting. I shook away the distraction of his eyes.

"Emily came to me and she said," I paused as I reached into my pocket for the piece of paper I had written her words on, "Everything you thought you knew is wrong. Get ready for it."

"That's...something," he replied. "Do you know what she meant?"

"Not completely, no. But right after she said it to me, I reached out to touch her, and she was taken away by something, or someone. I don't really know what it was because I couldn't see it, but it was like she was sucked back into some sort of vortex of darkness."

"Okay, that's very interesting."

"I chased after her, even out of the house—except I went out of the window and into the air. I was doing that thing—the astral projection."

"That's amazing. You're lucky. Some people try and are never really able to do it."

"Can you do it?" I asked.

"Yes."

"Are you good at it?"

"I've always done it, but I've been getting better."

"How did you learn?"

"It's sort of part of my heritage that I was explaining to you. It's part of *curandismo*. I never really had to learn, like I said, I'd always done it, it was always something I could do. I just fine tuned my skill by practicing. I knew that I was getting better at it when my mother said she had seen me outside when I was really asleep. It meant that I was able to project myself somewhere else, like a ghost almost."

"That's strange, isn't that like a sign you are going to die or something? It seems like I've heard that before."

"Well, those who are near death sometimes can inadvertently project themselves to places, because whether they know it or not, they are closer to the other side already. So it became a sign of impending death because there are sightings of other people right before they die. But you could do it too, if you wanted. It's possible for everyone."

"But you had an advantage because of your family," I searched his face for an answer.

"Yeah, but not so much so that I was great at it right away," he tapped his foot almost nervously.

Our food was brought out to us and we sat in silence for a few minutes while we ate. Dominic looked up and asked what I had already been thinking.

"So how did you feel afterward?"

I shrugged nonchalantly as I loaded my fork with eggs and grits. "I decided to just wake up and go for a walk. It was bizarre, because I felt this connection with everything around me—the birds, the trees, water, anything. I had an intense clarity. It's like, well this is going to sound stupid, but my sophomore year we had to research drug use for drug free week at school and my group was tasked with LSD. We had to read about what some of the users experienced. It was all supposed to be scary, but a few people had reported these miraculous experiences of being one with everything. I hate to say it, but it was like that, like I was high on nature."

"Then it's happening to you," he said quietly and sipped his coffee.

There was an awkward silence for a moment. "What?" I searched his face with wide eyes.

He laughed for a moment at my reaction. "You're becoming something more," he replied, lacking a desirable explanation.

"What? What am I becoming?"

He had finished most of his food and sat his fork down to look up at me with his full attention. "You have a purpose that is entirely different than what you may have previously thought."

"Explain?" I felt his intensity rise.

"It all makes much more sense to me now," he responded, leaning back as he untangled his thoughts out loud.

"My great grandma had always told my mother, ever since she was a little girl, before she knew she'd get married and have a boy, that her boy would be a part of something much bigger than she was, or anyone. She had all but forgotten most of it until she found out she was pregnant with me. My mom never fully understood what her grandmother was saying. Evidently, my great grandmother would sing a little saying, in Spanish. *Los dos, los dos, nosotros conoceremos*. It basically translates to 'The pair, the pair, we will know them'. Doesn't sound as good in English. When my mom would ask her what she was singing about, my great grandma would smile and say it was foretold already. My mom wrote it off to her being a superstitious old curandera that thought everything was significant andmagical. Even my own mother, who believed everything my grandma and great grandma ever said didn't really pay attention to it. In fact, it kinda caused a rift between them. We were just talking about it the other day, my mom and I."

"So you're saying…," I knew what I thought he was saying. I just didn't want to be the first to say it.

"You and I are the pair," he finished.

I placed my fork down gently. I felt my breakfast churning hard in my stomach. The whole idea, although seemingly contrived, felt too good to be true. What else could I want but to be something special with this person, this one person I suddenly felt like I couldn't be without?

"Like a pair of powers," he further explained with all seriousness.

"I see," I said, nodding and awaiting more information.

"If you're gaining the gift of sight and communication, and I'm developing my abilities, then together as a pair we can work to help people—and places—with problems."

"Problems?"

"Spells, hexes, demon possessions, hauntings, even problems like the one with your sister. Bad spirits, just about anything. Anything from the other side. Anything from the invisible world around us. You see, they can see us, people just cannot see them. Living in tandem is sometimes complicated. From what I know, there are people who are constantly seeking to cause harm to others using the dark powers. The pair works on stopping it."

"What if I'm not the other half of the pair?" I countered, looking for fault in his argument. It wasn't because I wanted him to be wrong. It was because I wanted him to be right so badly that I wanted all other explanations completely eradicated.

"Then I don't think you'd be sitting here right now," he replied.

I felt the greasy breakfast causing gestational complications. It was more than I was prepared to know all at once. "I need to go home," I blurted.

He looked slightly shocked at my sudden reaction. I was even in shock within myself at my reaction. I felt bad about it, but at the same time really couldn't control my sudden onset of a gurgling stomach and I was processing the truth slowly. It just didn't sound feasible to me. I thought about college, and what I was supposed to do there if I was all tied up in some sort of mythical problem solving lifestyle with Dominic, who seemed convinced that I would be a good match to this "pair". I wondered what he saw in me that made him know for sure. It was more of him just being kind. He was a genuinely kind person, and that is what someone like Chandra had misunderstood about him. I didn't want to make the same mistake.

"Jessica, I didn't mean to upset you...," he said quietly, looking up at me from his seat at the booth. He looked back down and tapped his coffee mug with his finger, waiving off the waitress who approached.

I looked backward behind me to see if anyone was around us and then back at him before I spoke in a shaded whisper.

"You didn't. I just don't want to let you down. I feel lost and found all at the same time and it's perplexing. I also feel sick to my stomach."

He nodded knowingly. "Do you feel like taking a ride to find Doña Carlota?"

I had all but forgotten the promise he'd made the day before to me about going to see her. "Sure. I guess we could," I replied, hoping I wouldn't vomit in the truck.

"Let me get you a soda to take with us to settle your stomach on the way there," he offered. He knew.

On the ride into Beaumont, we sat in silence much of the way as Dominic's truck had no air conditioning and the windows were rolled down. The wind billowing through the open windows caused too much extra noise for conversation. He turned the radio louder to make up for our silence, but we had trouble catching a solid station through the static.

I thought of what I knew about him and wondered what else he knew and just hadn't yet told me. His mother's side of the family sure did seem to think he had something. I thought so too, but it was more of a feeling than outright knowledge. I didn't discount the fact that he'd miraculously saved me from the unknown that night in the woods, but I didn't let my mind veer off too far to question him on how exactly he knew where I'd be and that I might need his assistance. It was too befuddling.

When we arrived in the city and started to slow down for traffic lights, Dominic started talking.

"Okay, so this is the side of town that I think we'll have some luck," he replied as he stopped at a red light. "Do you remember any landmarks?"

"I remember we crossed railroad tracks. As cliché as that sounds, it was literally on the other side of the tracks."

"Okay," he nodded. "That's a great indication of which way I should go."

He turned to the right and drove down the long street that entered into a neighborhood that was strikingly familiar. The vagueness of my knowledge of that side of town began to clear itself into a sharp recollection. There it was again. The keen sense of awareness I had experienced before. It was beginning to be there when I needed it.

"It was beside a yerberia."

"Yerberia del Sol?"

"It could be. I didn't remember every word but…," I paused and thought for a moment. "But that's it. Yerberia del Sol," I said with assurance.

"I know where that is. That's really ironic. My grandma used to buy stuff there when I was a really small kid. She'd take me with her, but she stopped going. She never said why."

He kept going down the street until he entered an intersection and made another right turn. We crossed over some railroad tracks. The bumps made me remember the way it felt riding with my sister that day. The emotion washed over me with the sensation of the road beneath us.

"Here we are," he announced as he pulled up to the storefront.

There it was. Just the way I remembered it from three years before. A tattered, old store front with little appeal. Desolate. We entered the store and a bell jingled above our heads.

A woman sitting at the counter looked up. I recognized her immediately as the same woman I had seen three years before. Her thick black eye liner and long red nails gave her away immediately.

"Hello," she greeted us somewhat suspicious. "Can I help jou wit 'sonting?"

"*Hola Señora, estoy buscando una persona, Dona Carlota. Es muy importante que hablamos con ella hoy*," Dominic rattled off.

"*Ah, sí. ¿Quién son ustedes?*"

"*Soy Dominic y ella es mi amiga, Jessica.*"

"*Y ¿porque necesitan ver Doña Carlota?*" she asked, tilting her head and squinting her heavily lined eyes at us.

"*Información*," Dominic responded, flashing twenty-dollar bills at her from his pocket.

"*Esperense*," she said, walking into the back through the beaded curtains.

"What were you saying?" I whispered to him, feeling inept.

"I greeted her politely, asked her for Doña Carlota. She asked me who we were and what we wanted. I said information, and I basically bribed her without saying anything."

"You're going to pay her?"

"If I have to. That's just the way it is sometimes around here. She went to go get her. She said to wait."

We stood in silence and waited. I couldn't resist any longer. I had to ask him again, "How did you know I was Emily's sister? That day in the parking lot? How did you know that?" Him just knowing didn't make sense to me.

"Because you told me you were."

"But I didn't tell you anything, I hadn't even talked to you yet."

"There's more about yourself that you don't even know yet."

"What do you mean?"

"I think you may have been astral projecting before you ever realized you were.

Remember me telling you I'd seen you in my dreams? Yeah, so there's that. It happened, and I can't explain it any more than you can."

My inquisition was cut off by chatter down the dark hallway where the woman with the thick eyeliner had disappeared. It was almost as if the two voices were arguing with each other. Their tones grew louder and more aggressive.

The woman with the thick eyeliner stormed back into the room, smashing the beaded curtain into the wall. She marched up to the both of us obviously trying to compose herself.

"*Ustedes pueden pasar*," she said, nodding at me.

"We can go in," Dominic explained in a low whisper.

"Yeah, I got it," I whispered back. I followed his lead. Down the corridor we entered a room to the left that was filled with candle light. There was no fan or AC, it was hot and the candles only perpetuated the heat of the summer. I could feel my shirt sticking to my skin as perspiration began to accumulate. I couldn't tell if it was sweat from the heat alone or the nervousness that I was trying to stifle.

I had intended on letting Dominic do the talking, since he spoke fluent Spanish. But upon approaching the woman who sat behind a small table full of cards, candles, skulls and crystals, I felt compelled to speak first.

"Hello, Doña Carlota. I'm the sister of Emily Carmichael," I said. I remember speaking clearly because

I wasn't sure how well she understood English, but Emily didn't know Spanish, so I was sure this woman had to understand me.

"Who?" she asked, looking up with a confused expression.

"She was a customer of yours, three years ago. She came to see you for a love spell. Dark hair, light eyes," I motioned to my own features as I described her. "You gave her a little black velvet bag full of crap."

Doña Carlota sat still for a moment, staring off to the right towards the ceiling. I noticed the sweat running down her heavy-set face. She was a large woman. Her hair was greying slightly around her face, and I could see her eyes moving around before they landed back on me as she spoke.

"I sell a lot of people magic bags, gringas and others. How am I supposed to know who she was?" she asked smugly, sitting with her arms crossed.

"I know you know who she is because she came more than once. And if you have kept up with the local news at all in the last three years, you'd know she went missing and you'd recognize her face. If you're really a psychic, or someone with any power at all, you'd know exactly what in the hell I'm talking about right now!" I clenched my teeth. I had to stop before she shut down on me.

Dominic stood by my side with his arms crossed, angry. We both stood and looked at her in awkward silence.

"Your sister wanted more than just a love spell. She came wanting power."

"Power? Well what did you give her?" I fumed.

"I gave her the things I would give anyone to conjure power, but I never thought she would use them correctly. Most girls wanting the things she wanted have no power to make any of it work."

"So, you conned her?" Dominic chimed.

"I con no one. But I cannot control all things, you see. Your sister, is she alright?"

"Well you ought to know. You're the one who's psychic or whatever, and sent her into those woods," I said, becoming daringly angry with her.

"The woods? I never sent that girl into the woods," she replied, offended at the accusation.

"Then why did she go? Why else would she have gone?" I screamed at her, slamming my fist on her table, shaking her candles to the point of nearly toppling over.

"*Mija*, there are things in this world that go beyond what you or I can control or even fully understand. Whatever happened upon your sister was by her own doing. She must have had a different intent—a stronger one." She stood and glared at me across the table.

"And why should I believe you?" I snapped back.

"Believe what you must believe to get through this life, but know that I only sold to her the same bag I sell all young girls coming here for love. Crystals, sandalwood and patchouli incense and Florida water in a bottle with a red candle! I slip in a card with an incantation and instructions on it, and I put it in a black pouch and charge twenty dollars for it," she sighed, admitting her tactic.

"Then why did she disappear? What took her?" I could feel myself breaking down emotionally.

I felt Dominic put his arm around my shoulder at the sound of my voice.

"Both of you, you must listen. The one which took your sister must be left alone. To unleash it would cause more damage. I've heard of things like this happening."

"Do you even know what it was?" Dominic fired at her, "Because you being fraudulent with your naïve clientele doesn't convince me that a word you say is true."

"I admit *mijo*, that my powers are weak. I could never make more than a flame dance at a true séance. My family, my mother and sisters, they had more power than I ever did. I learned the Tarot, but beyond that I am afraid to say that I have no true power. What I know is what was told to me. I inherited this store nearly 10 years ago, and have made it my life to keep it open. From what I can gather, your sister opened a door. She was using more than what I gave to her. She must have some powers within herself. If she's been abducted, you can guarantee that it was none of my doing, and it was not by any hands of this world either."

"How do you know that it's not of this world if you're not psychic," I growled.

She sighed heavily again, as if just simply talking to us was a workout in and of itself. "It's just a feeling. I know what I sold her, I remember what she wanted, and if she went into the woods, it's just likely that she encountered something not of this world."

"I think we should leave," I said, looking at her with the coldest stare I could muster.

Dominic and I began to turn away from her to leave. The woman with the thick eyeliner was standing on the other side of the door, having listened to what took place.

"If you truly want to find her," spoke Doña Carlota as we walked away, "you must go where she went. Something about the two of you together makes me think that this is not the end of your sister."

# CHAPTER 10

It was already mid-June, and the pressing timeline for when I was to leave for college was looming. The entire preparation for the process was fleeting from my mind. I had until August, I knew that much. Then what? I was already registered for all of my fall courses, I knew what I was taking and in which dorm I would live. But I didn't want to think of it at all. I wanted only to think of what I couldn't see around me but could feel with every breath I took. I wanted only to find time to spend with Dominic. I didn't want to be like Emily with her emotional attachments to nobodies, but I wanted Dominic and in that I refused to deny myself,

In an attempt to clear my mind and bring my life back to pre-graduation normalcy, I attended orientation at the state university with my parents. I had gladly missed the date to go with Sarah. I remember looking around at all of the other people who were just like me, but really weren't. No one there was anything like what I was becoming. I walked past booths for sororities with girls passing out information and thought about Sarah and if she had already come to orientation and begun her college endeavors. I thought about the way we had last spoken to each other and how people said that eventually you grow apart from some friends, but I didn't expect to grow apart from a friend in the way that I had from Sarah. It had just happened so suddenly. It was as if I had been in a fog for the years since Emily had gone away and I was just going through the motions in my everyday life. Maybe Sarah had never really been a friend, just a prop. Now reality was becoming something completely different than I had thought.

"Honey?" snapped my mother.

"What?" I chirped with a startled tone, almost irritated.

"She asked you if you were going to be looking into living here at Stratford Hall your sophomore year," she said, prodding me gently on my side. "Is that still what you want?"

"Oh. Sure. That's fine," I said, shaking myself out of my thoughts. I didn't know what I wanted. I couldn't see myself living there at all, really.

"Okay!" with a clap and a snap of the fingers, our peppy campus tour guide directed us along and we followed her inside to sign me up for my living arrangements.

"Alright, Ms. Carmichael," said the campus guide with a broad smile, "We look forward to seeing you August 24th."

It was a two and a half hour drive back home. I sat in the backseat of my parents' car on the way back, looking at the pine trees cast shadows from the sun. The light flickering through the trees in the late afternoon gave the effect of a strobe light, nearly intense enough to give a person a seizure. August 24th. That was the date I would start a different life and leave the one

I was beginning to become so familiar with now. It was almost July. I had a month and a half left to try and figure out my reality, and to be near Dominic.

Faking my life for as long as I had, I felt the rush come over me to make it the way that it should be. I knew that I needed to find Dominic and tell him that I wanted to know more about what he had talked about at the diner that day, more about some foretold pair. I felt a connection to that conversation that I couldn't explain. I was pretty sure that's why I hadn't really wanted to hear about it when he mentioned it at first. Something about it shook me to the bone and made me feel like that's where I was truly supposed to be. My thoughts raced on the way back home. I sprawled out in the seats, uncomfortably against the edge of the seatbelt that pinched my side, and pretended to sleep while thinking of all of the possibilities.

Maybe part of the entire reason my sister had gone missing was to awaken what was now within me. Perhaps everything was for some greater reason that we truly could not understand. But I felt like I was beginning to understand. There were too many connections for which I truly could not account with any type of rationality, but I knew that the feelings within me were too much to control and had to be harnessed and used. I could do the things that people had been trying to do and couldn't accomplish. I could astral project, I could move around outside myself and see things in that state. I could sense things now, stronger than I had ever been able to before. I had visions of how people died. I could tell while walking around the university which people were sick and which people weren't. I knew which rooms had bad energy in the dorms and which didn't. I saw a girl walk by with her father and saw the blackness around his liver and sensed the cancer that was taking over him…and I knew she didn't know.

The things I had begun to sense and feel but had tried to ignore all came flooding into my head. I rested my head against the window, looking up at the evening stars beginning to appear above the trees as we drove down the country roads back to the house.

"Goddammit, none of the stations are coming in," my dad mumbled as he pressed the screen on the radio console.

"Dad," I sat up, leaning into the middle of the console to talk to him.

"Yep," he replied, his usual distant self.

"Our family name, Carmichael, where's it from? Like our ancestors?"

"Hmmm…from what I know our people are from Scotland. The name is Scottish. We have a lot of ancestors from over there."

"What else do you know?" I asked.

"Uncle Paul knows a lot more, he did a lot of genealogical research a few years back. Evidently we can trace our ancestry back to the druids—before they were Christianized."

"Mom, what about yours?" I asked.

"I'm not sure sweetie—we'll have to ask Aunt Kathy," she seemed to try to blow the question off quickly.

"Really? You never listened to your family talk or anything? You don't know anything?" I asked her, vexed that she knew nothing. How could someone who hadn't been adopted know nothing?

"I'll ask her, if it means that much to you," she said with a cantankerous sigh.

"It does. I'd like to know as much as you can tell me," I pushed.

"Why the big interest?" Dad asked.

"I think it's important to know exactly where you came from, if it's possible to know," I answered. "My friend knows his heritage, and I thought it was interesting. I wanted to know mine too."

"Well, there are lots of interesting stories on our side, "my dad piped up. It was the first time I'd heard him truly engage in a conversation since before Emily disappeared.

"What sort of stories?" I asked curiously.

"Supposedly, out of all of the branches of Carmichaels, our ancestors were the ones who were the closest to the Druids, and who built places like Stonehenge. My grandpa used to tell stories about how his grandfather had heard that his grandfather before him knew the secrets that our family had."

"Whoa, what secrets?" I asked. I saw my mother roll her eyes as she turned her face toward her window. I looked at her with irritation. It was like she didn't want to hear him talk about it.

Focused only on the road, he spoke, "Secrets. No, really just more like Freemason secrets. We don't know what all they were or are. It had always interested me, but my brother and I could never get grandpa to tell us, mainly because I think he didn't really know, or was making it up. He said there were some interesting things that had happened in the past. Ialways wanted to know what the secrets were when I was little, and Paul and I would make fake treasure maps out at grandpa's place even though it was in the United States, and pretend that our family's secret legacy was a treasure that we needed to find," he laughed.

We laughed with him, but something about my mother's behavior made me feel an uncomfortable tightness in my stomach.

I pulled out my phone and began to write a text to Dominic. Before I could finish typing it out, I saw that I had one from him.

"Can I come and see you tonight?"

My heart fluttered. I had so much to tell him.

"Mom, my friend, Dominic, wants to come by when we get home. Is that cool?"

"Oh, Dominic? I think so. What do you think, Danny?" she asked, looking over at my father.

"Who?" he replied, keeping his eyes on the road.

"His name's Dominic, he's a new friend of mine," I sighed in irritation.

"What's his problem," Dad asked dryly.

"Danny, he just wants to come over and visit her. At least she's not out runnin' the roads like those Morton girls," my mother said as she adjusted herself straighter in the passenger seat. "And besides, he took her to the library the other day. Isn't that nice?"

"Yes fine, he can come by. I don't care," my dad answered, returning to his stoic state.

I didn't even really want to ask them permission, but I thought it would be the respectful thing to do. I'd never had guy friends come over to the house before, so it was new territory for all of us. It was always opposite—me leaving with friends. Dad evidently didn't know how to respond. Saying he didn't care wasn't exactly the caring, engaged response one would hope for from a father. I wanted him to care a little more. But still, he seemed numb to the world, to my mother, and to love and emotion in general.

"Yes, I'll be back home in about an hour," I replied back to Dominic.

The rest of the ride home seemed like it was moving in slow motion. I wanted to get back as fast as we could. I had a feeling come over me as we turned the curves of the winding roads in the piney woods. I blinked hard. I felt it come as it had before. A cyph, as it was later defined for me.

"Dad, stop the car!" I heard the guttural scream come from within a deep place inside of me.

Before he could hit the brakes, I felt a shock almost like static electricity that totally shut down the car and all of its mechanisms. My father cursed wildly as we screeched to a halt in the middle of the road, fishtailing a little. Everything had locked up. I released my grip on his shoulder as I saw that we had stopped.

"Jessica!" Mom yelled through heaving breaths. "What in the hell isit?"

I didn't know, but before I could respond to either of them, ahead of us on the road appeared four large deer slowly crossing out onto the road. They saw our head lights and moved across the road slowly, cautious of our presence. A pickup truck rounded the curb and before the driver had time to react, he plowed violently into the last deer remaining in the road. His truck screeched and we flinched at the sickening thud as he swerved uncontrollably down the road into our lane, but we had stopped far enough back to prevent him from slamming into us.

I sat back all the way in my seat. My dad started the car, pulled off the road and got out to check on the man who had hit the deer, yelling at us to stay in the car as he lightly jogged toward the truck. The man was fine, he just suffered some damage to his truck.

"Jeez—if you hadn't been stopped up there, I woulda hit you," the man said, shaken.

"Yeah, we had already...slowed down," my dad responded, glancing back at me in the back seat strangely.

"Sure you're okay?" Dad asked the man.

"Yep. Just glad our timing was the way it was. Something up there was lookin' out for us," he said, glancing to the sky. "I'll load 'er up and take 'er off the road so nobody else sees the mess. Keep them buzzards off the road," the man said, motioning over towards the bloody carcass.

"Alright. You need help with that?" Dad asked.

"Naw, I got 'er. Not my first time throwin' one in the back of the truck."

"Alright then, sir. You take care," Dad said, walking back to our car and getting in without saying a word to either of us.

My mother's voice was shaky as she spoke the words quietly, just before he opened the door, "You knew, didn't you?" It should have been a question but came out more like a statement.

"Yeah," I said from the back. I really didn't know what else to say. All I knew is that we needed to stop that instant before something happened. I hadn't known if it would be deer or an oncoming vehicle. Dad didn't say anything else to either one of us.

We pulled up to the house, and I went upstairs to my room to change before Dominic arrived. I heard the doorbell ring and walked outside onto the porch to see him.

He skipped formalities and got straight to the point. "Are you okay?"

"Yeah, I'm alright." I said, looking at him from the side and squinting, trying to decipher why he would ask me that before saying anything else.

"I knew, Jessica," he said.

"Knew what?"

"That there was danger. I could sense it. But you stoppedit."

"I know I did. I think I freaked my parents out."

"It scares mine sometimes, too."

"Right before you texted me, I was going to text you."

"What about?"

"You can't tell that without me saying?" I laughed, shedding some of the tension from

what had happened.

"I haven't quite figured it all out yet," he responded with a smile.

"I thought more about what you said about the pair—the foretold pair. I think I was afraid at first, but I'm not afraid of being part of it, if it's real. I just shut my dad's whole car down, so I think it's real," I said, taking a step closer.

"What made you think about it more?" he asked, hands in his pockets as he stood before me.

"Things have changed. I know things that I didn't know before. I have sensitivities to things that I've never had before. I can know things that other people can't know, plus the other things I told you, and it's been happening to me so fast." I tried not to speak too quickly because I wanted him to understand everything I was saying, but I also felt he understood without words.

"Well, like what I was telling you about at the diner," he started.

"Yeah."

"It reminds me of something else my grandma said about the legend of the pair."

"What was it?" I asked eagerly.

"We're not the only ones who know what we are," he replied, looking at me with a flicker in his eyes.

"What exactly does that mean?" I asked, unsure about what 'others' would know. Would this be a good thing, or would it lead to something more threatening?

"I'm not precisely sure" he muttered, letting a silence step between us for a brief moment.

Curbing my urge to hold onto him, I asked, "So, what do we do from here? If we're the pair?"

"That's part of why I wanted to come over and talk to you. Have you heard anything else from Vanek?"

"No, not since the weird messages."

"Well, as the legend goes, some force will try and stop the pair, because together the two can stop some, maybe not all, horrible things from happening. From what I was always told, the pair can stop the wicked, break cycles of curses, bring back lost souls, and send back the dark beings that enter into this world. But there will always be something trying to stop them."

"That's a lot," I gasped, nodding my head and looking down, wondering how I would handle something like that. I couldn't help but think about how difficult living a double life would be. What would I tell my parents? How would any of it work?

"Your sister could be saved," he revealed. "If we do this, it's going to be dangerous. I'm not sure if Vanek is the one sent to stop us, but he acts like it. It could get nasty."

"Nasty like how?"

"I'm not entirely sure, but from what I know, deadly. We've got to help protect each other. I think you know now at this point that I'll do whatever I can for you," he said smiling, motioning towards the woods from where he had rescued me.

"Yes, I have no doubt," I responded, looking down. I wondered if he knew about the dream I had about him. I tried to clear my mind of it, it was embarrassing but addicting to think about all at once.

"I also came over to give you this," he mentioned, coming closer to me. My adrenaline rushed as I flashed back to the dream I had that felt so real. I knew this. I felt what was happening.

He bent over, and I leaned up toward him, closing my eyes. I felt the cold chill of a chain fall around my neck.

"It's a blessed charm of Saint Michael. My grandma blessed it herself. For you," he smiled.

"Oh," I said, surprised. "Thanks."

"Saint Michael is a protector, and even though you're not Catholic, and neither am I, even though mom is, he's still a higher being of protection that you can ask to assist and watch over you, just personified as Saint Michael. You know, for protection when I'm not around," he explained. "My grandmother gave it to me when I was little, like seven. I've kept it locked up safely ever since. But she told me the same thing, that it would protect me when she wasn't around. But I want you to have it now. See his eyes? They're jade, and the wings are blue, they're made of labradorite. There's quartz in it, for protection. Each stone is meant to help you in some way."

"Wow," I breathed, looking down at it in my fingers. It was a beautiful little charm. I'd never worn anything like it before. "He has a sword, I love swords."

"Yeah, swords are sort of his thing. Saint Michael is the patron saint of warriors—not just against evils of this world, but of the other world as well. That sword is his weapon."

Besides a few heirloom pieces of my family, all of my previous jewelry had been gaudy and meant to match outfits for purely materialistic purposes. My eyes studied it carefully. The figure of Saint Michael was colored with exquisite detail. He had large wings, blonde hair, a shield and a sword. He was exquisite. All of the tiny, perfectly cut stones that created Saint Michael were set in beautiful, shiny gold. The eyes were cast in a jade color, making them glow as I shifted it in the light.

"What is it? You seem disappointed," he asked quietly. He stood very close to me, his hand on my shoulder.

"Disappointed? No! This is perfect, so thoughtful, so…beautiful," I thanked him, still holding it and studying it. "No one's ever given me anything meaningful like this before. Thank you. I just wonder what will protect you now? If this was yours for protection," I inquired, feeling my eyes lock onto the green jade, meeting their match.

"I think I've found what protects me. And there's something else I have to give you, before one more second passes," he whispered.

Before I could respond he took my head with his hand, pulled my chin up to his face and kissed me even more slowly and passionately than I had dreamed of so vividly before. I felt the air and sounds around me go still and quiet as I held on to him so tightly that I felt I was one with him. I felt like my entire body had vanished and I had melted into him with his touch. I felt like it wasn't my first time kissing him but knowing that it was, I didn't want the moment to stop. His lips caressed mine softly and I don't think I knew if my feet were touching the ground or not. His hand gently stroked down my back but stopped just at my waist, only to pull me closer to him for just a moment before pulling back. I was taken aback at the force between us.

We stopped for a brief moment and looked at each other, understanding exactly what was happening, and I leaned up and kissed him again, pulling him down to hold onto me and letting him pick me up and hold me right against him. I jumped up on him, something so uncharacteristic of me, and squeezed my arms and legs around him as I let his lips explore my neck and my jaw. My passion for him was explosive. I felt like it was almost dangerous. His warmth enveloped me with each breath we took of each other's. I slid down off of him, scared my parents would see me. He kissed my forehead and took my hand into his.

"Don't think I didn't want to do that from the moment I first saw you," he whispered into my ear.

With my eyes closed I felt his breath on me and tried only to feel the moment as much as I could while fully experiencing it at the same time.

"Don't think that I didn't want you either right when I first saw you," I responded, resting my forehead against his chin.

"Then you felt it too?"

"Right away. But I didn't know what it was."

"Everything that's happening—it's older than us. We've been us before. And here we are again. We always find each other. It's what we are meant to do. Now we're going to find your sister together."

In that moment, I already knew. I knew that I had known him and I knew that I was for him.

"I know," I said, "I feel it now. I know that I've loved you. I knew I loved you when I saw you. I knew you were for me somehow."

"Each lifetime that we come around, we find each other. It hasn't always been this easy. There have been lifetimes where we couldn't ever find each other. This time fate brought us together through your sister. It's all happened for a reason," he explained quietly and stroked my hair out of my face.

"Why didn't you say anything to me sooner?" I asked, the smell of his skin comforting me.

"I wanted you to start to realize for yourself what you are, and now that you're feeling it, you can feel the rest of what exists between us."

"It would have saved me a lot of craziness," I laughed.

"Was it that bad?"

"You have no idea," I chuckled, thinking of the longing I had within me for him.

"And now I know I can't be apart from you. I want every breath I breathe to be with you," I confessed, partly scared and partly addicted to the smell of his skin in the summer air.

"You'll never have to be separated from me," he promised, kissing my lips again. "You are my life. I can't live without you."

"Yes, it's more than love," I knew that one word just did not encapsulate what I was feeling.

"More than love," he repeated, "I more than love you."

"I more than love you, too," I replied, leaning into him.

"Can we talk to your parents?" he asked. I thought I heard him incorrectly.

"What, no! You can't tell them any of this!"

He laughed. "I wasn't planning on it. I just wanted to be a gentleman and talk to them, like a normal conversation, like a nice young man."

"Not a bad plan," I giggled, walking him inside the house.

"Hey you two," my mother greeted us as we walked through the house and into the kitchen.

"Hello, Mrs. Carmichael," Dominic nodded politely. I felt oddly at ease with him by my side. Knowing I loved him, and how much I loved him, didn't feel unnatural in the slightest to me. The old me would have said, "You idiot, you kissed him one time! You can't love someone you barely know!" But the difference was that I already knew him, some way, somehow. He was no stranger to my soul.

"Jess, I called Aunt Kathy, and she said she'd be able to drive in for a visit this weekend. She said we could use some sisterhood time."

"Really?" I asked, peering out of the side of my eyes at my mother. She had been very quick to jump on the request for information from her sister.

"Dominic," my mother gestured towards him with a cup of tea. He took it graciously. "Maybe you could come by and meet her too. She's a fun lady."

I looked back and forth at both of them, waiting for the world to collapse.

"Just tell me where and when, Mrs. C."

# CHAPTER 11

My world had begun to spin differently, tilted and in a different direction than the rest of the world. I could now look into the woods and see a glow that I had never previously seen. It was orange and would open up, almost like seeing the sun shine through the woods in the afternoon. I would see small lights come out of it. I knew it was a doorway, and I knew that my sister could have gone in and never come back out.

I could go to the market and smell the various scents of foods differently than I ever had before, and I could sense the emotions of the people around me while there. It made me feel what they were feeling. It had gotten so strong that I had to practice blocking them out.

I walked past an older woman slowly pushing a cart down the bread aisle. She looked as though she was in her early eighties. As she moved past me, I saw an old man appear behind her. He hadn't been there before. I stared at him. He looked back at me. His eyes were blank, void of any emotion. He watched me look at him and I watched him slowly turn away and walk behind the woman as she slowly made her way down the aisle. I had a brief flash of a vision in my head. He was in the hospital and the nurses were commanding, "Do not resuscitate." I shook it away with a slight motion and a blink. In my head I heard a voice say, "She's my wife, and I'm going to be with her until she comes back to me."

I felt happy and sad at the same time. He was still with her, but she was alone. I thought about how that must feel. *Death doesn't do you part*, I thought to myself. I knew that it didn't.

My phone vibrated in my pocket. It was Chris calling.

I answered quickly, watching the vision of the other man vanish with the breaking of my concentration.

"Hello, Jessica?" Chris asked through static. Everything electronic had now completely failed me.

"Hey, what's up?" I asked, walking toward the front of the store to try and get a better signal. It was pointless. I was interfering with the signal.

"Where have you been? We haven't seen or heard from you. Dana and I were wondering what was up."

"I'm sorry, Chris. I've been busy. My parents are making me do a lot of things for college, it's been time consuming." I felt bad for lying to him.

"We haven't seen much of Dominic or Vanek either. Have you heard from them?" he asked.

"No. . . no I haven't," I fibbed again. I didn't like not telling him what was happening, but I felt like there was too much to even begin to explain to him. Dominic and I had already decided it would be best for me to just avoid them, if not for our own good, then for theirs. Who knew what Vanek was capable of doing to them.

"Okay, well, if you want we're meeting up tonight again at my place," he replied.

"I can't come."

"Nine is when I'll be off if you change your mind."

"Okay, well, thanks Chris! I'll talk to you later," I nearly shouted over the static.

"Jess, just one more thing," he interjected through static before I could click to hang up.

"Sure, what's up?"

"I lied."

"What?"

"I have seen Vanek. He's been showing up at random places. Dana noticed the same thing. He hasn't been saying anything to us, just sort of—staring. Look if you see him, could you let us know? Something's not right."

"Yes of course, I'll definitely do that…," the phone died. The battery was completely drained.

I purchased my items and left the store, hoping to get home without any more incidents. As soon as I turned on my car, I could sense the radio was acting up. The static was too heavy to hear a song. I could hear a voice coming through again. It didn't scare me as much as it had the first few times it had happened. I listened hard and made out the words "Saint…church" and then the static stopped. I knew of three churches in town— the First Baptist, the First Methodist and Saint Mary's Catholic Church. I decided to drive by and see what the static voice was wanting me to know.

I parked outside of the church in the parking lot that held a few other cars. We didn't really go to church, so I didn't know exactly what I should be doing once there. I noticed on the marquee in front of the church that evening mass had just been held. I entered the church and walked quietly to the far left aisle. There were just a few people inside, and they seemed to be in deep prayer. As I walked slowly and looked around me, I took notice of the beautiful stained glass windows and the decorative statues and artwork. It gave the atmosphere a sense of majesty. No one who sat in prayer really took notice of me, so I made my way up to the front, to a statue of the Virgin Mary.

I admired the statue's perfection. Her face was so calm and serene. She held her hands out as if to welcome me. It was a comforting feeling to look up at the statue and feel the energy of the whole place coming together. I reached up to my Saint Michael charm that Dominic had given me and fumbled with it in my fingers. I stared at Mary's polished marble eyes. Although they were devoid of color, there was emotion carved into them. The emotion was so real. I saw, at least I thought I saw, a small tear in the corner of her right eye. It looked like a glimmering drop of water.

"Do you need to make confession, young lady?" asked thepriest, giving me a slight startle.

I turned to him, and when he looked in my eyes he took a slight movement back away from me, as if I had alarmed him. He was old, probably nearly eighty, though he seemed to still have his wits about him by the way he moved and spoke.

"My God."

I looked at him, unsure of why, as a priest, he would use God's name in vain like that, and in church no less. I didn't know much about religion, but it seemed a bit out of character for a priest.

"I'm sorry?" I said quietly to him, trying to decipher his fear.

"You are of the others, aren't you?" he asked.

"I'm sorry, um, Father. I don't know what you mean," I said. "Something told me to come here, so I did." I'd never really talked to any priest before, let alone one who seemed to know my deepest secrets, so addressing him was a bit of a conundrum for me.

"You are the Dhakris," he responded, still baffled at my presence.

"What?" I whispered sharply.

"There is a legend of the Dhakris that is told, especially to those who are entrusted to be Holy. It is kept a secret by those who know of it. It was said that this generation wouldhave you appear. I didn't know it would be here, but I felt it."

"What is a...Dhakris?" I asked.

He shook his head emphatically. "No one knows of the word's exact origin. It is said to come from a language older than recorded time. But that's the word; that's what you are."

I looked at him in confusion. He read my expression and, glancing around at the parishioners still kneeling in prayer with their rosaries he said, "If you have time, let's talk in my office, shall we?"

Nodding an acceptance, I followed him through a side door, down a short hallway to his office. The pungent smell of incense that had been burned during the evening mass, lingered

though out the building. Entering his office, the priest sat behind his massive oak desk in a worn, black leather chair. I took a seat in an upholstered chair in front of the desk.

"You're saying I'm the Dhakris?"

"I believe you are, yes."

"Why am I the Dhakris?"

"My child, you must be aware that there are forces unseen in our world which we cannot fight alone?" he inquired.

I nodded my head. "I know."

"And your partner?" he asked, I assumed referring toDominic.

"He knows."

The priest nodded in acknowledgment.

"So, you've found one another. God made man and woman at the same time originally, you know. At least if you read Genesis correctly. Genesis 1:27. It was later that someone came along and wrote that whole rib nonsense. It was for a good reason. He created man and woman at the same time, because the true partnership that is man and woman is strong and is one unbreakable, of equal importance," he whispered, looking me in the eye with each word.

"The Dhakris is you. You are the Dhakris," he insisted, becoming almost giddily excited that he had found me in his church.

"How come not everyone knows, but you do?" I asked.

"How could they?" he asked. "What do you think would happen if all the people of the world knew the truth?"

"But wouldn't it be better for everyone to know what reality really is?" I asked.

"Think about what you're asking," he suggested. "What would the people of the world do if they were told that what their religions have taught them have been untrue? What would they do if they truly knew we were not alone, not only on this Earth but in our Universe?"

I thought about his question. I thought about how people would be so completely lost if they knew that other beings existed. It would tear apart their belief systems. It could turn the world upside down. I could picture the crumbling of society upon knowing that everything they had based their world upon was a farce. The wars, the terrorism, the craziness that had all been brought about in our history—it was for nothing if the religion off of which it was based was not revealing entire truths.

"So, you knew about me, then? How come you know and others don't?"

"You've been here before, among humanity, and you've served your purpose at different times. Now you're back again, the both of you. You're lucky, actually, that you were born back into a situation where you could actually find one another. As it goes, sometimes evil will tear you apart first, and when one of you dies, you must be born again all over to find one another. We know about you, a select amount of the population. A very small, small selection of the population knew to expect you again."

I looked at him, wanting him to tell me more. "What else can you tell me? I thought Christians didn't believe in reincarnation."

Instead of answering the question right away he looked out the window with a distant air and asked me to take a walk with him. He gestured towards the door, so we left his office and exited the church through a side door. We walked in silence a short distance and reached a back yard of the church with a gravel path we could stroll along without interruption.

"It has been said," he spoke as we walked, "that some souls do reincarnate. When the Council of Nicaea created what we now know as the Christian Bible, many things were lost, thrown out, left out completely for reasons of propaganda. Not only that, but the tales of folklore, the tales that were told out of truth but passed on throughout generations, were ignored all together. The reasons for this had much more to do with political power than with religion itself. The Dhakris, you and your partner, were something kept secret among all holy keepers— the shaman, Egyptian priests, holy leaders of all creeds and religions. You always try to find one another in each new generation into which you are born. Usually there is a dramatic circumstance that will bring you together, a catalyst if you will."

He gestured with his hands as he spoke. "It is said that it could be in any country, in any time period that you are born into, that you will gravitate toward one another to fight the forces of the dark world. That is your whole purpose. You're a warrior."

"Who said it first? Where did you learn about all of this?" I asked, certain that he hadn't learned it in his theological studies.

"It is only spoken of, but not written down. There aren't many who know, like I said," he reiterated.

"Then how did you know it was me? How could you possibly know without talking to me or knowing what I've been through recently that I am part of the pair?" I asked, stopping to look at the Holy Man.

"The way it was told to me by my ancestors and passed down, something was to come at this time in our time cycle. It is not to be discounted that I am very aware of who is around me at all times. You are not a member of my congregation, but you entered the church for some reason, did you not?" he asked.

"Yes, Father, I heard someone, or something, tell me to come here. I'm sorry if that sounds crazy."

"Crazy? No. I've heard crazier things myself," he chuckled. I watched as his aged round face moved into a more solemn and stern expression. "It was foretold that you would appear in the 'new land', and those of us who knew of the tale assumed that was here in the United States, since it is considered 'new' to civilization. It is also told that the Dhakris have special eyes. Different eyes from most. Green eyes, unnaturally green."

"But lots of people have green eyes. How are mine any different?"

"When you see his green eyes, what do you see?" he asked me.

My stomach fluttered at the thought of the sight of them. They weren't normal green, that was for sure. They were like an emerald colored sea.

"They stand out."

"Well, child, so do yours. And you'll notice when you are more sensitive to your work, they will change, and they will become lighter and brighter. It is a mark of the sight of the other world. Some call it the second sight," he explained.

"Other world?" I thought of what I knew of Christianity, and it didn't add up to what he was telling me.

"My ancestors from Ireland called the people of the other world the Good People, the Muslim and our Middle Eastern brethren call them the Djinn, Christians often refer to them as fallen angels, the watchers or Nephilim, the Icelandic people call them Huldufólk, New agers sometimes refer to them as the Annunaki. Whatever you want to call them, they're the others that exist all around but are invisible to us. It was even said that a priest in Ireland could place his hand on his side, creating a space between his arm and his body, and if one were to look through that gap, it would be possible to see the Good People and the other world. These stories have existed for quite some time. But you and your partner, you have the sight to see them, at least you're developing it. You can see where they come and go, where there's darkness in their doings or not."

"What do you mean by this time cycle?" I asked.

"Oh, it can sound complicated, but think of time as overlapping circles that rotate—not a straight line. Time doesn't exist in a straight line as we would like to think it does."

"Okay, so cycles of time then, and this is our cycle?"

"It is. You may have just come from a cycle in the future or one from the distant past where you were the same soul but with a different family and a different name, a different race even, and you came together, or at least tried to, in order to work for our side."

"When you say, 'our side', you're just talking about what ordinary people see, then?" I asked.

"This side of our reality. The one where you can feel, taste, smell, hear normally like everyone else. The one where you were born, the one where I existed as a Priest and helped people find God's love through Christ, if that is what they so choose."

We slowly started walking again, back to the church.

"I've told you all that I can really tell you. Like I said, as far as I know, nothing's written down. It is all passed down orally. You are here now, so you have work to do. You may not have been successful in a different life, so it is up to you in this one to face the challenges that come before you and your partner, in order to keep our realm safe."

"What if we fail?" I asked.

"I've told you all I know. It is a blessing to be among beings like you; you are a helper of mankind."

"How did my soul choose to be me? And by pure, you mean we shouldn't…," I asked, confused.

"You should remain true to yourself. Like I said, each go-around the two of you try to find each other. Sometimes it works out, sometimes it doesn't. This time, you've made the first step. You've found each other. Your souls, both split, they lined up correctly to meet again."

We walked back in through the parishioners doors in the back.

"I must go now, child, and take confessions. I haven't any more time to speak with you. But I see you've got Saint Michael, the Archangel."

"Yes. It was a gift," I said smiling, thinking of the moment right after receiving it.

"Draw on that strength, for Saint Michael the Archangel is much older than religion itself, and it is he who made you for a purpose. The power of Saint Michael has always been there to protect and help all beings, and it must sometimes become incarnate. You are part of that incarnation."

"Are we safe?" I asked.

"Let us pray that you will be," he said, taking my hands. He began speaking in Latin, praying and tightening his hold on my hands.

When he finished, we made our way back to the statue of the Virgin Mary. I looked up at the statue that had held my gaze captive before the priest approached me. Her tear had dripped down her face and the stream glistened in the light. The priest took notice of it.

"It is a sign. You are to go forth now and begin your work," he whispered, so as to not be heard by the few people still scattered about the church.

"Thank you, Father," I whispered in return. I turned and walked slowly out of the church. I felt almost as though I was floating out. The good energy in the church was comforting, and I hoped it would stay with me as I drove back to the woods and to my home.

\* \* \* \*

"Aunt Kathy!" I threw my arms around her when I saw her. It had been a while. She hadn't been able to stay after my graduation to see me, as she had to travel to Sonoma for one of her excursions, as she called them.

"My Jessica! It's been too long!" She squeezed me tightly, leaving me slightly breathless.

My mother took my grocery bags as Aunt Kathy held my face and looked me over. "Good God, Jessica. What took you so long coming back from the store?"

I didn't even realize a half hour trip had taken me nearly an hour and a half.

"Oh, I ran into some people I knew, you know, and they were talking and talking…. "My mother looked at me dubiously.

"Oh, Celia, it's fine. She's here. We're all here together. Don't worry about it honey, we've had time to make tea and catch up," Aunt Kathy said cheerfully. I noticed the turquois bangles she had on both wrists that slid up and down her plump arms as she spoke.

"What do you want for dinner? We have salad, ham sandwiches; looks like she bought the makings for pasta…," Mom said as she dug through the grocery bags.

"Okay, Celia, let's cut to the chase. Something's going on here and that's why you wanted me to come."

My mother stopped what she was doing and looked up from the food at me.

I looked at both of them and couldn't figure out what my first words should be. I fumbled through different scenarios in my mind until something finally emerged from my lips. I had a feeling I wouldn't be inviting Dominic over.

"Mom brought you here to tell me something, and I want to know what it is." It didn't make a lot of sense, but both of them nodded as if it did. I felt a sigh of relief at not having to be more specific. The silence in the room was thick and tense. Someone had to say something first, and it wasn't going to be me. I waited until one of them broke.

"Well, Jessica, first of all I want to say to you that I know you've probably thought I was totally clueless since Emily went away." My mother's sudden blunt words took me completely off guard.

"I just wanted for you to have some sort of normal childhood, some sort of normal upbringing, some idea of normalcy before you changed."

"Changed?" I asked. "What do you mean changed?"

"I'm not certain," she replied somberly. Her eyes looked into the distance and not at either one of us.

"Neither of us were certain," Aunt Kathy chimed in. "Why do you think I never had any children of my own? I didn't want to risk what might have happened."

"Shut up, Kathy," my mother snapped sharply, cutting her off.

"No! I will not shut up! Why should I? That's why you invited me here, isn't it? She wants to know the truth, so we're gonna tell her! You can't back out now."

I stared, gawking at both of them, waiting for something to make sense. It actually made sense that nothing they were saying made any sense. It explained why everything was so strange.

Aunt Kathy turned towards me with a stern look in her eyes. "What your momma won't tell you is she knew all along she'd lose one of you. She just didn't know when and how. She told me when we were little that if we had children, they would be cursed. That's why I didn't have any. I didn't want to bring another cursed person into the world."

"Shut up, Kathy," my mother said again, this time through clenched teeth.

"Let her talk, Mom! Let her tell me what you won't, or can't. Who was she?" I had never been so stern to my own mother. Aunt Kathy gave my mother a nod and continued.

"When we were little girls there was an old woman who lived down the road from our church. Every Sunday, about the time we were going to church the old woman would be walking by towards town. She would stop and turn towards the church and watch the families enter. I don't recall if I ever heard anyone say anything to her— not even a 'good morning'. Your grandma would never allow us to talk to the old woman. Grandma would go so far as to try to hide us behind her if the woman was anywhere near us. Well, your momma and I couldn't help ourselves. We just had to find a way to talk to her. So, one day while we were supposed to be in Sunday school, we snuck out through the back door of the church and found her on her way back down the road to wherever it was she lived".

I decided to get a glass of iced tea and sit at the small breakfast table. I couldn't believe what I was hearing. Mom had poured a glass of wine and was standing with her back against the kitchen sink, swirling it around with an anxious motion. Aunt Kathy paced the kitchen with her mug of tea and continued her story.

"We stopped her in her tracks and without saying a word she turned around and looked at both of us, shaking her walking stick as she spoke. She said, 'Ah, I've been waiting on the both of you to come and see me. The two of you have the blood of the ones. One of you is going to suffer a loss of one of your own in order to bring forth what will save us all from this putrid existence. ' I remember the way she said putrid, and she looked right at you, Celia. When we asked her what she meant, she said, 'Don't worry too much, children, what is meant to be will happen. And when you think one of your own is lost, she won't be truly lost. For she will return. '"

I looked over at my mother, who now had her eyes clenched tightly with tears welling up in the corners.

Aunt Kathy looked around the room at each of us. "Wasn't that what happened, Celia?"

My mother had said nothing up to that point. It seemed like she was trying to hide inside herself for just a moment longer.

"Kathy," she murmured through sniffling tears, "I didn't want to believe her. She was just a strange old woman, after all. You believed her, I didn't. I didn't take her seriously and now it seems, as both of you can obviously see, that she was right."

I cleared my throat. "Did you know what she meant by 'the blood of the ones'?"

Aunt Kathy sipped her tea and shook her head. "I never fully figured that one out. When our momma found out that we had snuck away from Sunday school and chased down that old woman to talk to her she punished us—and severely. We never went to Sunday school after that. Momma made us sit right next to her every Sunday after that, in the regular church service."

Mom cleared her throat and said, "When Emily started exploring the otherworldly business, I knew, Jessica. Mothers know. We know more than you think. I've been trying to piece this all together for the past three years. Emily disappearing was part of what I assumed wassomething bigger. The old woman, she said that what was lost would return. I left everything the same because I expect her to return."

I was taken aback by her honest, calm demeanor. I thought she'd think I was crazy.

"Why didn't you ever talk about any of this?" my voice cracked a little.

"I may be an adult, a parent, but that doesn't mean I know what I'm doing," my mother said quietly.

Mother and Aunt Kathy gave each other a long look that I could only interpret as an affirmation between the two of them that all secrets needed to be purged. My mother came to the table and sat down next to me. "Something I've never told you is…," she glanced at Aunt Kathy who gave her a curt nod, "Grandma took her own life. I know you've always been told that she had a heart attack, but the truth is she drove off one morning, parked her car and walked into the bayou. A fisherman found her." Mom dropped her head and gave a shudder.

I looked from my mother to Aunt Kathy and asked, "Where?"

"Pine Island Bayou, at Caraway Park."

"Mom," I looked back at her and took her hands in mine. In that instance I could see what the fisherman saw. I saw her cold blue lips, her open, engorged eyes with their blank stare. I saw my mom and my aunt having to look at her. I hated seeing it and shook my head to try and get rid of the image. "I'm so sorry. But why? Why did she do it?"

My mother's face was twisted in anguish when she looked up at me. She shook her head as she said, "No one really knows. She didn't leave a note, or even an indication as to why she did it. The only thing I could figure is that she was sick and wouldn't tell anyone. But now I think it was because I was pregnant with Emily."

I may have been able to see the ghastly image of my grandmother, but I had no way of foreseeing that this was what had actually happened. I knew that my parents had married right out of high school, but I never gave it a thought, just chalked it up to young, high school love.

"So, she killed herself when she found out you were pregnant, she must have known something, like you said about the old woman, and you must have upset her, and she just couldn't take it...," I said to myself more than to them, piecing it all together.

In chimed Aunt Kathy with more information. "We don't know, we just don't know. We thought about it and talked about it for a long, long time afterward. The only conclusion we came to was that Momma knew something we didn't. She had tried protecting us all of our lives and it didn't work. She must have felt like a tremendous failure. But it all goes back to the old woman."

"Jessica," my mother spoke through sniffles, "we want to ensure you're safe, too. This whole lifelong saga, it's not something we would ever wish on anyone else or expect anyone to understand."

"Well, what would you say if I told you Dominic is helping me?" I asked.

"I'd say that whatever it is in your blood, he must have it, too. I knew it when I saw his eyes."

"I think that's why Momma dragged us to church so adamantly every Sunday," Aunt Kathy pondered out loud. "Whatever it was that she knew, it's like she thought if she took us to church enough it would stop whatever it was that she was afraid of from happening."

"I wish she were still alive to tell us," my mother said sadly.

I knew in my head what that old woman had meant, and why my grandmother was probably terrified.

"Look, I don't exactly know how to explain this to the both of you, but I can feel that I am different from everyone else. Dominic and I, we're both having the same experiences."

Aunt Kathy looked at me and smiled. "Just be careful. You know I will help in any way I can."

"I don't know if anyone else can help, Aunt Kathy," I said quietly.

"This isn't the life I wanted for you," my mother cried.

"Well, it's too late now. I'm in the middle of it, so please, just let me try and figure out what's happening."

"I can't let you. It's too late, Jessica. I've already made plans for to go to school out of state away from all of this."

"What?" My heart skipped a beat as my head tried to untangle what I had just heard. "Away from Dominic?" I almost screamed.

She looked at me with bloodshot eyes. "I'm trying to save you! I'm trying to keep you away from the same problems that keep manifesting themselves within our family!"

"Well save yourself then! I'm not going anywhere!" I roared.

"I've already arranged for your transfer to Northeastern University," she muttered, her voice crackling.

"But we just went to state the other day! You stood there and helped me plan moving in! When—why would you do this? How?" I was crying now, trembling with tears and confusion.

"Aunt Kathy is going to drive you at the end of the week."

"I'm doing whatever I can to make sure you're safe, butter bean," Aunt Kathy said with a guilty look in her eyes.

I shook my head in refusal. "It's like seven states away! It's so far! Why would you do this? Mom, you don't even know what's happening. You just think you do. You don't know the truth because no one has ever wanted to tell you, because this is how you react—terribly. Yourreactions are what push people away from you! It's why you just sit here alone and drink your wine every day!" I screamed through tears.

She ignored my insults. "Look, you had the grades, you had the letters of recommendation, all I had to do was pull a few strings and get your dad to make some phone calls and we were able to get you in. I knew I had to do something when you met Dominic."

"But...why?" I cried. They wouldn't answer. "You said you liked him, what's wrong with him? Why?"

I could hear them trying to console me, trying to reason with me, but I backed away and ran upstairs to my room. I had to find a way to escape.

# CHAPTER 12

Dhakris, Dhakris, Dhakris…The word repeated itself in my mind. It felt so familiar yet so exciting and new. I knew what I was now, at least somewhat. The sound of it helped numb the wound of knowing my parents were planning on sending me away soon, unless I could stop it.

It was a compelled gravitation, stronger than any other attraction that most people have for one another, that I was feeling towards Dominic. I suppose it was what made our souls try to find each other every time we were born again. It was something that was beyond our cognizant mind but existed somewhere deeper, in our subconscious. Now that we had found one another, we would seemingly 'know' when to come to each other. It began with Dominic coming to my window.

An old magnolia tree grew tall alongside the house where my bedroom was situated. When Emily and I were growing up, Dad had always kept the bottom section of the tree trimmed so that we girls could easily stand underneath the branches. It was our favorite place to play in the hot summer days. The shelter of the thick, waxy leaves gave us cool shade from the sun and kept us dry from light sprinkles of rain. Now the tree's branches gave Dominic an easy access to my bedroom window.

I had been in my bedroom for a little while, drying my tears and calming down, trying to make sense of everything I had been told when I heard a soft tap on my window. I froze in panic, thoughts zipping through my mind of the thing in the woods when I heard a familiar soft voice say, "Its me." I opened the window and let him through motioning to be quiet so that my parents wouldn't hear. I locked my door and turned my music on to cover the sounds of our voices, just in case.

"My grandmother is coming to visit. She's going to help us with getting to know what we can do," he said, and leaned in and gave me a kiss briefly.

"A lot has happened. Too much. First, I talked to a priest earlier today," I explained, feeling like it was a confession to Dominic.

"A priest, the priest here at the Catholic church in town?" he asked curiously.

"Yes, Father Dolan, I believe? Old man? Really nice?" I nudged.

Suddenly the intensity in Dominic's eyes changed. He had been stroking my hair gently, but he stopped. The look on his face sent my adrenaline into a rush. "Jessica, he's been dead for years. The priest at that church is a young guy that travels between this town and Beaumont to cover masses until they find a permanent replacement."

I cupped my mouth with my hands, leaning over trying to comprehend the implications of his words. Just like the other times, flashes of his end came into my head. He died peacefully in his bed, surrounded by close friends. He had kidney failure. But I had been with him, talked and walked with him. "What? Dead?"

"Yes. He's dead."

I shook my head and looked down for a moment, then looked back up at him. "He seemed so—alive to me. He had more than a lot to tell me about us. I guess he was right about my second sight then. I couldn't even tell him apart from a living person."

Dominic laughed quietly. "Great, he knew about us. My Weli, that's what I call my grandma, says there are a lot of people that know about us—the pair. She can't remember the old word for what we're called, but she said it wasn't Spanish."

"Dhakris," I said.

"Dhakris, is that what the priest told you?" He thought for a moment. "What else did he say?"

"Weli is your grandmother?" I asked.

"Yeah, short for *Abuelita*—like saying granny," he explained.

I nodded. I thought about the main points of the priest's conversation with me but I wanted to tell Dominic every detail. I began to recount everything the priest had told me, trying my best to speak verbatim. Dominic listened without interruption.

I closed my eyes and recalled the last thing he said to me.

"He urged that we have to remain true to ourselves, but I'm not really sure what that meant."

"I think it means that we have to always be true to each other," Dominic said with a smile and a kiss. "That's something else Weli always said. By the way, her bus gets into Beaumont around nine in the morning. You should come with us. We're leaving around eight to go pick her up."

"Well, I don't see how that would ever be a problem," I smiled, leaning into him and breathing in his breath. "I can't imagine a scenario where I'd ever want anything but you."

He held on to me tighter and I felt comfort in his beating heart. "So, you'll ride with us then?"

"Eight?" I asked.

"No, better make it earlier, come by seven. Mom drives slow."

"Hey, there's something else, it's about my mother. It's pretty terrible."

"What is it?"

"I talked with mom and Aunt Kathy tonight, or rather Aunt Kathy talked to me, and told me a story of when they were little. An old lady told mom and my Aunt Kathy that they'd lose one of their own one day. It made such an impact on Aunt Kathy that she decided to never have children. Mom didn't listen, obviously, and got pregnant with Emily her senior year. My grandmother was so upset she killed herself when she found out mom was pregnant.

She didn't leave a note or anything, but mom and Aunt Kathy both believe it was because of what the old woman said."

"I'm so sorry," he gently kissed my cheek, making my blood rush through me from head to toe.

"Yeah, but, it reminded me of what we were told about how forces try to keep us apart. It's as if that old woman was an early attempt at keeping me from being born. From existing." I took a deep breath, "Even worse, they're sending me to an East Coast college. They've already arranged everything."

He shook his head, thinking. "No," he said, "no you're not going anywhere without me. Don't worry about that."

"Why? How?"

"You'll see, when Weli gets here."

"I need all the help I can get," I mumbled.

"We definitely need my grandma for this. I think we're gonna get some answers."

"I can't believe my mother has already made all the arrangements. She knew something all along. She doesn't want me to be here, around you, around anything. Now I'm unsure if she's the force trying to keep us apart. It pisses me off even more because she acted as if she liked me being around you. The whole thing was an act."

"I don't think she meant it that way. Look, we'll find a way around this, I promise you that. You will never be alone. Never."

"Okay. You'd better go now anyway, before you get caught sneaking through my window," I laughed, nudging him towards his exit but hating to see him go.

He slid halfway out the window then leaned back in to give me another kiss. I felt like my soul was ablaze with tingling fire when his lips touched me. I didn't want it to stop, but I knew he couldn't stay. In the back of my mind I longed for the day that we could just be together, without worrying about the formalities of everything and everyone.

"Have sweet dreams. Listen, if you're gonna go anywhere in your sleep, at least come to me," he smiled and slipped out the window.

I watched him trail down the road to where I knew he had left his truck so he wouldn't be seen driving up. It was just too late for my parents to agree for him to be over, especially after the unveiling of my mother's plans. I smiled at his parting words.

I glanced out towards the woods and heard the loud chirping of the crickets stop. Silence permeated the air, and with that I knew whatever was out there was watching.

# CHAPTER 13

"The moonchild will be the one to try and stop the two of you—by whatever means," said Dominic's grandmother in one of the thickest Spanish accents I had ever heard. Nevertheless, she was fluent and articulate in English and had come with passion to help us.

"No one has told you about the moonchild? The moonchild is a mixture, a creature conceived from the seed of a human and one from the other side. My guess is that your sister and possibly others were taken for that purpose, to create more moonchildren. It happens more frequently than people would truly be able to understand," she explained, accentuating each word with long vowels and short consonants.

Weli was in the front passenger seat. His mom was driving. Dominic and I were in the back seat listening to Weli's lecture. We had arrived at the bus station just as Weli's bus pulled into the terminal. From the moment I was introduced to her I had a feeling of calmness wrap around me like a warm blanket. She began to talk about the moonchild as soon as Dominic's mother started the car.

"What exactly is a moonchild—what do they do, like their purpose?" I asked. "They sound so good. Moonchildren. It sounds magical."

"Oh, magical indeed—the real moonchildren are created for evil. They are sent here to help their counterparts—the other ones. They can exist within this frequency. The one where we live and see, hear, touch, smell. They are mortals, but very powerful mortals. Other people will tell you moonchildren are good. But this is like believing in a fairytale. A true moonchild was born of darkness. The moon has two sides, you know. One side we see, it is light, it looks clean and unspoiled. The other side is dark. It is never seen. No one knows what can truly exist there."

"So, if one is sent to harm us, how would we even know?" I asked, glancing at Dominic.

"The chances are that you may already know a moonchild," she said gravely. "I knew when Dominic was born that he was one of the Dhakris. I had known it since I was a little girl that my own child would bear one of the pair. And with that, I also knew that someone, something, would be out to destroy the child. That is why maybe he has told you that we have always been so protective over him," she said, patting my knee.

"I'm trying to think of who could be the moonchild," I said, thinking more out loud than anything else.

"Has anyone been in your life that has caused you trouble?"

She asked, turning in her seat and peering deeply into my eyes.

"The old lady my mom and aunt talked about—she tried to convince them not to have children of their own," I thought out loud. "Then evidently my grandmother killed herself when she found out my mom was pregnant with my sister. Now she is trying to move me far away."

"We must work fast," Weli muttered.

"Vanek." Dominic spoke up. "It's gotta be Vanek."

I held my breath, nervous at the thought.

"Who is this Vanek?" asked Weli, looking at all of us. "You must tell me now."

"He was at the meetings, where I met Dominic," I said, looking at Dominic.

"What meetings?" Maria, Dominic's mother asked, looking in the rear-view mirror at Dominic with concern.

"The ones I started going to, remember? The ghost hunting meetings," he reassured.

"Well what did he do to you?" Weli asked with growing concern.

"When I first joined the group for the meetings—he tried to scare me off afterward," I explained, trying not to stutter.

"What did he do?" Weli insisted on knowing.

"He—he sent me messages. I got them on my phone. He told me that he knew I was Emily Carmichael's sister, and that I ought to just stay away from trying to find out anything," I explained.

"And what reason did he have for doing that?" Weli asked.

"None really—none that I knew. Dominic knew who I was too, though," I said, glancing at his reaction.

"Yeah, I did, but I knew of what happened to your sister, and I knew what your last name was. So, I put it all together."

"Well, maybe Vanek did the same thing," I offered.

"Then why would he have bothered to say the things that he said to you?" he asked, looking over at me sharply.

"What do you know about this Vanek? Where does he live? Who is his family? Where does he spend his time?" Weli interrogated.

"We don't know, Weli," Dominic said, his voice sounding lost.

"Well, then I suggest you find out. That's your moonchild, that's your danger, and that's your mortal enemy. He's not one of us. He's a creation; he's a servitor."

"What's a servitor?" Dominic and I asked, in almost perfect unison.

Weli sighed. By her tone, I knew she was realizing just how much she was going to have to explain. "It's a magical creation, a synonym for moonchild. It can take on any shape and form its creator wants it to be, and it exists simply to work for its creator to cause an outcome."

Weli gave another long sigh, "That's enough for now. I want to hear more of what you actually experienced and know."

The rest of the car ride home was filled with details about every happening since we had met and other stories from the family's past. I sat and listened intently until we arrived back at Dominic's house.

"We're going to look into him," Dominic promised as he closed the door with force.

"I saw him walk away into the woods before, at the park," I said. "I always thought that was strange for some reason. Everyone else went to their car and left. There's nothing weird about taking a walk, but his overall vibes were just—weird," I shuddered.

"Yeah, not to mention his personal vendetta against you," Dominic said.

"What's his last name?" I asked.

"I always assumed Vanek was his last name. But I never heard. He never said."

"He was shuffling those cards, I remember," I murmured.

"Yeah every time I ever saw him he had cards—like a nervous habit or something. But he was never nervous, "

"Call Dana, maybe she knows more about him," I suggested.

"Alright. I'll be back." Dominic left to make the call inside.

I sat on his front porch and thought of what it could mean if there was someone out there created to destroy me. I thought about my sister being kept as a slave to some otherworldly creature trying to force her to carry a subhuman child to bring into the world. Perhaps wherever she was could be where Vanek went when he disappeared from our meetings.

"She said he'd never told her anything personal about him," Dominic's voice broke my thoughts. "She sounded surprised that I called, but I made it seem like I was trying to get in touch with him and couldn't."

"What about through the messenger app? The one that he used to contact me?" I asked.

"We could try that. It would be interesting to see if he responds."

I pulled out my phone and opened the app I had been using the day that he had contacted me. I looked for the last line he had sent. It wasn't there. Nothing was there. It was as if it had never existed at all. I scrolled up and down, beginning to look frantically for the conversation.

"It's not here!" I screeched desperately.

"What? How could that have happened? You just showed it to me the other day...."

"I know! I know I did!" I said as I frantically searched through the browser history on the phone looking for any sign or any inkling that I'd ever had a conversation with Vanek. Everything was gone.

My mind felt like it was spinning furiously. I didn't understand what could have happened, but I knew it was something Vanek had done. Dominic and I spent the rest of the morning sitting in his mother's kitchen listening to Weli's stories and the mysteries surrounding Dominic's birth.

"He was born red headed," she said as she rolled out the dough for a pastry. "And that was one of the signs. I know—lots of people are born red headed. But this baby was special. The day he was born there was to be a hurricane making landfall. Maria was in labor and we had to rush her to the hospital as many of the people were evacuating. When we arrived at the hospital, the lights went out. But there, in the room where he was born, the lights flickered and came back on. The backup generators were working but provided only dim light to the hospital.

Not in the room where we were, it was bright—filled with light. He had the energy to make the lights stay on."

"Weli!" Dominic smiled with embarrassment. I'd never seen him embarrassed before, he never let his confidence crack.

"It is true, and that's when I knew that everything I had heard was real," she shuffled over to the oven and popped her pastry dish in the oven to bake.

"And what about you, Jessica? What star were you born under?" she asked me, in all seriousness.

"Truthfully, I don't know much about it at all. I know my mom always said I was an easy baby. I'll have to ask her," I mused, thinking about what else she and Aunt Kathy could be keeping from me.

"You should ask her. Because the way it was told to me, one child or the other comes in through a difficult birth, under the easy stars. The one who doesn't usually comes in through an easy birth, but under difficult stars."

"Hence the hurricane," Dominic quipped.

"Exactly. That storm brewed in the gulf with hardly any forewarning. It appeared almost like it came out of nowhere," she said, settling the mixing dishes into soapy water in the sink.

"What do you think we need to do first?" I asked her.

"If legend holds true, you must first conquer your most prevalent foe. If it is this Vanek, then so be it. If it is the captor of your sister, then it is so. Either way, you have to use the combination of your strengths to work together. You are human beings, but you exist to work with the other side."

"I thought the other side was evil," I said.

"Why would you think that?" Weli asked me as she shuffled back to check on the pastries.

"It seems like everything bad comes from the 'other side'."

"While that is true, there are also the good ones on the other side that work with us, just as good and evil exist here among humans. People throw around that word, 'others'. It has different meanings. The others to which you are referring are in the middle with us, most of the time. Those who have had experiences with guardian angels or spirit guides, those are examples of the good on the other side. There are many levels of existence that we cannot see. But all the while where there is positive, there is also negative. As for worlds—anyone can fight the evil in this world, because it can be seen and heard. Not everyone has the capability to fight the otherworldly evil."

"What's the middle level you mentioned?" I asked.

"There are upper, middle and lower levels of existence. The middle level is where we dwell, along with many other beings that we cannot see," she explained.

"You and my grandson are members of a very special chain of reincarnation that assists the middle level in all of its plights. The moonchildren are creatures that exist in between the worlds in the middle level. They can slip in and out of our reality and the other reality."

"Can we?" I asked, watching Dominic pour a glass of milk for each of us as I awaited her response.

"Yes, but if you haven't learned how to shift already, you'll need some work. If you go without knowing what you are getting into, you risk not ever coming back. You could be captured, like many people who strangely disappear. You have to build your strengths. That is why I came here on such short notice. As soon as my daughter called me to tell me that I was correct and that something was happening with the Dhakris, I came to assist you," she explained.

Dominic sat glasses around the kitchen table before each of us and asked "So Weli, will the moonchild try and stop us with everything we do?"

"My boy—what you are not understanding is that the moonchild is one of many. There are different beings in this middle world that create them. You will always have to battle them. Look what Jessica learned about her mother and aunt being stopped by an old woman. That is the work of a moonchild. But what I fear the most is the one that is closest to you now. The one you mention, Vanek, he has already closed in on your existence. He has no trail for us to find him, but has found you. You must watch out, both of you. It is up to you to take care of each other," she said as she pushed back from the table and pulled the fresh pastries out of the oven. The room now smelled of cinnamon and vanilla. I wasn't sure what it was, but it was deliciously warm and gooey and filled with a sweet cream cheese-like mixture. As we ate, she continued on with her advice for us.

"Today, I want to work with you both on energy protection. It is something that I have had to use as a curandera in some of my experiences. There are beings in the middle level that want to harm. They seek to harm. It is your first step in being able to slip in and out of the worlds."

"I need to say something," I spoke up, wiping the food from my lips.

"Well, yes, go ahead *mija*," Weli gestured for me to speak.

"I feel the changes, the changes that have begun, and I can accept that I am meant for this greater thing. But I am completely terrified of my family moving me away. My family, everyone I know, expects me to do that and live that life. How am I supposed to be the Dhakris and also be what my family expects me to be and go to some university on the other side of the country?" I asked, looking around the table.

"You are not the first to have such struggles, and you won't be the last. This is your awakening. These things always have a way of working themselves out. I have a feeling your mother already knows."

"What if her family doesn't support this? What if they refuse?" Dominic spoke up. "She's going to live three thousand miles away from here. How are we supposed to protect each other when there's such a distance? How is this supposed to work?"

"You will see," Weli gestured to Dominic. "Everything is already in motion."

Weli looked over at Maria who had remained quiet for the majority of the day. We all looked over at her. Unwillingly, she spoke.

"I'm having a difficult time...," she began, wiping a tear from the corner of her eye, "...accepting that all of this is true." She leaned over for a moment in silence and then pushed back from the table and looked around at all of us with fierce eyes.

"Mama," she glared at Weli, "It's true I called you here, but...you raised me with all of these superstitions and then brought me up through the Catholic church at the same time. I always thought the superstitions were just stories and I accepted them as only that. Now I know people came to you and believed in you, but I didn't think anything of it. Now there is talk of danger, other worlds, my son, my only son, working magic with a girl, a girl who I do not know, and I am scared. I need to be able to understand it but I—I just am having a hard time. All of this goes against everything I have ever known, truly believed in. Yes, mama, you told me all of this before. But I never really believed you. In fact, people would talk about you when I was growing up and say you were crazy, that you weren't really a curandera at all, just a crazy woman. That always hurt me to hear. So, I pushed aside what you had said, and I chose to believe only in the Catholic faith because that was more real to me. Now this—all of this, if it is true...I just don't know what to believe anymore."

She sat quietly and stared off at the table, not looking any of us in the eye.

"Crazy woman?" Weli asked with exasperation. "*Crazy* woman!" This time louder, with a shock. "They may have said that I was a crazy woman, but it was I who brought comfort to the people when they needed a remedy that medicine could not provide. It was I who they came to when they thought they were cursed. It was I who they approached when the priest couldn't make it down to the houses in the rural parts to say the last rights over the dying. So maybe it embarrassed you to hear people say I was a crazy woman—but I say that crazy is mocking something you don't understand and blindly believing anything anyone tells you. I may be a crazy woman, but I know what is real and you see before you now, Maria, that what was said would happen, is happening before us now."

I sat silently, looking down at the crumbs on my plate. I felt uncomfortable being in the middle of their family conflict and thought maybe that I shouldn't really have said anything at all. I didn't realize how protective Dominic's mother was over him and that she didn't want him leaving his life to be with me, regardless of if we were special or not. Our mothers had more in common than I thought. I didn't have any idea that she never really believed anything her mother had told her. I looked at Dominic who was looking down as well. He looked up and his eyes met mine. I felt a tingling down my spine and knew that everything would be alright somehow.

"I'm sorry, Mama," Maria said, getting up and kissing her on the head. "I didn't want to hurt you with my words. I will try and understand this," she said with a drawn out sigh, collecting our plates and heading towards the sink with them.

Weli looked at both of us with stern eyes. "Now. The two of you need to be ready to listen to me and to remember the things I say to you. And you, Jessica, have no fears of what is expected of you. You're not going anywhere alone, unless you don't listen. Learning to embrace being the Dhakris will give you all the answers you need. Now that you've found one another, other gates will open for you. It is perfect. No matter where you go, you grow as the Dhakris. It doesn't matter whether you moved to a foreign country or stay right here. "She stood up and gestured for us to follow her outside.

We walked with her into a nearby clearing behind the house near the woods. It was more like a pasture with tall grass. The overcast day helped stave off the heat, but the sound of the crickets and cicadas could be heard stirring all around us from their hiding places.

"Take off your shoes," she instructed.

We both looked at each other and removed them without question.

"Feel the ground beneath your feet. That is the energy from which you will find your protection. It is always there to protect you, but you must first harness it. It is told that many pairs of the Dhakris were unsuccessful because they were unable to understand how to properly use energy and therefore found themselves trapped or killed before they were ready to use their powers. I do not want that to happen to you, you must learn now how to protect yourselves first and before all else," she said.

"Now," she began, slipping out of her sandals and standing bare foot with us, "close your eyes and feel the energy of the Earth crawl up your legs, as if it were filling up your legs like water into a jar. Visualize it as white, clean, pure protective energy. Feel it come up as it surpasses your knees and into your thighs, past your stomach and now up to your chest and neck, into your head and down your arms. Feel it make you glow. You are now covered with white energy. You must be able to do this yourself without guidance, so remember the way it feels."

I opened my eyes and looked around in this altered state we had conjured for ourselves. Everything looked brighter, sharper, as if it had a glow to it. Looking across at Dominic, he looked illuminated, as did I as I looked down at my body.

"Now, walk towards each other," Weli instructed. "Reach out with your hands as if to press them up against each other, but stop just before you touch, you will feel the energy."

We did as we were told. As we came closer to each other it was as if there was a static between the two of us, it was like electricity existed there, the energy was so powerful I thought it might thrust me away.

"Feel the energy of each other, so that you are familiar with it. Each of you registers at the exact same frequency of energy. Every person has their own energy frequency. You both

share. Become familiar with this feeling. Understand how it makes you feel so that when you need it, you will know when you have it."

Eyes closed, we let our energy bounce off one another and I concentrated on memorizing every subtle detail of the energy I felt.

"Now," she said, "touch hands."

As our fingers came together, I felt my body jerk upward without my effort to do so, my feet came straight off of the ground. I gasped for air as I opened my eyes and looked down to see that we were at least a foot off the ground, no longer bound to the Earth.

"The Earth energy has given you this energy," she said calmly. "It is a gift. You are experiencing the art of levitation using your protective energy. This is a sacred practice, a sacred art," she murmured, watching us in awe.

I could feel the power we had conjured buzzing in my head, as if I was plugged into something gently electrocuting me. There was no pain, only the feeling of radiating energy.

"Focus your mind now. I want both of you to visualize slipping through a curtain, a veil, into the other world. It is not unlike the world we see around us, but you will know when you see it. You will feel it," she coached. The tone of Weli's voice had slipped into that of someone in a trance like state as she guided us. It was as if she was meditating and had hypnotized herself to give us the instructions.

I concentrated on what she had asked and began to feel a heaviness set in around me. Still hand in hand with Dominic, I opened my eyes to see around us. Everything had gotten darker, but there was still light out. It was like viewing the world through a filter that dimmed everything. The sound of the cicadas and crickets had stopped. Weli's voice sounded as though it was in slow motion and I felt a wind around us, one that seemed to have been forced from an entirely different world.

"Both of you, now, look to the left towards the edge of the forest. Look for the duende at the edge of the woods," she said, sounding like a slowed down recording on a tape. Time seemed to be warping around us.

We moved our heads and looked towards the edge of the forest. There, still within the trees but at the edge of the line, I saw a small person, smaller than a human. It wasn't human looking at all. Its face was different. Its pale grey skin was glowing in my vision, which blurred in and out. Its eyes were black, dark black. I saw no movement of an iris, only blackness. Its thin mouth opened slightly as it watched us. It wore a hood of some sort, covering its head mostly. I knew it was what people see sometimes, the times that they can't quite explain what they saw.

"Duendes dwell all around us. Little people. He is the messenger to the colony of duendes in this forest. Look him in the eye and tell him you are the Dhakris, with your mind."

She spoke slowly. There were sounds in my ears of different frequencies and pitches, like one would hear when televisions are on with no sound but amplified greatly. My hearing seemed to ring and buzz with the high-pitched frequency sounds. I concentrated on telling the duende what we were and that we meant him no harm.

*We will help you find the one you seek.* I heard the words echo in my head in a strange voice that came through the frequencies. I watched him turn and walk back into the forest.

"Come down now, with your mind. Come back out to me," instructed Weli. I felt myself lowering and the ringing in my ears fading away.

"Duendes are not always friendly to outsiders, but they will not harm either one of you now. They recognize what you are. You must respect them, and they will respect you back. Don't expect much more from them, they have their own survival to worry about," she explained.

As the light came back around me and we slowly snapped out of our altered state, I felt nauseated and weak. I leaned over and started heaving from the heavy feelings. I felt Dominic patting my back.

"You don't feel sick?" I asked him.

"My head hurts pretty badly, I've never seen anything with that clarity, but we'll both get used to this," he said half assuredly.

I looked around and noticed that the position of the sun was very low.

"What time is it?" I asked.

Weli looked at her watch. "It is ten until six, "

"What happened? It was way earlier when we came out—we've been out here for four hours, five almost?" I asked, slightly panic stricken.

"When entering the other realities, you will find that time does not follow the same rules that you have grown accustomed to in your upbringing, *mija*," she said calmly.

"So, because we were looking into the other realm, we lost almost five hours?" Dominic asked.

"That is correct, but lost is not the term I would use.

You didn't lose the time; it was still there all along. Time is not in a line like you think it is *mijo*. It deviates, it changes, even overlaps. In this case, no time at all in the other world can be much time spent in our regular world. Just be aware of it. There are many stories of people who have experienced this missing time and didn't understand that they had accidently entered the other world. It is more common than you think," she explained.

"Then when will we know that we can enter that realm safely?"Dominic asked.

"There is no such thing as safe," she replied. "You're not truly safe anywhere, at any time, there or here. Are you safe when you drive on the freeway? No. Something could happen at any moment. There are things we can control and things we cannot. It is the same there as it is here. It is always up to you to control what you can control. One thing you can control is your personal energy and protection which is why I'm showing it to you now, today," she said sternly.

Everything she said at that moment resonated with me and I felt I understood it perfectly. After my conversation with the ghost of a priest, and him essentially explaining time the exact same way, the reality of it all began flooding in and overtaking me. I felt that something terrible was about to happen while at the same time overwhelmed with emotions of happiness and excitement. I did not yet know or understand how to interpret the emotions that came to me with such force. I was about to get a crash course.

The first cue that my newfound natural awareness and precognition was on point came after Dominic dropped me off at my house after our lesson with Weli. When I got home, I had a certain sense of dread welling up within me, but I couldn't pinpoint the cause. I wasn't sure if it was because I was about to have to explain to my parents where I had been for hours or if I thought something truly bad was going to take place.

As I let myself in through the front door, I heard my mother yell from the kitchen "Jess, is that you?"

After confirming that I was home, she came out from the kitchen and my father came out from the living room with concerned look on their faces.

I could smell in the air that my mother had cooked some sort of chicken dish for a meal. I was surprised that she had cooked at all; I couldn't really remember the last time she had made a full meal for us.

I sat my bag down by the door just as my father asked me where I had been. I could hear in his voice that he was irritated, but I never irritated my father. He was usually so aloof that his emotions never broke through like that.

"I was with Dominic, at his house. His grandmother came to visit from Mexico. We were with her all day," I said, glancing at my mother who stood awkwardly with a spatula in her hand.

"Why weren't you answering your phone?" she asked me, furrowing her brow intensely.

I was confused. I hadn't heard my phone make a sound all day long.

"I never saw that I had any calls," I blurted with irritation.

"What is the deal with this guy, Jessica?" My father asked me point blank.

"He's a friend, a good friend. That's it, that's all," I said, taken aback at their sudden concern for the company I kept.

"Oh, really? Tell me again when and where did you meet him?" he asked, visibly upset.

"I met him through some friends of mine. He doesn't live far from here—really just on the other side of the woods, like fifteen minutes from here," I explained. I made every effort to remain calm and not blow up at them.

"Well does he know you're going to college very soon and you sure as shit don't have time for a relationship?" my father snapped at me.

I looked at my mother. I needed her to defend me. Aunt Kathy was nowhere to be seen. I needed someone to advocate for me.

"Mom, what is wrong? With both of you?" I burst out. "Why do you care if I spend any time with Dominic before you ship me off to east Jesus nowhere? He doesn't drink, he doesn't smoke, he doesn't have wild pool parties with all sorts of crazy stuff going on...why do you care? You never cared about any of the other people I spent time with! Do you know how bad my other friends were? Do you have any idea what they're really like?"

They ignored my rage and continued on with their own.

"I lost one daughter goddammit, and I won't lose another one, not like that!" my father exploded. His face was flushed red.

"Not like what, because of a boy? I'm not Emily! I'm not like her! I have a different life and am completely different from her!" I yelled back, not wanting to say anything else. All

I could think about was proving to them I was doing something good, that I was trying to bring her back. It hurt me that I couldn't tell them that I knew where she had gone.

I stormed past them and up to my room, slamming my door behind me. The swish of air from my slamming door set some papers on my desk floating around, and I noticed a flash of something odd fall with them on the floor. At first glance I thought nothing of it, but upon closer inspection I realized it was a playing card. An ace of spades. I felt my stomach drop to my feet and I shook with fear.

That night I was physically spent. I lay down in my bed and held the card up to examine it. He had been there, somehow, someway, in my room. It bothered me on a deep level. I thought he could even be there right then and kill me as I tried to sleep. But something within me could feel the lack of presence in the room. I just knew he had been there. I wanted to call Dominic, to tell him right away, but I didn't have the energy. It felt like something was holding

me down and draining my energy. No matter how hard I tried, I couldn't function normally. Instead, I was welling up with anger. Vanek was the creation, the servitor, the moonchild of some strange being. He was sent here to stop the Dhakris, and was most likely sent out to kill me. If that were the case, then I wondered what had happened to my sister and was she in danger of bearing a moonchild herself? I could feel my energy building up within me now, all of the tiredness shedding itself from my being. I had to see for myself what they had done. I wanted to slip in between worlds in the woods, now that I knew how.

Barefoot and in only jeans and a T-shirt, I slipped out of the house silently and ran into the woods. Feeling totally consumed with lethargy, I forced each step with all of the energy I could muster. The summer air was cooler than usual and a soft breeze blew my hair back as I approached the main trail into the dense brush.

I remembered Dominic finding me the first time I had tried this, and carrying me out of the woods. That wouldn't be necessary this time, I felt more confident, more aware of what existed here. I ran down the trail with deliberate speed, not feeling the dry pine needles and sharp points of the pine cones underneath my feet. I was determined. I thought of Dominic and my feeling that I loved him, but felt that I had to go in to this alone. This was my own mission, my own proof that it was all real—the Dhakris, the moonchild and my destiny.

I came to the clearing where I remembered the incidents from before; where the light had been glowing in the woods. I stopped there in my tracks and began grounding myself with my bare feet on the earth, remembering how Weli had instructed to pull the earth energy up through my feet and into my body for protection. I closed my eyes and concentrated, feeling a tingling sensation at the soles of my feet and gradually begin to travel up through the rest of my body. I imagined a white shell forming around me in a protective layer so that nothing could truly harm me in my state.

I focused on slipping into the other world around me. I could feel its electrifying presence. I felt my ears buzz with the pitches of strange frequencies and I knew I was reaching the gateway. I felt an inner vibration all over me as my molecules danced their rapid dance and sped up to make me shift. I slowly opened my eyes to see a strange glow all around me as if the sky was illuminated with radiance akin to a midnight sun. It was different though—there was no sun.

"You'll find no sun here in our world," I heard a voice say in my head. I spun around to look for the source.

"Look, over to your left."

I looked over my left shoulder. There was the duende. It looked to be the same one I had seen earlier with Dominic and Weli.

"Yes, that is correct, it is I, Rau, the same one you met earlier. You can think of me as a forest being if that will make you more comfortable," he said tome.

I felt anxious not to scare him away. Not knowing exactly how to communicate or where to begin with the endless questions I had, I spoke to him with words. "Why doesn't it get dark or light here?" I asked, then felt inept that my first question was so basic.

He took a few steps closer to me and I could better see his features. His skin, a pale and pasty blue grey color, looked surreal, as if it wasn't real skin at all. It almost looked like if I reached out and touched him, his skin would peel away. His small mouth seemed as though it was incapable of moving to talk, yet he spoke to me clearly. He was short, maybe three feet tall, and his body was covered by a black cloak. The cloth looked old; it reminded me of what monks used to wear in medieval times. But the most mesmerizing and strange part of his appearance were his eyes. They were filled in, all black, almost demonic looking, but I knew he wasn't there to hurt me.

"You are in the middle world; there is always dim light, never sunshine or darkness. Time is different here, as you learned earlier. I see that you have come alone. Why would a Dhakris do such a thing, may I ask?"

"I needed to see for myself. I want to find my sister," I said to him.

Rau tilted his strange, pasty head as he looked at me and communicated with slow words in my head "Your sister? You mean the one who made a pact with Nachmei?"

"What is Nachmei?" I asked, peering into his cold blackeyes.

"Who…you mean to ask who. Nachmei the ancient one. Nachmei the trickster. Nachmei the hidden and the majestic."

"I don't know. She came here and never returned home," I said coldly, hoping I would have enough energy to return.

"We try to warn those who wish to make a pact with those hidden beings of our realm," Rau said. "Not all heed the warnings. You coming here alone—that is very brave, but also very stupid. You had to practice, I see?"

I nodded tiredly. "Where's Emily? Has he—made her have a moonchild?" I asked hesitantly?

Rau ignored the question. "Not all Dhakris' have to train you know, some can do it naturally. Like your partner. He has always slipped in and out. You have to work at it a little harder, don't you? Others before you have just come naturally into our world."

"You didn't answer my question," I said, ignoring his implications that I wasn't a strong Dhakris and perhaps I wasn't capable.

"You coming here alone, you are asking to be a victim. No Dhakris is strong enough without the pair!" Rau's eyes became fiercely focused on me, angrily focused.

"Nachmei is watching, with his servitor. Nachmei knows you're here and if you don't leave now you may not ever—like your sister! Don't be stupid and ruin what you must accomplish. I warn you, as it is my job. There is more behind this veil than you can know. We see all that happens between the here and there and so does he. Heed my warning to go back to your realm now, I say it with the most genuine care for your well-being. There is a reason you are a pair." He bowed his head to me as he said this.

I looked around, hearing his words echo in my head. I could see black beady eyes beginning to emerge from all around the edges of the clearing in the woods. They were all watching, and for whatever reason, were silent. Rau seemed to be their leader. They were strange little beings. Behind them I saw what looked like taller, human forms. I gasped at the sight of them. They seemed to be in a trance, almost like zombies as they approached and stood behind the duende to observe me.

"Who are they?" I asked Rau.

"They are with us," he replied with disdain and without further details.

I looked at each figure, then I asked, "Is Caroline Tarney with you?"

"That one, no, she never survived here," he answered without emotion.

I felt my palms tingling. I saw her, Caroline. She had suffered. I couldn't see her as clearly as I had seen others, but I saw her shriveling up. She must have died from sheer exhaustion, dried out, and turned to dust. She had become nothing. I slung my hand down with infuriation for his irreverent disposition for the her.

Like the crack of a whip, energy popped the ground and sparked with a slight tinge of electricity as if I had thrown a lightning bolt. For a moment, I saw the faint outline of what looked like a sword.

"Ah," he smiled. "There it is."

I looked at my hand with awe, as if it belonged to someone else. Perhaps that was his purpose in his distant demeanor, calling me stupid—to get me upset so that I could comprehend the power hidden inside me. I realized then exactly why I interfered so terribly with all of the electronics in my presence.

Rau began to back away from me slowly, his eyes never wavering from mine. I put my mind on returning to my side of reality. I felt myself fading into darkness, which soon became dawn as I realized I was back in my own realm of the woods. I heard leaves rustle. A bird flew over my head and startled me. I ran back along the trail as fast as I could to get out of there thinking that Nachmei and his minion could be watching.

Sneaking quietly back into the house, I quickly padded up to my room and saw that I had missed calls on my phone. They were all from Dominic. I felt panicked. I couldn't believe I had missed all of that time. Dawn had come and gone while I was in the woods; it was almost seven in the morning.

# CHAPTER 14

Steady rapping on my front door snapped me out of my panic into a new one. *Who could be here this early?* I thought to myself, quickly padding back down the stairs to beat my parents to the door as I heard them getting up when I passed their bedroom. I had been ready to drop into bed from no sleep, but I was wide awake now with anxiety.

I opened the door with its oil-begging squeak to see Dominic, disheveled and on edge, standing before me.

"What happened?" I gasped, reaching out for his arm. He was visibly out of breath and pale. I heard my parents rushing up behind me to see what was happening. They looked at the both of us and each other in confusion.

"This happened," he said and whipped out a playing card from his pocket. It was an Ace of Hearts.

"I don't understand...," I heard my father begin behind me, "Why are you here so early? What's wrong?" he asked confusedly.

"My grandmother is dead!" he cried, choking up with his words.

I felt overwhelming sadness consume me and I fell into him weeping. My parents stood there, slightly stunned at what was happening.

"Oh, Dominic, we're so sorry," I heard my mother say. Her words seemed distant. I felt far away from everything at that moment. We just held each other and cried.

My father left the entryway to go get dressed and my mother shuffled to the kitchen, presumably to start the coffee. Dominic pulled back from our embrace and held me by the shoulders, looking intensely into my eyes.

"It was…horrid. It was something no one should ever see. She was dead with her eyes wide open in her bed, Jessica. But her eyes, they were scared, and filled with black where the white should've been. It looked like dried blood was coming out of them. Her mouth was gaping open as if she were trying to scream for help, but we never heard anything! Her face, it was just so contorted," he choked a little and I patted him for comfort. "Her muscles were frozen on her face, like, like an expression of terror. It was like something had…had dislodged her jaw. No one's mouth is supposed to open like that. It was just hanging down, open. Her mouth was blackened, too. Christ…her face…I can't get her face out of my head. All the color

was drained from it. She wasn't normal. She was green, or grey. . . Something completely unnatural happened. The card was right beside her," he whispered with sobs shaking him.

I could see it, exactly what he was talking about. He didn't even have to describe her to me. She may as well have had hands rip her mouth apart. It shook me to the core and I fell to my knees, trembling with fear. I sucked in a sharp breath, "Then he's after us, because when I got home last night, there was an Ace of Spades in my room," I told him, trying to put everything together in my head.

"What? Why didn't you let me know? I had a feeling something was wrong but I thought maybe it was just from the intensity of the day," he said, shaking his head angrily.

"I couldn't, I just…couldn't. It was so strange, as if I had no will to let you know. So, I went out into the woods. I wanted to see something for myself."

"What? What did you do, Jessica?" he asked. His eyes were bloodshot from his tears, making the intensity of the green in them stand out even more with contrast.

"I went out to the woods alone again, and I did everything Weli told us to do yesterday, but alone," I confessed, humiliated that I might have caused something to happen.

"Jesus, Jessica, you could have been taken. Something could have happened!" His voice rose angrily, but I could tell that he was scared behind it all—scared he could have lost me. He gripped me tighter in his arms.

"I met Rau again, the duende we saw," I said, ignoring his anger and trying to stay focused.

"Rau? That's what he's called? Does he know what could have happened? He told you

his name?"

"I guess it's Rau, that's what he told me. He told me that those woods are Nachmei's woods, Nachmei is the being that we've been warned about. He said that Nachmei is the one who watches and makes moonchildren. He said he's ancient. But Nachmei wasn't there, and I didn't see Vanek. I saw more of the duendes…and I, I found out I can shoot electric voltage from my hands." I stammered with my words. "You probably can, too."

"I think I know where Vanek is," Dominic said, hanging his head. "I just can't believe I wasn't able to sense it, to stop it. Maybe if we had been together…."

"I can't believe this happened, but I didn't have any way of knowing I should've been with you to help stop him. How's your mom?" I asked.

"She's in shock, really. She won't say much, but I know she knows it has something to do with us, with all of this," he said.

"Why us?" I asked.

"I don't know if we'll ever know. Weli never said why, she just said it was so. I guess there's no way to know why and who becomes the Dhakris. Maybe it has something to do with where it will be needed the most in this lifetime. I don't know." he said, shaking his head and leaning down on me.

"So, we're like a weapon. A biological weapon."

"That's what it looks like. In a weird way, that's what we are. A hell of a lot of good it did us if we couldn't stop Vanek from hurting Weli."

"There's gotta be a way to find out why and who becomes the Dhakris," I said. I wanted to know exactly why this was happening to us and not to anyone else. I wanted to know why only we had the burden to bear.

We both turned our heads to see my parents looking at us with their eyes wide and their mouths open. They'd heard everything and we'd been talking so rapidly we didn't even notice.

"Sorry, guys, we need a moment," I said, pulling Dominic outside. They didn't protest this time.

"One thing Weli said after we took you home is that the Dhakris was kept secret in most societies. She said there wasn't much writing hinting towards it or that it was encrypted or encoded so that the true identity of the Dhakris wasn't shared, so that they wouldn't be compromised by humans or by anything else. It was bad enough, she said, that the beings from the other world would be out to get them."

"That makes sense. But if we find Emily," I said, checking that the front door was totally shut for privacy, "what next then? And how do we explain to people that we found her in another earthly realm and brought her back, without her aging three years, without her knowing anything about her disappearance?"

"Weli said what comes to be always makes sense. She didn't go further than that. But she said that it plays out and people don't notice the difference," Dominic said. "She said time and purpose always have their ways of working out, and that it happens constantly and none of us know the difference. But I have a feeling the disappearance of your sister and getting her back is really just the tip of the iceberg. If legend holds true, the Dhakris basically dedicate their lives to stopping anything evil from wreaking evil onto humanity."

"The truth is a lot scarier than the fiction. What is a moonchild besides a hybrid human—other being?" I could barely talk I was so saddened.

"From what I know, they're here only to assist their otherworldly parent. They work to do the parents' dirty work."

"What kind of dirty work?"

"Anything you could think of, really. Destruction, madness, pain, suffering, even to assist in sacrifices—which may be where the whole vampire idea came from, the idea of taking a human's blood for their own needs. Plus, some beings just enjoy watching the world and its people suffer."

"How do we stop him?" I asked.

"We kill him. A moonchild servitor can be killed like a normal human, because that is how they mainly exist, flesh and blood. But Nachmei will still exist."

"Well, what else are we good for then?" I asked, feeling defeated already.

"We are meant to help all of humanity. Until the day we die."

The front door opened, my mother stood there with two cups of coffee steaming with milk and sugar. "Here, come inside," she invited. We followed her in to the living room and sat on the couches with her and my father.

"Dominic," my father began, "I'm terribly sorry to hear about your loss. We're here for you bud," he said endearingly.

"Yes, sir. I wish I had the chance to meet you before. Each time I've come by to visit our timing has been off," Dominic said, shaking a little as he spoke.

"I'll also admit that I was a bit upset she had spent so much time with you and I didn't know who you were," he said, glancing over at me. "We'll do anything we can to help with your grandmother. Does your family need anything?"

"No sir, but thank you. My father drives trucks long distance—he's on his way back now but is at least a day away from arriving home. We're waiting on him to get here to help my mother with arrangements. I know that mom wants to have her buried in the family plot in the cemetery."

"What happened—if you don't mind my asking?" My mother interjected.

Dominic around at all of us with a pause, "Stroke, we think."

"Well, we know how hard it can be to lose a family member," my father said uncomfortably. "If there were a way to bring them back, we would."

Dominic and I looked at each other and then back at him uncomfortably.

"You two kids—you sweet on each other?" my father asked awkwardly. It sounded completely unnatural for him coming out of his mouth as it did us hearing it. My mother even looked at him strangely. It was the worst timing ever.

I looked down at my necklace he'd given me and then back up at my dad. "Dad...," I half smiled, "we're just—really close. We're best of friends. And, and he needs me right now," I said, looking back at Dominic.

"We just—get each other. And I do need her right now. My grandmother—she was my rock. And now she's gone," he finished, looking back at my father.

"I get it, bud, I do. Look, she's going off to college as I'm sure you know," he glanced at me sharply, "but a death in the family is something you need support with. You can't do it alone."

"Did you give her that pretty necklace?" my mother asked, leaning forward to get a closer look at it.

"Yes, ma'am, I did. My grandmother gave it to me when I was young," he answered.

In that moment, I realized my parents didn't really know that nothing would be the same, and that I wasn't going to be able to follow their chosen path for me.

"I was hoping I could take Jessica with me for the day," Dominic broke the silence, looking at both of my parents. "I could really use her company right now. Would you mind if she came to my house for a while?"

"I don't see why not," my mother said as she sat back and sipped her coffee, adjusting her bathrobe over her pajamas.

My father sat silent for a moment, staring off into space.

"She's the only one I've got—take care of her," he finally said, looking at Dominic.

"Thanks dad," I said, going upstairs to grab my things. Dominic followed me up to my room.

"I'd keep you with me always if I could," he said and pulled me close to him, tilting my chin up toward him. We lingered there for just a moment. "I could have lost you yesterday too, you know."

He kissed me softly and held on to me with both of his hands. "I'll die without you," he said to me.

"I think I would, too."

"No, I really would. You would, too. We die without each other. If something happens to you, half of my power, my protection, is gone. Without you, I will die. Alone, we are vulnerable and we will be hunted down and killed. That's one of the last things Weli said to me before she went to bed last night. She warned me how important it was for us to protect one another. We're not on our own. The best way I can think to honor her is to kill this bastard and do everything she said," he said. "So don't go into that world without me again, it could be the death of us."

"I won't. I won't go anywhere without you again."

# CHAPTER 15

The winding road seemed especially long as we made our way on the two-lane highway back to Dominic's side of the woods. I let the wind whip my hair around wildly and smiled as Dominic reached over for my hand.

Even though he had just experienced something so profoundly tragic, he was still able to make me smile. He looked over at me and something caught my attention ahead of us.

"Stop!" I screamed. He slammed on the breaks as his truck swerved off of the road, leaving skid marks and the smell of burned rubber.

Ahead of us were a man and woman standing in the middle of theroad. My heard pounded wildly in my chest. I felt like it was in my throat.

"Are you okay?" Dominic gasped at me.

"Yeah, yeah I'm fine. Who are they?"

"I don't know," Dominic mumbled, opening his door with a loud squeak and getting out of the truck.

The male approached Dominic casually. "Sounds like y'need some doubleye dee forty, there, dontcha?" The Irish accent was unmistakable.

"What?" Dominic asked, cautiously. I caught up to his side and stood there on the side of the road as the female walked up to join us.

"Yer door...it's a wee bit squeaky. Sounds like ye need some oil," the stranger stated.

The girl swept her auburn windblown waves from her eyes revealing one of the most beautiful faces I had ever seen.

"What were you doing in the middle of the road? Don't you know we could've run you over?" I asked, heart still pounding.

The girl spoke up. "We wanted to stop you. We got the call for help. We're here to help you." She looked us both up and down.

"Help us?" Dominic took in a big breath of air, clearly flustered.

"We know who you are," the beautiful girl said. "We are part of the Dhakris, too. Our circumstances are a bit...different. But nonetheless, we've been sent here to help you. You are about to face phenomena in which you have no experience. You will need our help."

"You're a Dhakris too?" I asked in awe.

"Yes. Came from the same line as both of ye," answered the male.

"So, it's nice to finally meet you, Dominic and Jessica. I'm Brisen," the beautiful girl nodded.

"I'm Keagan," the Irishman smiled, stepping up alongside her. As the shock from the abrupt encounter began to wear off, I observed them more closely. They were young, late teens or early twenties. He was dressed like us in jeans and T-shirt. She was dressed in a beautiful flowing kaftan dress with leather sandals. The pair definitely had a strangeness about them.

An unseasonably cool wind blew our hair around wildly as we stood beside the road. It sent a chill down my spine as we all met eyes.

"Take us with you," Brisen gestured toward the truck. "We have work to do. Whatever your plans were, consider them changed now."

Without questions or discussion, we squeezed in together into the cab of the truck; me beside Dominic, Brisen to my right and Keagan on the far passenger side.

"Funny way to get around," Brisen laughed.

"Aye, not everyone knows how to move like you," Keagan replied, nudging her a little with his shoulder.

I didn't ask how they knew we would be driving down that particular road because I understood that however they knew, we would soon be able to know, too. It occurred to me at that moment that I was among equals, albeit slightly more experienced equals.

Brisen's long auburn waves touched gently against my arm as we sat close together in the cab of Dominic's truck. It was so soft I almost felt compelled to reach out and touch it. In sunlight the auburn locks shone red, but in the shadows, the strands appeared virtually ebony black. I shifted a little in my seat and my arm rubbed against her bare skin.

"Whoa," I said, unexpectedly. The tingling sensation was still fiery on my skin as I pulled my arm away from her.

"It happens when I touch—people," Brisen said, and smiled softly at me. Her eyes were green like ours, very bright. But there was something different. I noticed a vibrant hue of violet purple outlining her pupil. It made her all the more alluring with her olive skin tone. She looked like she could be from a number of different places in the world, or none at all. She had no distinct accent, only perfectly calm speech. It piqued my interest, but she didn't seem very open to conversation.

Her eyes moved from me to the road ahead. "Wait, stop here, pull over here," she commanded to Dominic in her calm, low tone. She had a look of keenness in her face and I could tell that she had a very specific reason for her request.

We scooted out of the truck and stood alongside the road as Brisen surveyed the area around us. It reminded me of the way a wild animal sniffs the air and pauses before moving into a clearing, checking for danger. Brisen and Keagan began walking into the field, hand in hand. Dominic and I followed behind the pair.

Brisen whipped around suddenly as she approached a patchy, grassless area.

"This is one of the gateways. It will be easier to enter here," she closed her eyes and knelt down, spreading her hands along the ground using her tactile sensory to gently feel the ground.

"Do y'wanna go now?" Keagan asked gently. He had the hair of a schoolboy, shaggy and wavy brown. He was built like a man though, I could see the strength he possessed through his thin t-shirt. His muscles tensed up beneath his shirt as Brisen stood up quickly.

"No, not yet. These two need orientation," she said matter-of-factly.

"What do we need to do then?" Dominic asked. He sounded dismissive and impatient. I really couldn't blame him.

Brisen gave us both a straight forward look and spoke clearly and calmly. "What you've experienced today Dominic is not your complete reality. We exist in multiple realities in multiple forms. What's happened to you in this reality hasn't necessarily happened in all of your realities."

My head spun with the thought of what she had just said.

"I know it sounds confusing now, but it will be clearer to you as we proceed. Although the loss of your grandmother here is devastating, I need you to relinquish those thoughts of loss and focus on our intent. There is an evil presence in this area that has done much harm to humanity. This you know, as Jessica found out for herself. He, Nachmei, is powerful in many ways; but not powerful enough to withstand the Dhakris. He has sent his own creation out into this realm to try and thwart you, but it can't stop us. We heard the call and have come to help."

"What do you mean about our realities?" Dominic asked.

"You'll see as we go. But first, you need to learn to shift," she said. "It should come quite naturally for both of you. Jessica, I'm sure you've been getting your cyphs, at the very least."

"Is that what all of those feelings are—and the electricity?" I asked.

Her expression as she raised her eyebrows at me indicated that I had answered my own question.

*Rude*, I thought to myself.

"No, I'm not being rude, Jessica. I'm here to help and there isn't much time. Your words have meaning, choose them wisely. Speak with knowing."

Keagan smiled a boyish grin and glanced up at me, knowing I was embarrassed by her epic shut down. So, she was able to read my thoughts…that was going to be something I'd have to learn to protect.

She gestured for us to come forward and hold hands in a circle. Dominic and I both jolted a little as she grasped our hands. It was like feeling an electrical shock. She glanced up at us as if to caution us to not comment about it.

"We're going to change our vibrations. As you know, your entire body is comprised of atoms and molecules. They are moving and spinning constantly. Everything you see, feel and touch is because your vibrations resonate on an equal level with the environment around you. We are now going to change that. You are going to speed up the vibration of your own matter. It can be done with your thoughts," she spoke with the words of an old soul, calmly and scientifically explaining the process.

I felt her squeeze my hand as she continued. It burned but didn't hurt. "Do not close your eyes. Instead, clear your head and focus only on imagining you can see your molecules moving. You must envision them moving more rapidly, faster and faster."

Dominic and I followed her instructions. It was innate within us to naturally be able to obtain this altered state of existence. I felt myself grow warmer and warmer as I envisioned the speeding molecules of my physicality spinning faster. It was different than when Weli had showed us how to shift—this time, we were stronger. I felt more like myself than ever before.

The four of us rose up off the ground. I felt myself suspended in the air and smiled in awe.

Noticing my amazement, Brisen whispered "this is only the beginning of what you can do."

In the distance, I heard the whirring sound of an engine.

"Oh, no!" I gasped.

"They can't see us, Jessica," Keagan replied calmly.

"We're vibrating out of their level of perception," Brisen continued. "At most, a finely tuned person might see a flicker of something, a faint indication of something different in the air, though that is unusual. We are invisible at this frequency."

"C'mon then, you two, come see whatya can do," Keagan said as he flipped backward in the air as if he were suspended on strings.

I followed suit, moving my way behind him, gliding smoothly through the air. I was flying…not like I had imagined I would ever fly, but with my mind I could move myself wherever I needed to move.

"Brisen, Keagan!" Dominic shouted as I moved farther away and faster.

I turned around to see him rise up farther off the ground and position himself openly to the air.

"We don't have time for this. Whatever has happened, it's taking its toll on my family. My grandmother is dead. We've gotta do something now! Jess, show them what you learned to do yesterday?"

"Did you not hear a 'ting she said?" Keagan spoke up, moving closer to Dominic and stepping lightly down on the ground in front of him.

Dominic's landing back on the ground was more of a thud. He faced Keagan and was about to say something when Brisen suddenly appeared beside him, giving Keagan a look of warning.

"Keagan, don't," Brisen interrupted.

I wondered how she did that. She disappeared and reappeared. It was like she had teleported.

"One thing before we go…," Brisen started.

"Wait, you're leaving?" I interrupted her. "You just started helping us."

She turned to me with stone cold eyes, more violet now than green. "We cannot stay and help you on this particular assignment. Everything that transpires in this assignment must happen based on your own free will and actions. You have to do the work yourselves. What I was going to tell you was to remember how to shift like we showed you. That's the first step. There's much more but there isn't any way I can show you right now." She looked at Dominic.

"No!" I slung my arm down the same way I had the previous day. With the cracking force I had previously displayed, energy popped the ground hard, creating a reverberating shock.

Brisen stopped and looked at me pensively. Keagan smiled knowingly. Dominic sped up to my side.

"How'd you do it?" he asked with amazement.

"It's your gift," Brisen said. "She found it quickly. It hasn't fully formed into her weapon. But it will. So will yours."

"Have ye felt yerself breakin all of the plug-in 'tings?"Keagan asked jovially.

"I have issues with electronics," I acknowledged.

Dominic conceded a bit as well. "I haven't carried a cell phone in a long time. I kill them."

"This is good," Brisen said, circling me slowly, sizing me up with her eyes. "You're stronger than I had thought you'd be at this level. There is much more you will need to learn, but for now, you've got to do your work alone," she said, stopping her rotation in front of me.

"We can't stop you? You can't help us?" Dominic asked.

"Dominic, we have our own assignments and it is imperative that what is to transpire happens based on your own decisions. We have to go. Keep practicing everything. We'll be seeing you again," Brisen said. With a grand swooping motion, she whipped herself around in a circle with Keagan. As they embraced, they vanished before our eyes.

I felt myself cooling off slightly and we both noticed that we were sternly grounded on the earth. We were visible again.

"What just happened?" I asked, bewildered.

"Come on, let's go," Dominic hustled over to his truck. As we headed toward his home, I felt the feeling of being on the verge of something huge well up within me.

# PART III

# THE DEAL

# CHAPTER 16

My thoughts were zipping through my head as we drove to Dominic's house. I wasn't paying attention to the road in front of us when I heard Dominic whisper, "What the...?" As he began to slow the truck I saw looked ahead and saw why he was slowing down. A large log was jutting out onto the road, blocking our way. We couldn't pass. It was huge. Stepping out of the truck in synchronization, we both walked up to examine the large barrel trunk of the tree.

"How in the hell did this happen?" Dominic mumbled.

"It doesn't want us to get home," I said, feeling my truth. "It's going to keep trying to stop us."

"Then we're going to have to go through the woods," he said, staring at me. His eyes danced with a fury of green magic I hadn't seen before.

"Both of us together, we should be able to cut through," I said, hoping I was sounding confident.

"I hope to God so," Dominic said, grabbing a sheathed Bowie knife from his truck's glove compartment and clipping it onto his jeans' belt loop.

We began making our way through the thick brush, scratching our skin on brambles, but walking as fast as we could to make it over to his land. If we could just get to his land, we could run across the pasture and make it to his house in time to deal with what had happened to Weli.

I felt my energy begin to spike—not my physical energy, but my actual powers and abilities.

"What do you think Brisen meant by my weapon not being fully developed?" I asked.

"I don't know," Dominic grumbled, knocking low hanging branches out of our way as we walked. "I don't trust her."

"Why? She's one of us."

"Is she? How do we know that?"

"I just know, Dominic. I know she was telling the truth. She's just different because she's from somewhere else, like Keagan."

"Yeah, he wasn't as weird," Dominic noted, holding a small branch back for me to pass through.

"But even if he was different, why wouldn't you trust them? What did you feel that was so different about them that I didn't?"

"Brisen just felt different. She wasn't what I thought another Dhakris would be."

"She did, she did feel different. But don't you think she's known she was the Dhakris way longer?"

"Oh, definitely. She read your mind, that didn't piss you off?" he asked.

"It did, I have to learn how to block that. I don't want people knowing what's in my mind."

"Weli said you can block your thoughts by using the white protection she taught us to create," he said, stopping to cut through a thick spider web with his knife.

"I'll remember that."

As the forest thickened around us, the daylight dimmed to a point where it was hard to see anything. That's when we saw it—the same thing I'd seen the first time I'd ventured out alone. The yellow flame.

It approached us with such speed that at first I thought it was going to ram into us. I then realized it was quite the opposite. It dipped down towards us with immense heat emanating from it. I felt myself respond immediately with a low dip, seeing my legs meld into the ground beneath me. We were no longer in a state of solid matter. The laws of physics as we knew them ceased to exist. It raced past us into the forest.

The yellow flame came back around from the distance and was fast approaching with what looked like the intention again of ramming us. Dominic yanked me up by the hand and we flew off the ground together, narrowly dodging its path of destruction.

Dominic yelled angrily, throwing his arms open and shouting

"Show yourself to us!"

We dropped back to the ground, looking around in silence for just a short moment.

Then it appeared again a short distance away in small clearing. Ablaze, it began to take the form of a human man. The blinding yellow light slowly trickled out from him until only a glimmer was left in his eyes and on top of his platinum blonde head. It was Vanek, in full incarnation.

His normally clear blue eyes retained the light of the yellow flame that had burned violently as he had attacked us only moments earlier.

"You cannot stop it. It doesn't matter what you do. What we are is older than what you know and can possibly understand," scoffed Vanek. "We came before you, before humans, and we are a part of this land—of all the land. We are all over this planet and have been since the beginning of its existence. You can't stop us from what we do."

"Then why take my sister? To make another one of you? Why does your kind need humans if you are so powerful?" I yelled, leaning over as if I were ready to physically attack him.

Vanek laughed and the sound of his voice echoed through the now still woods around us. "We're ensuring our existence forever. We're peopling the world with a new kind. My kind," he retorted.

"What good will that do?" Dominic asked, keeping his hand on my arm to hold me back from charging him. "What does it matter if you people the world with moonchildren and the blood of—of whatever your maker is? You're just a servitor, you aren't even real!" Dominic yelled with passion.

"You don't even know what you're up against, do you?" Vanek laughed. "They send you here to fight us and they don't even tell you what you are supposed to destroy," he mocked. "My father can be seen and heard in legends across time and cultures. He is that which the natives of this land spoke of in legends of tricksters. He is that which the Christians attribute to demons; he is that to whom Lilith ran in the stories in Judaism; he is that which the Muslims call the Djinn or the hidden ones. The fallen, the dark ones, the shadow people, the watchers— call it what you want—it is one in the same. He and his kind once held their own place in the human dimension but were banished. In order to regain their rightful place, they are creating a hybrid race. I am of that race. Your sister is blessed with assisting in this cause, she offered her powers to help," Vanek said, looking straight at me with a sinister smile.

"Then take me, take me instead!" I screamed at him. "Your father can have me; just give my sister her life back. She didn't deserve to be taken like that; she didn't know she was signing her life over to this!" I shrieked at him.

"Jessica, what are you *doing*?" Dominic screamed at me, reaching for me as I moved away from him. I looked back at him over my shoulder. "If I'm the Dhakris, then I'll be able to fight it, Dominic. Just let me do this."

"No, I can't let you. We're in this together," he pushed forward towards me as I walked over to face Vanek.

"Let me see her. Let me see Emily," I demanded, face to face with him. His breath was cold on me, not human, not of life.

"What makes you think we would want you as a mother, as a sister, as a maker of one of our kind," he sneered down at me.

"I'm trading one life for another—that's all I'm asking," I said calmly.

I recognized the blue light that began to glow faintly in the distance behind Vanek. I saw it move as a flame dancing through the woods, much in the same way that Vanek moved before he appeared before us. I had flashes of the slit-up face I had seen in my dreaming state, but I felt it was not coming to attack, but Dominic clung tight to the knife in his hand behind his back regardless.

There, before us, the blue light transformed into a dark figure, tall and domineering in his presence. From his feet he began to emerge into a human like form but with skin that glowed with a blue tint to it. He wore dark blue robes that billowed in a wind that we couldn't feel but seemed to envelope him. As his face emerged, so did his tantalizingly sharp features. He had dark eyes, almost fully filled in, like there was no iris. They were dark sapphire eyes, not black. It was not a human eye color. His glowing skin was offset by his shimmering hair that seemed to flow behind him with his energy field. He was beautiful yet nightmarishly frightening all at the same time. It was definitely nothing like I had seen before.

"You would rather take the place of your sister, you, even as the born Dhakris?" he spoke, moving fluidly around us, his presence almost like that of a flame in the wind. His voice was robust and velvety.

I couldn't feel or hear anything else around me it seemed, I was enraptured in the presence of this luminescent and domineering being before me. "I will trade places for my sister's life. Just give her back, she didn't understand what you were. I do," I said. It felt like I was speaking in a slow motion wind tunnel.

He wrapped his energy around me; I could feel it like a cold embrace that was neither evil nor good. It was only enticing. I was scared somewhere in my mind, but my actions did not show fear.

"You think you understand me," he whispered, and his voice became like a whirlwind all around me.

"Father, she is a Dhakris, meant only to destroy us. Why are you even considering taking her?" Vanek growled. He ignored Vanek and focused only on me.

"Show me my sister," I commanded, feeling weak now, unable to control my body the way I had before. I could see Dominic raging, desperation in his beautiful eyes. I knew he'd understand later.

I looked to the left as I began to feel the presence of someone else emerge. I saw Emily, her glowing pale skin illuminated like everything else around me at that moment. She smiled when she saw me, her grey eyes lighting up with joy. I couldn't hear her voice; it was as if I was deafened by the presence of this being that had me enraptured. Everything around me was roaring.

Emily stepped forward, stumbling in some sort of white dress toward Dominic, who reached out for her to take her into safety. She cowered behind him, watching the events unfold.

Everything was happening so slowly around me, I didn't feel like I was in myself at all, I felt out of myself, like I was watching everything happen from someone else's point of view.

I could see that Vanek was trying to get his father's attention, trying to stop him from making the trade. I felt myself being pulled away with a forceful magnetism that was beyond my control. As I began to be sucked into the new realm, I saw Dominic begin to whip his arms around. The electricity was building up in them. He reached up toward the sky, screaming, and the whip of electricity that streamed from his arm, like it had with mine, formed a glowing sword of green jade color, sparking in the dim light that hit it as he wielded it. It whipped through the air with narrowly focused power, rotating and spinning.

I watched, unable to use my breath to scream out. Dominic's electrified sword swung with all his strength, and he struck Vanek through the top of his head, stunning him. Dominic swung again, hard like he was hitting a home run, slicing through Vanek's side. Vanek looked whole and complete for just one brief moment. Then, the top half of him began to slowly slide, and he fell into two pieces, legs and torso separated. Once his body settled, it began to crackle into papier mâché looking dust. Dominic had wounded him before he could change himself from flesh and blood. I saw the shock in Vanek's face he disintegrated in front of us; the confusion in his eyes spelled it all out to me. He was a bloodless creation of the mind, and now he was gone. The trade had been made. One life for another. As playing cards floated gently to the ground, around where he had been, I floated away from Dominic and Emily, until they completely faded from my vision.

# CHAPTER 17

The roaring had stopped. I felt my normal sense of emotion numbed. I felt panic, but could not react to it. I was stoic. The world around me had taken on a darker hue. It was the same earth, same plants, same trees, same smell, but different feel. It was as if the air and my body were one; our molecules dancing together rapidly so that I could flow however I wished, like being able to swim through water. I saw only a blurred vision of the forest, a softened one, as if it had been painted before my eyes. Everything seemed to exist in slow motion here.

"You are brave, so it seems," said a voice from a direction that I could not quite pinpoint. I felt myself flow around in a spin motion, looking for the source.

"Where are you?" I asked, "Come out…" I beckoned, but felt myself losing my energy as I spoke.

The blue glow began to grow again before my eyes and I watched as it developed into the male form of the being who had taken me in place of my sister. There he was again, in all of his grand stature. His dark eyes, filling his whole eye where white should have been, softened to the point that they looked more human—less frightening. His long hair loosened, and I could see that it fell behind his shoulders—very large and broad shoulders. His skin still aglow with a blue hue, I stared at him in curiosity and awe. I had never seen such a creature before in my wildest dreams.

"Who are you?" I demanded to know.

"Don't play stupid. You know who I am. I have many names—as my child told you in the other realm."

"What do you want me to call you, then?" I asked.

"Nachmei," he responded. "Unless you'd like to call me something else…something

more personal, perhaps?"

I ignored his velvet voice of charm.

"What language is that?" I asked.

"One much older than those known to humans," he replied arrogantly.

"What is it that you wanted her for, what do you want me for?" I asked, holding my knees in front of me and feeling like a child in his presence.

"My kind—we simply want what was ours from the beginning. Our lives are better lived in your realm, enjoying all of the pleasures and fruits to experience and behold," Nachmei replied.

"So how does kidnapping people to have your half-children get you back into our realm?" I asked.

"There are many other ways to do it. Not everything has to be so black and white, Jessica. Kidnapping is such a primitive way to think about it. Haven't you ever heard of the incubus and the succubus? They come and visit humans in their sleep, implanting their seed for our posterity," Nachmei said. "But I prefer to take you to my side of reality."

"The pain you caused—you must realize how terrible it is to people," I said.

"Pain?" he asked, coming closer to me, our faces almost touching. His speed startled me, but I did not budge from my position. "There is no pain here." he said, taking my hand in his and pulling a blade from his garment. He ran the blade across the palm of my hand, puncturing the inside of my forearm slowly with the tip of the blade. I winced and gasped, anticipating the sting of the injury.

"See, you do not flinch with actual pain. You feel nothing here like pain," he showed me. I watched blood trickle from my hand and he placed his other hand over the wound for a moment and when he removed it, I had no cut, no scar, no sign of having ever been damaged.

"How did you do that?" I asked, amazed but fearful of his intent.

"My kind can do many things to which you are not accustomed," he said and pushed back from me. He seemed to flow backward like we were in water. I watched him move around the perimeter like a spirit, then land firmly on the ground and stand before me.

"Then why did your son feel pain? I saw Vanek die," I said, eager to provoke some sort of emotion from him other than his clever act of seduction he was posing. "And I wasn't talking about physical pain, I was talking about emotional pain. My family—they thought their child died."

"My son felt pain because he was not yet all the way through the worlds as we are now. He was trying to come through, obviously displeased with my decision to take you in return for your sister. But he was not across the threshold before he was—lost to me. He was also not my son. He was a servitor. Every servitor is created with their death already an inevitability," Nachmei said, not showing emotion when he spoke. "Besides, I would rather have you instead. The emotional pain you speak of—it is all relative."

"And what if I just kill myself, so I can come back as a Dhakris in the real world," I dared.

"I just showed you that you cannot die here. You're welcome to kill yourself in your realm. Then you will just come back as the same thing. Always the same thing," he replied, smiling with a cunning grin.

His words had a strange effect on me, like an incantation, mesmerizing me.

"Same damned thing…." I muttered, staring blankly ahead. I shook myself back to my questions. "Why was he considered a moonchild, Vanek?" I asked, forgetting my argument about emotional pain.

"He wasn't a moonchild. That's a misnomer. If your sister had borne my child, then he would have been. But there wasn't enough time."

He moved towards me again, graceful, with the stature of a Greek God and the flamboyancy of an Arabian Genie. He seemed to embody all mythical things at once and yet none to be exact. Each timeI looked at him long enough, he seemed to grow more human, more attractive. I wasn't sure exactly how he was doing it, but it was enigmatic.

My mind gave way to an image of Dominic. I thought of all he was probably going through, having found my sister and losing me all at the same time. I wanted so badly to tell him that I was sorry, but I needed to save Emily. I wanted to see him just one more time.

"Do not fret for him. You have made your choice," Nachmeisaid.

"How do you know what I was thinking?"

"There are no secrets here. I can hear your thoughts. I can taste your every breath. I can feel what you feel for him, what you want to feel from him...." he said, moving closer to me.

Anxiety welled up within me. I wanted out so badly but couldn't take back what I had done. I had underestimated what it would be like to be his prisoner here. I was weak. I wasn't myself.

"But you didn't get that far, did you? You didn't give yourself completely to your Dhakris. No...no you, you are a difficult one," Nachmei analyzed, surveying me through and through.

I wanted to cry, but I knew it would be futile.

"Don't worry," he said with facetious undertone, "there's always the next lifetime for you," he whispered as he held me down to the mossy floor of the dreamlike forest that encompassed us. Everything looked different. The trees were much larger, droopier in their stature, not like normal pine trees. Moss hung everywhere and there seemed to be trails weaving in and out of the forested surroundings.

"How long do you keep people here?" I looked at him, trying not to be afraid of his strength or his possible underlying motives.

"How long?" he replied, "How long? That is not really the correct question to ask, for here, there is no time. Time does not exist. You can ask how long but no answer would ever satisfy you. There is no answer."

Looking around, I couldn't imagine a way of escaping. I had the strangest sensation of voices ringing in my ears. It was faint, but definitely there. I wasn't sure if it was from creatures that existed there in that reality or if it was an overlap of the world from where I had been taken.

"Then what happened to Emily? Why did she come to you?" I asked, feeling the words hard to speak.

He looked at me, keeping me in my place down on the forest floor. "She came to me for a favor, as humans always do—users with no means to their end," his voice trailed off.

He knew I couldn't run from him. I had no idea if I could hide. I thought of the power I had gained with electric voltage but quickly put it out of my mind. If he wasn't bluffing and he could read my thoughts, I didn't want him seeing that. The problem that I began to encounter was his physicality. His presence was so demanding, his gaze so strong. It was like he was a magnet for my eyes. I tried not to look or let him feel anything I felt.

I weighed out my options in my mind, all the while wondering what Dominic was going to do with my sister and if there was any hope of being saved from this world where I now found myself. The pervasive stare of Nachmei kept me wondering also if he knew my thoughts as I realized them. I could see how girls could come to the woods and be wooed by his promising charisma. He wasn't a forest monster like Sasquatch, that was for sure. I had a feeling he could be whatever he wanted, though. I thought back to when I saw the horrible, twisted and distorted face in the woods the first time I had ventured out by myself. I wondered if it had been Vanek or Nachmei that I saw, trying to scare me away. Nachmei didn't seem interested in scaring me now, if it had been him. He only studied me as though I was a specimen of undulating interest and desire to him.

"It doesn't matter if you try to keep me here, they'll come and find me," I said to him. "Dominic can find me, and he will."

"Ah, the love of the Dhakris for one another. There is no real stopping it, is there?" he replied, never taking his eyes away from mine as he spoke. By now, he appeared as a strikingly intense man, still aglow with his power. His dark eyes had an iris now that I could see clearly and his human-like physique was now more apparent. He looked physically strong, too strong for me to physically fight. He had high cheekbones, I noticed. He was unidentifiable by any known race yet beautiful all the same.

"No, I don't think there is," I replied. "And why did you prey on my sister's innocence? Why would you take someone like that? She was young, she didn't know what she was doing. I don't think you really know a thing about love."

"She knew exactly what she wanted," he responded.

"The love of another? She obviously didn't know what love was, what it really meant. She was being a stupid girl and you took advantage of that," I accused.

"You don't know what she really wanted—I do," he said fiercely. "She came out here to me looking for a power to help her. But it works both ways. I needed her power, too."

"What power?"

"The power to bear a child, like I mentioned. A Servitor— they aren't as strong. She was capable— and so are you. My kind will return to our rightful world, permanently. None of the Dhakris can stop us for good."

"She also has the power to kill that child!" I mouthed back.

"Our children aren't the same as normal human children. It would kill her before it let her kill it. That is a guarantee. Now before you continue to shout at me about your power, know that you are now powerless here. Nothing you do will get you out. You are dead to the world you knew now."

"Are there no females of your own kind that you can use to populate your own world?" I dared to ask.

"Well of course there are, and what do you think they do?

The same thing that I do. But there are no Banshees here. Only me."

"My sister couldn't have wanted something that evil," I whispered.

"Look at me," he commanded.

"No, I don't want to anymore, "

"Afraid of me, then?"

"No. Why? Are you afraid of me?"

He laughed. I didn't expect a real answer from him, or I expected him to be insulting to me instead. He wasn't.

"You don't know who she is, who she really, actually is. You never had any idea. You have no idea now, even with all your newfound wisdom," he smiled.

He frustrated me and my weakness overwhelmed me. I had a wary feeling about my sister. I couldn't pinpoint the exact emotion, but I knew that she wasn't who I thought she was entirely. Nachmei wasn't lying.

"My beauty, you could stay with me here without worry and together we could reign, I as king and you as queen, and the power of the female Dhakris with me combined, consider how invincible we will be. I can help you with what you already have. You must only learn to relinquish your emotions attached to your counterpart. Let him go and you can begin to see what we could do together."

"Wouldn't that just make me a ghost? A dead girl who is seen in the other world only. Why would you think that would even slightly be appealing to me?" I asked, still not looking at him.

"But you would be so alive—more alive than you ever felt in your world. And besides, you chose to come here," he coaxed. "Nothing just—happens. All of this happened for a reason."

"I thought the whole point of this was for you to regain full access to your place in my world," I said.

"It doesn't matter if I do it now or later. I'm not alone in that venture. As you well know there are others like me. What I'm trying to get you to understand is that emptiness you're feeling now can be completely replaced with an everlasting ecstasy."

"And only I, you say, can feel that way?" I asked.

"You...you are something special. You always have been, from what I've known. You made an enormous sacrifice...being here now. But that isn't unlike you. You've done that sort of thing before, you know."

I paused for a moment and reflected on what he had said. I scratched the ground with my foot and noticed its strange iridescence. "What do you mean?" I asked, intrigued but not enough to allow myself to look at him.

"I'm not talking about you as Jessica Carmichael. You, the Dhakris, in the past. You have always been a special one. I was warned that when you came again, you'd have a reason to come for me. But I was always intrigued by it," he said, placing his hand on his chin and continuing to stare at me. I glanced up but looked back down. I didn't want him to be able to read me at all and I felt the only real control I had was my eye contact.

"Why don't you let me show you what exists in the beyond," Nachmei spoke with such charisma, shaking me from my concentration.

"Why don't we not. I'm fine here," I said. If I had to spend an eternity in the netherworld, I didn't think it mattered where it was exactly.

"You're not seeing the full picture. There is more to this side than just a veil through the woods. Do you think I just live here in woods? Wait until you see what really exists here," he said, approaching me.

"I don't want to see it; do you understand me? Do you understand what that means?" I asked, breaking my concentration of staring at the ground and glaring straight at him. I could feel my eyes burning into him with rage.

"I understand what you really want," he said without missing a beat in the cadence of our words. "I understand more about you than you think. You were born of flesh and blood and know only those things which have come to you in your five senses but now you can see the rest of it all. So, come, take a look, it won't make a difference if you're already here anyway. You're the one who chose to be here. You're the one who wanted to see what would happen."

I felt terrible inside. The anxiety welling up within me for having left Dominic to trade myself for Emily was now overwhelming. Being a Dhakris was something so special and I had just given it up…who knew when it would come back again—when I would come back again. What if he now had my soul here and the Dhakris was over for good? I also wondered what had happened if Dominic had brought my sister back to my family. What would they have said when they saw her? What would the story be? My mind twisted with the confusion of thoughts flooding into it. Worst of all, I had a terrible feeling about Emily.

I looked up slowly at the beautiful hand stretched out before me, daring me to stand up and take a walk.

# CHAPTER 18

It didn't feel how I thought it would feel. The world just wasn't the same at all. The abstracted feeling of being alive was still there, but in walking it took on a new meaning. I thought I felt where I walked before I stepped. The steps were just consequences of the actions I thought I was taking.

One of my first slips into changing was when I had become so weak that I had to relinquish my stubbornness toward Nachmei to survive. I felt that I had no other choice. I felt that he could keep me alive, and if he could do that—then he could keep a living chance of me returning to Dominic.

Nachmei had changed himself from what he had originally seemed to be. He no longer seemed threatening to me. He was like a prince from a fairy tale, moving me along through this strange world by which I was now surrounded. The forest had transformed into a world that was completely unrecognizable to me. The thick underbrush of the forest had diminished into an iridescent moss of sorts. In the dim lit world, everything smelled sweet like roses, even the same moss that covered the ground beneath my feet. Everything glimmered gently, not invasively. I couldn't quite capture the exact color. It would seem green at one look and then at the next seem blue or purple. The limbs of the trees curved over like old oaks around us and I felt like the trees were alive and aware of our presence, but that was just the woods and the gardens. The places Nachmei had built were almost incomprehensible.

The moment I let go and decided that I had to give into some of Nachmei's world was a defining moment for me—a painfully beautiful one. I had come to notice afterward that even my hair was different, it was perfect in that realm, falling into graceful waves of shimmering beauty. My skin took on a glow not unlike Nachmei's. I took notice of it but avoided the fall into his trap that he was creating.

Nachmei led me through the forest to a clearing, where before us stood the most amazing castle I had ever seen. Nothing in the human realm compared to it. It shimmered with sapphire sparkles and violet speckles. The ground around it looked like marble but it was crystal...combinations of moonstone and fluorite that made everything glow in the dim, sunless atmosphere.

"Why is it so different here?" I asked as we walked.

"It is no different, really. What you want to see is what you see. This is what you imagine it could be like," he replied.

I was confused. I didn't think I had imagined anything at all.

"I didn't imagine this. I've never seen a world like this. Where are the pine trees? And this castle of yours, you're telling me it's not real? I can see it, touch it...."

He stopped and turned to face me. "You only see what you wish to see."

"Well, what if what I wish to see is my sister, and Dominic?" I retorted, forgetting who

I was with and the reach of his power.

"Then I think you'd be slightly disappointed," he replied without hesitation.

"And why would I be?" I said angrily, stopping all movement forward with him.

"Because you've changed everything. You've changed the entire timeline in which you existed by switching places with your sister. Your timeline is now altered. That's the way the world works. What you remember happening in the past is now not what was. What you think you know in the real world is not necessarily the same."

"How is that even possible?" I stammered. I couldn't think all of the sudden. I was finally in love and I had taken it all away, sacrificed it all. I felt a terrible sinking feeling within me. I knew what he was saying and I didn't want to accept the implications. I shook my head in disbelief and felt as his arms moved around me in an effort to comfort me, as if it were even possible.

I jumped away from him with a shove. "Don't touch me, you snake! You absolute snake! My life is over now! I have nothing that I had, I lost everything, everyone! I'm dead now." The sudden outburst of energy made me collapse back down after my words.

"No, you are very much alive," he said calmly, standing and watching me from the distance I had created between us.

"I don't want to be then, not anymore. Not if I'm here and I have to endure an eternity with you. You've taken everything away from me! I had love and now it's lost! I had my sister back and you decided it would be better to keep me as your prisoner!"

"You're not my prisoner. And once again, my beauty, you chose this. You decided it would be better this way," he replied with the same calmness.

"Then tell me why am I here and why can't I leave?" I demanded.

"Jessica, or should I call you Yasmei? Or Sarso? Or Elnok? Or Thalia? Or Iasha? Should I keep going?" he said, taking a cautious step in my direction and looking at me daringly.

"You don't have your full memory, and I know that. But you have been here on this side before, it isn't your first time. And you and I have met before. Where you came from is from where you last disappeared."

"Who are all of those people you named?" I asked breathlessly.

"They're you. Your soul as the Dhakris. In time—as they say from where you come—you will begin to understand that there is no real time as you thought of it previously. If you were to cross back over, it could be into the same world from where you came but a completely different line of time. Your Dominic could have a completely different situation than that which he had when you fortuitously crossed paths. And let's not forget that you crossed paths only because of my interactions with your sister."

I looked at him and felt the energy drain from within me after hearing his metaphorical slap of reality. I felt as if I had been hit with it in the gut as hard as someone could hit me without killing me.

"Jessica," he moved towards me so rapidly that I never saw him approach. He tilted my chin up towards him as I attempted to look away from him. "Just let me show you."

His lips were up right against my cheek as he spoke. The touch of them against me sent electrifying chills down my spine, but I couldn't tell if the chills were that of fear or exhilaration. Whatever they were, they gave me energy back that I had lost.

"I don't understand…" I said, closing my eyes again for fear of looking at him.

"Why won't you look at me?" he asked.

"I just—can't," I said.

"Are you afraid that you might like what you see?" he asked.

I didn't respond. I felt his hand slide from my chin down my arm and into my hand as he gently pulled me to follow him further. Reluctantly, I stepped forth with him.

If nothing else, his energy at least allowed me to move more normally, and I took advantage of it. I needed it.

"Open your eyes," I heard after what felt like a long time of walking blindly.

I held them shut tight. "There's nothing left for me to see."

"Jessica, you have to at least look, come now, don't make me beg. It's unbecoming of
me."

"This is ridiculous," I said out loud. It was. He was playing games with me and I knew it, but I couldn't stop it.

I inhaled deeply, wondering for a moment if the air I breathed in was the same as the air from my own world.

Upon opening my eyes, my eyes didn't know where to look first. He had taken me inside his grand palace. There was everything one would imagine a palace containing. Every food I could want to eat was spread out before me. Windows were all around us, tall and shimmering. Two winding staircases led upstairs to what I could only imagine contained more enigmatic things. It was shaped more like the Taj Mahal than a European castle, but it didn't have an architecture to it that was precisely recognizable. It didn't have a complete roof. It was like an open atrium, in a place where it never rained but everything remained fresh and beautiful. The walls shimmered inside like they did from the outside, with violet from what appeared upon closer examination to be purple amethyst and sapphire.

"Is it real?" I asked.

"It's as real as you feel right now," Nachmei replied, walking around to face me. I looked straight at him now, unafraid.

"This isn't where you kept my sister," I said. It couldn't have been. Why would she have ever wanted to leave such a mesmerizingly beautiful place? Especially if Nachmei was being as hospitable to her as he was to me.

"Your sister was never here. Only you are here now," he replied.

"What does that mean? You had her. She was here, where we are now," I argued.

"Jessica, there are different existences for all of beings. This is your existence here. Not anyone else's."

"Are you trying to say that what I see is not what shesaw?"

"There's more to all of it than you seem to understand at this time. Your world bears far more mysteries than you have yet to grasp."

I prayed in my mind that Dominic would find a way to rescue me, to bring me back through whatever door I had entered. It didn't matter how beautiful of a place I was kept, I was still away from my love.

"Everything's changed now, Jessica."

"Changed how...."

"Dominic was here in this world when you traded yourself for your sister. When they went back, they arrived on a different timeline."

"You keep saying that—different timeline—what does it mean when you say it...."

"Line of time, a different time cycle. They entered back into the world at precisely the same time that Emily disappeared. You, however, are now gone. You are the one who has disappeared. You are the one for whom everyone you know will search and mourn. You are the one they've decided is now dead. What you've found between you and Dominic—it no longer exists," Nachmei said.

I hung my head and felt weak all over, losing the energy I had gained. The weakness now consumed me. "But he has to remember."

"It doesn't work that way. Now that you're here there is no time as you perceive it to be. We could go back, go forward, it doesn't matter. There are many levels of existence occurring simultaneously all around us right now."

I felt pain within me. It was deep, writhing pain but with no physical indications. It was my soul that was hurting. Different than any other pain I could imagine having to feel.

Flashes of what I had experienced over the previous month ran through my head carrying on like an old film on a home video. I could see Dominic helping me out of the woods, the comfort he provided, my realizations that I was supposed to be with him, the first time he touched me, the first time he kissed me. I reached up and touched the necklace around my neck, holding on to it tightly. I still had that. I still had that one piece of my former reality. I clenched it even tighter. Why did I still have it, I wondered? It seemed like everything about me had changed.

I felt the world spin around me, it was nauseating. I closed my eyes to avoid the feeling. When I opened them, we were outside his palace, in a garden full of hammocks and giant crystals all around us.

"How'd you do that?" I asked.

"It will be more comfortable for you here," he said, walking past me and over to what looked like a pool of water inside the large, elegantly sculpted room. Gargoyle style faces carved into amethyst and sapphire scowled and smiled at me with a myriad of different expressions. Their stare was unavoidable.

"I can't see myself being comfortable anywhere here...," I muttered to him—but it wasn't the truth. I loved it, I realized. I loved the feeling of comfort with which I suddenly felt provided. I felt like I was some sort of queen.

Before I could see him move he was completely in my face, leaning in to me to the point I could taste his sweet breath.

"You chose to come here, remember?"

I couldn't argue with him. Anything I could try and use as a rebuttal was a moot point.

I followed him back inside to a room where there was a large mirror on the wall. The floors beneath my feet looked like they were made from sheer amethyst. They changed as I walked on them. Nothing was truly real looking in the sense of solids like I was used to seeing. A corner tile caught my glance and I padded towards it. I placed my bare foot onto it and saw it dance like a pool of water, and I caught a glimpse of asphalt. A road! An actual paved road! I could hardly believe what I was seeing. We were in a parallel plane overlapping another existence.

I felt impotent and tired, suddenly aware of a need to sleep.

"I wish I knew what you were looking for," Nachmei said, unexpectedly.

"A way out of here," I quipped back with the small amount of energy that remained within me.

"No, that for which you are truly, deeply searching," He responded with a melancholy tone. He gestured towards the large mirror in front of us. As I stood with him I saw the version of ourselves he had created. It was no mistake he wanted me to see how beautiful the both of us could be together. Our skin aglow like warm pearls and our eyes twinkling, we looked like a king and queen of a world unimaginable. I shook my head and turned away.

"I found what I was looking for. And now I've lost it all. So why are you worried about it? Just let me be. Let me rot here," I said. I had all but completely lost my fear of him. He had begun to become more and more human like, transforming into a being that almost seemed to have a soul.

"If you're going to be here, you might as well be happy, contented. And you can't rot here—not possible," he said, moving closer to me.

"I can't be. Not here, not now. I can't see what's happening in the world that I'm from. I'm trapped in a different dimension," I said contemptuously.

"You can see them, if you want. If it is what you *truly* want," he said intensely. "Follow me."

He led me by my hands through the spacious interior of his strange shimmering abode. I felt his elegant fingers gently pull me to the center of the atrium, where he ushered me to a pool of water incased in crystal. It was beautiful and sparkling, both inside and out. He motioned for me to come closer with his eyes.

"Look into it. Think about those who you wish to see, and you'll see it," he said.

I leaned over, cautiously. I could envision him shoving my head in to drown me but then I realized he seemed to want me living. I looked in to the water and saw Dominic in mymind. I thought hard about him, about the feelings he gave me when he touched me, about the allure of his skin, the gaze of his eyes. I felt sick to my stomach. Within the reflection of the water, I began to see images appear, almost like watching television but the color was much different, more vivid, three dimensional.

I took in a tight gasp of air and held my breath as I saw what was happening. I saw Dominic, very clearly. There was no doubting that it was him. There was a female on top of him, in his lap. I concentrated to see who it could be. Maybe it was a vision of us from the past. But I didn't have a memory of that time. I convinced myself quickly that maybe it was a memory of us together in a different timeline—but I continued to look.

No, there she was. It was Emily. Her hair swayed gently in a breeze. It was dark, moonlit almost. I saw her slip her straps from her top and lean in towards his face.

Anger, jealousy and rage all began to swell up within me. I could feel it pulsate through my veins. I swatted the water as hard as I could, cursing and splashing the image away from my sight and my mind.

"It's not real!" I screamed at Nachmei. "You're just showing me that so that I'll stay here with you and hate what I love the most!" I fell to my knees on the grassy floor of the atrium. Its velvet softness didn't comfort me in any way. I felt a tear well up in one eye, and then the other. In no time at all tears poured out of my eyes without me trying to stop them.

Nachmei looked at me calmly. The calmness was eerie; he knew something I didn't, and I could sense it. "What you're seeing is real."

I wished I hadn't broken down in front of him. I didn't want him to see the hurt that was created. It couldn't be taken back.

"To them, you're missing, and you have been for some time. They bonded over your disappearance. It's only human nature, to bond like that," he said, approaching me slowly, watching my eyes to gauge my pain. "Humans are simply the worst at bonding. They do it with all the wrong people. Then they are miserable for the duration of their life because of their primordial thoughts on companionship."

"How long have I been gone to them?" I asked. My voice quivered as I spoke.

"Does it matter to you?" he asked back, coming down to my level on the ground, kneeling beside me.

"Of course it matters. Why wouldn't it matter? You wouldn't know what betrayal was like on my end, would you? You monster," my voice had changed to an almost inaudible whisper. I hoped he would just kill me somehow, so that I wouldn't have to feel the emotional pain of losing everything, losing Dominic.

"Why do you think me a monster?" he asked.

"You steal women, you want them to have your children, you hate humanity—sounds like a monster to me," I said, letting the tears flow freely.

"What makes you think I stole anyone? Oh, for the love of all that is, you have such primitive thoughts," he groaned. "Furthermore, my darling, your sister came to me—not the other way around. We've had this exact conversation over and over again. I'm not the only thing that lives beyond your world, you know. There are other beings besides me," he explained.

"Doesn't matter—you stole my sister."

"She offered to come in exchange for love."

"Well, look at her now then. She got mine," I said through the hurt, clenching my jaw tightly—because that was what it had all come down to for me. Emily was exactly where I should be.

"I admit, I took her offer, yes," he said. "But I'm not a monster. I have a soul, just the same as you. I have my own existence to experience. It is just much different, much longer than yours."

"Vanek was evil. You made a monster, a murderer," I said.

"To you, I suppose he seemed that way. He knew no better. He knew only to fight for our kind's existence. I could think you evil for wanting him dead. But what my servitor was truly looking for was to serve my purposes— nothing else. Besides, that woman had long known what she was in for in her line of work."

"Well that's not how it's viewed. She may have known her work was dangerous, but he killed an innocent human. Don't you think that is a monster?" I asked.

"No. I don't. I don't see you that way. And you and your other half killed my servitor. By your logic, that would make you both monsters as well," he spoke calmly.

"In what way do you see me?" I whispered, keeping my head down, buried in my knees with my arms gripping my legs tightly.

"Differently than I've ever seen any other human. Most every human has always seemed the same to me. Curious but clouded by fears and religion. Lost in their emotions, unwilling to try and understand the truth of what exists beyond their senses. Lost, always lost," he mused.

"What makes me different than any of that then?"

"You—you have the ability to transform yourself, beyond just human understanding."

"Oh, right, being the Dhakris," I said facetiously.

"Don't believe me?" he asked.

I shrugged, wrapping my arms around my knees as I sat, "I don't care anymore. It didn't do me much good to ever believe that I was special in some way to begin with. I'm obviously replaceable. I lost my life before which was strange enough, but now everything is lost, every... single...thing...," my voice trailed off into silence.

"You can't blame human nature," he said, knowing I was talking about what I had seen.

"I still don't know that what I saw was real. You could still be tricking me. Either way, it doesn't matter."

"Everything matters on some level," he said. "Everything you do is somehow meaningful. Every thought which you create is a real thing," he said passionately.

"So, everything you've done counts against you in some way, too? You're held accountable for what you've done?" I asked.

"You could say that," he said. "Look, Jessica, I don't want to harm you, I don't want you to suffer. I have my own existence here that I want you to understand. Besides, the things that you consider so evil, they may not be. Evil is subjective. Everyone has their own idea of what defines it. Sure, you have your basic standards— murder is evil, charity is love and so on, but everything in the middle...there is subjectivity," he explained.

I heard him, but I dismissed him. "Why isn't there anyone else here but me?" I asked.

"There are others. Like me. Like the inhabitants of the woods that you've seen. There are other beings, you would probably consider monsters, hairy beings that meander about the land."

"Why can't I see any of them now then?"

"You're inside my dwelling. They are not."

He stared at me while I sat. I tried not to look back. He was no monster to look at. He must have been what Zeus looked like when he came down from Mount Olympus to fornicate with the humans. From what he had begun as, he was now transformed. His beauty shone like that of a perfectly carved statue. I wanted to look at him but didn't let myself. I felt like it was the equivalent of me cheating on Dominic—even though I'd seen him holding on tightly to my sister. I didn't know what that was, a vision, a mirage sent to me from Nachmei just to make me angry and want revenge. I couldn't be sure so the easiest way to cope was to clear it from my mind.

"You look worried, tired," Nachmei said, reaching out and stroking my cheek gently. His hand tingled against my flesh. I recognized that sensation of tingling.

"Don't touch me," I snapped at him. I didn't care if every time he touched me it brought me back to life, and I didn't care if he was the most strikingly beautiful thing I'd ever seen. I would have rather turned into stone than let him keep trying to comfort me.

"If that is what you wish. I couldn't help but to touch you, you have a different aura than anyone else I've ever encountered."

I pushed myself back from him and looked right into his eyes, sitting up slightly but remaining on the soft ground.

"What is this? What does that even mean?"

He seemed to switch subjects. "You know, Jessica, in some world, you and I already have been together, been through something tremendous. You may not understand it now, or know about it. But reality as it seems is not what you think you know."

"I've figured that much," I said. "How else could I be in a different dimension now, here with you?" I asked. I finally stopped fighting it and looked up at him. Purple. The inside of his eyes around the pupil were purple, with flames of indigo dancing around the very outer rim of the iris. I held my breath. Brisen. Did she send me here to get trapped? I was more confused now than ever. If Nachmei could indeed read my thoughts, he wasn't bothering to tell me any answers to my inner questions.

"That's right. We're all alive and dead at the same time, somewhere," he said with a smile.

"What I saw in that water—you said it was a different timeline?" I asked with overwhelming curiosity.

"Perhaps. It may have shifted in favor of a different outcome," he said.

"Then is Emily the Dhakris in that timeline?"

"No. You always were and will be. Your soul is what it is, and it's unchangeable," he explained.

"But then it's the lifetime where we don't find each other," I finished.

"The cycles overlap and overlay each other throughout the continuum. If you go back to your realm and you die, the next cycle could be at any point, really."

"Why isn't it like that here?" I asked.

"Here is different, it's more of a middle ground, so to speak. It's in between what you experience and what the higher ones experience."

"Higher ones?" I looked at him for an answer.

"The beings that have no physicality, that are but consciousness and have moved to that level," he explained. "There are many, many layers to existence, and many levels as well. Here, where you are, you've barely scratched the surface.

It was all quite a lot of information to take in at once, but my brain was now open to receiving much more than it ever had been. I wanted to know more about Emily even though I felt rage toward her.

"What about my sister?" I asked, feeling my stomach knot up in sickness at the thought of her.

"She came to me for love, as you already know. I explained to her that I needed her as a carrier of my kind into her world. She was hesitant. That's what took her so long. That's why she was here for so long in your reality. She couldn't have a moonchild. So, we created Vanek."

"What, and you didn't force her?" I asked punitively.

"Jessica, I am not what you think," he said, trying to show a convincing side of himself.

"If you created him together then, how did you do it?" I asked.

"When a servitor is created, it needs to be grounded, or housed if you will, in something material. Your sister, for some reason, had brought a deck of cards with her, in her collection of magical things. We decided to develop him from the deck of cards, in the sense that it would be his materialistic stronghold and ties to the tangible world," he explained.

"So, what if we had taken his cards away?" I asked.

"He was made to fight, and had the ability to vanish, but if his material stronghold was destroyed or taken, he too would be taken away. The brilliant thing about the cards is that there were so many of them. Each time he carried out a duty of his servitortude, he left one behind," he said.

"Then after 52 times, he would vanish?" I asked.

"Essentially, yes," he moved a little closer to me as he finished his answer. This made me want to shift gears back to my original thoughts of Dominic.

"Well, what if I go back now, to that timeline?"

"Why do you want that, really? With all of the emotion and hurt? You can stay here, as long as you like, and you won't ever need to worry about those painful emotions. And I would never again need to take anyone else, I would have you. You would stay as you are now, never age. You would evolve yourself to have powers beyond what you are capable of imagining. There are beings over which I rule, and you would, too. You could be my queen," he finished, sounding almost desperate.

"And what about the Dhakris? It would be your way of destroying us, if you just keep me here for yourself."

"There are other Dhakrises. Did you know that?" he asked.

I nodded yes, but looked away from his enigmatic gaze.

"What you do know is true about there being two people with one soul, the Dhakris is a pair. But there are other pairs. All over the world, and on multiple timelines," he explained.

"How many?" I asked.

"Always seven," he said.

"Why seven?"

"Seven is a very sacred number, and that holds true for many different reasons. For the Dhakris, you were created into seven pairs by the higher ones. Well, a specific higher one. He sent you out, and knew you would suffer and find love and lose love, lose yourselves in battles with the dark side. I think it's a shame, really. You were created with such potential, only to suffer from the trials and tribulations of the human condition over and over again," he said.

"So, you're trying to convince me that if I stay here with you, I won't be missed, because you're telling me there are others, and that it's really just better for me to live in this dimension because ultimately, I'll be much happier," I surmised.

"You don't believe me. Trust. A very trying human trait. What will it take to earn your trust?" he asked.

"I need proof. I need proof of everything you're telling me."

"What would be valid proof for you?"

"Something I can see in reality, not in water. Something I can hear with my own ears," I said.

I stood up, tired of his mind games and overwhelmed by everything he'd told me. He stood up with me, following me as I walked back over to the pool of water. I leaned over it again and wished to see him, telling myself it would be the last time I looked at Dominic if this is how it were to be. Maybe part of me was dead and alive at the same time.

I looked away quickly, closing my eyes and shaking the vision from my head. The tears came. It was a different reality entirely.

I spun around and looked dead at him, allowing my eyes to explore everything that was before me.

"Don't shed tears. Look through your tears, look past them," he charmed, reaching up to touch my cheek again.

This time, I didn't flinch away from him. I let him touch my face and feel the electricity that buzzed between our touch.

He wiped the large tear that had dripped from my eye. He took the moist tear onto his finger and tasted it, gently placing his finger in his mouth. Each motion he made resonated with me deeply. I felt like time had passed, but I wasn't sure how much. I felt dizzy, overwhelmed and weakened.

"I'll show you what we can be," he said. I was weak, much too weak to protest. He took me by the hand and pulled me to walk with him. I still needed hydration, nourishment. My body was feeble after all I had endured. He led me down a path off to the side, into what looked like a garden, in what I could only assume was the back side of his palace. There were plants, flowers in full bloom all around us. They were larger, more extravagant than what I had seen in my own reality. I started to fade in and out of consciousness. Blurred colors began to take over my sight. I thought if it was death then I would welcome it. I felt moistness up against my lips.

"Drink," he commanded.

I relented, I felt that I had to in order to survive. The flavor was sweet, like honeysuckle that as a child I used to pull from the fence when it bloomed. I felt my body tingle with rejuvenation. As I opened my eyes I could see more clearly, sharper. I felt more alive. I saw Nachmei go from a blurry figure to a clearly sharp and striking creature. I could see he was feeding me from a cup formed from a flower, its juices flowing from the broken stem. He held the flower upside down with the petals closed to let the juices fill and then turned it over, more of the drink sat in a cupped puddle. I sipped the rest of it eagerly, feeling it dribble down my chin.

"This will heal you," he said calmly. His eyes sparkled and his sharp jawline formed a sweet smile.

"Heal me? I'm not hurt," I said.

"From the inside—you are hurt from the *inside*," he said.

"Why are you being this way to me?" I asked, sitting up to notice I had been laid on a garden bed, covered in thick layer of soft moss.

"You still think of me a monster," he said, taking the drained flower and setting it gently alongside the bushel from which he picked it.

"I don't know what to think of you," I mused, feeling better as the juices flowed through me. A euphoric feeling set in, like morphine rolling through my veins.

"What did you give me?"

"It is from a flower from my garden. The dragonia," he said. "It grows here, on this side. It has been used by all who dwell on this side to heal, help. It is very potent."

"I can tell," I said, straightening up and looking at my surroundings in wonderment. "But you still didn't tell me how I was hurt in the inside."

"You were dehydrated, your cells were dying from the inside because you're not used to vibrating at this level in this dimension for this long. Most get used to it quickly, but you were suffering, losing your sight. I didn't want you to suffer. Not if I could change it," he said kindly.

"Come, follow me," he said, reaching out for my hand. I was feeling better, I was no longer weak, but I followed him reluctantly.

"Do not fear; I have no intentions to ever cause you harm," he assured. "I think I've made that clear to you."

We walked down a path that looked like a dreamy fairy world to me. I thought to myself that it must have been similar to where the people said they went when they followed fairies, or where Morgain la Fey went in the Mists of Avalon when she came across a fairy fort. Perhaps this was where the missing sometimes went, with no desire to return. I still hadn't finished that book.

"There, ahead of us," he pointed to a clear pond that sparkled in the glowing light of the strangely beautiful world.

"I see it," I said.

"It is for you, you can cleanse yourself there," he said.

"In the pond?" I asked, confused.

He walked up to it and I noticed for the first time that he wore clothes that were similar to someone from a long time ago. Just white cotton shorts—or were they pants? I couldn't tell.

They were different. His shirt was billowy, like ones I had seen in really old photos of people from a different era. Almost as if it was all wrapped together from one big piece of fabric. He slid it off to reveal himself. I could see his toned flesh, shimmering in the dim light, each muscle perfectly proportioned with his body. His dark golden skin was almost blended perfectly with his honey colored hair. That's not what he had looked like at first. He had changed so much, but I hadn't noticed it. It was curlier towards the ends as it grew out, almost shoulder length. More wavy than curly, really. There were bronze highlights in it that caught the light. He turned around to look at me, the sapphire raged in his eyes against the glowing allure of his skin. He dove into the water, disappearing beneath its pristine surface. I waited, anticipating his return for air. It seemed like he didn't need it. It felt like an eternity, standing on the shore of the strange and sparkling pond. I looked into the water for him.

I heard a ripple and was startled as he appeared by a rock a few feet away from me.

"This water is warm. I think you'll find it suiting to your needs," he gestured for me to enter.

I thought about the last time a male had wanted me in warm water. It hadn't ended well. "How did you hold your breath that long?" I asked.

"You'll see for yourself, just stay a little longer," he coaxed further.

I closed my eyes, took in a deep breath, and jumped in with him, diving head first into the warm water.

I felt the water envelope me fully, like a soft hug that enraptured me completely. It was the most liberating experience I had ever felt. The cleansing was not only occurring on the outside, but within as well. I opened my eyes underwater to see an array of aquatic growth that was mesmerizing. There were glowing organisms that looked like translucent fish, there was a grass growing down at the bottom that was blue in color. I was fully encompassed in taking in all of the wonders I could behold. I pushed through the water with my arms and feet, moving through it effortlessly. I looked up to the shimmering surface, in awe of its beauty. I pushed back down through the water, amazed at the experience.

Through its clarity, I saw him swim up to me. I made sure to keep my eyes on him only, not his body. I didn't want to be like that.

Nevertheless, under that water, everything changed.

He embraced me, holding me tightly. I knew I wouldn't drown, I could feel it. Our hair swirled around us in a whirlpool of lust as he kissed me. He kissed me, and I kissed him back, water filling our mouths then releasing as we came together with our lips. There was nothing I could do to stop it and there was nothing to stop me from it, either. I just let go.

I pushed through the surface and took in a breath. He was right there with me. He pulled me up on him and swam with me on his muscular chest to the shore. He then drew me on top of him, giving me flashbacks of what I'd seen in the mirror pool of Emily and Dominic.

Instead of anger taking over my emotions, I indulged in every good feeling I was experiencing. It was my own revenge. I didn't want it to feel so good, but it did. I didn't care anymore. I didn't think about anything but that exact moment; not the future, or the past—just that exact moment. It was everything I had never experienced and more. Anyone who I had known who had indulged like this could never have imagined this type of experience.

"Different than the usual swim, is it not?" Nachmei whispered in my ear. The chills that followed were the answer.

"Do you feel like yourself?" he asked, pushing his lips against my ear, causing me to cling to him more tightly.

"Well I don't feel like anyone else," I said, letting him take complete control of me. The irony of giving in so easily when I finally had the strength to fight back did not occur to me in that moment. It may have well been hypnotized.

I felt myself feeling comfortable for the first time in the strange place where I found myself. It wasn't that I was comfortable with what had happened—no, that wasn't it at all.

It was instead the feeling of not fearing anything. For just a short, minute instant, I had lost the anxiety that was all encompassing. I felt the pain of losing my life with Dominic subside. For just that moment, I didn't want my life back.

I stopped myself briefly, looking at his sapphire eyes with their gleaming sparkles of purple. "What is the purple in your eyes?" I asked.

"It's the mark of the others," he whispered, smiling coyly.

I thought about Brisen again. She had the same thing. I tried to shake the memory from my mind.

"Don't think about them, just lay here. You changed me," he said, looking deeply into my eyes.

"How did I change you?" I felt the tips of my feet touch the water that washed gently against the mossy shoreline on which we lay.

"I may be made of fire, of a different breed altogether, but until you made your decision, I felt like a stone—cold and impossible to penetrate without destruction. Now I feel like gold, the softest of the most beautiful metals you have."

With the word gold I felt the necklace, the Saint Michael necklace, burning around my neck. It too, was gold. I looked at it and sat up, moving my body off of his.

"Where are you going?" he asked, catching up with me faster than my eyes could see him move.

"I just need to go, I just need to be alone," I said matter-of-factly.

"Wait a moment," he said, stepping in front of me. I noticed the way his shining hair, golden in the light, had dried and framed his face, almost touching his broad and muscular shoulders. Water dripped from his skin— his very normal, human looking skin with its perfect smoothness. All of his changes were apparent now. All of his blueness had converged into a home in his eyes. I was intoxicated by staring at him. Maybe it was the drink he had given me earlier, or the impossible-to-compare love making he had made happen on the shore of that beautiful water. I didn't quite know.

I paused in my tracks, waiting for what might happen next, feeling slightly dizzy yet fresh. I had never been intimate with anyone—and it was something I cherished deeply. Now I had been, and although I felt no regret at the moment, the burning necklace reminded me of the one I was supposed to be with.

"Let me see your necklace," he demanded more than asked.

I looked down, avoiding the memories it automatically conjured. I reached up to touch it but before I could grasp it, Nachmei's finger lifted it up.

"The warrior spirit, the protector, your creator...my old friend," he said.

"Saint Michael," I said.

"Archangel Michael," he corrected.

"Saint Michael," I countered.

"It is an Archangel, completely different than those considered saints to humans. It is different—older than what you know of religion. Who is as God, as he is known. Sabbathiel," he said. "Why do you wear it?"

"It was a gift."

"Gifts are but tokens of materialism. You are more than just material," he said. "Besides, I can have finer things made for you."

"I know that gifts are material," I said, "But from where I come it is the thought that counts, no matter what the material thing is."

The memory of that first kiss that I had with Dominic when he had given me the necklace hit me like a rock on the back of the head. I realized I couldn't give up. I had to try and get back to that timeline, the one where we were together. If what Nachmei had told me was true and if time was truly cyclical, then that had to mean there was a chance I could go back and exist from my original time line. I could be myself again, unused. But perhaps to get there, I would have to make some sacrifices of my own.

I closed my eyes tightly and felt the sensation and burst of energy as he gently placed his lips on my eyebrow. It was a kiss…a very gentle kiss. Then next my cheek bone, just below the eye. Next my neck, completely skipping my mouth—but not for long. Chills moved through me as I let him move me. I didn't want it to stop, and that disturbed me. I closed my eyes even tighter. He could sense I was disturbed.

Grabbing the sides of my face, he held my face up to his.

"Look at me, look at me, look at me," he whispered, each time the words growing with fierceness.

"No, no…," I whispered back, shaking my head adamantly. The kind of guilt and shame I was feeling was something he was sure to have been able to pick up on. I couldn't control those emotions.

"It's alright to just let go. Let go of all of it, everything will be different" he pleaded.

I opened my eyes and looked into his deep sapphires of eyes. His black pupils dilated and enlarged then shrank back. Not human, that was for sure. I worried that if I let go of myself even more than I already had, I might never get myself back the way I had been before. I was in a different world now—different rules—different feelings.

I looked at his face. I studied each feature slowly. His chiseled features were magnetically enticing. My eyes moved along from his brow to his nose, down to his lips. The perfection of this monster was insurmountable. He kissed me very, very softly. The electricity of his touch traveled through me, making me forget where I was, and most importantly, what was at stake.

# CHAPTER 19

Now that she, that sick sister of mine, had my place, and my time, she had everything I wanted and when and where I wanted it, there was no tomorrow for me or a yesterday. I only existed…and in Nachmei's eyes, I now existed for only him.

I couldn't feel how long I had been there, only sense that time didn't seem to pass at all. It was as if I was stranded, hanging by invisible strings that drained my energy and allowed me to barely move, unbreakable by whatever force it was I couldn't see. I was scared and too weak to wander off too far. Dense fog seemed to fill the creases of the outer-lying areas and I felt like I was already lost deep enough as it were. My reasoning, my logic—came from what I had learned thus far.

I had earned my way into his world by fair trade—and now only to be fair I did what no other Dhakris had ever done before.

My old clothes had become tattered and I now wore loose fitting clothes of a cotton like material that Nachmei said came from the forest people. He said they sent it as part of their pact. He gave me stones from the earth that were cut to sparkle, that any normal human would worship.

He had the forest creatures make me a full out diamond and sapphire undergarment that I wore underneath my robes at all times. It was something I would normally have considered tacky, but I had to wear it for him. It wrapped around me like a halter bra with bands of large diamonds that didn't exist in such quantities in the normal world supporting my bust and wrapping exotically down my torso and arms, neatly crisscrossed around my wrists and fingers. It went from my stomach and dangled down along the sides of my thighs like a flapper skirt from the 1920s, so that I would sparkle at all times for him, dressed or not. He insisted I never take it off because he said I was too beautiful a creature not to be wrapped in the finest of things. He brought me large rings, also diamond and other stones like ruby and opal, and my fingers were heavy to lift with them.

He forced a forest creature to come and paint my face with minerals and make my skin dazzle at all times. They would come and tend to my long hair, interweaving jewels through intricate braids so that my hair made its own crown of sparkling glory. He insisted they make me what would almost be considered shoes, except they didn't protect the bottom of my feet. They were an exquisite leather wrap that accentuated my feet and legs, studded with diamonds he had forced them to mine and chisel to perfection. He said my feet would never touch ground that was dirty anyway, so I didn't need to have shoes like other people, I only needed the finest of décor, fit for the queen of his world.

Once, a forest creature had brought an undergarment for me made of amethyst instead of whatever other jewel he had wanted, and I watched from behind a tree as he bashed the small creature to a brutal pulp of death for his mistake. I tried to cry, but I felt my breath catch and my body freeze in horror instead.

Underneath my jewels, my body had changed to that of a smooth and perfected statue. I was hardened by the emptiness of it all. Inside of my head I knew I had changed. I was no longer the eighteen-year-old girl that had disappeared. I was no longer the Dhakris who traded herself for her sister. I was older in some way yet ageless all the same. One thing was certain, I wasn't 18 year old Jessica Carmichael anymore. She was long gone forever.

Each time I walked through the halls of his palace, I would turn my head away from the atrium with the pool of water. I knew what power it held and what I could see if I looked into it. I didn't want to see him again, Dominic with my sister. The last time I had looked I had seen what no other woman in love would want to see. My mind flashed with the visions of them embracing—kissing—him undressing her slowly—I shook my head rapidly. It was a different timeline, I told myself. I could go back to what had been real to me somehow—someway. Besides, I had no way of knowing if what I was seeing was what was really happening in any timeline or if it was some sort of illusion meant to confuse me.

But my reality stood before me. Nachmei came to me and asked what bothered me. I thought to myself how I could explain that I was haunted inside my own head by my life. Nachmei knew though, without me really saying anything. When he approached me, I let him pick me up and carry me to a place where I could rest. The feelings within me were so twisted and confusing, but so enticing all at once. Part of me felt that I was taking revenge by reveling in my relationship with my monster. I was a rebel in my own mind, rebelling against all of what had happened to me. Besides, I needed his touch for energy. I would avoid him until I couldn't anymore because I needed to be able to move, walk, think clearly. Something in his touch gave me that energy.

"Do you find me a monster?" he would always ask, after feeding me, giving me more jewels, touching me gently or romancing me beyond my wildest dreams.

I would only respond with "No," and either indulge in the attention he gave me or bury the feelings within myself. His kindness was a drug, an addiction, and most definitely a substitute. I wanted to love something, but I couldn't figure out what, exactly. Accepting that I was there with him was all I really could do. Strained and emptied like casting off what a human should feel like, I let myself just be—emptied and in my own personal purgatory.

I had come to realize was that unless Nachmei was directly next to me, he couldn't tell what I was thinking like he said he could when I had first arrived. I had tested it with certain encounters with him. When I discovered that the farther I was from him physically, the more I could think freely, I took the chance to walk and think alone any time I could. When I was close to him, he did his best to make me happy, so I pretended to be happy.

One particularly empty passing moment where I felt a brief moment of energy, I decided to take a walk by myself out into the forest. The enjoyment of walking alone was cut off shortly when I heard an odd rustling and whispers around me. I stopped and looked around me, startled. Closing my eyes in frustration, I knew it was either Nachmei stopping me or something worse. Even though Nachmei had told me there were other inhabitants of the forest, I never saw any of them. From the beginning of my time there with him I felt like there was no one else around at all. If I was about to be destroyed by an evil creature, I wanted it to happen fast.

I slowly turned to see if I could find the origin of the sound. It seemed to be coming from everywhere and nowhere all at the same time.

"Jessica." I heard my name from what seemed like a disembodied voice.

I turned to try and find it. I felt a tap on my shoulder and spun around swiftly.

"Rau!" I exclaimed with excitement. It was the first somewhat familiar face I had seen since I had begun my self-enlisted imprisonment. He had never been particularly kind to me but seeing him was the closest thing to an old friend I could have imagined at that moment.

He shushed me harshly.

"Do not say *anything*! You foolish, *foolish* imbecile of a girl! Do not speak a word out loud. Only listen," he sharply instructed. I nodded my head in agreement. He began talking inside my head.

"If he hears you, he will kill me when he finds me, and believe me, he will find me if I stay much longer. You've seen how he kills our kind whenever he feels the need, and I'm in violation of our pact as we speak," Rau clenched his small mouth tightly with anger as he spoke.

I nodded my head and furrowed my eyebrows in acknowledgement of what he was saying. Rau took my cues and continued.

"You think it is safe with him, but what he allows you to see is not what is real. You are needed back in your own realm. I have seen your other, Dominic, and you as the other part of the Dhakris are needed. I have come to make sure that you are safe, and I see that you are, for now. Continue on like you have been but know that if he lures you any further, the ultimate goal has been met," he said, almost as though he was taking notes out loud to himself.

I looked at him with wide eyes, dying to speak but making sure I followed his instructions. I bit my lip forcefully to keep myself silent. I motioned with my heavily jeweled hands for him to tell me more, holding my breath to avoid any inadvertent words.

"I cannot stay but a brief moment longer. If I'm caught, my kind will be destroyed, starting with me. I must go. What you think is happening here isn't really happening—you are losing power and you have been since you arrived. A Dhakris like you should be able to shift like you learned before and we should be able to communicate without words. That is how you are being affected. You are losing yourself and it is no fault of anyone but yourself. It is all in your head, Jessica. Every time you let him touch you and you feel energized you are losing your own energy. Look at you! Look at what you are! He's taking it from you. Why do you think you haven't been able to shoot out energy like you were before you came here? Know that you are missed, and there has been much work to seek your whereabouts. Try not to eat or drink anything else in this realm, or you may be too powerless to ever leave. That's how most become trapped here. It makes you feel whole here, but it is draining you of the real you. Stop immediately, no matter how bad you think you feel. When you can, focus on your strengths."

I nodded my head in understanding, feeling panicked knowing I had already given away so much of my power.

"Plans are underway as I speak with you. You must have many questions, of that I am sure. But do not fear, you will be rescued."

I was reeling with agitation that I couldn't ask him any questions about the timeline, to what timeline would I return and what was happening from where I had come. I wanted to know, at the very least, if I was dead or alive.

He took one more look at me up and down and shook his head. I could tell he was upset with my appearance. Like a queen of all that was evil, I stood before him glowing and ostentatious. With that, he vanished in front of me, sort of just dissipated into thin air. I gasped, startled by the whole incident. I felt relieved and confused at the same time. But more so, I felt overwhelmed with the idea that Nachmei was more evil than I knew—truly evil and I had been taken by him and had given my entire self to him.

As I began my trek back to the palace, I concentrated on protecting my thoughts so that he couldn't read them. If nothing else, that was the least I could do to protect myself.

I felt my stomach churn with both excitement and fear, a sign of life within me that I hadn't felt in quite some time.

# CHAPTER 20

Without being able to sense how long I had been there in human time, it was hard to try and gauge the time I was missing in my own world. What if it had been a month, or even years that I had missed in my world? It also could have been no time at all. I tried to shake the thoughts from my mind because I knew there was no way I could truly know, so there was no reason for me to bother with letting the thoughts consume me. I would often stop and reflect in my thoughts the idea that I would be saved somehow. The sensation of the thoughts would invigorate me with such energy that Nachmei would mistake it for me being happy. I let him think that way. He had done nothing to even remotely make me think he would harm me in any way since I had begun to engage with him in any type of intimacy.

Nachmei didn't question it. He brought me things to eat, delicious delicacies that grew only in that world, fruit that was sweet and succulent, juices that would nourish and reinvigorate me, but I barely touched any of it. I could tell he took note of it, but I kept my mind clear of any thoughts that he could decipher. That was the most difficult part of all. I replaced my thoughts with images of sweet baked delicacies from my realm, cupcakes, coffee and teas. Things he could not provide me. I concealed my real thoughts.

I awaited a coup. In my mind, when I felt safe, I could see it happening a million different ways. Maybe the world around me would just dissolve, and then I would arrive back from where I had come and everyone would be the same as before. But then what? Here I was. Was it the same where I was lost? Could I go back there and have things back the way they were or was I going to have to live watching my sister with Dominic?

I started to take longer walks, and when I felt I was far enough away, I'd build up my strength and manifest my jade sword. I could see it for just a few moments, make a few moves, then it would vanish with crackles like the end of a transformer exploding. I knew I at least had something left in me.

Nachmei was patient and began to care a little less that I took long walks, because I always came back to him and gave him the attention he desired. But he noticed my dreaming thoughts one day, catching me off guard.

"In your mind are you somewhere else?" he asked me after watching me pretend to eat.

"Always," I said, knowing that was a mistake. I should have been more patient.

He moved closer to me, face to face. I felt the tip of his nose touch mine. It didn't make me shudder or make me want to move away from him, but I felt nervous nonetheless. I wanted to hide that from him.

"Where do you want to be then?" he asked softly.

"I want to be alive somewhere—anywhere," I replied back, my voice shaking slightly.

"What is it. Do you wish to show your exotic attire to the world from where you came?

You know they'd think it absolutely glorious. No one's ever seen anything like it. You look absolutely royal, more royal than anyone who is considered to be so there. It's all overrated you know—that life you left."

"It's not like I left it on purpose. I didn't just decide out of nowhere to come here. You know that. I know that. We don't have to pretend," I said coldly.

He looked at me blankly. I turned away from his stare.

"And you still think that man of yours is going to come for you?"

I heard him say behind me.

"I have no way of knowing anything. I only know what you tell me," I said.

"And have I ever lied to you?" he asked.

"How can I know that? I only know what you tell me," I repeated.

"Turn around, please," he asked with a pleading desperation in his tone. I wondered why he would ask that if he could just as easily appear right in front of me. Or even worse, brutally force me to look at him. He wanted so badly for me to trust him. If I turned on my own free will, it would indicate how much trust he had gained.

"Look at me and tell me you see a monster," he commanded. I saw the fear now in his eyes— the desperation from his voice.

"Why?" I turned cautiously towards him, "So you can actually be one? Would it help you to be more like yourself if you could stop putting on an act around me?"

"Tell me I'm a monster so that you will hate me. I've tried to make you love me and I don't understand why you just won't," he hissed, his inner hatred seeping through.

I found myself to be speechless. I hadn't realized it, but he wanted me to love him so badly he was doing anything to make that happen. But he didn't know with what—or whom—he was truly dealing. He didn't understand human emotions either, or how people fell in love. Most of all, he could never understand the Dhakris. He only had people come to him for things, things he could manipulate. But he couldn't manipulate me. At least not the same way he had expected to be able to. I looked down at myself in disgust. I let my hands dig past all of the large cut diamonds until I touched the necklace that was my one and only physical connection to Dominic.

"I don't know what you expected from me," I said. "I came to you as a prisoner, not as a—a wife, or a queen. I came because I wanted to save her. I don't know—I can't feel how long I've even been here."

"So, you've felt nothing for me this entire time you've been with me?" he asked. I sensed pain in his voice.

I didn't want to say anything back to him; I feared what his reaction would be. I had mixed feelings of how exactly to regard him. If he was a monster, he sure didn't look like one.

But falling in love with looks alone never yields genuine results. He had taken care of me when I was at a very low point—yet according to Rau, that was only a ploy to rid me of any power I had left. He could have let me die in his secret world. But then he had brought me up, taken care of me, healed me—only for me to tell him I thought he was a monster.

He walked up to me, taking my head by the jaw and touching his lips against mine. I wouldn't kiss him back, not this time. He trailed his finger down my lips and neck, and stopped at the touch of one of my necklaces. The one I arrived with. With the rage I had released in him, he yanked the necklace violently from my fingers, breaking the chain from behind my neck. He heaved heavy breaths of anger that he had been holding back and he threw the necklace with a guttural scream into the forest, the echo of his voice bouncing off of the invisible walls of our hidden realm. His entire body was flexed with rage, his face contorted into a screaming mask of fury.

I grasped my head in my hands and tried to hide all my emotion. It was, after all, just a material thing, and I was still dripping in diamonds that earthly women would kill for. But it was my last real thing I had to cling to from Dominic. It was my last hope that what we had together was real and that I wasn't dead to him.

# CHAPTER 21

The parties that had searched for me had long given up in the world which I had left so abruptly. The timeline shift had occurred much as how Nachmei had said it would. It was the same day, but with a different history. I had now gone missing and Dominic and Emily, who had met through their friendship in the witchcraft group, had grown closer in their efforts to find me.

Dominic had never known me in this time line. He only knew of me through what my sister had said about me as he had helped her and my family search for me after I had disappeared in the woods.

Emily sat on the back porch of our parents' house looking out into the ominous forest. It was late October, the 27th, almost Halloween. She thought of her friends' costume parties. She didn't want to go to any of them—not unless Dominic would come. It was pointless, meaningless to her unless he wanted to go. A breeze caught her long wavy chocolate locks and blew them across her face.

Dominic came out of the house from behind her, but she stared blankly ahead.

"Dom," she said without looking at him.

"Yeah, Em," he acknowledged. He was kind to her—same old Dominic. Ever since they had first met there had been a connection between them. He knew he wanted to keep her safe, so he had always stuck close by her side.

"I want to go out there and look again, just one more time," she said, fiddling with her fingers. Her long, pretty nails were blue near the cuticle. It was chilly outside; even East Texas could feel cold sometimes.

"We looked. We looked for months and months. Everyone did. You came out here two months ago by yourself. What did you find?" he asked, stroking her gently on the back for comfort.

"Nothing. I know. I just want to go one more time. I keep having dreams. They're of Jessica. I really wish you could have met her Dom, she was something special," she said. He moved her long strands of hair out of her face.

"I wish I could have, too," he said.

"Sometimes I feel like it's my fault."

"Why? You didn't do this. You didn't make her disappear."

"I don't know. I'm not sure really. But sometimes I just get this feeling that if I had never messed with, you know, spells and stuff, this wouldn't have happened to her," she admitted self-consciously.

"Oh, Em, I know what you mean but, you never did anything bad, you never worked on a spell of any kind that was negative or could come back on you, did you?"

Emily was silent.

She shook her head and then finally answered to him. "No. But before I met you, when I was just working alone, I envied her."

"You envied her," he said, begging the question.

"I envied the life she had that I didn't. She was popular, beautiful...."

"...you're beautiful too...," he interrupted.

"No, let me finish. She was the All-American kind of girl. Something that no matter how hard I tried to be, I wasn't. We've never—we were never the same. I saw her, younger than me, going through the years that I went through with such difficulty with such ease. I didn't even get invited to senior parties when I was a senior; Jessica got invited as a freshman! To my classmates' parties! Everything that was so hard for me she went through so easily. And smart! She was so smart. She made wonderful grades so easily. Like it was nothing."

Dominic listened to her, looking at her as she spoke.

"If she had a crush on a boy, you'd never know it. All the guys in my class and hers wanted to take her out. She brushed it off. She didn't even realize what she had. If—no—when I had a crush on someone when I was her age, I'd just dwell on it and feel invisible and wonder if that person ever saw me. She didn't see it. She just breezed through all of it. Her friends had money and alcohol and threw house parties all the time. I never went anywhere when I was her age. I came home and dwelled on everything that had happened to me each day and just let things fester within me. I envied her. And one night, I envied her more so than I should have."

"You did it with intent," he said with resounding inquisition.

"I guess so. Now that I know more about what it was I was doing—how powerful thoughts can be. I did it with intent," ashamed, she looked down at her feet. She couldn't look him in the eye and admit to it.

"What sort of intent? My Weli, she might be able to help. I haven't spoken with her in a while, but I could ask my mom to let me call her."

"She could help?" Emily asked, almost choking on her words.

"She's a *curandera*, a healer, they know about spells, they deal with things like this," he said, standing up. Emily looked up at him with pleading eyes.

"Okay, let's go have another look," he said, unable to refuse her begging grey eyes.

Reluctantly, he led her into the forest.

The dead pine needles and oak leaves that had fallen crunched heavily beneath their feet as they began their journey into the woods again looking for the last known place that I had been. Emily never knew why I had gone out there, but she had assumed it was to meet up with someone. After all, the woods opened up on the other side where lots of people knew, Dominic knew them well.

"So, if you grew up out here, how come I never saw you before? Emily asked as they
pushed through the twigs.

"I don't know, I guess I never thought about it," he said, moving some brush out of her way so she could walk without getting her arms scratched. "These woods are pretty big. Plus I didn't go to school around here. I told you, dad drove me up to Langsbury. I was around a different crowd."

"Well, did you ever know of anyone going missing or see anyone weird out here? Like creepy old men?" Emily asked.

"Nope. My Weli never likes these woods when she comes up to visit. She said they are cursed and won't go near them."

"Do you really believe in what she said? Everyone thinks my sister was abducted by somebody, someone who took her away somewhere," Emily asked, stopping and looking at him to see his face while he answered.

He furrowed his brows again pensively.

"I think there's something to it—to what my Weli said. She knew or saw something the rest of us didn't…and she's usually right whether we want to believe her or not. I just know I grew up hunting and fishing out here, I know my way around pretty well. So regardless of what is out here, seen or unseen, it has left me alone so far. I don't think I've ever seen anyone suspicious though, like you said they had…."

It hit him faster than either one of them could see. In fact, neither one of them had seen it coming at all or even heard it. It was as if it had just appeared out of thin air.

Dominic yelped with a curse. It had almost knocked him onto the ground. He stumbled around for balance, reorienting himself.

"What was that? Did you see something fall?" He touched the side of his cheek and saw the blood that was trickling from the deep scratch on his face.

"What!" Emily stopped, frozen in her tracks. "What in the hell was it? I didn't see anything!" she cried, terrified.

He put pressure on his cheek to stop the bleeding and turned around slowly. "Something hit my face. Something with a sharp edge, I'm bleeding."

"I'll look around for it. Maybe, I don't know... maybe it was one of those stray bullets people hear about, falling after someone shot straight up," she said as her voice faded from his ears.

Dominic didn't respond. He held his face to put pressure on the wound and let his eyes move around the forest floor in search of a foreign object.

"I'm really freaked out Dom, what happened?" Emily shuddered, ready to sprint away as fast as she could.

A glimmer caught his eye. He approached it slowly, not sure if he was seeing what he thought he was seeing.

"Holy shit," he said, picking the object up.

Emily turned and walked towards him, studying the cut on his face after he released his hand to hold what he'd found.

"What is it, a necklace?" she asked.

"Yeah. Not just any necklace. It's my necklace, from my house. My Saint Michael necklace," he gasped.

"Are you sure that's what hit you?" she asked, trying to find the most logical explanation. "Maybe you had it with you and didn't know it and it fell out of your pocket when something else hit you."

He focused in on the charm in his hand intently. "No. No, I know where I kept this. I know I never, ever, took it out, ever."

"How did a necklace leave your house and come and smack you in the face, Dominic?" Emily asked dubiously.

"I don't know, but I do know it's a sign. My Weli always said there will be signs. I never knew what she meant. I don't really know what she means now. I just know this is what she was talking about," he said, almost giddily.

"Let's get out of here—I think your Weli was right about this place," Emily said, adrenaline beginning to rush through her veins. She started back down the path to her house, trotting and then sprinting when it was clear. Dominic followed after, glancing down at the sign given to him so fiercely. He didn't understand what it meant. He only knew he had to find out because if what his grandmother had always said was true, then it was really happening.

# CHAPTER 22

"I didn't like that girl. When your mother told me about that girl I just had a bad feeling. I didn't like her—there was something—not right about it. Then when I saw her picture—no, no. It is close, but not quite right *mijo*. Now I'm telling you, what has happened to you is more than just a sign. Objects appear, and they disappear, people have it happen all the time—they don't understand why," Weli poured out as much information as she could through the static-filled phone line. Dominic strained to hear her voice, her thick Spanish accent accentuating each word with its importance.

"*Mijo*, did the charm fall? Did you see it? Where were you when it happened?" she asked quickly.

"I—I was in the forest where that girl supposedly disappeared. I was with Emily, the sister of the missing girl. We were walking towards the clearing…," he stopped when he heard her gasp.

"Dominic, *escuchame*, listen very carefully. It was dangerous for you to go out there. That girl, Emily, she has been there before."

"Well, yes, Weli she lives out there, it's near her house."

"No, *mijo*, that's not what I mean. She's been there before. So have you, and so has the girl. That necklace? That was no mistake. It came from her. Jessica, the missing girl," she said slowly.

"I don't understand."

"I understand everything now. All of the signs that I have been telling you and your mother about for all of these years, they're happening," her voice became garbled over the phone.

"So, Jessica was trying to get Emily's attention, to let us know she's out there? Her ghost?" he asked, reaching up and touching the scab on his face.

"No!" she exclaimed emphatically. Her voice could strike him through the phone like a whip. "Listen, before we are cut off. Because what I'm about to tell you is going to sound like I have become crazier than your mother already thinks I am. But Jessica, you gave her that necklace."

"No, I didn't—Weli—I never met her. I met her sister, I'm seeing her sister, yes, I know you don't like that," he said calmly.

"Shhh! *Mijo*! We don't have much time! I know now why I did not like her for you! You gave Jessica that necklace in a different dimension, different timeline. You gave it to her as a gift and she wore it when she disappeared. Everything I have seen is somehow happening. I've always told your mother this, that you were one of them. And now, I think Jessica is too.

You have to help her *mijo*, that necklace is proof. Whatever you're doing with Emily, you must stop now. Jessica helped Emily in another time, but there was a mistake and they took her…whatever is out there took her in place of Jessica. She is what you are, *mijo*. She is the other one. This is beyond time and space."

Dominic's hand trembled holding the phone as he felt his heart pound on his chest. The crackles and static began to shift into the conversation, breaking up the connection.

"I—I don't know what to do Weli. What do I do?"

"You will know what to do when you unravel yourself. I will be coming to help *mijo*. Take care, *te amo.*"

The line disconnected. Dominic felt a chill run through his every being. He had sweat beading from his forehead.

It was all becoming so strange to him. Ever since he had met Emily, he had felt a strange feeling towards her. His grandmother had an inexplicable aversion towards her since she first had seen a photo of her a year before. Dominic had sent it to her in an email and had his aunt in Mexico share it with her. He remembered her reaction to it when she came to visit.

"*Mijo*—that girl is no good for you."

"But Weli she understands all of the same things that you and I understand, she's into it, you know?"

"No, *mijo* there is something not right. I am not sure exactly what it is yet. Be careful."

"I will, Weli," he remembered saying to her. He brushed it off as her typical paranoia and reaction to him having a serious girlfriend. No one wants their twenty-year-old grandson to become too serious with someone that's no good for them.

The trouble with Emily was that it was easy for her to become serious with Dominic. Emily had always been looking for someone to love. She craved it, craved the attention and the feeling of the rush of it all. That's what had gotten her into spells and learning about how to get what she wanted through intention—and it was what had led her to Dominic.

When I had gone missing, Emily needed affection; she needed someone on whom she could lean. She found that in Dominic. He was sympathetic to her pain and helped tremendously in the search for Jessica. He knew the woods like the back of his hand. He helped lead search parties through the woods with the county sheriff and had assisted when the prison loaned their bloodhounds to the search parties to sniff for my scent, too.

The bloodhounds had picked up my trail, but it had ended in the clearing. No one understood what had happened after that. There had been no heavy rains to wash away the scent and there were no other scents picked up or tracks seen. It had been a complete and tragic mystery. There was an anomaly once, when the dogs suddenly found my scent further away from the clearing. They all ran about a half mile into the woods and led everyone to a tree. They could smell me even on the other side.

After Dominic had stayed around to help so fervently, Emily began to see something in him that she had seen in others before. She started to feel something for him that she knew meant she wanted to be with him. It was a tingle in her stomach when she saw him, one that would rush up and down her when his eyes met hers. Then, they started hanging out with the occult group, and it was another excuse for Emily to spend more time with him.

Dominic had become so familiar with the family that my parents treated him like he was part of the family. He would come over for dinner and talk with our dad about things that he and his father would do together when his father wasn't off driving long distance loads. The fact that her father was so comfortable with Dominic had made her crave him even more. He was accepted by our family. That made her feel like he was hers.

One particularly strange night, Emily was having a rough night coping with everything. She picked up her phone and called him.

"Hello?" he answered, it sounded as if he'd been sleeping.

"Dom, can you come over?" Emily said, slurring her words slightly.

"Em? It's already midnight, are you okay?"

"No...no not tonight. I feel—I just feel so bad. I miss her. I'm so upset, I'm upset with myself," she cried, her voice trailing off on the other end.

"I'll be over. Give me fifteen minutes."

He came expecting to comfort Emily in a time that she needed someone to support her. She was outside when he arrived, standing up on the tailgate of our dad's pick-up truck.

"Hey," she said to him, jumping down off of the tailgate and walking up slowly and with a twist to her step as she approached him.

"Hey," he replied, putting his arms out on her shoulders to slow her down as she leaned up to his face.

"Are you okay? You sounded awful on the phone," he said, looking at her through soulful, questioning eyes.

"I'm better—now that you're here," she said in a whisper. She reached up to him and kissed his soft lips, twisting her tongue out to let him feel what she wanted.

"Woah," he backed away, holding her off at the shoulders.

"Are you—have you been drinking?" he asked.

"Just a little..." she confessed with a giggle. "I'm having a hard night." She looked at him with her best don't judge me eyes.

Disturbed, Dominic decided not to leave her to her own devices in that state. He sat on the tail gate next to her as she talked about looking up at the stars and wondering what all was out there.

"I just—you know—wonder if there's other layers of this world or if there's other worlds out there...," she said, sipping from a wine cooler she'd taken from our parents' refrigerator.

Dominic nodded. "Yeah. I know you miss her."

"Yeah," Emily said, sweeping her long wavy hair off of her neck, revealing her shoulder in the small summer dress she was wearing. She looked over at him from the side of her eyes.

He could sense her seduction. They had spent so much time together, but he was still surprised that she was coming on to him that strong. He began to regret coming to see her. She tossed the empty bottle of wine cooler she had just finished to the ground and then made her move. She swung her leg over the top of him and straddled him on the tailgate. Dominic knew he couldn't push her off or she'd fall off the end of the tailgate. He pushed himself back away from her, but she mistook that for him encouraging her to grind further on him.

She leaned forward and kissed his ear, then whispered, "I want you," heating his ear up with the steam of her breath. "Help me forget everything."

"Emily, you're drunk. Just—just...."

"Shhh...," she silenced him, pushing her finger up against his lips sloppily, then slipping it around the edge of his bottom lip in seduction. She slowly slipped off the straps of her dress, revealing a bare chest, and leaned over further on him, reaching for his shirt by the zipper of his pants and tugged on it, suggesting he take it off. She took his hands and forced them onto her thighs, wanting him to grip her. He removed his hands from her and tried to figure out how to escape.

"Emily—" this time he said it more forcefully and scooted himself back to where she was forced off of him.

"What is it, Dom? Don't you want me?" she asked, tilting her head to the side with the hurtful implication of rejection.

He sat up and got on his knees and came over to her, pulling her straps back up and putting them in place, covering her nakedness.

"I'm here for you Emily, you know that. You know I'm not with anyone else. I spend so much of my time with you. But this isn't right, not like this," he said.

"Not like what?" she asked.

"Not here, not with you upset, drinking, at your parents' house."

"We could go somewhere else," she suggested.

He looked down, eyes cast to the ground. He didn't want to embarrass her but hoped she would just sleep it off.

"Emily, I'm not going to take advantage of you when you're like this."

"You're not taking advantage, I'm offering," she countered.

"It just doesn't feel right. But clearly, you had other intentions."

"Dominic wait...I—I...." he didn't stop to listen. He climbed into his truck and drove the winding country roads back home, wondering what it was that was had really been stopping him from letting a beautiful brunette take advantage of him.

Thinking back on that entire experience now, it all made sense to him. That's why he couldn't do anything with Emily that night. He knew now that something rang true in his grandmother's words, he just had to figure out what, exactly, that was.

The next day, he stayed in his bed and thought about everything that had happened. His mind wouldn't allow him to see Emily anymore, at least not for the time being. He felt that being close to her was almost poisonous, like his grandmother had suggested. He had seen photos of me in passing, in Emily's house and on search photos. He knew that people thought I was beautiful and he knew that I had been full of potential at the time of my disappearance. What he and no one else could figure out is why I would have gone into those woods alone. He couldn't shake my image from his mind.

Grasping the Saint Michael charm, he looked at it in his palm. The chain was broken, he noticed, like it had been ripped. His grandmother's words echoed in his head. You gave it to her. When had that happened? He wondered about all of it. It just didn't seem plausible, yet nothing his grandmother had ever said to him would seem plausible to the average person. Ever since he had been a little boy able to have full memories he could recall her saying that he was "one of them". He didn't know what that meant.

In his late teens, he started to talk to people who were into witchcraft, spells and dabbling in the occult. He never practiced spells like some of them did—mainly because of the tales his grandmother had told of opening doors that couldn't be closed. But he had met Emily there—curious Emily—seeking knowledge about that which she couldn't understand. She had been practicing pretty heavily when Jessica had disappeared.

Dominic tried to think about what his grandmother had meant about unraveling himself. He knew she meant metaphorically, but the metaphor didn't make sense to him. It wasn't like a riddle. It meant something deeper, he knew. She had given him the Saint Michael necklace when he was a little boy, only seven years old.

He remembered that day. It was February and cold, she had come to visit from Mexico and the family had been outside saying their goodbyes before his father drove her to the bus station. She had pulled the charm necklace from her pocket and said, "This is for you, *mijo*, because you're special. This represents something that will mean more to you as you get older. Take care of it. *Te amo*." Then she left with a kiss to him on his forehead.

He had always kept it put up in his room. He had always cherished it. He knew that Saint Michael was important to the Catholics. He had been raised moderately Catholic. He wanted to know why he would have given me such an important thing, something he held so dear. He wracked his brain. It must have been for a good reason. He had held on to the thing for so many years, keeping it tucked away in a wooden box where he kept his most cherished small things. A ring from his grandfather, an arrowhead he found on a hunt with his dad, and that necklace, a gift from his beloved grandmother. He hardly ever opened the box. Yet, it had gotten out, flown through the air, and cut him in the face.

Or—according to his grandmother, he had taken it from the box in an alternate reality and given it to me, who he had adored and wanted to protect. He wouldn't have given it to anyone else for any other reason.

He saw calls from Emily on his phone. He was not answering them. She was calling to check on him—he knew that. She had seen what had happened in the woods. She wasn't going to stop calling. He figured he'd better answer.

"Hey," he said hurriedly.

"Dominic, where have you been? Are you okay?" she asked.

"No, yeah, I'm fine. I'm sorry. I talked to my Weli."

"Oh, really? What'd she say?"

"It's quite a lot. My Weli can be longwinded. But Em, I need to have some space for a while, in case you think I'm ignoring you, I'm not. I need to figure some things out. It's all connected to what happened. But it's gonna take some time for me to—figure out," he said.

Emily didn't handle any sort of rejection well. She didn't understand the concept of "space" when someone asked for it. It offended her that she couldn't be involved. Her voice shook as she responded.

"Okay. Well, just let me know if you need me for anything. I feel like this is my fault since I wanted to go out into the woods."

"No, nothing's your fault. You have to stop all the self-blaming. It's not healthy. Let me take care of this and I'll explain everything to you. Please, just trust me. I'm going to figure this out," he reassured.

"Alright—bye," she said, hanging up her phone. "I love you," she said after the fact. She didn't think she could ever tell him to his face for fear of rejection again. But she had fallen for him, the way Emily did so well—deeply and obsessively.

# PART IV

# TIMELINES

# CHAPTER 23

Dominic thought it would be best to investigate why Saint Michael was so important to his grandmother, and now why a Saint Michael charm was playing such a central role in this new mystery that had been unveiled to him.

He went to the local library. He had long since cut off most connections with Dana, Chris, Josie, Chandra and Vanek. They had been good company to discuss things with at first but now he found them to be centrists, each focused on their own personal agendas. Vanek made him feel the worst out of all of them. He seemed to be almost pleased when he found out that Jessica had vanished. He never offered to help and came around less and less. No one knew anything about him other than he would meet up with the occult group and listen, scolding those who were wrong in his opinion about a belief or practice. He took a certain interest in Emily, and Emily sort of gravitated to him, too. He thought he was protecting her by keeping her from Vanek. Emily had gotten extremely jealous of Chandra and argued with her once at a meeting, so Dominic decided it was best to just part ways. Now after what Weli had told Dominic, he definitely didn't want to talk to them about any of it.

Upon entering the library, he headed straight for the section on religious studies. There were books written about angels, demons, fallen ones, watchers, spirits, and all of their counterparts. He pulled out a book written about angels.

*Michael is an archangel, considered a saint by Catholic tradition. Michael was worshiped by Chaldeans prior to Christianity*—he read to himself, *Chaldeans worshiped him like a God, as he was in charge of the virtues, the seven virtues...* He read on, See appendix for more information... He flipped to the back of the book frantically, looking for the information on the virtues. It referenced a different book. He went to the computer and searched the Internet for information on the seven virtues and Archangel Michael.

Michael was supposed to have emerald green wings, emanating the emerald glow. He continued reading. There wasn't much information on the seven virtues other than what had been recorded in Judeo Christian Islamic texts. He felt he needed to go deeper than that, but there was nothing other than meaningless forums where anyone could provide any information, falsified or true. It was impossible to tell, and he didn't have the time to find help.

His phone suddenly vibrated, making him jump. His bright green eyes lit up, seeing that it was his mother. Perhaps his grandmother was near with answers. He answered with a whisper to evade the harsh stare of the librarian.

"Hello, mom?"

"Dominic, I'm picking up Weli at three. Do you want to come along?"

"Would you mind if I went and just got her by myself?" he asked in a hushed voice.

"Why?" she asked, irritated.

"I'd like to just have some—you know—one on one time with her," he mumbled quietly, not wanting her to ask questions. He clicked to print the pages of information he had found.

"Okay, Domi, that's fine. I can get started on supper while you get her," she acquiesced.

He paid for his copies of paper and almost ran from the library. It was already past twelve in the afternoon, so he'd have plenty of time to go and get her. He was eager to ask her about everything he had found. It all was coming together, he could feel it.

* * * *

"Ay, *mijo*, you look so handsome! Look how your eyes sparkle!" Weli greeted him at the bus station with a kiss on the cheek.

"Hey, Weli. I'm so glad you came," he greeted her with a huge hug.

"Don't tell your mother—you haven't told your mother why I really came, did you?" she asked with all seriousness.

"No. No, I thought you told her, so I haven't said anything to her."

"Good. Keep it that way. She already thinks what I know is crazy. I don't want to perpetuate her notions about me."

Once he had helped her up into his truck and climbed into the driver's seat, he handed her the papers he had printed from the library.

"Weli, I want to know why you gave me Archangel Michael when I was seven. I kept that necklace locked in a box," he said, looking straight ahead at the highway.

She looked over the papers, read what he had printed about how far back Michael had been worshiped, and what his purpose was.

"I gave you that necklace because my best friend made them. She made it for me to give to you. She didn't say why, or for what. She said the Archangel Michael would protect you. So, when I came to visit you, I gave it to you. Why?"

"There's no other history beyond modern religion about him, really. But I think there's something else to this, that necklace was special to me. I kept it in a box. I was afraid I'd lose it if I wore it," Dominic said, glancing over at her as she looked at his evidence.

"Well, she made good jewelry. She used the best of everything. It was a nice necklace, I remember. Your mother was going to be taking you to your classes for Confirmation, so I thought it would be nice for you to have it," she said, shifting through the papers. "Why?"

"Everything I told you on the phone. It hit me. It hit me in the woods. It came out of nowhere, and it hit me in the face," he pointed towards the scrape along his cheekbone. "I kept the necklace in the box, the box! I don't know how it got out or where it came from."

Weli's eyes widened. She sat in silence, thinking of all of the different possibilities the necklace could entertain.

"What am I, that you kept saying all of these years that I was? What am I that you say Jessica is the other part of?"

She took in a deep breath, preparing herself for the best lecture she could give.

"I had a feeling about you asking this. When I was growing up in Mexico, the priests would often talk, and so would others who were shamans, *curanderos*, people of higher knowledge. They talked about the seven virtues. There is a word for what you are—I cannot remember it right now. It will come to me, I'm sure. But you were born under the right star as one of them. My mother and my grandmother always told me that they had been told and foresaw that you would be one of them."

"One of what?"

"These seven virtues. Angels, but incarnate. You see, angels are neither male or female. They have almost like, a mix of both. We talk about some angels being female, some being male. But these virtues were angels that were neither. To do their proper work here in our world, they must split into two beings, a male and a female. You are the male."

"And Jessica is the female," he finished.

"Yes. I believe that is why all of this has happened. She has disappeared in this timeline, but in a different one, you knew her and you both discovered what you were. You have lost what abilities you had there," she sighed heavily.

"And there are others?"

"There are seven pairs, yes. And Archangel Michael is the higher being watching over it all. That is the way it was taught to me," she explained, her tone changing to a darker seriousness.

"And why isn't any of this written down, Weli? Why is there no research, words, scripts, evidence?" Dominic asked desperately.

"*Mijo*, it cannot be written. It just *is*. You all were created to help keep our world in balance from evils. There are different kinds of evils that exist and there are some that only a special kind can eliminate. You are that special kind. The evil that exists in those woods where Jessica disappeared—it is one of them. I came in such a hurry because I need you to understand that she needs to be rescued, and you are the only one who can do it," she said, running out of breath with all of her words.

"I'm an angel?" he asked, unsure of his words.

"Not entirely, no. You are flesh and blood and can be killed. The evils that exist, many of them like to mate with human women to create hybrids that can blend and seek out the virtues and kill them. They called them— moonchildren I believe. Anyhow, once one of the pair of the virtues is dead, they must wait until reincarnation to try and find one another again. It is a cycle. You knew Jessica before in another life, and even on another timeline. You must save her, *mijo*. It is up to you, you and Jessica," she closed her eyes as if in prayer.

She let out a breath of relief after giving him all of the information.

"Why didn't you tell me any of this when I was younger?"

"There was no reason to tell you. From what I know, the ones who are what you are, they don't know it until they are older, late teens, early twenties, young adults. They don't discover one anther until then, usually. What good would it have done for me to tell all of this to you and then your mother…oh your mother would have thrown fits. All this time, you've lived across the woods from Jessica and her sister—who I hope you have stopped seeing by the way—but you never knew them until now that you are older," she explained, her eyes filled with hope that he was comprehending everything she was explaining so rapidly.

"I was never really seeing Emily, not like that," Dominicsaid.

"Well *mijo*, you have to understand how dangerous it could be. In another timeline, she was the one who was missing. The evil one took her to make a moonchild. It didn't happen the way it all was supposed to happen. Whatever occurred, now Emily is blocking your abilities. I can feel that. She is a negative force. Jessica traded herself for her sister. Now she is waiting," she said somberly.

"How do you know that?"

"I was told. By guides, spirit guides," she sighed again, desperate to be understood but knowing she couldn't fully explain all of the things that she saw in her mind's eye. "At first, I didn't know how to interpret what I was seeing but once you told me what had happened with that necklace, I knew. Most of the puzzle in my mind came together. It all made sense to me. Now I know what to tell you to do. But I also have a sense of dread. Dominic, *m*

*ijo*, this all can be extremely dangerous. I want you to know that I love you very much and I came knowing that I might have to die for you," her eyes expressed that she wasn't simply being dramatic.

"What? Weli, no. What are you talking about?"

"In a different timeline, I died."

"But you're here now."

"Yes, in this timeline. I don't profess to be an expert in the workings of the worlds and the timelines, but I'm telling you what I know. I was dead there, I'm alive here. I'm both dead and alive at the same time, and for all I know, we all are."

He swallowed hard. The thought of losing his grandmother was deeply upsetting to him. He felt like she was all he had now, the only person who could completely understand what was happening to him. "Alright. What next?" he asked, breathing in deeply to process all of the information that had been given to him.

"We have to carefully unravel your true self. And in the process, go and get that girl," as she spoke, her eyes widened.

# CHAPTER 24

Emily was shaken at the sudden absence of Dominic in her life. She felt like she had been so close to having him but had never felt more far away from him than she did now. When she hadn't heard from him in three days, she began to grow desperate. She didn't want to seem desperate though. That was the problem. If she showed up at his house, she knew that it would be out of place. She couldn't call him anymore; he'd already explained that he wouldn't answer.

It hurt—and it hurt deeply. This beautiful green-eyed man that had given so much of his time to her did not seem to think of her the same way that she thought of him. She thought of what she might be able to do to earn his love, make him love her somehow. Was it possible? She had heard of such things happening. There were spells, incantations that she could try. But no—why would she want to do that? It could backfire—she'd read about that happening. Some people—mostly girls—had tried to get the love of another man by using a spell. But whatever one chose to do to another could come back on that person three times over. If she tried to use magic to get Dominic to love her, it could come back on her in a bad way. She could possibly be made somehow to love someone that she would not have wanted to love. She knew not to mess with free will.

It was all so messy, so tumultuous. She missed me and wished she could talk to me about her problems, but at the same time thought that if she had just been like me, she probably could have what she wanted. If she only knew…

Dominic didn't waste any time trying to unravel himself as his grandmother had instructed him to do. Part of his mind thought of Emily and how he was hurting her by not talking to her—but he had to have confidence in what his grandmother had said. If she said that Emily was not good for him, there had to be something to it. It was more than just her being stubborn or controlling, she had a true feeling that it wasn't right. And if that weren't enough, something had come through time and space to hit him with it.

"Dhakris!"

He heard his grandmother yell from down the hall in the guest bedroom of his parent's small house.

"What, Weli?" he yelled back, looking through a book he had checked out from the library on Archangels.

He heard her feet come shuffling down the hall in her loose house slippers.

"Dhakris," she said in more of a whisper this time. "That is what you are. I couldn't remember the name of it—the word for the ones. It is Dhakris."

"What language is that?" Dominic asked as the word resonated with him.

It comes from a time much earlier than languages with which we are familiar. It is older than time. Each language uses the same word—there is no translation. It is only Dhakris," she said in almost a whisper.

"That's what I am, then?" he asked.

"No—that's what you and Jessica are, *mijo*. I know this now," she said with her hands outspread in desperation.

Dominic looked away from her, staring off towards the floor. A girl he didn't remember knowing. A girl whose sister he knew had feelings for him. A girl that was thought to be dead.

"What is our real purpose, if Jessica and I are this—this Dhakris."

"In my lifetime, I have never seen it at work. But my grandmother had heard a story once of what happened when a Dhakris had existed in a village not far from where she grew up. It was said that the village was tortured by evil spirits.

There were all sorts of negative things that would happen to the people of the village. Babies would die. Older people would suffer terribly, more so than with the normal ailments of growing old. They would be tormented in their sleep. Evil spirits were trying to take their souls. Younger people would do strange things. There was a man who broke every plate in his family's house, every single dish, can you imagine? And he said he was told to do this by the devil himself. He said if he didn't do it, then he would be made to kill his family. You can imagine *mijo*, the feat that arose within his family upon hearing that their own father could strike them down. There was a child who was with his friends who followed a snake he had found into the bushes. His friends refused to follow. When he finally returned from his search, he had gone mad, completely insane.

Then the Dhakris arrived. They were two young people, a man and woman. The way my grandmother told me the story was that they seemed like a married pair, together, no children.

They came to the village and offered help. They used their combined powers to stop the evil spirits from torturing the humans of the village. They banished them from ever returning. That was their purpose there. It was said that they traveled elsewhere to do their work thereafter—not staying behind for too long, although the village offered them a place to live and they were to be treated as royalty for the rest of their lives. The pair turned down the offer and said they had other work to do, but they thanked them for their kindness. The village was left in awe and forever obliged to their work. The pair only said to thank Saint Michael, and to always give him thanks for what he had done."

"Nobody knows what happened to them?" Dominic asked.

"No, not from what I was told. But the shamans and the *curanderos*, whenever something really bad was happening while I was growing up, would talk about the Dhakris. It was rare that they would call them by that name, Dhakris, which is why it was so hard for me to remember. Mainly they would call them the pair. The priests, as I said before, also knew of the Dhakris and would consult with the shamans and the *curanderos* at times, sharing what they knew, but no one knew when a pair would be needed or return again," she finished.

"Can you tell me why I need to stay away from Emily? I mean, this is about her sister, I think she'd need to know this—"

"No! Dominic, *No es amor*. There is something very volatile underneath her pretty face. You must trust me. There is an imbalance at work. You have no way of knowing what has happened and what exists on the other timeline I have explained to you, but you must believe me that telling her will do no good—no good will come of it," she warned.

"What if she stops by here to see me? What would happen then?" he asked. It wasn't far from her house. He knew she was capable of just coming over if she wanted to badly enough.

"Then we must get to work quickly now, *mijo*. We're going to pretend everything is normal, okay? Do not tell your mother about this. She doesn't need to know right now. Let me take care of it when the time comes. Meet me in the morning, outside, six sharp, before your mother wakes up. We've got work to do," she smiled broadly as she shook his shoulder.

Dominic couldn't sleep well that night. He tossed around frequently in his sleep and had waking dreams of different things that he had never seen and couldn't really explain. They were the kind of dreams that seem like they'll be easy to explain later but the details become fleeting as the hours pass. I was in them, and he knew it. He would see my face and then he would wake up, trying to recall the details. I tried to speak to him, but there was a barrier between our two worlds that wasn't allowing me to get my message through. I wanted to tell him in his dreams which way he should come, when he should come, what he should expect—that Nachmei could change in a split second and become a complete monster. But he would wake up only having seen me, and my voice only made inaudible echoes in his mind.

It was hot, at least he was hot. He couldn't seem to feel comfortable in his sheets as he twisted around in them. He woke almost on the hour each hour and noted the time.

At 5:00 AM he decided to give up his attempts at sleep. He wanted to meet his grandmother out on their land and see what she wanted to show him. His stomach felt weakened, but not with fright, more with excitement than anything else. His last dream's image had been one of me, and I smiled at him.

He left the house in the early dawn hours before six to find her. The grass was moist and dewy as it always was that time of year. The chill in the air was only in the mid 50's but because of the humidity it felt much colder. He swept his dark brown mid-length waves of hair from his face and shuddered a little as he looked for signs that she was out there somewhere.

He heard her gentle murmur, out near the edge of the grass by where the underbrush of the woods marked its entrance. She was sitting on the fresh earth and speaking softly, saying prayers that Dominic didn't understand but knew were significant.

Opening her eyes slowly, she looked up at him and gestured for him to come over and join her.

"We're going to open a...small window," she said before he could ask her anything.

"Small window," he repeated, searching her face for more information.

"Small window into the other side. You see *mijo*, it takes so much of a person's energy to see into the other realm. You have what it takes, but you haven't tried it yet. What I want— what the guides are also saying to me—is that it is best to first show you what we want you to know. We want you to see what we see," she said with words that almost seemed trance-like.

"You mean Jessica," he felt his own anticipation rise in his voice.

"We have to see. You need to see, more importantly, so you can feel it," she said, this time more like herself and less trance-like.

He sat down with her, not questioning anything they were doing or where they were. He thought maybe they'd go somewhere deeper in the woods.

"What do I have to do?" he asked.

"What I have asked of the spirit guides with whom I always work is to help build your energy. You can only see what you allow yourself to see, whether you know it or not. So when we begin, you need to be fully prepared to see beyond what one normally sees—and I can't tell you how to do this, you have to feel it. It is different for each person," she emphasized strongly.

"Okay," he agreed, trying to hide his apprehension towards failure.

"I'm about to begin. We're going to look at the space between us and concentrate only on that space," she explained. He nodded in agreement.

"Focus all of your energy, feel it pull up from the earth and flow through each part of you until it needs to escape from your fingers and your eyes," she commanded.

He focused on her instructions, noticing the electric tingle that seemed to flow through him easily as they sat together, concentrating on the empty space between them.

"Slowly, lift your hands. We're going to hold our hands out to create the space we want our minds to enter," she explained.

He did as he was told. Between the two of them, only a couple of feet away from each other, he began to see his grandmother disappear in front of him. He lost his concentration as she faded from sight. Suddenly she snapped back into his vision field in clear focus.

"*Mijo*! Don't stop! Continue!" she demanded in a hushed irritation.

He shook away his fear and began centering his mind back on what she had told him to do. Just as she had before, his grandmother began to slowly dissolve into thin air before him.

This time, he noticed that the space where she had been was no longer empty or void of her presence; rather, they had created a screen of sorts. He could see into something—something not unlike a wormhole but not tunnel like either. It was a landscape slightly different from the one that surrounded them. He saw the beauty of it, the different greenery, the different fauna that scattered the landscape. He sensed he wasn't alone.

*Look deeper*, he heard a voice say. He wasn't sure if it was his grandmother or if it was someone else, but he concentrated his vision on the wave like screen that had been created out of thin air before him.

He saw himself as though he were in a movie. He saw his own face as he looked at me for the first time. He saw me, and he felt an immediate blood rush flow through him like burning opium through his veins, setting him into a euphoria that could only be explained by those who experience it firsthand.

He watched himself find the Saint Michael charm necklace in his box where he always kept it and bring it to me, giving it to me gently. He watched as he kissed me for the very first time, seeing that he had an unbridled passion for me that was something he was lacking in the world in which he now existed.

He watched me disappear into a blur of light in the woods, with the world around him shaking as though it had been hit with a sonic boom. He never realized what had hit him, only that he had come out of the woods with Emily knowing a completely different history than what had happened prior to that moment.

Last, he was shown me. It wasn't me in real time, as though I could see him through a mirror—but instead me in my state of timelessness with Nachmei. I sat on a mossy rock, able to lean comfortably on to it as though it was a chaise lounge almost. I was dressed loosely in the robes that Nachmei had provided me and my long blond hair flowed loosely down my shoulders and across my chest, framing my face gently in the strange dimness of light in which I had become accustomed to living. He watched me look up, my green eyes glistening. He caught his breath but forced himself to hold his concentration. He saw my solemnness, that I was distraught. He saw me reaching up to touch my collar bone, motioning to the area. He could tell I was looking at something—someone.

From the vantage point he had, he watched my eyes focus in on what I was seeing. Nachmei came up to me slowly. Dominic focused hard to see what this thing was that was approaching me. He recoiled a little—but stopped himself from losing his concentration.

"Who is that?" he murmured out loud to himself. He felt the strangest sensation. Trying to pinpoint it, he could only describe it as jealousy. He saw only the back of the man that stood in front of me—at least what looked like a man. Nachmei the monster knelt beside me—Dominic could see that much. He saw disgust on my face as I turned away from the man creature.

It grew dim—harder and harder to see. The face of his grandmother came back in to focus in front of him.

"Did you see what I saw?" he asked her.

"I did," she whispered back.

"What was it? Do you know?" he questioned her, desperate for answers. He felt a wave of exhaustion set in from the exertion it took to see what they saw.

"All I know is that is Jessica, and she's been there waiting. The being in the woods that has her wants to keep her because he knows what she is—what the both of you are. How do you feel, *mijo*?" she asked softly, reaching out to touch his hand gently.

"I feel—tired. Overwhelmed. I don't know what to feel," he said, his face drained and empty for a moment.

"What did you feel when you saw her?"

"Like I should be there. Like I should save her. She looked like a princess, but so...sad. I felt like she's mine, not his," he answered.

"Well, you have your Saint Michael back...that means something. It means you are ready to be rejoined," she said assuredly.

"I don't have all the answers I want—but I know I have to do this," he said.

"The answers will come. There are others—like I said. You aren't the first one to feel these things. Just be happy that you are able to know what you are. Some haven't had such luck."

He put his head in his hands, exasperated with not knowing what to do next. The answerless questions nagged at him like mosquito bites as he tried to filter everything out. "But what can I do for her now? How do I get to her?" he asked, his voice cracking a little.

"The same way that we saw into the world—it's the same way you go in," she answered matter-of-factly.

"I could have gone in then, right there."

"No. No, that was too small, too weak of a portal. It was all I could do to create for you to see into what exists beyond. But you are going to have some help getting her."

"Help? From who?"

"There are others in the forest, the duendes—that's the word I know. They exist—in between the here and there," she explained. He looked up, his interest piqued.

"They know what has happened because they have seen it all occur. There is one in particular. He is a forest creature, he communicates himself as Rau. He sent me a message, last night. He sent word that he had spoken with Jessica and that although she was unharmed, her spirit was damaged by being held by the monster— Nachmei he called him. He said that Nachmei is trying to force Jessica to stay with him and convince her that she is more powerful there with him than back here with you. He said she hadn't fallen for it completely but was very weakened by him, and that her state of isolation and loss of power had blinded her. She cannot see as much as she was able to see before she was taken there. He is afraid she's fallen into his complete control."

"What do you mean?"

"Ahh—I forget. You, my grandson, had built up a better ability to be in tune with the invisible around you in the other timeline. Here, without her presence, your female counterpart,

you haven't developed properly. Plus, with that negative one blocking you now...," she trailed off for a moment. "...in the other timeline, you both had developed nicely. She had begun to see spirits and other beings around that others could not see. You had the—excuse me—have the ability as well. But you feed off of one another, you see. You embody both of the male and female aspects of the archangel. You are both in one," she said in a hushed but exuberant whisper.

"Well, if I get her back?" he asked, raising his eyebrow inquisitively, almost daringly.

"Then both of your powers will be restored," she finished, nodding her head up and down.

"I want to do this," he said looking at her intensely. "Weli I want to do this as soon as I can. Can I do it now?"

"I want you to do it, too *mijo*, but you need to build up some of your abilities without her before you go to the other side," she cautioned, shaking her head slowly.

"What is that going to take? I want to start now."

"One thing is to clear your mind. You want to have those abilities back, you need a clear mind, a clear body, a clear soul. Start now. Take your shoes off and go for a run, a hard run, through those woods...with your mind concentrated on your intention. You need the intention to be that you are gaining your clarity and abilities. You'll see that it will come to you," she said fervently.

"Barefoot?" he asked curiously.

"Be one with the earth energy. You need to be as close to the energy of the world around you that you can be."

He shook his head in acknowledgement.

"Come back to me when you believe you have gained something." she said, "I will know when I see you back at the house. Don't worry, I'll tell your mother I sent you out there for Yaupon blossoms or something."

# CHAPTER 25

Dominic entered the woods, feeling the coolness of the late October air chill his skin. He began to trot down the trails, feeling the ground beneath his feet crunch as he moved. He didn't worry about hurting himself. He only thought of what his grandmother had told him to do.

He sped up to the point of running, feeling his body heat up underneath his clothing. He yanked his shirt off over his head and ran without it, wiping the sweat from his head with the cotton fabric. Running in the chilly air seemed to enhance the strength of his contracting muscles as he made his way through the overgrown trails, each part of him flexed and strong as he increased his speed.

He cleared his mind and thought only of gaining what he had lost. In his mind, he let the words See the other side, make me what I am, help me save her, over and over to himself.

He ran hard—to the point of pure exhaustion. He didn't want to stop, but he knew his body was losing water with his exertion. He listened hard for the trickle of the creek that he knew ran through the woods. He heard it further up and ran as hard as he could until he was at its edge.

Falling hard to his knees, he knelt before the water and heaved in breaths of air in and out. He leaned over the water and looked with amazement. What was normally murky mud water in those parts was crystal clear. He immediately dipped down and scooped up a mouthful of its clear flow, then splashed more onto his face and through his dark, long hair.

After he had taken in the water, he closed his eyes and repeated his mantra again and again, begging whatever power it was to help him.

"I can't do it alone," he said out loud. "Just help me... whoever you are. Archangel Michael, if that's what you are...I need you now," he said.

Leaning back over the water and peering into his own reflection, he was taken aback to notice someone standing behind him over his shoulder. He spun around quickly to face whatever had found him.

"Do not fear me," said the creature. He was short— elf like almost. That skin—that pasty looking skin—kept Dominic captivated. He couldn't tell if it was brown or grey; it seemed to shift in the light.

Dominic froze, waiting for it to speak to him again.

"You asked for help, this is part of it. I am called Rau. We have seen each other before, but you do not know that time. I am an intermediary of sorts. I know what you seek."

"You spoke to my grandmother," Dominic said, wide eyed.

"Yes. And now you are regaining your abilities, I can speak with you, too. You are the Dhakris, and you need your other counterpart. She knows that you are coming— but has no sense of time. For her, days are like years or minutes—there is no sense of time," his voice sounded so somber.

"What do I do?" Dominic asked.

"You've taken the first step...you can see me, hear me. Look around you, feel around you with your mind's eye. It is there, your ability. She is near, but not where you can sense her...yet," Rau said calmly.

"I feel like I need to do this fast," Dominic said, feeling like there was no time to be wasted.

"Your sense of urgency is understandable. But you must be prepared before you continue. Nachmei—what he is—is more powerful than you are now. If you were to step into that realm, I'm afraid you may never return. He is a jealous, vengeful creature. It would be a sad loss for this cycle, as there are many other callings for you in this timeline, in many timelines."

"What is he, this…Nachmei?" Dominic asked.

"He is many things to many cultures. He has been called a demon, a shadow person, a genie, a Djinn, a dark spirit…there are endless names to his existence. There are others like him. But he reigns here. Even I—as your intermediary—must avoid him at all costs. I took a large risk with my own existence in contacting Jessica. He is perilous when exposed for what he truly is."

Dominic nodded in understanding, gesturing for more information.

"In order to defeat him, you must match his power. When you have Jessica, your power will immediately double. Nachmei has been fighting for this not to occur for as long as he has existed. It is why he settled in these woods. But it is only recently in human history that he has felt much more threatened. He could ward off Native Americans, but the new generations, building all around him and closing in on his woods, without any understanding… he wants to remain where he is with no risk of exposure. He likes taking innocents for his own needs but will make things much worse if he feels threatened. The Dhakris is one of his only real mortal enemies—therefore if he possesses one half of a Dhakris, he feels he has won."

"What do I need to do?" Dominic felt like he had asked for the hundredth time.

"You need to learn how to fight like one of his kind," Rau explained, with an almost irritated tone.

"And how is that?" Dominic asked back, almost just as irritated.

"Energy fighting," Rau said bluntly.

"With weapons?" Dominic asked, becoming more irritated. Everyone seemed to expect him to already know everything.

"Energy is your weapon. You must learn how to manipulate it."

"Can my grandmother help me?"

"She knows of techniques. But after witnessing what happened to her in the alternate time line, it would be preferable if she is not involved," he said, lowering his eyes. Dominic understood what that meant. She had died trying to help him before and would probably do it again if she was allowed the chance. He stood up, looking down now at Rau.

"Continue to focus your mind. Come back tomorrow and see what you can do," Rau said, and he walked away into the woods, disappearing before Dominic's eyes.

"Wait!" Dominic shouted into the empty air. "Wait, come back! There's no time, no time for tomorrow!"

Even in the empty silence, he knew he had succeeded at something.

\* \* \* \*

"What took you so long, *mijo*!" Weli shouted as Dominic came back through the back door into the kitchen, barefoot and shirtless. His mother turned around from the stove and gasped at seeing her son so scantily clad in the chilly air.

"I don't know. But it was worth it," He said, moving past them and down the hall to the shower.

"That girl Emily came by—looking for you," he heard his mother's voice. He stopped in his tracks, bothered.

Walking back toward the kitchen he asked, "Emily?"

"Yes, she was worried, she said she hadn't heard from you in a few days and that you usually talked to her every day," his mother said, her eyes scolding him harsher than words ever could.

The look was nothing compared with the staunch disapproving glare that his grandmother shot in his direction. He knew that it was trouble. He had to stay away from Emily while he worked on finding me. Emily somehow was a negative energy towards him being successful, but neither he nor his grandmother fully understood why or how.

"Well if she comes by again, can you just tell her I'm visiting family or something?" he asked, turning away from them to go take a shower.

"I don't like you lying to girls Dominic, it's not how I raised you! And you're going to get sick running around outside without a shirt and shoes!" his mother shouted at him from the kitchen. He knew better about the first part, too. He wasn't the kind of person to hurt another, but something innate within him told him to avoid her at all costs—emotionally or any other way.

He stepped into the hot shower to wash the dirt from his body after his nature run, now feeling like he better understood why everything was happening the way it did. He could almost feel himself connecting with me, there in that hot shower. Like a daydream, he imagined what it would feel like to see me, even though he had never seen me before in his current timeline. He had such a burning feeling within him, one that couldn't be contained. He didn't want to sleep, didn't want to eat; he only wanted to find me.

* * * *

The following dawn, Dominic ran from the house in nothing more than jeans and this time having properly hydrated beforehand, to clear his mind with a hard run through the forest. He returned to the stream where he had last seen Rau.

Again, his body heaving for breath and moist with sweat, he leaned over the water, unmistakably clear and out of the ordinary. He put his lips right up to the stream, forgoing the use of his hand. He sipped up a gulp of water and rolled over onto his back by the water, lounging by its trickling whisper.

Closing his eyes, he spoke out loud to whoever was listening. "Help me...help me save her please. Help me find my powers. I need to save her and I don't know what I'm doing."

He lay by the water until his breathing had calmed to a steady in-and-out pace. He felt his body tingle with almost an electric feeling. He reached up and touched the charm around his neck. He had put it on before he had left the house that morning. He felt that if he had it around his neck, it made him closer to me somehow.

With his eyes still closed, he felt something else touch his forehead, right in the middle above the space in between his eyes. He opened them with a surprised gasp.

"Shhh...Dhakris boy!" the tiny figure hushed him. It was a being that looked a lot like Rau but more effeminate, almost...pretty. She was small like Rau, her skin had a bluish tint to it, but it didn't appear to be almost falling off as Rau's did. Her eyes were larger than human eyes and her hair was dark brown and dirty looking. She smiled, revealing a kind grin that would make anyone smile back. Dominic thought to himself that he must be hallucinating or that she was what people must have thought fairies looked like.

"Rau has sent me. I'm Kele."

"Why has he sent you?" he asked, still lying flat.

"You want to know how to defeat Nachmei...well I am knowledgeable with regard to that," she answered. He sat up to look at her. She wore the equivalent of the brown attire that Rau had worn but this revealed more of her skin, like a dress but short so that she could maneuver her legs and arms. Her skin glowed blue and greyish in the light of the early morning and she had dark blue hair pulled back tightly in a bun, almost making her look like she'd had a facelift. He nodded his head at her words while he studied her.

"I am a healer and a glass maker. I know and have seen many things between this world and the one which you wish to enter," Kele said.

"Why'd you touch my head like that?" he asked, feeling dizzy.

"I'm helping open up the third eye. You'll need your full awareness to be successful, and I don't do this for just anyone," she answered flirtingly, pulling something from a pouch as she spoke.

"Here, drink this," she said sweetly, handing him a small vile.

"What is it?"

"It's a cocktail to revive you for now, you'll need all of the energy you can muster for today's lesson. I make them myself and I make the vials," she said.

He drank the potion cautiously, worried about how it would affect him.

"Do not worry, Dhakris boy, it is made for you specifically. You will thank me later. The vials are just as important as the drink they contain," she explained busily, taking the empty vial back from him and placing it in her pouch.

"Thank you," he replied back, beginning to feel alert and in tune to everything around him.

"No need—I'm grateful to be able to work with a Dhakris—it is a very rare occurrence, you know," she replied.

"What is such a rare occurrence?"

"Firstly, the odds of the Dhakris successfully finding each other. If you find her and save her, all seven of you will be paired up simultaneously on this earth plane. That hardly ever happens. It can take many cycles for this to occur," she explained, gently sweeping her bare foot around her, forming a circle in the dirt.

"And, me being able to serve you is an honor. Our kind is here to serve," she said, gesturing with her hands for him to come closer to the circle she had created. "And I have to say, you make me wish I was the Dhakris." Dominic thought he saw her blush, if that were possible.

"We're going to revive some of your energy," she said, changing the subject and positioning him to stand in the center of her circle. She levitated herself off of the ground and floated up to his face.

"There has been much negative energy thwarted upon you in recent times. It has affected your own abilities. We must heal you, give you back your second sight," she said, taking Dominic's sharp jawline in her two small hands and pulling gently on his face. "It is true what they say about your eyes," she commented.

"What about them?" he asked.

"They're a—different kind of green. Very interesting, I wish I could make a vial with that color, but I don't think I could replicate it," she said as she rotated around him.

"Don't try to watch me now, you'll become dizzy. Simply close your eyes and feel my energy transferring into you," she instructed as she rotated faster and faster around him. He could feel the wind she was creating, but also a deep blast through his body. It began down at his bare feet and came up through the top of his head where she had touched him.

"You will feel this every time you begin to conjure what you need to use," she said. "Feel the way it feels."

Dominic nodded his head and let her complete her cycles around him. He could feel her come to a stop. He could see her come to a stop but knew that his eyes were closed. He could see with his eyes closed. He knew now what was all around him. He could smell the life of the forest, see it without seeing it.

"Now, open your eyes," she gently directed.

He stopped breathing. He could barely take in what was occurring around him. He had the vision of something else. He could see so much more. He could hear the colors and smell the sounds, he could sense everything. He could hear animals moving, smell them nearby. He looked around in wonder, amazed at everything he beheld all at once.

"This is only the beginning," she whispered to him in his ear. "You will do so much more," she said emphatically.

He began to feel a throbbing throughout his physical body that wasn't painful. It was a throbbing of energy — unbridled energy that wasn't just physically exerted, but mentally.

"What you are feeling is your true self coming to life.

You've got your sight back now — the way you had it before," said Kele in the same whispered voice. She backed away from him slowly and motioned toward him with her finger to come toward her.

"If you want it, come find it," she daunted as she turned and took off from him.

Startled, Dominic shook himself from the trance of energy and followed after her. She darted mischievously through the trees of the forest, up and down, faster than he could run. He had to run hard again, until he was breathing at a steady heavy pace. He felt that the breathing helped direct his energy as he ran.

She brought him to a standing halt in the middle forest clearing — the same clearing in which he had been hit in the face with the charm.

He stopped, breathing in deeply to control the air as sweat trickled down his bare chest in front of her. She hovered in the air in front of him.

"Did you ever wonder why nothing grows here?" she asked, lowering her hand and caressing the barren ground.

"I haven't ever given it any thought, no," he responded.

"Because this is the doorway. Most doorways can never fully grow this realm's greenery the way it grows elsewhere.

This is where you shall come—again—for you have been here before. Come tomorrow to the same place for your final lesson."

She turned from him and floated away slowly, just above the ground, dissipating into the woods from his sight.

Sweeping the hair out from his eyes as he looked around him, he took off running back the way they had come. He knew more and felt more now than he had previously ever experienced, but he knew he didn't know how to handle Nachmei—whatever he was. It would take a different lesson for that knowledge. He felt impatient, but he knew that he had to wait. He had no choice.

Dominic returned to the stream the next morning the same way he had for the last two days. Again, after a hard run, he felt completely exhilarated and open when he stopped to drink the water. Since meeting Kele, he had been able to tune in to the environment on a much deeper level. When he had gone home he had needed to sleep heavily to refresh himself, but he knew that his final day would yield amazing results.

Now, lying down on the chilly ground, he felt the air around him change, heard the slight vibration frequencies in the air alter themselves. He was in the presence of another who would normally be invisible to most.

"I know you're there," he said out loud with his eyes closed.

"I see that you are coming along," he heard a frail voice respond. Dominic wasn't sure what to expect upon opening his eyes. He sat up and looked around him, taken aback at the sight of the ghoulish figure before him.

It was another one of them, like Rau and Kele, a forest person. He was small, very old looking. His hair was white and grey, long and tattered at the ends. His blue skin was now grey and weak looking. The only thing that gave him vibrancy was the twinkle in his dark enlarged eyes. He still had quite the spark behind them.

"I am Moscha. I am an elder of my kind," he said, extending a frail hand up in a greeting. He stopped Dominic from introducing himself properly, waiving his hand in protest and distorting his face.

"I know who you are, Dhakris boy. You are ready this time. Last time, there were too many obstacles."

"Which time."

Moscha laughed. "That is a good question my boy! It is! You've come, as you know, as a reincarnated soul. I've been around long enough to know that the last time you came into a time cycle you lost your Dhakris completely. You had to come into another lifetime, just as you have now."

"So you weren't talking about the other timeline, the one where I already knew Jessica…."

"No, well, I suppose I could be talking about that, too—if you think of it that way. That time," he looked deeply into Dominic's eyes, "you are reconciling with in this time. It will all make sense soon, my boy," he explained with a kindness in his voice that wrapped around Dominic like a blanket. "Each time, these past two days, I know you've been impatient. But we've been charging you."

"Charging me?"

"With as much new energy and power as you could handle. If we'd done it your way, all at once, we might have fried you. It takes a lot of energy from us, too. You've done well to be patient," he said slowly.

"Okay, so I'm charged. So why did they send you? I was supposed to get my most difficult lesson today, to learn how to fight with energy...that's what Kele said," Dominic asked, beginning to feel the chill in the air.

"Oh, yes, yes, your lessons today will leave you fully prepared, you can rest assured of that my boy. But you must let go of any preexisting expectations to which you may be subconsciously clinging before we begin," he said with cunning in his eyes.

"I'm not thinking anything—I don't think," Dominic responded. Would this be a battle of wits or brawn he wondered. He felt as though he had a massive amount of energy that needed to be expelled, but he didn't know how to release it.

"Kele helped you feel what power is within you yesterday during your time with her, that second sight, so to speak," Moscha began. "But first, do you have any questions for me?" He took a seat across from Dominic on a tree limb that had been knocked over by a storm.

"Well, how old are you?" Dominic asked, wondering if it would come across as offensive.

"Old. That much is for sure. I've been an elder of my kind for as long as there have been warm conditions in this land. My kind, we came here with the ancestors of the ancestors of the Natives, as your kind calls them. But we have been around as long as man."

"How come no one ever acknowledges your existence?" Dominic asked.

"How do you know they don't?" replied Moscha.

"Well, no one has ever written about your kind or says anything about there being other human-like beings in the woods. I grew up running through these woods and I never, ever saw anything like your kind," Dominic countered.

"Maybe not in the timelines with which you are familiar—but there is much more to this complicated world than you know. But you will know. A Dhakris always does," he replied keenly with a nod.

"Well, if you've seen it all then, what is it all about?"Dominic asked.

"Ahhh...that is the age-old question, my boy. There's always the question of why? What is the purpose? Why are you the one and what is even to come of you being the Dhakris?"

"I've thought about that, but my grandmother always told me that I was one of them. She said it had been told to her that way."

"It is the same as your scientists asking why light can be both a particle and a wave at the same time. They don't truly understand how. But they must acknowledge that anomaly to continue their work," Moscha explained.

"I think you understand what I am telling you. There's more to everything and you're a large part of that. Your soul was created by the being known as the Archangel Michael. It and six others—long before my time. The seven souls contained the divine feminine and masculine oneness. He saw that within them, just like he is himself both masculine and feminine—as all archangels and beings of that nature are. He knew that in order for the souls to do their work among humanity they needed to take both forms. That is where the Dhakris began. He split them into their masculine and feminine forms, choosing to let their first birth and reincarnation occur through bloodlines and in completely different areas of civilization. He knew you would be needed all over the world."

"My grandmother always told me I was born during a hurricane and that was why I was one of them," Dominic said, feeling like he'd told that story before somehow, some way, like déjà vu.

"Indeed, my boy, many cultures have their secret legends of how the Dhakris comes about. It could be that you were born under a special sign, or that it was a coincidence of the forces that it happened that way. Either way, synchronicity is almost always at play in between the here and there, the timelines where you also exist," Moscha answered.

"When will I be ready?" Dominic asked him.

"You already are, my boy. It isn't that you ever weren't. You have been. But sometimes, it must be something that occurs to oneself before one realizes or understands that they are ready, an awakening, if you will," he said, straightening his posture.

"Am I supposed to kill Nachmei?" Dominic asked, feeling his blood pulsate stronger through his veins as he awaited the answer with anticipation.

"The Dhakris only kills when absolutely necessary. There are many forms of punishment that you can use to control your enemies. Death of a supernatural being can be complicated, as Nachmei's lifespan and mortality are much different than that to which you are accustomed. You will find that throughout time, there have been many different methods of banishing the evil beings from taunting humanity." He paused for a moment, letting silence set in uncomfortably. "Didn't you ever hear of genies in a bottle?"

"Well, yes."

"That in and of itself is a form of banishment. But once the genie is found it can be released to wreak more havoc, therefore creating more work for the Dhakris. But the cycle is not in vain, it is part of the greater cycle, that of which you are now becoming aware," Moscha explained.

"So, when it comes down to rescuing Jessica, there is no sure answer of what I need to do to him?" Dominic asked, shaking his head with confounded thoughts.

"My boy, you will know. You will just *know*. It is part of your second sight. And we, the forest beings, we will help however we can. As I have told you, we have been here for many, many Earth years. We were protected by our Native human peoples in this land for a long while until Nachmei rid them of this land. We stayed only to protect others who might cross his path. We do what we can. That is why we are blessed to have the opportunity to assist the Dhakris. We've needed you for some time."

"Why does he look human? My grandmother worked with me to show me the other side, and I saw Nachmei."

"Yes, I do know of this. She is a powerful woman in her own right. Nachmei can look like whatever he wants to look like. To Jessica, he shows himself as a powerful and attractive being, hoping to will her to stay and make alliances with him. To others, he can appear as pure evil, hideous in the most grotesque of ways. He can change himself into a serpent, a dog, a shadow that plays with light—whatever he chooses. Most often he chooses the dark owl."

"And me, what can I be?"

"Excellent question, my boy. You will grow with time to see your abilities. For now, be only the Dhakris. You can be successful with the knowledge you are gaining now."

Dominic felt thwarted by the lack of information in the last response. "What if I'm not successful? Then what happens?"

Moscha nodded his head in acknowledgement of what Dominic was asking. "Then you will either wait for another life cycle or you will watch Jessica make alliances with Nachmei, destroying your existence in all timelines until she is free. It is a trying situation—this one—though not impossible to resolve."

Dominic sat still, absorbing all of the information he was obtaining. It would have been overwhelming if it wasn't all making so much sense to him. It was as if pieces of an infinite puzzle were falling into place and he could understand more now than he ever had before. The odd sense of déjà vu hadn't left him and he knew that the other timeline was there, surrounding him and awaiting his arrival.

"Have you any more questions, my boy?" Moscha asked kindly.

Dominic sat pensively for a moment, looking down at the ground. He started shaking his head to motion to the negative.

"No, no I don't think so. So, what's the lesson?"

"Then the lesson is finished. Go forth, my boy. We and all of the positive beings will be with you," he said feebly.

Dominic watched as Moscha stood slowly and crept back into the dark brush of the forest, disappearing from his view.

The energy that he felt upon Moscha leaving was almost painful to contain. He knew that he had to do something to quell it.

As Dominic stood in the forest, alone with his sharp abilities to perceive the tiny animals around him, he swung around at the sound of a rustle. A jolt of electric shock slung from his left arm, hitting the ground.

"What the hell," he said to himself. He felt a relief at the purge of the energy. He whipped his arm again, but nothing happened. There was something about the feeling, the feeling of fear, or of excitement, or anything that got his adrenaline going that made the difference. Wondering if it had been a squirrel or possibly something more dangerous like a hog, Dominic repeated the motion. This time, the electricity stayed with him, down his left arm.

He focused on it hard as it began to shape itself into the form of a sword, a long sword. The light from the electricity began turning green. He could see it now, perfectly clear, and in his hand. He swung it, hitting some greenery from a tree. The leaves disintegrated instantaneously in front of him.

"Don't use that thing so frivolously," a tiny voice spoke from behind the leaves.

"Kele, is that you?"

She revealed herself from behind one of the larger trees.

"I had to come see what you could do after visiting with Moscha. You know, it isn't just his words that are important. He radiates a certain—power. When you are in his presence, you gain wisdom and strength that you do not even realize. He just charged your entire being up thoroughly. He is kept separate from the others for that reason. Not everyone can be in his presence without him accidently harming them. Moscha is our elder, but he is so precious to us that he must be protected, and we all do our part to ensure his well-being. We keep him in a cavern of black tourmaline so that he is safe and his power stays within him. Believe me, he may have seemed innocent and mundane, but you being able to wield your weapon now, that is his doing. Go forth without forgetting this. You have what you need now, sweet Dhakris boy. She waits."

"Wait, Kele," Dominic stumbled forward after her. His sword had diminished, but his sharp intuition told him that she had answered any questions he may have had, other than where he was supposed to go to find me.

\* \* \* \*

"Boo!"

Dominic was surprised to open the door and hear such a greeting. It was Emily. She'd found him.

"Hey," he said unavoidably, standing in the doorway to block her entrance. It had already been dark when he arrived home from the forest, but it wasn't that late yet.

"I know you said you needed some time, but it's Halloween!

I thought maybe we could go out, take a breather from everything. Have some fun?" She persuaded, batting her long, overly fake eyelashes.

"I don't know, Em. I've got Weli here, I just don't think I can," he dissuaded. He hadn't even realized what day it was. Everything had kept him so preoccupied.

"Really? You can't leave for an hour? I think it would be good for you," she coaxed, yanking his sleeve.

He thought of what his grandmother and the others had said to him. It didn't seem right—but she had such pleading grey eyes. She was lonely. She had relied on him for company for so long, what sort of person would he be if he just shut her out?

"I can't Emily. I just can't. I'll see you—later," hesitant with his words.

Her face twisted with hurt. He knew she didn't understand.

She wouldn't understand. She wasn't the kind of person that could understand rejection.

"Fine," she retorted with a shaky voice. "But you don't know what you're gonna miss," she said, walking back toward her car, her revealing costume showing her legs in the dim light.

She stopped and turned to walk back, just as he was trying to close the door.

"Just be honest with me, Dominic. Is there someone else?"

"What?" He was taken aback by the accusation. He hadn't had any time away from her or for himself, let alone time to find a different girl. And why would he want to? He had enough on his plate.

"You're pushing me away, and I don't get to see you, to go in your house...this is what happens to girls when there's someone else," she said through tightly clenched teeth.

"Emily, I'm not interested in anyone else. I've spent all my extra time with you and you know that. I've tried to help you find Jessica…," his voice weakened as he said my name. Emily had no clue what was happening in reality.

"It's just so stupid, Dominic. You make me think that you want me. Then you turn around and push me away. You're a dick," she said, looking down away from his eyes.

"I have never tried to mislead you in any way. All I have ever done is try and be there for you—be a real friend. Something you obviously don't understand," he fired back harshly.

"Well, I fell *in love* with you, Dominic. You happen to be all I can think about. I guess you don't feel the same way, but now you know where I stand. So fine, this is how it's going to be. I'll leave you alone. But I hope you know what you've done," her tone was very stinging, very powerful.

"What I've done?" he asked, shaking his head. She had gone from one end of the spectrum to another. She was blaming him now? He just didn't understand. He watched as she stormed off back toward her car, looking over her shoulder shooting daggers through her eyes.

He closed the door gently, leaning up against it as it clicked shut. She was upset, she was furious. But there was no way he could explain to her everything. It was too much. He never had cared about Halloween anyway, not even being interested in the occult had ever made him have an interest in the festivities of Halloween. He didn't know what she had in mind for him leaving for an hour. It took at least fifteen minutes to get anywhere down the country roads anyway. Maybe she would meet up with friends, her friends from the meetings. Surely there was someone out there to keep her company for the night.

A voice broke his pensiveness. "That girl keeps coming back. I saw that look she gave you."

Dominic turned to see Weli standing in the doorway of the back door to their kitchen.

"I know Weli. I spent a lot of time with her before. Believe me, I wish I hadn't."

"Big mistake. Stupid, I'm sorry to have to say it," she said, casually sipping tea from a mug.

"I know that now. I don't know what I'm going to do with her. What is she going to do if she sees that I rescued her sister and now need to spend time with Jessica and not her?"

"It has been nagging at me, *mijo*. I'm not sure exactly what. I told you, I can't see exactly the things that are going to occur. But I do know that because of that, there will be a paradox of sorts created. You need to be careful," she warned, taking another casual sip that juxtaposed her seriousness.

"I'll be as careful as I can, I guess," he said, unsure of what exactly she expected him to do. He walked slowly to his bedroom where he attempted to rest. It was going to be a long night, that much was for sure.

# CHAPTER 26

Dominic's eyes flashed open and his heart beat fluttered with adrenaline. He looked at the clock beside his bed.

The clock read 3:07. The witching hour, he said to himself.

*Now is as good of a time as any*, he thought. He got up out of bed and prepared to leave for the woods. It was November 1st, All Saints Day.

Leaving his silent house behind, he knew that his grandmother would know where he had gone once she saw his empty bed. He brought nothing with him but the knowledge that he had gained in the last three days.

Running through the woods, he felt the heat rise through his body as the chill wore off around him. He searched in the moonlight for the clearing. He knew where it was and remembered what Kele had said about it. It was time to enter through it.

He stopped at what he perceived to be the center of the circular clearing in the moonlit woods. The sound of crickets stopped, the rustling of the breeze in the trees halted. Everything seemed to be frozen except for him.

When he first began to see the portal, it appeared as heat rising from the metal of a car on a summer day, waving and creating the appearance of a mirage. He knew that once he stepped in, there was no turning back. He approached it without heed to caution; he knew he would find me through it.

Upon his entering my realm, I felt it in the waves of my existence begin to shift. Something all around me changed. The cyphs had come back to me. I could feel the electricity running through my veins. It has been so long since I had felt them. It was like knowing someone was in the room with you with your eyes closed, sometimes you can just hear it.

I opened my eyes. They had been closed for some time, but I wasn't asleep. I felt that I had been though, and I felt my body ache terribly in all of the strangest places. I hadn't been moving enough, I was resting, I was in limbo, I was dead to the world that knew me. I had been only thinking of what Rau had told me was going to happen and trying to imagine all of the different possibilities.

There was something else different about me, too. I felt like I had actually been missing time, even though there was no time, so to speak. I had this strange feeling that I had been out, completely out, for a long while. I tried to move, but pain struck me down, and the heaviness of my chains of diamonds made me feel trapped.

Eyes wide open with awareness now, I could feel the forces begin to change. Where was Nachmei? I feared for Dominic. I knew Nachmei was powerful, but I didn't know what his full capabilities were. I looked around me, feeling the pull of something different in the stale air. Each direction seemed to tug at me to run, but to where I had no clue.

Dominic was slightly surprised at the sudden onset of light as he entered the dim lit netherworld where I was being kept. His sight keen and his senses on overload, he felt the plexus of his body pull him toward where he felt I might be. He looked behind him, noting each detail around him to recall exactly where he would need to bring me to pull me back through to the other side.

The strangest sensations began to pop through my body. It was like electric crackling in the air. I was beginning to feel stronger, more like my formal self, not so much like a cold statue that existed like a ghost. I could feel the blood in my veins stir at a different rate. He was near me.

Dominic pushed forth through the different plants and growth that existed in the in-between world. He could feel his heart rate change, he was close and he knew it.

I heard the softest rustle. I feared Nachmei had come to stop me. I turned to face whatever it was. Maybe it was only Rau. Maybe this was what Rau had set in place to happen, although it was different from the ways I imagined it.

"Jessica," I heard a soft, breathless whisper. I turned around and met the same green eyes which I also possessed. It was Dominic. He had found me.

Without words I jumped at him, holding him as tight as I could grasp him. I felt myself melt into what finally felt like skin. I felt alive, truly alive. He held my face and looked in my eyes. Finally, finally at last. It was real and I wasn't dead. He was there for me. I kissed him the way I remembered kissing him the first time. I felt the world tilt and spin around me.

He heaved with heavy breath from his journey to find me. I felt how cold his skin was, but it was alive with the sweat from his plight. My blood began to pulsate strongly through me as if it had only been a trickling current and was now a raging river.

"You're alive," he whispered, his face touching mine and his hands on my head as though he needed to feel that I was real. Without another word, he leaned in to hold me up against him. He touched me, holding my hands and examining my rings and all of the adornments on my body.

"What is all of this?" I said playfully, "It's in style here." My joke landed empty as he stared in awe. "Don't worry about any of it, it doesn't matter. Only you being here matters, I said, and I started removing the ringsand the chains and all of the adornments I was wrapped in so that I could hold onto him.

Our long awaited embrace created an onset of powerful visions. Suddenly both of our minds were inundated with the happenings of both of our timelines and experiences. Without words between one another, we saw everything. Every single experience merged together to the point where we both understood why we were there and what had happened to each of us. Dominic flinched, and I feared he saw what I had done. But he didn't say a word.

Dominic saw that I had seen him with Emily and had been made to think that he had been with her intimately and shook in my arms. I saw that it had never happened the way that I thought it had and I clung to him tighter, all the while never parting our lips.

I saw that his grandmother was still alive, not dead from the wrath of evil that surrounded us, and tears escaped the corners of my eyes for the first time since I had been there. I scolded myself in my mind for having doubted for a second that what we had was real.

He saw that in the other timeline he had given me Saint Michael as a gift and that he had kissed me, falling in love with me since the moment our eyes had met. He knew that Emily had entered into this strange world originally and that we had given our best to get her out— crossing the timelines into what they were now.

I could see that he had become stronger, more in tune and more than I had even imagined was possible. I could tell there was more, but each moment was becoming more precious and I could feel that we needed to escape. After all of the visions stopped to the point where we were now, we knew we had to go.

"I came from this way, I think it leads back to the portal," he whispered and pulled my hand to lead me out. My second sight was coming back stronger, slowly. At each moment that we touched I fed off of his abilities to regain those of my own. My cyphs were coming on stronger. But now, instead of bothering me, they gave me more energy.

We ran, the ground under our bare feet barely registering to our senses, speeding up as fast as we could go to escape. He pulled me down the path he had followed to find me. The fog that always surrounded us thickened. It looked more like what I was used to—a thick foggy forest from which I could not escape. I could feel the heat of the portal approaching, its electromagnetic waves registering at a frequency that our ears could now hear with our abilities to sense the other world. The high pitch screamed in our ears as he led me to it. I couldn't believe it was happening so quickly. We were there, I could see it. How had I not been able to do this on my own since I had become a prisoner here? He must have taken everything from me.

Grasping hands tightly, Dominic yanked me and we leapt through the illuminated screen of heat in front of us. Landing hard on the ground on the other side, I could see that it was dark, very late at night.

"It has to be the next day already—the Day of the Dead, "

Dominic said, considering how time passed on the normal plane of existence in comparison with that of the in between world. He took my hands and pulled me from the ground, noting with his eyes my white cloth robes I was wearing.

"Also in style here," I joked again, this time getting a smile.

"You think you're pretty clever, don't you?"

Dominic looked at me, and I looked back at him. The voice had come from neither of us.

"Pretty easy to leave my world and come back into this one, didn't you think? Did you really think it would be that easy? Jessica, you made a deal with me. You gave me yourself for your sister," Nachmei appeared before us, as a man, but much taller and larger than a normal man—much more domineering than he had made himself appear to me.

"These woods are mine, and you are mine now, too," he said, stepping casually towards us, reminding me of all of my foolish sacrifices.

"The deal's off. This is a different timeline," Dominic retorted, stepping up to Nachmei but not letting go of my hand. I could feel the electricity in the air start to build, like feeling a thunderstorm begin to electrify the sky. I was nervous, we were very close to the portal and I worried he could pull us both back through.

"And what do you expect to happen? Do you want to fight me, Dhakris man? You are but a mere human, regardless of the maker of your soul. You weren't given a different anatomy," Nachmei mocked.

"No, but I was given a partner," he said, pulling me to his side and standing shoulder to shoulder with me to face him. "And together, we're one. One that is stronger than you."

"She's mine now. She gave herself to me. Furthermore, I can give her things you'd never imagine even existing. She's much better off with me, you are useless to her now."

"Don't listen to him, Dominic," I whispered.

"Concentrate on the intent of defeating him," Dominic whispered over to me. We glared at him with our eyes, focusing on weakening him.

He seemed to appear smaller before us, just slightly, not as grand as he had at first. I heard a clink down at my foot. It was a strange sound, like a glass bottle, but I didn't want to take my eyes from Nachmei and let him regain any strength.

"Get it," I told Dominic, nudging him toward the sound,

"I've got this," he swept his hand down quickly and picked up the tiny vial. It was a glass vial of vibrant colors with a tight, flip-top cap held in place with a latch. It contained beautiful blue colors that glowed from thereflection on the glass. I had never seen anything quite like it before. I glanced toward the direction from which it had come, sensing a gentle presence.

"Kele," Dominic said. "She's giving it to us to use, "

I unlatched the top off of it and held it open. The aroma coming from within it intoxicated my senses. It was energizing and I could feel that whatever was in it had been charged with extra energy to help us.

Nachmei looked at it with a short glance. He knew what it was as well.

"Damn those creatures. I should have killed them all."

"You'll never be able to harm them. You don't have as much power as you think, monster," I said, looking at Dominic hold the bottle out towards him.

"Monster?" he laughed as he retorted. "You didn't think me a monster when you let me take your body and…"

"Shut up, monster!" I screamed. I didn't want him to say another word. I knew what I had done was bad enough and I didn't need him making me feel any worse than I already did.

"Get him in it!" Dominic screamed. The wind and static noise seemed to swirl around us. Nachmei was ready to fight. He disappeared before our eyes.

"Is he? No—no he's not—where…?" My questions and voice were cut off short as I saw an unnaturally large black panther leap onto the ground from the trees, landing before us and ready to pounce.

"He can change…into anything he wants to be," Dominic explained. "We have to get him, his essence, into this bottle. It was made for that purpose…."

"I know him," I said quietly, my eyes wide with anxiety. "I know what he can do, I've seen it."

We began a dance that only evil knows. Circulating around one another, we stepped at a rhythmic pace, waiting to see who would take the first chance. I looked at Nachmei in his cat eyes. They were still his eyes, sapphire and glowing. Dominic didn't remove his eyes from Nachmei either. We stepped backward, round and round, slower and slower. I could feel tension mount.

For a moment, we were all frozen. There was no time, there was no sound—it was only the three of us. I could feel my energy burning within me, ready to explode. I heard Dominic in my mind. Not yet, he said. Wait until he moves.

Knowing that Nachmei was able to read thoughts, I worried for a moment that he could infiltrate our heads. It broke my concentration, I glanced away from his sinister glare to the woods around me, for a brief moment I was able to see the crowd that had gathered. It was the others, they came to watch. We weren't just doing this for us, but for them as well. Their existence was constantly under siege because of Nachmei. They needed us to take him down.

That brief moment of distraction was everything it shouldn't have been. Nachmei pounced at that moment, digging into Dominic with his claws. Dominic moved quickly enough so that he wasn't penetrated, but he was scratched along his side. Nachmei was fast, he could win. I couldn't let that happen—no, I couldn't let him win. I grasped the bottle tightly in my hand and leapt toward the giant cat as he prepared to lung at Dominic. I tackled him and rolled with his massive fur body. His weight took the breath from me as we tumbled. I slid away from him as fast as I could. I couldn't get on my feet fast enough. He swiped at me, cutting into my shoulder with his long claws and leaving a gaping would, flesh hanging from my left arm. It burned and I immediately felt dizzy. Adrenaline kept me going. Dominic, injured but still moving, helped me to my feet as quickly as he could.

Nachmei prepared himself to pounce on us again, this time I didn't know if I could handle another injury. If he couldn't have what he wanted, if a deal couldn't be made, then he wanted me to die.

*At least if I die, I did what I could to save everyone*, I thought. Dominic heard the thoughts.

*No! God, no. I can't go through this again. Without you, I'm half, only half. You're sentencing me to death*, he said.

*Swords*, I said in my mind.

We drudged up our electricity, bloodied and weak. From our arms and out through our fingers, we manifested our glowing jade blades.

Nachmei made his move. He lunged toward us with an immense power and speed. I felt a push from the plexus of my gut, almost a visceral power. I didn't move away from him. I slashed my blade at him, taking strong strides forward to attack. The blade sliced into him with a voltage that would kill an average man, knocking him to the ground. The smell of fried hair filled the air.

Dominic circled around him and approached from behind, wielding his jade blade above him like an axe, and smashing it down onto him, cutting into him deep. Sparks flew as he lifted his blade and smashed him again. He cut through Nachmei again, making his animal form howl in pain. He still wasn't dead.

"Why won't he disintegrate?" Dominic screamed.

"He's powerful, he's much more powerful than anything we've dealt with," I explained with huffed breaths over the roaring sound of our powers. "We have to get him into this bottle," I grunted through difficult breaths. My arm was a gruesome sight and it was slowing me down.

Still holding the bottle, I tossed it underhand to Dominic, then I collapsed to the ground out of weakness. Still conscious, I watched as Dominic caught the bottle and I motioned for him to hold it up. He tried to come to me, but Nachmei began changing forms again into that of a large man, and Dominic ran straight toward him, cutting at him with his sword to stop him. We had lessened his ability.

Nachmei's injuries restricted his ability to completely transform. He was stuck between a man and a panther, giving him the appearance of a centaur except he had the legs of a large cat. His breath was now coming in rasps, but his dark eyes still shown with a desire to destroy us.

I dragged myself with my right arm and my legs over to Dominic, clawing at the dirt for support, filling my fingernails with earth and feeling them bend backwards as I felt my energy dwindle. I was fading in and out, thinking of how wrong it was all going.

"Together," I shouted breathlessly. "Command him into the bottle."

With heaving breaths, I pulled myself up to a crouched position and reared my right arm back, then thrust it forward towards him as if I was throwing a javelin. From my hand came a long whip of electric current that struck Nachmei and held him in place. Like an animal being tased, he fought it with strength that I couldn't contain for much longer. My left arm had lost feeling and I felt my loss of blood making me dizzy. The voices of the duendes in the forest buzzed in my ears. There was excitement and rustling all around me and I felt everything begin to spin.

Dominic looked at me and knew I was fading. The strength I had couldn't hold him much longer.

"Throw the bottle," I grunted. "Throw it out near him."

Dominic looked at with worry but did as I said. He tossed it near Nachmei.

"Lead him into it, with the…" I tried to finish talking but I needed all of my strength to hold the current.

In my head I said, *Do what I'm doing*.

He knew, whipping his arm out and with a much stronger current, creating a line of voltage, sparking and popping, that assisted my weak one in holding Nachmei in place.

From my knees, bloodied and battered all around, I held out my good arm and directed the current flowing from it, as did Dominic. Nachmei as he clawed, hissed and fought our electric grip, but he was unable to control our ability to move him.

"Visualize shrinking him," Dominic commanded, and I focused only on watching Nachmei try to scramble away as became smaller and smaller. His half man, half animal form began to wither and writhe like a snake as it turned to an almost vapor form. The bottle in front of him began to glow.

Like a roaring wind during a tornado, everything around us seemed to spin and blow. My hair billowed in a wild, electrical frenzy as I gave the last of my energy to vaporizing Nachmei into the bottle. Dominic jumped toward it and flipped the cap over to seal the opening.

I let myself fully collapse. I couldn't do anything else. I tried to sit up but felt the restraint of my body's failure keep me locked down in a pool of my own blood.

"Kele!" Dominic screamed desperately. "Kele I need you!"

He scooped me up into his arms and laid me down on the soft ground and ripped a piece of my robe to make a tourniquet at the top of my shoulder.

"That will stop some of the bleeding," he said gently, holding me in one arm and the vial in his other. My vision faded in and out. Everything became quiet.

"Open your eyes," said a voice coming from a small face that hovered above me, my vision focusing more clearly. Her soft bluish hands waved over me as though her whole being was a wand.

"Thank you, for what you did for us," said Dominic as she worked.

"There is no need to thank me. I had been working on that vial for quite some time. It only needed the right forces to make it work. It was made for the purpose for which it wasused," she said assuredly as she worked over me. Never once did she touch me, but I could feel my wound tingling without pain as she worked.

"Will she be alright?" Dominic asked, stroking my hair and my cheek.

"I'm fine, I feel fine, I'll be fine," I said softly, but I didn't know for sure what was happening to me.

"She will be fine. I am healing this wound. You will someday learn to do the same," she said. "I will take care of your cuts as well."

Grateful, but weak, I watched as she erased my wounds from my body.

"It's gone, it's gone!" Dominic exclaimed. Just as fast as Nachmei had ripped through my flesh, Kele had healed it. There was no sign of scaring, but I could feel the tingle of where my nerves had been torn. I could move my arm and my fingers with no pain, as if nothing had ever happened. Blood drenched the white robes I still wore. Dominic lifted me up into his arms and kissed me, but for the first time, making me feel more alive than ever before. He held me tight as Kele hovered in front of us gentlyand worked on closing his wounds. I knew then that I would have waited until the end of time to feel that moment.

"I thought we lost everything," I whispered, clinging to him as tightly as possible.

"No, no it has only just begun," he whispered back, his warm breath bringing me back to life. I leaned into him and let myself feel comfort. He was my home.

Kele looked up from Dominic's side, her dark eyes widening with fear. She looked past us, just behind where we were and sputtered with a whimper, "They saw."

# PART V

# THE AWAKENING

# CHAPTER 27

"You!" I heard Emily scream. She was mortified to see me, as if she was looking at a ghost and her mortal enemy at the same time.

"You had her here? No, wait, you're—you've been with her this whole time? You knew where she was, and you've been with her and that's why you couldn't be with me?" Emily's words were spouting out of her confused mouth with twisted anger. Her raging jealousy masked any happiness she had to see me alive. In her mind I had now betrayed her in the worst way.

I stood still, like the statue I had almost become in the middle world. I looked at her as she glared at me with hatred.

"Emily, I know you have no way of knowing what happened…"

"Dominic!" She screamed, closing her eyes and taking in a choked breath, "Say that I'm not seeing what I'm seeing…say you remember that we had…something…," she said, fumbling her words. Her face was wrought with betrayal and an uncanny sense of evil.

From behind her emerged Vanek, tall, blonde and his blue eyes just as clear and frightening as ever, he was very much alive in front of me.

"He's not dead in this timeline," I whispered, gripping Dominic's shoulder.

"No, I'm not. I'm very much alive and well, thank you," he said with a cunning smile. "But nice work, before. You were stronger than you thought, weren't you?"

Emily looked up at him, with a sense of satisfaction in her eyes. Her hurt was covered up by the look she gave him. Her eyes said something else. Dominic and I both felt the unease of what was happening. Vanek slid his hand around her waist, giving her a tug towards him.

"You don't have to hurt for him, Emily," Vanek said.

I was filled with a fury of mixed emotions. There she was, my Emily. I had traded my own life for hers and she hated me. She hated me because she loved Dominic. Some people were just that way, I realized. She was an obsessive lover. It's what got her lost in our first timeline and now what was causing her such anguish in this one. She didn't care that I had returned and had no way of knowing or believing that I'd given myself and my own happiness for her before. There was no way to make her see it—at least not now. She was lost.

"I'd like my creator back," Vanek said, gesturing towards the vial Dominic clasped tightly.

"It can't happen. It's over, Vanek," Dominic said. "I always knew there was something off with you."

"What, that I was not fully human? How'd you guess, that you just couldn't figure out how I was so powerful in the meetings, how I knew everything I knew? How I was just more intelligent than you and everyone else?"

"You always shuffled those cards," I said.

"Oh, perceptive one, aren't you?" he said, glaring at us. He turned to Emily. "You must be very confused by all of this."

"My sister's been hiding and has stolen the man I loved," she snarled, grabbing her head in fury. "So, no, I'm not confused. I just don't know why you'd want to hurt everyone like this Jessica, especially me. And Dominic, what a phony. You're the fakest fucking person. You really had me. And what the hell is that? You gave her a ring?"

I glanced down at my hands. I had forgotten to take one off. A large diamond that would rival any engagement ring sparkled on my pinky finger.

"Emily, he didn't give that to me, I've been trapped...," I said, trying to slide it off.

Dominic was nearly speechless, his eyes said it all. Knowing his other timeline history with me, he couldn't think of anything to say to her that would quell her anger. "It was never like that," was his only response. I didn't want him to say anything else to her. It would have been pointless. She was blinded by rage.

"Shut up, both of you. You both are dead to me. You're dead," she roared.

The tension was mounting. I could see Vanek glaring at the vial. He knew what to do with it—how to get his maker back. If Nachmei was released, there was no telling what wrath he would bring with him. I imagined the destruction he could cause if unleashed.

"Emily...," I said, almost helplessly and most definitely uselessly, "I did this to save you. Dominic and I did this to save you. All of this is for you! You want the ring?" I pulled it off, finally, and tossed it at her feet. "Take it! It's nothing to me because it came from something horrible."

She sneered at it and looked back at me. "What? You little liar. You took him from me!" she screeched through clenched teeth.

"What about Jeremy? Jeremy Mullins, was it?" I asked, provoking her.

"Who?" she asked.

"Jeremy, the first one who you came out here for—the one you made a deal with your little devil for—so you could be with him," I said calmly.

"I don't know what you're talking about—but soon enough everyone's gonna know you've been hiding out here making everyone think you were gone all along," she sneered back.

Vanek looked back at Emily. "You want them to feel how it feels?"

"Yes," Emily sneered.

"They will," Vanek said. With that, he charged at us quickly, almost inhuman like. Kele's voice came in to our head. Run and take it far away. You will need to take it to where the others are kept.

We ran as hard as we could, leaping over branches and whipping past vines. Vanek trailed us closely. I could feel his presence nearing me with a coldness that was unnatural, and Emily was not much further behind. We were about two miles deep into the woods. Brambles and bushes flew by us as we ran faster than I could have imagined running normally. Kele and the forest beings made their own attempts to thwart Vanek, tripping him with branches and scraping him with twigs as he charged after us, all the while clearing what they could in our path to help us.

We began to see the clearing and I could see the dim light of dawn emerging through the thin trunks of the trees and brush as we came out on the other side.

"Get in now!" screamed Weli. She had Dominic's truck parked right at the edge of the clearing from where we were emerging with the passenger door open. Inside sat two recognizable faces. It was Brisen and her sidekick Keagan.

Keagan drove the truck out and down the rocky driveway, leaving Vanek and Emily heaving in the dust. I turned and looked out of the back window, panting for air. I watched them fade out of our sight, still in pursuit.

"Weli!" Dominic gasped breathlessly. "I was worried he got her again." He looked back at her longingly, and she faded into the distance as they drove away. He turned to Brisen. "Will she be alright without us?"

"She'll be fine," Brisen said calmly. "I've cast a binding over Emily and a protection over your grandmother. Emily and Vanek didn't even see her. What happened in the past won't happen again this time."

"How did we outrun him?" I asked.

"You're much faster than you think," Brisen said, staring straight ahead and not looking at us as she spoke.

Keagan sped rapidly down country roads lined with heavy thickets of East Texas and I worried a little about the curves and the turns.

"Don't worry about his driving," Brisen said, turning her head to face me with a coy smile. "He's been around long enough to know how to handle things."

I could tell he was driving the truck south. Weli had left fresh clothing in the truck and I changed clothes mindlessly in the cramped cab, not worrying about anyone seeing me but hurrying to feel the feeling of normalcy envelop me. I needed to get out of the blood-stained mess I was wearing. Dominic did the same, trying not to hit the gear shift in the front as we wiggled and moved. The jeans were a little big on me, but I was happy to have them, anything that reminded me of being back in my own world. She'd packed me one of Dominic's old T shirts and it clung to me like a soft familiar blanket, the smell of it giving me immediate comfort. He reached down into the pocket of his dirty crumpled jeans and pulled something out. He took my hand slowly and slipped the necklace into it.

"You found it?" I exclaimed. I thought I'd never see it again after Nachmei threw it into the ether."

"It found me," he replied, pointing to the scratch on his cheek. "I thought you might want to have it back."

"I remember the first time you gave it to me," I sighed, reliving the memory.

He leaned over gently and kissed me, making my every atom light up and spin like I was about to explode. It was even more intoxicating than the first time.

"Listen," Brisen interrupted, keeping an eye on the road head of us as she spoke, "this pursuit isn't over and it won't be for some time. We have to place that bottle in one of the safe houses."

We looked down at the vial.

"It wasn't as hard as I thought it would be," I said, referring to trapping him, not being attacked.

"Besides the fact that you almost let him rip your arm off, you're right. That is because of what everyone has been telling you both all along. You are extremely powerful together. That is why you are what you are and there are only seven pairs in existence. You understand now?" She looked at us, flashing a spark of purple in her eyes. It was off-putting to me. Something was off.

"Yes," we said in unison.

"To your family, you are still missing Jessica. You're gone to them just the way you have been for some time now in this timeline. They do not know you are back and will not believe Emily if she tries to tell them."

"Will she try and tell them?" I asked.

"I don't know, but Vanek being a servitor will only want to serve and help his creator. They could be communicating somehow right now for all we know. We know much information, but we don't know every single thing," she said calmly.

"Will they try and find us and the vial?" Dominic asked.

"They will, yes of course," she answered. "Thus, the need of my help for you to escape."

"Escape?" I asked? Dominic looked confused as well.

\* \* \* \*

I awoke to see the first shimmers of the sunrise at dawn as we drove down a road facing East somewhere along the Gulf of Mexico. I could feel that I felt actually rested, finally.

"Where are we?" I looked around for landmarks.

"We've come down the coast," Keagan answered.

I looked over at Dominic. He was sleeping softly and I didn't want him to wake up.

"Why are we here now?" I knew we needed to put the vial somewhere with others.

"There is a beach temple, not far from here," Brisen replied in her melodic yet mysterious voice.

I didn't question her source of information. I nodded to her that I understood what she was saying.

"Boca Chica," She whispered, pointing ahead on the road to where we were fast approaching. "It was sacred ground for the Karankawas. The Spaniards named it, but the Karankawas knew it was something special long before that.

I gently shook Dominic awake. I wanted him to see what I was seeing. The sunlight dripped over the surroundings, illuminating golden sand and dark water.

He opened his eyes and squinted at the light but then smiled.

"Did you know we were coming here?" I asked him.

"No, but in a way, yes. I don't know how to explain it. It seems like we're heading into familiarity though," he said.

I agreed. Something in the pit of my stomach felt excited, like I was about to be comforted. Keagan diverted off of the main road and onto a sandy beach road that seemed to take us nowhere. As we jostled and bumped down the road, we slowed as we approached two people who stood on what looked like a sand dune.

"From here, both of you walk. Grab the waters," Brisen gestured down to a bag underneath my feet.

We followed her instructions and took the water bottlesout.

"Take that tobacco, too," she said, gesturing to a different bag tucked neatly down on the floorboard. We didn't question her, just looked at one another and did as she said.

"There, those two people, you will need to speak with them," Brisen commanded gently.

"Aren't you coming?" Dominic asked her.

"No. It is not permitted for me to go. I will wait here. But you both should go now. They are waiting on you," she kept her eyes straightforward. It continued to unnerve me.

# CHAPTER 28

"You have arrived safely," I heard the man speak. Next to him stood an exquisite looking woman, both with eyes of sparkling jade.

They both had richly dark complexions, and spoke with an accent that seemed African, and their beautiful skin glowed like smooth velvet in the morning light.

The wind whistled and whipped our hair back and forth, the smell of the ocean leaked smoothly into my lungs. I looked at them with curiosity but without fear. They were like us.

"Come now, we haven't much time before the tide comes in," the woman instructed.

With that said she began kicking and sweeping with her foot at the side of the sand dune until a hole was revealed.

"This cavern is unknown to most. It was first discovered by the Karankawa, but they feared it as it will fill up with water and drown those who are inside at high tide," she explained. "Come, we must enter now, the tide will drown us if we do not hurry."

With slight reluctance, we followed the two of them down into the cavern, which shocked us with its very existence.

"You're wondering how such a cavern can exist here?" the man asked.

"Yes, it seems impossible, I always thought nothing like this could exist on this type of land," Dominic said.

"The clay reinforced itself over many years, and the sand is not a natural occurrence here, it was brought in to the beaches by humans, so the cavern stays empty at low tide, except for the natural wonders within it."

"It is a wonderful blessing that you have made it this far. We know of the tribulations that have occurred for you to get here. We know of the time jump. It has happened to others as well," The woman said, gently touching my left arm where my wound had been.

"Do come sit with us, join us. We are awaiting the arrival of the others." the man said, leading us into a moist, dark cavern below. Low flickers of sunlight made it possible to see.

We came closer to them and sat, forming a four-person circle.

I clenched the vial tightly, protecting what had done so much harm to me. Now that we were here, I didn't want anything to happen to it. We had come so far.

"I see what you have there," the woman said. She motioned with her glowing eyes to my hands clenched around it.

"I can't let anything happen to it," I said.

"Well, you've come to the right place for two reasons. First of all, this cavern is a sacred place where the Dhakris can keep those bounties of their work protected as they move forward with their other assignments," she said with a smile that crept across her face mysteriously.

"There are others just like that one kept here," said the man. "This cavern is a place of protection, a temple. That is why it is not known to the outside world.

"We are Lekon and Abele," Lekon said, introducing himself and his partner.

"We come from West Africa, to this place now. It is one of our spiritual meeting locations as the Dhakris. You, Dominic and Jessica, will learn all of the locations, and how to get to them regardless of your timeline and situation," Abele explained.

"Shhh…Abele, you're explaining too much at once," Lekon scolded, looking over at her harshly but with kindness in his glowing eyes.

"They can take it," Abele retorted, waving him off with her hand.

He looked back at the two of us. "There are some interesting tricks to being the Dhakris. Luckily, you've already used one to avert a separation," he said.

Abele moved her eyes away from us at the sound of the word "separation". I couldn't help but study her.

"It can be devastating to our kind, a separation. You must learn how to withstand, to come through a separation and find each other again. It can take more than one life time, if your jumping isn't well timed. And then, even then, it can be difficult. Things happen, life happens," she said, looking straight into my eyes.

"You're doing it again," Lekon looked at her. He looked back at us. "We are the oldest of the Dhakris at this moment, and we wish to share our secrets with you, as we have with the others that you will meet."

"Well, how old are you then?" Dominic asked. I was relieved he asked first because I wanted to know just as badly.

"Our human age in years, had we stayed on the same timeline, would be three hundred and seven years old. We try to not count them, but it is without a doubt that we recall our struggles from the time we were born until now and cannot help but be aware of our true age."

"How is that possible?" Dominic asked, again, taking the words from right out of my head.

"It is possible the same way it was possible for Jessica to leave one timeline and come into another, finding you in both, making it through. In that realm one can move forward or backward in time, or stay in the same era. We do what we must," again she shot daggers through her eyes at me.

"But she's in the same era of time now that she was in when she left," Dominic said.

"Only because of the particular set of circumstances in which you both found yourselves. It could have been different if it had needed to be. Abele and I, we both had our share of issues in our homeland, and you had some extra help from the two that brought you here," he finished.

"Yes," interrupted Abele, "My village thought I was a witch because of my eyes. I was born with them this way, of course, and they only intensify with strength. When I was just a baby, they wanted to burn me alive. They thought I was worse luck than anything else and that I would bring death to the normal children. My mother took me and hid me, far away from the people who wished me dead. She told the witchdoctor where I was, and he found me and secretly cared for me, knowing what I was truly meant to be. He told the village he drowned me with his own hands as a sacrifice so that they would not fear my existence or punish my mother. I would have been dead if it wasn't for them," she said through her thick accent, her voice rich with compassion.

"My story was almost the same, but I was never in danger from my own people," Lekon said. "I was born into a family of witchdoctors in my village. They had authority over the people and no one could question why I had different colored eyes. In fact, I was revered as someone powerful and magical. My family, witchdoctors near us, they knew what I was. When we were around twenty years old, the witchdoctor that cared for Abele brought her to me. We began our work together then, so long ago now. It wasn't always perfectly safe. To be around as long as we have, we've jumped timelines many times, and avoided certain death. We know some of what you've already been through."

"It is so much harder to come back together through rebirth. It takes so much more time and work," Abele chimed.

"Yes, that is what separation is to the Dhakris. But through death comes rebirth. Other Dhakris' have had to come back together through rebirth, and it has taken until now that all seven of us are back together on this earth plane again."

"So, in essence, we've been waiting for you, and many things transpired while you were in the other realm, Jessica," Abele said, looking at me curiously. "Come, I've got a place for your possession there," she gestured to my white knuckled grip on the vial.

Lekon stood up after her and Dominic and I arose up with them. Looking around, I wondered where on Earth they were talking about, because inside the cavern, I could clearly see only the rounded rocky walls and there were no shelves on the wall or doors leading elsewhere. Lekon and Abele walked to the center of the cavern and looked up.

Dominic and I followed their lead, looking up to see the object at which they stared so intently. I could see trickles of daylight on sparkling oyster shells. Beneath my feet, there was a low rumble, gently vibrating like something was shifting.

"Watch your step," Abele said, "the stairs are open now."

Where there had been solid ground there was now a staircase, matching that of the oyster shells beneath our feet. We crept slowly down the twisting spiral of stairs into a bottom layer of the temple.

Lekon had brought a torch and proceeded to light the closest light. I could see that it was a tunnel, not a room.

"Follow," Lekon instructed, "we haven't much time." We walked in a line behind him—Lekon, Abele, myself and Dominic. The tunnel almost scraped my elbows as we walked through it. It was not for the claustrophobic—that was for sure. We took a right turn, then a left, leading to the east, as I presumed from where we had started.

The tunnel began to gradually widen into a larger chamber.

I couldn't see exactly how large until Lekon lit up more torches. The size took my breath away. It was almost like a medieval castle, except I knew we were under the ocean. There were more doors along the walls and I wondered if each of them led to places where no one knew there were secret passageways.

We continued to follow Lekon to the left side of the chamber where he counted to the third door. It was a wooden door that smelled strongly of cedar. He gave it a push and we followed him into a small room with shelves all around the walls, shelves from floor to ceiling. All of the shelves were spaced so that they held containers of all sorts. I evennoticed what looked like a soda bottle on one shelf. It had to have been old—but still, it was strange.

"Choose where you would like to keep your vial," Lekon said to me.

"Does it matter where I put it?" I asked, examining the shelves all around me in the room.

"Typically, we keep the forest devils over on the shelves toward the back," Abele said, walking slowly in that direction. "But please, do hurry, "

"We, the Dhakris, do much more than bottle these beings. But the way we ensure their safe keeping is to keep them in places of sanctuary. Places that have been used for their special earth connection since the beginnings. Here, this temple was closest to you. There are temples all over the planet located where the ley lines intersect. This one is very well hidden. None of these are touched after a Dhakris sets them down. They are guarded by those who help humanity. The Little People, the spirits, and the chosen Day and Night keepers—and us of course. All of us. The entrance can only truly be seen by one who can see at its vibratory level."

I took the vial and set it down in an empty space on a shelf near my eye level. I watched the dark blue of the glass for a sign that something was inside of it. My body jolted as I saw the blue electrify itself to a lighter shade then calm back down to its darker tone, and with it I felt a wave of static in my gut peak and dissolve.

"Nachmei is in there for good," Dominic said, resting his hand on my shoulder.

"That was the spirit letting you know," Abele said. "They do that sometimes, especially when they're fresh."

"Come now," Abele instructed, "the tide is coming, we don't want to drown." She led us up and out of the cavern. I was surprised to see it was now dusk. I worried for Weli's wellbeing, my own family's wellbeing, regardless of what Brisen had told us, but I saw that Dominic was calm.

"Now," said Abele, looking straight into my eyes with the same eyes as my own, "there is something else that is happening with the two of you."

\* \* \* \*

"I see," nodded Lekon. Abele sat next to him, absorbed in thought.

"So basically, my sister fell in love with Dominic the same way that she fell in love with a guy in the first timeline, well, she really doesn't fall in love. She becomes...."

"Obsessed." Finished Abele.

"Yes," I concurred. "It was what got her caught up with Nachmei in the first place and what led to everything unfolding how it did."

"I can't say that it didn't happen for a reason," Lekon said, pondering the situation. "There is always a catalyst that brings the two together. This was obviously yours. It is amazing that you had two timelines that ran together to bring you together. Now that is something rare. Normally switching timelines is something we do later, in situations where it is absolutely necessary."

"This was necessary," Dominic said. There was a defensive tone in his voice, as if he was angry we had gone through everything we had been through.

"Of course it was," Lekon agreed. "But now, Emily will be coming for you."

"But when we left her, she was with Vanek, the servitor of Nachmei, what does she plan on doing?" I asked.

"Right," Abele spoke up, "And now they're on the hunt for you. You see, the deal went through. Her deal with the devil, if you will. Brisen helped as much as she could and as quickly as she could—but the two of them, your sister and the servitor, are powerful together."

"What do you mean?" I asked immediately, shaken.

"Everything went through the way she wanted it to happen."

"But we stopped him," Dominic interrupted.

"She has now become a more powerful witch. Nachmei knew what he was doing, your sister was born with powers too, but she was not the Dhakris."

"Yes, that part is true, and it is because of your powers. But he didn't let Emily go without reason. The deal happened. She wanted the powers of a witch and he gave them to her. She already had ability enough to conjure him up out there. You, Jessica, he took in return knowing what would happen by sending Emily back. He tried to stop the Dhakris by keeping you, but it was a gamble—one which he was willing to take. By sending Emily back out and giving her the powers she wanted he was preparing for the possibility that he would be taken in the end by you and Dominic, ensuring his posterity within this timeline at the very least."

"Maybe she'll become as obsessed with Vanek as she did with me, or the guy from the other timeline," Dominic suggested.

"Or, she'll work to become powerful herself for the reasons she was so angry. Dominic, it is no longer safe for either of you because of what has happened," Abele said in a whispered hush.

"Wait, how could she become powerful? She's just a normal human." I was perplexed at the suggestion of Emily being powerful in anyway. All she'd ever proven to me was her weakness.

"Did you not hear what I told you about her being powerful? There are exceptional people. People who learned to hone in on their inner powers. Your grandmother is one of them," she looked at Dominic, "But someone like your sister, she could make herself powerful if she wants to—and whatever Nachmei has given her has only created more power with her. Vanek has his own powers as well. Together, I'm afraid they'll seek you out."

"How do we avoid them then? How do we stop it?" Dominic asked.

"Together you are much more powerful than they are. And with the help of us, and the others, you'll be safe," she assured.

"Human obsessions can be strong," Lekon inserted. "They are not love, but most ordinary humans confuse the two. As long as the two of you are away from where they are, they shouldn't be able to inflict harm upon you. I only worry about what Vanek will be able to detect."

"Do we stay here? Where do we go from here?" I asked.

"Now that you've put Nachmei where he belongs, we're going to take you to meet the others. It is rare that we all convene together but your presence in this timeline marks the calling time."

"What's calling time?" I asked.

"You'll be given your first real calling, beyond what you've already accomplished. It will be time for the two of you to begin your work all over the world. Our services are always needed. There are always occurrences happening that demand the use of our abilities."

"Will we live as long as you?" Dominic asked, taking my hand in his tightly.

Abele smiled. "As long as you can skip time like you've done so far. But all things must come to an end eventually. You are still flesh and blood, mortal."

"We knew you before, you know," Lekon said. He had a hint of nostalgia in his voice.

"Who were we?" Dominic asked.

"You will discover that. It will be part of your journey. Time does not hold your soul, your shared soul."

"Come now, with us. We'll take you to the others. We shouldn't stay here any longer," Lekon said, sniffing the salty air, motioning for us to stand and follow him.

"How do we get to leave, to travel with you?" I said, looking at everyone in the room. We had no money.

"The logistics of our needs are accommodated by the major religions of the world," Abele said with a slow nod.

"Major religions?" Dominic asked, both of us were astounded at the notion.

"All religions, regardless of name or belief system, are a part of the same world and exist among the same beings. It was agreed upon a very long time ago that funds would always be available to accommodate the Dhakris, no matter where we are needed on this Earth. Whether Muslim or Christian, Buddhist or Jewish or whatever else anyone chooses to believe, there are spiritual challenges brought on by the evil beings. We are always secretly supported, because we are always secretly needed," Lekon explained.

"Then it will be our entire life?" I asked.

"Yes, if you like to think of it in those terms, you won't hold a career like the average person. Your whole life will be being the Dhakris," Abele finished for him.

"You will one day be able to say farewell to your loved ones, but not now. It is not the time," Abele said.

We walked briskly with Lekon and Abele. I felt for Dominic's hand. He held it tightly as if to say to me that he wouldn't let it go again—not like he had before. We knew now that there was more to life than anyone else knew. We felt the thoughts we shared as we melded together as one.

# CHAPTER 29

Dominic swirled me around in a large, swooping motion as we stood in the sands near the ocean. We had done it—what we were meant to do. Pulling me close to him, he whispered to me that nothing would be able to tear us apart again. I hoped it were true.

The stories of the other Dhakris' would not stop haunting my thoughts. They hadn't had it as easy. Time line jumping, death, rebirth—every time I stopped to really think about all of the implications, I felt like my head would explode. There was so much involved and so much risk.

"Come, the two of you."

We looked up to see Abele motioning us to walk with her down the beach.

"Brisen and Keagan have arrived with you, the others could be arriving soon," she gently spoke as we walked.

"What do you mean by 'could be'?" I asked her.

"If they have no issue, no danger. It is hard for all of us to find a safe place to meet, and something quite important has just happened here, so it might draw some otherworldly attention to these parts," she explained.

We approached a beach campfire that Lekon had lit and tended to as everyone gathered. Brisen sat calmly on the white sand, her skin almost blending in with it. Her dark hair reflected red with the light of the fire, matching it in vibrancy. She looked up with her dagger-like eyes, the violet flickering in the flames.

"Don't feel so safe just yet," she said calmly. "But I'm glad to see you've made it this far."

Walking up from behind her a voice emerged from the shadows. "Don't scare 'em, Brisen, they've already been through enough. "Didn'tcha hear what Lekon was tellin' ya?" Keagan asked.

"We're glad ye made it all the same. After what your sister pulled we were afraid ye might not," Keagan said, plopping himself down next to Brisen. The waves of his dark hair defined his chiseled features in the firelight. He had the skin of a person who worked in the sun often. His eyes lit up all the same. "And this darlin' here thought ye might have troubles," he put his arm tightly around Brisen and she leaned into him. She seemed so aloof, like there was much more to be said but she had disconnected. I wanted to know more about her because I could sense that she wasn't the same as everyone else.

"If the others don't make it, we can't stay much longer."

Abele said, stoking the fire alongside Lekon and looking at all of us in our glowing eyes.

"Why not?" I asked. I could feel that I was the equivalent of a baby to them. I had so much to learn in a short amount of time.

"When we convene like this, it isn't long before the others find us. Our energy field is strong," Brisen said.

"Wait, who are the Others?" Dominic beat me to it. I knew it was what Abele had been explaining to me earlier.

"Some of my kind," Brisen said wistfully.

"Shhh!" Lekon stood up. "That is enough for now. We must arrange our next meeting place. The Others will find us here before the rest of us arrive. We will not be able to convene as we had wanted."

I glanced nervously over to Dominic. He was staring into the fire as if in a trance. I knew he was thinking deeply.

"What is it?" I whispered to him.

"I'm worried," he confessed.

"About what?"

"Everything they're saying. Vanek is still out there, with your sister, and then the Others, whatever they are...," his words trailed off into the air.

"Why don't you just ask?" Brisen interrupted. Her eyes shot straight into us and for just a brief moment, I thought I saw the flicker of violet grow stronger behind them. My stomach dropped at the severity of her words.

"What did you mean *your* kind?" Dominic asked. I felt him squeeze me tightly as the heat of the fire lit up our faces.

"I'm not all human, like the rest of you," she started to explain.

"Not now Brisen!" Abele interrupted. "We are losing time. They're not going to make it and now we must leave. Up! All of you." She whipped her arm around in one grand motion and extinguished the fire before us. "I'll expect you to meet us at this location on the day written in the scroll inside the bag."

She tossed what looked like an old canvas book bag toward Dominic "Look inside, you'll have what you need for now."

He dug inside, inspecting the contents quickly. There were our passports and an address book. Earmarked on one page was an address. Dominic pulled out a black plastic card.

"Your funding. Use it carefully, discreetly," Abele instructed.

We all stood up in the darkness that had fallen upon us and glanced around the circle of the six of us who had made it. I worried about the other Dhakris'.

"We all have our means by which we travel," Lekon spoke in a quieted whisper. I expect to see you all on the promised date. Until then, do not let the darkness fall upon you. I am sorry, but we must all go our way now."

Abele was already tugging his hand toward the ocean. The two of them waded into the waters. I watched, half horrified and half mystified as they disappeared into the sea.

"You'll know soon enough," Keagan said to us with a smile as Brisen pulled him toward her quietly. "But don'tcha go tinkin' they won't be after ya, they will. We'll do what we can to help, just stay together."

"And don't ever, ever let down your guard," Brisen warned, checking us both in the eyes.

"But we'll be seeing you again," she said almost sweetly. With her final words she embraced Keagan tightly, and they began to fade into the ether.

"No wait!" My voice quivered. I felt panic in my throat. They came back into clarity.

"Why did you help us so much? From the beginning, until now, you've helped us. But you won't tell us what is different. You're part of the Dhakris, but I know you're different, and you did so much for us. I just—I just need to know before we go why you helped us so much."

Brisen took a step towards me, leaving Keagan slightly in her shadow.

"Because," she said softly, stepping toward me and touching my hair gently, letting her eyes flicker from green to violet without hindrance, "a daughter always does anything to help save her own mother."